GILDED TREASON

CHAMPIONS OF FATE: BOOK 3

NOEL COUGHLAN

GILDED TREASON

Cover Illustration by MiblArt (https://miblart.com/)

Edited by Proofed to Perfection (http://www.proofedtoperfection.com/)

Proofed by Proofreader Alexa (https://www.facebook.com/alexaproofreader/)

Published by Photocosmological Press (http://photocosm.org/)

Paperback Edition: ISBN:978-1-910206-24-9

For Nick.

MEMBERS OF THE VICENARY JURY

Osro Onez – The Ducal Steward
Thespenilea Reiner – The Grand Parsimon
Devaner Tiranicon – The Justiciar General
Nacyn Revistan – The Dragon Keeper
Greny Scylax – Cordent General
Opriet Braesum – Cordent General
Posaleum Minol – Cordent General
Thaxen Savarel – Intelligencer General
Elca Trajar – Intelligencer General
Griman Epitan – Ambassador General
Inamyr Minan – Censor General
Leca Monem – Governor General
Zizor Findel – Inspector General
Anyrim Norcaro – Conflagration Marshal
Drona Torn – Conflagration Marshal
Egava Sipian – Conflagration Marshal
Cenmis Velso – Jurist
Aretro Falier – Jurist
Okia Vavar – Jurist
Ederion Visentar – Jurist

SERVANTS OF GRENY SCYLAX

Scylax Tower:

Chemp – Most Senior Servant and Chief Bodyguard
Deetch – Butler
Zueel – Palanquin Driver

Queek
Zetch
Treek
Dweed
Sneeth
Kleest
Feerth
Qweelch
Geekel
Sheeg
Eedee
Steevig
Evreet

Inkeep:

Mileek –Warden

Riskeel
Kreevest

I have teams of ratchers covering every exit from his den. Once you and your daughter are safely clear, we'll close in and deal with him."

Ecethor nodded. "Dragons protect us from these foreign criminals."

Greny put away his lampstone, leaving only the ball of light in Ecethor's hand to pierce the gloom. He watched Ecethor shrink into the distance until she disappeared around a bend, plunging the tunnel into sepulchral darkness. Shallowly breathing in the tunnel's dank, sour air, Greny strained the surrounding sounds for any hint of the reception Ecethor had received from Dronan, but he could hear nothing beyond echoey drips, the burble of water along the tunnel, the distant roar of greater courses spilling into the Void, the furtive patter of scurrying rodents.

A claw-like hand tapping his shoulder made Greny flinch. One of the ratchers, most likely Chemp, had heard something. It would be marvelous if Greny possessed his servants' keen senses. Except for smell.

After what felt like an eternity, awkward splashes announced Ecethor's return. She lurched back into view, alone and weeping, the lampstone clutched loosely in her hand, throwing curves of light onto the tunnel walls.

Greny hastened toward her, stopped some distance away, perplexed. Aside from his mother grieving his dead sister in the Scylax family crypt, he had never witnessed a meritocrat crying before, and it disconcerted him. His class was supposed to be made of sterner stuff. His mother certainly wouldn't have approved.

"Dronan has Cibiela chained and prostrate at his feet like a pet," Ecethor said. "She begged me to take her home, pleaded for my forgiveness, but he won't release her unless..."

"Unless?"

"I have to give him something incriminating on other meritocrats," Ecethor said. "I won't do that. I can't."

Would she be so resolute if Greny weren't here? Remembering she had thrown away her handkerchief, he reached for his own, but the oppressive malodor put him off offering it. "You won't have to. Did Dronan tell you what exactly he wanted?"

"He said, 'The sort of secrets that would make a meritocrat come down here.'"

"How many thugs are with him?"

"I saw seven."

"How are they armed?"

Ecethor squeezed her eyes shut. "Two carry springbows. The others are armed with swords and clubs."

"You're going to go back to Dronan and offer calumny about other meritocrats. Make up whatever salacious nonsense you like." Greny smirked. "Tell him I sleep with ratchers." That slander already circulated in the parlors and dining rooms of meritocratic Gyre. Greny heard, no matter how low it was whispered. Dronan would love a compromising secret on a cordent general. "Say that you want to be sure that whatever incriminating material you bring him will be enough to secure Cibiela's freedom. We'll be right behind you. I'm using you to light our way up the tunnel and hide the sound of our approach. When the fighting starts, take cover. For dragons' sake, don't run to your daughter. You'll end up getting one or both of you killed. Lie against the tunnel wall, crawl into the nearest crevice. If you get caked in dirt, it doesn't matter. The main thing is that you and Cibiela get out of here unhurt."

He and the ratchers quietly followed Ecethor down the tunnel. At the end was a round chamber, illumined by sunlight streaming through a large, circular opening in the floor, that acted as an outflow for this section of the sewers. Dronan, a muscular man with green-black skin and tightly curled black hair, looked every bit a monarch on his wicker throne. Typical of the man's arrogance to have such a ridiculous piece of furniture down here. He wouldn't deign to stand like the minions clustered around him. Cibiela sat at his feet, legs crossed, head bowed, her red hair spilled over her face like a veil.

As Ecethor entered the chamber, the Rhumgadians ceased their banter and turned insolent grins toward her. Dronan hopped off his throne. Cibiela's chains rattled as she crawled out of his way. "Back so soon, I see," he said. "What do you want?"

"I want your guarantee that the information I give you will secure my daughter's freedom," Ecethor said. "I have a love letter the cordent general, Greny Scylax, wrote to his ratcher lover. Possessing it would put him forever in your debt."

Dronan's hearty laugh filled the chamber. "A letter like that certainly would be worth your daughter's freedom."

"Don't do it, Mother!" Cibiela cried. "They were laughing at you. They—" Dronan's yanking of the chain cut her short. Squealing in terror, she pulled at it as he dragged her near the edge of the hole.

"Don't hurt her," Ecethor pleaded.

Dronan laughed. "I expect collateral from you as well, Meritocrat. You must have some documentation relating to your brineflower smuggling operation."

Cibiela's head twitched. She couldn't be enjoying her dirty secrets being aired before another meritocrat, and, worse, a cordent general.

"Very well," she said with weary resignation.

Now that the clump of thugs had dispersed a little, the two with springbows were easy to pick out, but Greny hesitated to order the attack while Dronan had Cibiela within the immediate vicinity of the aperture.

"Get him nearer to you," Greny whispered with as much volume as he dared. Had Ecethor heard?

She stretched out her hand to Dronan. "Then come to me and shake on our agreement."

Dronan sauntered leisurely toward her, dragging her daughter along behind him. He froze, his eyes rounding. Greny blew his whistle that no human could hear. A bolt struck the forehead of one of Dronan's springbowmen, knocking him to the floor. The springbow of the other exploded in his hands as a bolt punched through it. A third bolt made a loud crack as it hit his arm. A fourth hit another thug in the chest. Three other Rhumgadians scarpered down other tunnels, forsaking their leader. The last of Dronan's crew drew his sword and charged, only to be felled by four bolts in rapid succession.

Ecethor, frozen amid this carnage, unwittingly shielded Dronan. Signaling the ratchers to stop shooting, Greny joined her. "Are you okay?"

"I couldn't move. It happened so fast," she said. She looked stunned.

Dronan stretched Cibiela's chain over the hole. The bedraggled girl sat on its lip, body quaking, her face bathed in the unsleeping light of the inner sun a frozen mask of abject terror. If he tried to drop her into the inner sun, would she even think of trying to cling on for dear life, much less have the strength?

"If you release Meritocrat Orom's daughter unharmed," Greny said, "I'll let you leave Gyre in similar fashion. You have my word."

"Why should I trust you?" Dronan demanded.

A distant scream echoed from one tunnel. Evidently, one of his associates had met his end at the hands of another ratcher party.

"Cibiela's safety is my paramount concern," Greny said. "And once you've left the city, you're no longer my problem."

Dronan gave the chain a savage yank, making Greny flinch and Ecethor yelp. "I want a hundred thousand ducats," the Rhumgadian said.

"I'll give you a thousand ducats and you'll consider yourself lucky to have it," Greny said. Ecethor's eyes bugged in startled disbelief, but she had the sense not to contradict him.

Dronan bit his lip. "Do I really have your word?"

"You have it," Greny said. "Let the girl go."

As Dronan dropped the chain on the ground and sidled away from Cibiela, two ratchers seized and bound him. The girl struggled to her feet and, wiping her eyes, sheepishly approached her mother, her chain rattling behind her.

Ecethor plucked her emblem of merit off her head and waved it at her daughter. "Your conduct has besmirched the Orom wyrm." Spotting dirt on the gold disk, she rubbed it feverishly against her dress.

"Please forgive me," Cibiela begged. Dronan smirked like a fool behind her while ratchers collected the bodies of the men he had led and tossed them into the hole.

"There can be no more of this foolishness," Ecethor said. "You mightn't be so lucky next time."

"There won't be a next time. I promise."

"I'll have a ratcher escort both of you out of the sewers," Greny said.

"Thank you," Ecethor said, venomously eying Dronan. She broke into an unconvincing grin and leaned unnervingly close to Greny, her florid scent cutting through the sewer's stench. "Of course, you already know about the brineflowers. You know everything that happens in Gyre."

So, she was trading contraband goods from Rhumgad. Surprising that he had missed it, that the likes of Ecethor could hide it from him. "It's something I've been planning to talk to you about."

"My contacts on Rhumgad have no connection with its tyrant," Ecethor said. "On the contrary, they may prove a useful ally should we invade the shard."

Detecting a hint of the sewer's stink on her breath, Greny covered his mouth with his handkerchief. "This is neither the time nor place to discuss this. We'll talk later."

The rudeness of the gesture was not lost on Ecethor; she regarded him with quiet horror, then ice-cold hate. "You always were honest to a fault."

As she flounced away, dragging her daughter along by her chain and forcing the ratcher Zetch to scurry ahead of them to act as their guide, Greny shook his head. Her ingratitude didn't surprise him.

"I know all about her operation," Dronan said. "I can give you names. For a price, of course."

Dronan posed a greater danger than all the brineflowers in Rhumgad. "You're very talkative for a dead man," Greny sneered. "Feed him to the inner sun."

"What!" Dronan roared as the ratchers dragged him toward the hole. "So, a meritocrat's word means nothing!"

"To a scoundrel like you, no," Greny said.

"Liar!" Dronan roared, his cry echoing as he writhed against the iron grip of his captors. "Liar! Liar!"

Greny stalked over to him and slapped his face so hard he hurt his hand. "The time to take me at my word was when I warned you to leave Gyre. We meritocrats rule this city from top to bottom, from the tip of the Grand Preservatory's highest spire to the lowest depths of the sewers. There's nowhere for your kind in the Halcyon Republic except..." He gestured at the hole, a great mouth of light.

The ratchers threw the throne into the Void after the last of the corpses. Greny stood as close to the edge as he dared and watched the seat shrink into the distance. Great tresses of water fell down into the sepia cloud below. It was hard to believe that the city's effluent could create such beauty. The scene mesmerized him until Dronan's desperate chatter intruded.

"You're not listening to a word I'm saying," he bleated.

"What you say doesn't matter anymore." Greny signaled the ratchers, and they shoved Dronan over the edge. His scream fell away until the roar of the waterfalls swallowed it completely.

2

———————

Drinith stared at the empty seat at the other side of the table. She rubbed her hands down her face and exhaled. *I shouldn't be here.*

She hadn't set foot in the safe house on Wealgiver Street since the Crevastival attack over two years before. It was here that she had slain the treacherous Zin, only to suffer a far more terrible betrayal. The post to which her former advisor Gelasin had bound her had been repaired, but the notch remained where he had stabbed a dagger high above her before leaving to carry out mass murder in Crimson Plaza.

She directed an irritable glance at the closed shutters. The gloom weighed on her, but it wasn't safe to open them. Nobody other than her network of sympathizers must know she was here. From outside came the cries of merchants hawking their wares. They could just as easily sell word of her whereabouts. Almost anyone in Gyre might become a spy for the right price.

The four youths Woad had stationed downstairs didn't make her feel any safer. Despite his training, they were still untested boys and girls, certainly no match for a skilled assassin. *Why is Woad taking so long to arrive?*

At the sound of the front door opening downstairs her hand tightened on the haft of the knife in the concealed pocket of her dress. *One can't be too careful.* She stared expectantly at the door as boots tramped up the stairs. Drinith exhaled a long-held breath as Woad strode into the room, doffing his hood to reveal his bald pate. The beaded braids dangling from the stocky blue-black lowlander's chin had recently been shortened. A second hooded figure followed him, head bowed in funereal solemnity.

"Sit down, boy," Woad snarled. "And tell the meritocrat what you've done!"

The youth sank into the chair opposite Drinith and slowly pushed back his hood. Jathar bit his lip, his blue-black face darkening at Drinith's gasp of horror. His cheeks sported two white tattoos bearing pyratic symbols for justice and loyalty.

Drinith pressed her hands to the sides of her head. "Gods! What have you done, Jathar? What utter foolishness is this?"

"We are the new Warserks," he said meekly.

Drinith tapped a finger on the table. "The Warserks of Kaplar obey commands. My instructions were to avoid attracting attention. Those tattoos on your face are more than a simple proclamation of fealty. Warserks only receive their tattoos after killing at their emperor's behest. Have you slain anyone on my orders? Have you?"

Jathar's dismayed gaze fell to the table. "No."

A tingle shot up Drinith's spine and reached into the roots of her hair. "Have you killed someone? If you've done something stupid..."

Jathar regarded her with wide-eyed panic. "No no no. I haven't. I haven't. I promise!"

You're not even from Kaplar. Your parents were lowlanders from Erdabo. It was best left unsaid, given that her followers came from every realm on Rhumgad. Some even hailed from Javlohm, the heartland of the tyrant Magian's empire. "Are there more like you?"

"No," Woad said, his corded arms folded above Jathar. "He's the first. There were others intent on following his example, but I warned them off. Those tattoos need to go. Not just for his sake. If people outside our organization see them, they might become a fashion trend." He smirked. "I knew a man once who had tattoos like that. He chiseled them off with a dagger. Left nasty craters in his face."

Jathar stared up at him in absolute terror.

"I don't need a reminder of that traitor," Drinith said. "We'll send Jathar to the Grand Preservatory. The preservators can remove the tattoos in a far less barbaric fashion, and we can depend on their discretion."

"Cheaper just to…" Woad grinned evilly as he flicked a dirty fingernail down each cheek.

Jathar gaped as he looked to Woad and then to Drinith.

"The preservators will deal with it," Drinith said firmly.

"Thank you, Your Imperial Majesty," Jathar said.

"My title is Meritocrat. On Gyran soil, at least," Drinith said.

"Of course, Meritocrat." Jathar lifted from his seat, froze in a posture of uncertainty.

"You may leave," Drinith said.

He fled toward the doorway, mumbling thanks.

"You're right to be grateful," Woad growled after him as Jathar thumped down the stairs. "I wouldn't have dealt with your stupidity with such generosity. Wait for me with the others." Shaking his head, Woad shut the door and sat down in Jathar's vacated seat.

"You could have resolved this matter yourself," Drinith said.

"Your chastisement carries more force," Woad said. "I've heard some rumblings that things would run better if you took direct charge in the Blue Quarter. This incident will serve as proof that we're of one mind on matters of discipline."

"My coming here is a risk," Drinith said. "If our network is uncovered, we all could end up being shunted off the Plank. You know that."

"I know. But it's hard on our people. They're getting impatient. They crave change."

"There's little that can be done until we reach Rhumgad."

"Any word on when that might happen?" Woad asked.

Drinith winced. How many times had she been asked this question? "The Parliament of Merit remains deadlocked on the matter." The grouping that supported a military campaign in Rhumgad, the so-called New War Faction, was large, but an equally popular coalition, the Short War Faction, opposed it, preferring to continue the two hundred-year-old conflict on the shard of Noster. *Only in Gyre could there be two factions competing for different wars and none for peace.*

"Our people won't wait forever," Woad said. "We might look back on this incident as mild in comparison with what could follow. Gyre is the only home many of the younger ones have known. Rhumgad was little more than a fable to them until they joined us. Now their every hope awaits them there. If they decide they'll never get there, they'll start agitating here. They already hate the Meritocracy. Even the lowest native beggar looks down on them. You're the only reason they're willing to stomach Gyran oppression. If they choose to take on your colleagues, we'll all be in the bowels of Empyrosis."

"I'm frustrated too," Drinith said.

"But you have the sense and the discipline to not act on it."

And I'm living in opulence while they are forced to eke out a precarious existence in the Blue Quarter slum. "I've devoted every ducat I can spare to the welfare of our community. I've advocated for the Blue Quarter in the Parliament as much as I dare." *Which has achieved less than nothing so far.*

"Nobody questions your efforts. On the contrary, Drinith, our people love you. But that devotion holds its own danger. It can't be bottled up indefinitely. Eventually, it will break through in ways we won't be able to control. Last week..." The beads in his braids clinked softly as he stroked them. "Last week, I had to tear down a shrine devoted to you."

Drinith must have misheard. "A shrine?"

"Somebody drew the Hax emblem on a wall and flowers and candles and other offerings quickly accumulated beneath it. They even drew a red crown on the alerion just to make it doubly clear it was in your honor. I had to distract a cordent patrol while I got rid of it. It's only a matter of time before one of these spontaneous outbursts of adoration comes to the attention of your meritocrat friends."

Snide rumors already abounded in those circles opposed to the Rhumgadian War that Drinith had carved out a private domain in the Blue Quarter. Her enemies would seize upon any open displays of veneration of her as proof that she posed a threat. The Meritocracy detested monarchs beyond all else.

"If I can't convince the Meritocracy to dispatch an expedition to Rhumgad, what do we do?"

"We'd have to hire a dragon or two and go to Rhumgad by ourselves. Your meritocrat friends might even pay to be rid of us. But the chances of success..." Woad shrugged and pulled a face. "We'd have a better hope of beating a dragon by wrestling its tongue."

"I haven't created this organization to get all its members killed in some vainglorious gesture," Drinith huffed.

"Then you need to break that deadlock. You need to get those missing votes from somewhere."

DRINITH'S casquar palanquin crossed Hax Plaza toward her mansion when the door flung open, slapping the cab's flank with a bang. Drinith drew her knife from its secret pocket, ready to spring at whatever assassin was about to assail her. Meanwhile, outside, her driver, Nosdan, wrestled with a young maroon-faced woman—her former maid, Perian.

"Unhand me!" Perian cried, squirming as Nosdan locked his arms around her. The blue-black Rhumgadian dwarfed her and easily lifted her off the ground. She kicked his shins so hard he dropped her, sputtering a torrent of oaths. Two burly male servants rushed from the Hax Mansion to his aid.

Drinith alighted from the cab and strolled by them with pointed insouciance. "I'll walk from here."

"Why did you dismiss me?" Perian cried.

Because you're a spy.

"You replaced decent Gyran servants with oafish Rhumgadians for red months!" Perian yelled. "I stuck up for you all that time. I stayed while the clever ones sought employment elsewhere. And what is the reward for my loyalty? I'm out on the streets with no job and no reference."

I'm sure your spymaster will find you employment elsewhere. "This sort of unseemly spectacle is exactly why I discharged you. Take this as a lesson for your future endeavors."

The butler Fenvar waited at the mansion's front door, a hint of anguish on her usually placid face. "I apologize, Meritocrat," she said as Drinith entered. "I knew she was waiting out there, but I never imagined she would stoop to such an outrage."

"She's a spy," Drinith muttered. "How much lower could she be?"

She glanced back at the human knot by the palanquin. Perian was lost in the middle of the scrum, but her voice filled the plaza as she protested her dismissal.

"She's putting on a good show," Drinith said.

Fenvar shut the door. "I am as disappointed in her as you are, Meritocrat. Despite her excessive talkativeness, I regarded Perian as an exemplary servant and even a friend. I was shocked when I spotted her taking money from that man."

Drinith patted Fenvar's shoulder. "You did the right thing by telling me. At least I have one servant who I can absolutely trust."

The faintest of smiles softened Fenvar's face. "It is my honor to serve House Hax."

"Where are Jarma and Quiescat?"

"The meritorian is currently with her mathematics tutor. The Oracle is in the library. Shall I summon them?"

Drinith glanced at the longcase clock decorated with a gilded alerion besting a winged jackal in a fight. It was almost noon. "Leave them be. I must ready myself for Parliament." Today's session was one she could not miss. A delegation from Rhumgad was to attend and all manner of rumors swirled through the Parliament of Merit as to its purpose.

3

———

The Parliament of Merit, like all the palatial buildings clustered around Crimson Plaza, looked from a distance as though it had erupted from the shardlet's dusky yellow bedrock. As Drinith's cab drew nearer, statues and reliefs emerged from its walls as if by magic. The sculptures depicted dramatic events of Gyre's history: the laying of the foundation of the city by Olympeda Wealgiver and her pyrates; Thaxen the Iron's defeat of the Second Skyshore League; the toppling of Gyre's final monarch, Karis the First and Last, off the Plank; the establishment of the Parliament of Merit and election of the first ruling ducalion, Ecethor Trajar; the marriage of one of her successors, Emenis Braesum, to a Nosteran Emperor to save the city from being sacked by his army; the fall of the last Mock Emperor of Noster at the hands of Gyre and its allies.

The palanquin passed by the imposing main entrance with its three bronze arched doors and stone canopy shaped like an upside-down crown, on which stood the statues of the Seven Martyrs, and turned down the gated lane reserved for arriving meritocrats. Drinith waited patiently for her turn to disembark, then hopped out of the cab.

A hooded figure in black stood in the doorway. The old woman, shriveled and hunched, leaned on an ornate sword forged from blood-red orichalcum. It looked too heavy for her to lift, much less wield. On her forehead rested a medallion bearing the image of a scytale. Tival Ronad, the Arbiter of Merit, regarded Drinith with half-closed eyes. "Who are you to enter here?"

"I am Meritocrat Hax," Drinith said, strolling by her. The challenge was an empty ritual, dating back to more fraught times.

The emblems of the meritocratic families tiled the walls of the corridor. A few symbols had been scratched out. Drinith slowed as she scanned the wall for hers, the Hax alerion.

"Drinith, how marvelous to see you!"

Drinith cringed. "Hello," she said, turning toward Elca Trajar. The meritocrat's large pale eyes still discomfited, but Drinith's experiences on Ophigee had dulled their mesmeric quality. She could maintain eye contact with effort.

Elca's black dress had an iridescent green sheen. Much of the cleavage above its low neckline was smothered by an ornate necklace in the shape of a peacock's tail. Her black hair was wound around her head into tight braids except for two white-tipped tresses hanging loose down her temples.

Her face was a constant source of fascination now that Drinith could focus on it. Over time, the starry freckles that covered her purple face slowly drifted, so she never looked quite the same at each encounter.

Elca leaned close, her cloyingly sweet breath tickling Drinith's nose with the urge to sneeze. "Any word of what His Immortal and Infinite Majesty is up to by sending a circus for our amusement today?"

"I'm sure you know better than me."

Elca's pale eyes narrowed a fraction with appraisal. "The rumor is that Magian has sent us a troupe of dancing girls for our entertainment. I can only hope it proves to be true. The Parliament could only regard such a spectacle as an appalling insult. An unparalleled diplomatic blunder like that would surely win us the remaining votes we need to overthrow the tyrant."

"Don't underestimate him," Drinith warned.

"Or me," Elca said with a simper. "I've studied Magian's history closely and have become quite an expert on him. He's up to something. That much I know. How goes your hunt for his agents in Gyre? Apparently, Greny eliminated a cell in the sewers yesterday."

How had she learned of that? Even Drinith wasn't party to the exact details. "My understanding is that the group were common thieves looking to establish themselves in Gyre. They weren't agents of Magian."

"Pity."

"We have uncovered several spies."

Elca shook her head. It wasn't the answer she hoped for. "If espionage was enough to spark a war, Gyre would have exploded years ago. We need proof Magian has both the ambition and the capability to destroy us. Only then will our adversaries in Parliament regard him as a pressing threat."

A snow-haired meritocrat joined them. Okia Vavar's maroon face, crinkled like a dried apple, evinced a roguish amusement, but a hardhearted perspicacity glimmered in her cerise eyes. On her forehead rested her emblem of merit—a dragon holding a rose. She had a gold rose pinned to her plain black dress.

"You're looking well today, Okia," Elca observed.

Okia grinned as she leaned on her cane. "Spare me your flattery! I look like a haggard crone. Can't be helped." She looked Elca's artificially preserved body up and down. "To think we were born the same year."

"I have the preservators' arts to thank for my looks," Elca said.

"As have I for this." Okia dismissively waved at herself. "They have maintained me in this state of polite decrepitude for many years." She fixed an admiring gaze on Drinith. "Ah, to be young and carefree again. Enjoy your youth while you have it, Drinith. You'll miss it when it's gone."

"I don't understand," Drinith blurted. "You could afford…"

"I'm already the wealthiest meritocrat in Gyre. I can't be the most beautiful as well. You know all about the jealousy of others, eh, Elca?"

"That's in the past," Elca said. "I am an intelligencer general now."

"A reward for a job well done," Okia said with a smirk. "I'd say quite a few mothers, sisters, and lovers gave sighs of relief when you ceased to be Arbiter of Courtesars. The carnage you wrought in that position will live on in legend long after we're both interred on Mount Riddle." Her playful nudge sent a shiver through Drinith. "Elca's charms pitted sons against their mothers and sisters, and brothers against each other. I don't think there's a house that crossed her with a male descendant left."

Drinith had heard vague rumors of her past fall from grace, but it was a revelation to her that Elca had wielded her dalliances with courtesars as a weapon against her enemies. In retrospect, such calculation and callousness very much chimed with Drinith's impression of her character.

"Only the ones who threw their swords away and melted into the shadows," Elca said. "I saved courtesar lives, too, on occasion."

"I will be forever grateful for the help you extended to my willful great grandsons," Okia said.

"And I always played by the rules."

"You certainly did. To great effect. Speaking of which, Tomyr Pitero will sit with the Short War Faction today." Okia spoke with such clear glee, Drinith wondered if she had heard right.

Elca's deep frown hardly rumpled her forehead, frozen by the preservators' magicks. "I fail to see how losing one of our key supporters is a cause for celebration."

"It's all to do with the Olapsin seat coming vacant last night."

"Ronel Olapsin passed away? How sad," Elca said with a smile. "She had lost interest in life after her grandson, Muenthax, died."

"Sad indeed," Okia said, without a hint of sorrow. "As none of her family survives her, and she never nominated a successor, her demise leaves the Olapsin seat vacant. Osro Onez told Tomyr if she throws in her lot with the Short War Faction, they'll support the election of Tomyr's sister, Gafyso, as the new Meritocrat Olapsin. Of course, Tomyr's true loyalties lie with us and so will her sister's. In trying to steal a vote from our New War Faction, Osro will have secured us an extra one."

"Delicious irony indeed," Elca said. "But how do you know Tomyr isn't tricking us into giving her sister the Olapsin lynx?"

"Our side of the chamber is her natural home. Most of her friends sit with us."

"Most, but not all. The others could just as easily switch to the Short War Faction when Gafyso has secured her emblem of merit."

Drinith listened to their discourse with a sinking heart. It was like being trapped in the cogs of a clock, subject to the relentless tick, tick, tick of politicking, the heartbeat of Gyre.

"They won't," Okia assured Elca. "I have *good reason* to trust Tomyr."

Drinith grimaced. Plainly Okia had some hold over Tomyr. It might be a debt or a favor owed, or something more sinister. Elca and Okia weren't the sort of allies Drinith desired, but repudiating them would end any chance of freeing Rhumgad.

"Sounds like you have everything in hand," Elca said as the three of them proceeded down the corridor.

"I wouldn't say *everything*." Okia waved a fist in front of her. "But on the particular matter of Tomyr, my grip is iron."

A portly woman with a broad, handsome face breathlessly demanded their attention as she caught up with them. Her dress had a rather large cutaway below the collar but was otherwise plain, aside from the row of brass buttons typical of most meritocrats' outfits. Braids of red and blonde hair were twisted into a layered bun upon which rested the Tevalen emblem of merit, the double-faced lion.

"Meritocrats, I ask only a moment of your time," she said.

"And you shall have it, dear Isalar," Elca said sweetly. Drinith nodded along with Okia.

Isalar Tevalen heaved a sigh of relief and smiled. "If truth be told, I find myself in a quandary. For many red months, your faction has promised to open up the Leonine Theater again." She paused for effect, then declared triumphantly: "But now the Short War Faction has offered the same."

Drinith fought the urge to scream. To think that the future of her people might depend on satisfying such whims....

Elca blinked in surprise. Taking Isalar's arm, she hastily drew her to a shallow alcove, away from the traffic of meritocrats heading for the chamber. Exchanging worried glances, Okia and Drinith joined them.

"Our faction is your natural ally," Elca said. "Did Thaxen Savarel ever show even a passing interest in the arts? How many times did you beg Osro Onez to rescind her predecessor's prohibition, to no avail?"

"Thespenilea..." Isalar said, invoking the name of one of the Short War Faction's greatest advocates.

Elca leaned close to her and murmured, "Thespenilea, like the thespians you admire, has a penchant for sweet words, but there the similarity ends. Her promises might scintillate now, but they'll fade to black nothing if her faction wins."

"And what of your promises?" Isalar muttered truculently. "You've promised me the theater would be reopened for red months."

"Our efforts have been stymied by the very same people you now put your faith in," Okia said plaintively. "Dragon's hot kiss, look at their supporters! Do you imagine Inamyr Minan or Thaxen Savarel would open the theater again? What about Drona Torn?"

"I suppose," Isalar said, wavering.

"The Short War Faction desires the status quo—the same old war, the same old laws, the same old prohibitions," Elca declared. "They don't see the need for change. On the contrary, they fear and despise it. I grant you, Thespenilea *may* be sincere in her offer. She *may* genuinely believe she can deliver on her promise. But the other leaders of her faction—pah. I have it on good authority that one is even quietly lobbying for the theater to be re-purposed."

"No, they couldn't," Isalar said, her voice trembling. "What could they possibly use it for?"

"Space is at a premium in the city. The theater has been derelict since the Silverfish Revolt and it's next to the Temple District."

"Inamyr Minan must be behind this," Isalar said. "She's the Censor General."

Elca shook her head sadly. "Inamyr hasn't the imagination for something like this." She leaned in and whispered in Isalar's ear too softly for Drinith to hear.

Isalar's eyes bulged. "I can't believe it."

"It's what I heard," Elca said with a shrug.

Isalar glanced guiltily at the three meritocrats. "You've given me a good deal to think about."

"Can we depend on your support for now at least?" Okia asked.

Isalar blushed and nodded. "I'll see you in the chamber," she said as she rushed down the corridor. The three meritocrats trailed after her at a more sedate pace.

"I know you find these trade-offs distasteful," Elca said to Drinith, "but they are unfortunately a necessary part of getting business done in Gyre."

Tick, tick, tick.

As they strolled by a gaggle of gossiping meritocrats, the group fell silent. A few blushed as they eyed Drinith and her companions, but the svelte middle-aged Nosteran woman at the heart of the knot acknowledged the passersby with a casual nod. Thespenilea Reiner's thick dragon-spike eyebrows were unmistakable.

"Thespenilea's popularity is such an advantage to the Short War Faction," Elca observed wistfully after they had ambled a safe distance beyond the group. "Thaxen Savarel is disliked even by her allies. Osro Onez's role as Ducal Steward forces her to maintain some distance from political machinations. Cenmis Velso is a lightweight. Thespenilea is the velvet cord that binds the Short War Faction together."

"We have Aretro Falier on our side," Okia said. "Everyone likes Aretro."

This wasn't mere hyperbole. Since Aretro's resignation as Ambassador General, her popularity had risen substantially in the Parliament to the point she had been reelected to the Vicenary Jury, the clandestine body charged with the security of the state. Her diplomatic successes could be recognized now that she was no longer considered a threat and her humility was seen as charming.

"Indeed, dragons bless her," Elca said. "But if I had the choice of the two, I'd prefer Thespenilea on our side."

Okia shrugged. "Unfortunately, you don't always have a choice in your friends."

Never was a truer word said, Drinith mused bitterly.

4

———————

Alone, Greny entered the parliament chamber. The stepped rows of seats were arranged in a horseshoe. At the center stood a white marble throne, its back shaped like a lion's paw. Behind it, an angled shaft descended to the double doors by which the Ducalion accessed the chamber. The blackness of the meritocrats' clothing against the dark furniture made them appear as disembodied heads. The Short War Faction gravitated to the left side of the chamber, while the New War Faction gathered on the right. Fashion, too, distinguished the groups. The Short War supporters tended to wear high collars while the New War Faction generally preferred lower necklines.

Spotting Ecethor in the midst of the latter group, Greny stalked up the steps to her. Her feeble attempt at a smile failed to conceal her disgust as he sat in the empty seat alongside her.

"How is Cibiela?" he asked.

"She is doing her best to put yesterday's trauma behind her, as am I. I trust the matter is closed."

"Not quite. There's the brineflower smuggling."

Ecethor stared at him with open-mouthed horror. "I had hoped we had come to an amicable understanding on that matter."

Greny's sitting beside Ecethor drew quizzical glances across the chamber. He usually sat in the very back row in the neutral space between the two factions.

"On Cibiela, yes, absolutely. But you'll have to come clean about your Rhumgadian venture to the Vicenary Jury."

Ecethor blanched. "The Iron Circle? Is that really necessary?"

"I'm afraid it is." He gave her arm what he hoped was a reassuring pat, but she recoiled from his hand.

"I'll be ruined," she said.

"Aren't you being a little melodramatic? You'll get little more than a slap on the wrist if you put the right gloss on it."

"I've sunk a large part of my wealth into the operation. Its loss would bankrupt me. At least, give me a little time...."

"If Dronan knew about your operation, then others must as well. It's inevitable that rumors of its existence will spread through the city. Once it becomes common knowledge, it will be too late for this matter to be resolved discreetly. Those meritocrats who lost sizable portions of their income playing by the rules will demand your punishment for profiting off their sacrifice." Seeing Ecethor's look of dismay, Greny raised a mollifying palm. "You're not bereft of friends among the Vicenary Jurists. I'm sure you'd get a sympathetic hearing. If your associates on Rhumgad prove as useful to Gyre as you believe, the Jury mightn't even close down your operation."

"Don't dare pretend that you're doing me a favor. We both know the Iron Circle will confiscate my enterprise and I won't get a black serpent of its earnings."

"The Iron Circle will take it either way. I'm offering you a chance to save face. For Cibiela and the rest of your family."

"Why? What could you possibly gain from such generosity?"

"Despite what you might think, I'm not ill-disposed to you. I've always considered you a friend."

Ecethor snorted. "Friend? You don't have any friends. Aside from those flea-ridden rodents you keep as servants. Go away."

· · ·

Greny rose stiffly to his feet. *I saved your daughter, safeguarded her good name, and you repay me with hate.* "You have until the midnight bell tomorrow night. After that, I'll be forced to bring this matter to the Jury's attention."

He missed her retort as he hurried up the steps to his usual haunt.

Below, Drinith, Elca, and Okia entered the chamber through the main door and sauntered up to the middle rows on the right side. A couple of meritocrats rose from their seats to let them sit dead center, but Elca didn't follow her companions. She proceeded up the steps, her pale gaze fixed on Greny. He looked away, feigning ignorance of her approach.

The hem of her dress brushed against his legs as she sat beside him. The coercive intoxication of her pungent scent immediately put him on edge. She inhaled to speak.

"What do you want?" he asked, forcing himself to stare into those pale, pale eyes.

"Can I not check in on an old friend?"

The echo of his previous conversation with Ecethor made him wince. He looked about with theatrical exaggeration. "I don't see any friend of yours around here," he said with mock puzzlement.

Elca chuckled. "We are on the same side, you and I."

"Really? And what side would that be?"

"Gyre, of course."

Greny gestured at the chamber. "You could say that of any meritocrat."

Elca sniffed. "You smell surprisingly good for someone who spent yesterday in a sewer."

So that's why she's here. She can't have learned it from my ratchers. Drinith has already ejected Elca's agents from her staff. Elca must have spies in Ecethor's household. "I'm surprised you would take an interest in such an inconsequential matter."

"Drinith tells me the issue that sent you there had nothing to do with Magian."

"She is correct," Greny said emphatically, hoping he might bring the conversation to a swift conclusion.

"Because it's important that if there is any evidence—"

Greny sneered. "Getting nervous, are we?"

"We both know Magian is a threat, despite the wishful thinking of some of our colleagues. He must be dealt with before there's another attack like Crevastival."

Greny arched an eyebrow. "I'm under no illusion about the menace he poses. But I can only present the evidence I find to Parliament. I'm not going to fabricate proof."

"I would never ask you to," Elca said. "But are you sure Holver Dronan wasn't one of Magian's agents?"

How is she always so well informed? The whole city must spy for her. She would certainly make a formidable cordent general if she could be trusted with such power. "Dronan was a common criminal. Nothing more."

"Then why did you waste your time on him instead of focusing on the task the Vicenary Jury assigned you?"

"I need no lecture from you about my duties as a cordent general, thank you. It's exactly this kind of overreach that precipitated your previous fall from grace."

"I came here to offer the hand of friendship, and all you do is fling insults at me," Elca huffed.

"When I have conclusive proof that Magian is actively plotting against us, I will, of course, inform you and the rest of the Vicenary Jury. Until then, I suggest we keep our private interaction to a minimum. We wouldn't want Thaxen or Thespenilea questioning my impartiality."

With a derisive snort, Elca headed down to join the other leaders of the New War Faction. She sat between Drinith and Okia. The seat to their right had been left vacant, presumably for Aretro Falier.

Two leaders of the Short War Faction sat directly across from them on the opposite side of the chamber. The austere, gray Thaxen Saveral cut a striking contrast with the easy affability of her neighbor, Cenmis Velso. Cenmis's face possessed a plump, winsome beauty like an eternally ripe fruit.

Thespenilea Reiner hadn't arrived yet, while Osro Onez in her elbow-length ceremonial white cape sat alone on the stool reserved for the ducal steward by the white throne.

Greny couldn't help but grin. Aside from Drinith, neither faction had an inkling of the truth about the Crevastival attack. One of Drinith's advisers, an ex-mercenary called Gelasin, had instigated it. Drinith had stopped him, but she had gone along with the fiction that Magian had been behind it.

Timing is a funny thing. If Greny had learned the truth before Magian's machinations in Ophigee had been exposed, he would have sent Drinith to the Plank. But the nature of Magian's scheme had given him pause. Drinith and her network of Rhumgadian exiles had their uses sniffing out Magian's spies, and she didn't pose any risk to the Halcyon Republic while she remained ignorant of the proverbial knife Greny held to her throat.

5

———————

Drinith tucked her legs to one side as Aretro shuffled past her to take the empty seat to her right.

"I've heard a disturbing rumor," Aretro whispered as she brushed a couple of whitish red curls off the centicore medallion on her forehead. A blush tinged her orange cheeks. "About Tomyr Pitero."

"I heard something similar," Okia said breezily. "As far as I am concerned, she can sit with whomever she chooses."

Aretro's soft green eyes widened with surprise. "One of us should talk to her. Try to make her see sense."

Okia made a batting gesture with her hand.

"She has many friends in our faction," Aretro said, glancing around.

"The dragon's already taken flight, I'm afraid," Okia said.

"But who knows where it will ultimately perch?" Elca added with a sly grin.

Why didn't they tell Aretro the truth? They either feared her disapproval of Okia's scheme or simply couldn't be bothered. *What secrets are they keeping from me?*

"I'm more interested in whatever stunt Magian has planned for today," Elca said.

"The delegation hasn't stirred from their embassy since they arrived," Aretro said. "Its female contingent, fifteen girls about Drinith's age, wear splendid gowns and fine jewelry, but they are forced to share two cramped rooms, little better than prison cells. The windows are shuttered and barred and the beds were removed, so they must sleep on the floors."

"This is all fascinating," Elca said. "But what is the point of their visit?"

"If I knew that, I would tell you, of course," Aretro said with a hint of ire. Did she suspect that Elca and Okia weren't being forthright about Tomyr's impending defection? "Perhaps if you listened to what I say, you might answer your own question with the clues I've collected. There's a third room in the embassy, kept under guard. Fifteen red incindar chests are deposited there, one for each girl."

"And what might those chests contain?" Elca asked.

"I don't know," Aretro admitted.

"Those chests could contain anything," Okia opined.

The mesmeric pallor of Elca's eyes didn't entirely distract from the avaricious lick of her lips. "They must hold something very precious. Red incindar is the most valuable of all Rhumgadian woods. The Rhumgadians say it is the only wood fit for the cradles and coffins of kings."

Drinith stared incredulously at the mention of kings, a shocking breach of etiquette in this chamber. Aretro shifted uncomfortably in her seat and nervously glanced around.

Okia stared at Elca with bulging eyes a moment before breaking into a smirk. "You could have phrased that a little better, don't you think?"

"But it is the phrase," Elca said with a frisson of mock naivety. "What other way should I say it?"

"Monarchs rather than kings, perhaps," Aretro said.

"Rhumgadians are traditionally ruled by kings, not queens," Elca said. Directing a sidelong glance at Drinith, she rested a silken hand on hers. Drinith's spine tingled at the buttery softness of her touch. "Drinith shall be the first ruling queen of her people," she whispered.

"If they accept her," Okia said with discomforting gruffness. It was not reassuring to hear one of the New War Faction's leaders express such doubt, even in passing.

"Of course they will," Elca said, removing her hand to give Drinith's knee a few gentle pats. "After their tyrant emperor is deposed, they'll be delighted to have her."

Across the chamber sat two leaders of the Short War Faction. Cenmis Velso's plump countenance, with its large, soft brown eyes and the permanent hint of a smile, evinced an innate amiability. Thaxen Savarel looked as gray and grim as ever. Even across the chamber, Drinith could feel the cold hate in her black eyes.

Thespenilea swept into the chamber, accompanied by Tomyr Pitero.

"This is going to be embarrassing," Aretro muttered as she sank into her seat.

Cenmis's loud applause was taken up by several grinning meritocrats around her. Even Thaxen joined in, her face briefly transformed with uncharacteristic, though still malevolent, delight.

With predatory intensity, Elca sat forward and quickly performed a head count of their clapping opponents.

"By my reckoning," she said, "they number about four dozen, pretty much the same as us."

Okia grimaced. "A third of the chamber supports our faction, a third is firmly theirs, and a third continue to dither."

"Mark my words," Aretro said. "If we suffer any more notable defections like Tomyr, our faction will crumble."

Drinith did her best to conceal her unease. "Has everyone forgotten the attack at Crevastival?" she demanded. "Has nobody learned from Magian's machinations in Ophigee?"

"Our opponents, like us, recognize him as a threat," Aretro said. "But invading a shard the size of Rhumgad is a daunting prospect, even with the support of our allies. Many meritocrats are content to rely on the blockade of Rhumgad to neuter Magian's ambitions."

"So instead of freeing my people, you want to build a prison around their prison?" Drinith shouldn't have said that. Gyre's welfare was meant to be a meritocrat's paramount concern.

"Save that fire for the next debate," Okia said with distaste.

"Or better yet, keep it to yourself," Elca muttered, "or you may burn us all."

Drinith fought the reflex to apologize, which would be an admission of weakness.

"We're all on your side, Drinith," Aretro said, always the peacemaker.

"I didn't imply otherwise, did I?" It was the best non-apology Drinith could put together. "This waiting about makes me testy."

"It appears that we won't have to wait too much longer." Elca pointed to the throne. "Osro is strapping on her gold sword." The jewel-encrusted weapon was far too big for the Ducal Steward to wield, its purpose being purely ceremonial.

"I've often wondered, was the sword originally intended to defend the Ducalion from us or us from her." Okia smirked. "It appears little more than a pointless flourish now."

Osro pounded her gauntleted hand on the double doors behind the throne until they opened. The Ducalion entered, dressed in opalescent silk and fretted silver. She wore a white lion skin as a cape, its head drawn over hers like a hood. The thick mask of white powder on her face and elbow-length gloves made her look like a living statue as she glided toward her throne. Everyone rose from their seats in a show of respect as devoid of substance as Osro's sword. Countless whispered conversations filled the chamber before she had sat. Several meritocrats had already settled back into their seats before Osro's booming voice bade them to do so.

"A delegation from Magian the Infinite, the self-styled Emperor of Rhumgad, craves an audience with our parliament," she said. "Shall we admit them?"

The meritocrats shouted their assent, and the doors reserved for visitors opened.

The ambassador, a burly Rhumgadian highlander named Lysan Moylar, entered, followed by more than a dozen girls, dressed and bejeweled more opulently than the Ducalion. Each carried a red incindar chest.

Bowing to the Ducalion, Moylar grimaced as though the sign of respect due to Gyre's head of state was beneath him. "I bring salutations to the Halcyon Republic from His Imperial and Immortal Majesty, Magian the Infinite, King of Javlohm, Emperor of Rhumgad and its many kingdoms—Skander, Valmer, Eswonim, Ifar, Lenrath,..."

Gods, he is going to name every realm on the shard! A blush stung Drinith's cheeks as she guessed which he would mention last.

"... Chaden, Chanent, Jover, Egada, Starm, Tirem, Geltan,..."

She sat bolt upright, determined to deny him taking pleasure from the slightest hint of her chagrin.

"... Lemibus, Erdabo, Zadmy and Kaplar."

Drinith ignored disapproving glances from a few meritocrats on the opposite side of the chamber. Everyone was well aware the Blood Crown of Kaplar was her birthright.

With a triumphant sneer, Moylar continued: "His Imperial and Immortal Majesty requests that this unnecessary and provocative blockade should cease"—a few titters rippled through the audience; everyone knew Rhumgad hadn't the dragons to take on Gyre and its allies—"and friendly relations be restored between our shards."

Moylar's restless gaze moved about the chamber, doubtless searching for hints of sympathy among all the hostile faces. "He is aghast at the outrageous slander his enemies have spread about him. He swears in the names of the gods of his shard he had no part in the thwarted attack at your Crevastival celebration." His gaze suddenly fixed on Drinith. She met his sneer with haughty defiance, though behind that mask, her heart squirmed. She knew well he spoke the truth.

Elca stood. "And what of the mesmeric creature Prystian that attempted to topple Ophigee?"

Moylar shrugged. "You have only the word of the same person who blamed Magian for the Crevastival incident."

Thespenilea rose. "A meritocrat's word is beyond reproach. Our guest would do well to remember that."

The ambassador answered her with a brazen grin. "*If* anything I've said is untrue, I apologize."

Drinith didn't find much comfort in Thespenilea's support. Meritocrats would never disparage one of their own in front of outsiders. The pointed questions would likely come after Moylar departed.

"It is in all our interests that this conflict is resolved amicably," Moylar said. "How can His Imperial and Immortal Majesty prove his good intentions to Gyre, so that we can put this rancor behind us?"

"What does Magian offer beside platitudes?" demanded someone in a higher row behind Drinith. Approving murmurs rippled through the assembly.

"His Imperial and Immortal Majesty has sent his vassals with gifts from their kingdoms," Moylar said. "From Skander, Princess Ecawar brings a chest of dreamist. From Valmer, Princess Tavrar brings a gift of ground soulnacre. Princess Gerthar of Eswonim offers powdered monoceros horn...."

Each princess offered a rare spice, aphrodisiac, medicine, or narcotic native to her realm or the shard of Rhumgad. Drinith couldn't focus on them, forgetting their names as soon as she heard them. She was waiting for mention of one realm in particular.

"And last is Princess Eslaf of House Sathbad, *rightful* ruler of Kaplar."

Drinith straightened in her seat. House Sathbad, her house, her name. Who was this timid child who dared to claim the Blood Crown? Probably an unfortunate pauper that Magian's servants had foisted into the role.

"She bears a phial of dipsa poison," Moylar said with a grin. The serpent had a reputation for killing its victims before they noticed it had bitten them. Only assassins had a practical use for its venom.

Drinith concealed her ire at the calculated insult with a dismissive smile.

Aretro rose. "Is this all you offer us? Gifts for the Ducalion are all very well but—"

"Perhaps I did not make myself clear," the ambassador said. "These are given as samples. In exchange for peace, His Imperial and Immortal Majesty offers Gyre the monopoly on the trade of these substances."

"And if we refuse?" Aretro asked grimly.

The ambassador grinned. "Then, His Imperial and Immortal Majesty will extend the same offer to whichever of your allies is more amenable."

A collective gasp filled the chamber.

"We have a choice to make, it seems," Osro Onez said, her hand squeezing the hilt of her sword. "We will consider your emperor's offer. Leave us now and enjoy the Ducalion's hospitality. We will summon you in a few days when we have reached our decision."

"Quite an offer," Okia said. "The Halcyon Republic could profit hugely from such monopolies."

"Can Gyre be bought so easily by its enemies?" Drinith demanded.

"Come now. Don't be so naive. A blockade of Rhumgad can't be maintained indefinitely. Either we overthrow Magian or we must eventually come to some sort of accommodation with him."

"This proposal is an admission of weakness," Drinith said.

"True." Elca examined her long, sharp nails. "But the Short War Faction will argue that our position is also precarious. Our allies are former enemies. Any of them might be seduced by Magian's overture. Even the Shopkeepers." And with that capitulation, any chance of liberating Rhumgad would evaporate. "This offer is calculated to shred our alliance, regardless of whether we accept it. Magian is as subtle as dipsa venom and just as deadly."

"We can't give up," Drinith said, feeling useless.

"Of course not," Elca said. "But this makes uncovering Magian's efforts to undermine our republic all the more critical. We need to prove he is a persistent and unequivocal threat. You must uncover a plot equivalent to the Crevastival attack fast or events will overtake us and all hope of an expedition to Rhumgad will be lost."

Drinith glanced behind her for Greny Scylax, but the rows of chattering meritocrats obscured him. Somehow, she needed to secure credible evidence that Magian threatened the republic's survival. But if she failed to discover it, what then? She would have to manufacture the proof. She'd have to risk the same course that turned Gelasin into a monster.

6

His hands clasped, his elbows resting on the arms of his chair, Greny stared out the bay window of his study at the city far below. Beyond the reach of the inner sun's dull glow, lampstone constellations beaded the restless night, mapping out the streets veining the floating islands, giving shape to the architectural sprawl. Yes, light and dark would restlessly lie in each other's arms until dawn. In his youth, Greny had sometimes spent the entire night watching the ebb and flow of shadow across the patchwork of shardlets until the rising outer sun finally burned it away. He preferred to view Gyre from this lofty vantage in Scylax Tower. It looked so ordered, so peaceful.

The darkest spots were where the meritocrats' mansions clustered. Night was a commodity, like everything else in this floating city, to be hoarded and traded. It was fortunate for Greny that his family had inherited this ancient tower, a relic from the Age of Queens, and now the second tallest building in Gyre; only the Grand Preservatory was taller. Once such towers had been common, but the others had been felled by war, structural flaws, and other misfortunes. Scylax Tower's lean was noticeable, particularly at this height, but Greny never gave it much thought.

Well shielded from the inner sun's intrusive light, the tower had been built of imported black stone as if hewed from the night itself. At least here, high in the nocturnal sky, he could scrape together a few hours of sleep each night that irritating nether glow might otherwise deny him.

Not, of course, that he would get much rest tonight, he suspected. His conscience would nag him for a few nights after what he must do tonight. Still, it had to be done. It was his duty.

He took a deep breath and swiveled around to face his prisoner, a young girl shivering in a black nightdress, chained to her seat. Thean Rerato's maroon face was undeniably plain, but her indignation gave it a regal beauty. It was a pity Gyre hated all things royal.

A pair of ratchers in black and yellow cordent brigantines stood by her side, their clubs at the ready in the unlikely event she made trouble. Greny took pride in being able to tell their furry faces apart. The slightly taller one with the graying muzzle was Deetch, Greny's butler and more senior servant after Chemp. His younger, pale-blue companion, Queek, a recent addition to Greny's staff, had such earnest soot-black eyes. Both still possessed their long, slender tails. Gyre had always expected the ratchers it hired as executioners to dock their tails to make them look more human, but Greny never saw the point in it.

"Why did you drag me from my bed in the middle of the night?" Thean demanded.

"It's not your bed." How best to break the unpleasant news? "I'm afraid your time under my roof must end. The Vicenary Jury has ordered that you walk the Plank this very night."

She looked dazed, as though physically struck. His guests always did when their end came. They never heeded his warnings that execution was inevitable. Hope got the better of them.

He picked a scroll off his desk and waved it. "I hold your death warrant right here."

"My mother is an important woman…"

Greny suppressed a smirk. So much for all the blather about equality. *Faced with death,* he mused, *she turns to her former status to save herself.* "All meritocrats are. That is the nature of the Meritocracy."

"A meritorian can't be executed without the consent of her meritocrat."

"That doesn't apply to treason. Besides, your mother's seal is on the death warrant."

Thean gaped, her eyes bulging with horror. "No, she would never..." Turning her gaze to the floor, she burst into tears. "You made her do it."

Not Greny alone. The entire Vicenary Jury had prevailed upon Thean's mother, Nyriam, to condemn her traitorous child. But it hadn't taken that much persuasion. Nyriam was a patriot, and she had other daughters.

"You brought this on yourself," he said, vexed by an errant urge to comfort her. "You betrayed her."

"I didn't. I fought against this rotten government, not her."

"But *she* is the government. Don't you understand? All meritocrats are. You betrayed her. You betrayed your whole class."

"Meritocracy—what a joke! You should appreciate that better than anyone. You're a..."

He frowned, folding his arms. "I'm a what?"

"A man."

"My maleness is inconsequential." He tapped the metal disk on his forehead. "I'm a meritocrat, first and foremost."

She sneered. "If your mother had a daughter, you wouldn't be. You'd probably be long dead, gutted by some rival courtesar."

A memory came unbidden of his weeping mother crouched over the ledgerstone bearing her daughter's name in their family crypt. If Greny's sister had survived, she would indeed be standing here now instead of him. Or his mother might have passed over him and chosen his older brother Erphel instead. He had always been her favorite. But for whatever reason, she hadn't. She had made Greny her successor, and he had proved the wisdom of that decision a hundred times over by his service to the Halcyon Republic. By his sacrifice...

Rage made him unfurl the scroll with a snap. "See what your mother thinks of you!" He stabbed the Rerato seal, the grinning crocotta, with his finger. "She has endorsed your banishment to the penal colony of Beamstone."

Thean sighed with relief, exactly as he hoped she would. The best way to hurt her was to tease her with hope and then snatch it away.

He snickered. "Beamstone is a myth. There's no such colony."

"But..." She stared agog at him. "But my friends were exiled there. I've seen Beamstone on maps."

His guffaw filled the room. "If you took a dragon to the spot indicated on any of those maps, you'd find nothing but cliffs. Beamstone is a convenient fiction to conceal your execution. Troublemakers like you among the meritorian class, if they are caught before they gain notoriety among the common folk, are dispatched without fanfare. No point in highlighting the inconvenient fact your type exists among us. My ratchers will toss you off the Plank this night like a common criminal."

Thean attempted to leap from her chair, but the chains held her with a resolute clank, forcing her back into her seat. The ratchers raised their clubs, but Greny's headshake made them lower their weapons to their sides.

"I won't go quietly," Thean declared. "The whole city shall hear me tonight. Its streets will echo with my condemnation of a corrupt and venal system."

Greny sighed. He had heard variations of this speech countless times. At his signal, the ratchers grabbed the girl. Chained, Thean could do nothing but scream. Queek roughly pinned her arms behind her while Deetch fixed a wooden clamp over her mouth, stifling her screams.

"You were so certain of everything," Greny said, "and yet you understood so little. Get her out of my sight."

As the room filled with the clangor of chains, he turned his attention back to the city through the window. He tried to ignore her writhing reflection, translucent like a ghost on the pane. Despite her mouth being clamped, she managed an eerie moan as she was dragged from the room. The scuffling terminated with a decisive bang of the door.

Greny poured himself a bowl of hard, blood-red tea. It was cold and bitter, but he drank it anyway.

He should have been a little kinder to Thean. She was naive, almost to the point of absurdity. Her plot to assassinate the Ducalion had been so half-baked and wrongheaded, in less fraught times, the Vicenary Jury might have dismissed it as youthful exuberance. She might have made an able meritocrat someday. After all, the Meritocracy had little attachment to the present incumbent of the Leonine Throne. Greny certainly wouldn't mourn the Ducalion's death, given how close she had come to ruining his family. It was certainly ironic that she had become the target of a new generation of younger revolutionaries.

Greny began to sift through the batch of papers on his desk. It was part of his nightly ritual to review his spies' reports of the comings and goings of other meritocrats. He had fallen asleep reading them occasionally, but more often, the tea and some intriguing tidbit of information kept him awake for most of the night.

The first report he plucked from the pile bore the Hax alerion, though it might as well have displayed the Kaplar Blood Crown. Drinith had visited the house on Wealgiver Street, apparently to deal with a follower who had let his zeal override his good sense. What would she think if she realized that Greny had a transcript of every word exchanged there?

He scanned the other reports. On the surface, they comprised the usual mundane litany of visits, dinner engagements, and apparently random encounters, but the names of faction leaders popped up again and again. Over the next few days, both sides would work to win over the uncommitted and potential waverers by every lever at their disposal.

Magian posed a far greater threat than the likes of Thean Rerato or Drinith Hax. His divisive offer to the Parliament had set Short War and New War factions at each other's throats.

For the Short War Faction, the gain Magian offered was clear;

moreover, invading Rhumgad with Gyre's unreliable allies, even against Magian's paltry conflagration of dragons, posed great risk while offering dubious benefit. By themselves, the monopolies the tyrant had proposed wouldn't make amends for the foiled attack at Crevastival two years ago. Magian would have to execute a few of his senior servants to mollify Gyran indignation. Maybe that preening windbag, Lysan Moylar, could take the fall. He had been in Gyre at the time. He could have conceivably organized the attack. Magian wasn't the sort to balk at such petty sacrifices to get what he wanted.

The New War Faction's strongest counterargument was that Magian's attempt to destabilize Ophigee proved he couldn't be trusted. The reports also hinted that Elca and Okia had also turned to calling in old debts and favors owed to bolster their support.

Of course, Greny would maintain scrupulous impartiality, but he and the other cordent generals needed to keep a close eye on this politicking. The last thing Gyre needed was for the debate to turn violent.

The ratcher Chemp announced his intention to enter with a light knock. The black ratcher shuffled into the room with an apologetic squeak, carrying an envelope on a silver tray. The ratchers usually opened correspondence to check for poison before presenting it, but, laying the tray on the table, Chemp signed that he could smell the quick-fade ink normally reserved for messages from the Vicenary Jury.

Ratchers' understanding of human speech was exemplary, but they could not mimic it. Greny had mastered but a little of theirs which consisted of chirps and clicks, whimpers and hisses, grunts and growls and even sounds inaudible to human ears, so master and servants had turned to a complex system of hand gestures to bridge the gap.

The envelope was tan instead of red so it wasn't an official communication. The seal was stamped with the winged siren, the emblem of the Ducal Steward, Osro Onez. If she had written it, she was determined not to leave Greny in possession of anything incriminating.

At Greny's gesture, Chemp sliced through the wax and removed the letter. After sniffing it carefully, the ratcher returned it to the tray with a reassuring nod. Nonetheless, Greny slipped on a pair of gloves before picking it up. It was not beyond the bounds of possibility that one of his many enemies might coat the letter with something novel from a distant shard that might confound Chemp's sensitive nose. Greny quickly scanned the already fading writing.

> Greny,
>
> I write to you on a matter of utmost gravity that imperils our beloved republic. This is a new threat, entirely separate from our Rhumgadian entanglement, but its roots are old. Given its seriousness, I dare not commit its details to writing, but I urge you to visit me at my mansion in Woodshard this very night, alone, after the midnight bell. Trust nobody, not even those flea-bitten rodents you love to keep as pets.
>
> Osro.

THE NOTE HAD DISAPPEARED COMPLETELY before Greny had finished a second reread. He tossed the blank vellum sheet on his desk and drummed his fingers on the table meditatively. The letter certainly had the ring of something Osro might write, particularly her dig at his ratchers. But, if the danger was as great as she claimed, surely she would have come to him directly instead of sending this theatrical invitation. It might be bait in a trap designed to kill him or compromise him in some way.

He daren't risk going, and yet he couldn't ignore the urgency of Osro's summons. He would have liked to send his most senior cordent, Nayz, but he couldn't entirely trust the man, and Osro would be grievously insulted if an inferior answered her summons. There was only one person Greny might send in his stead.

He picked up his quill and scrawled orders to go to Onez's mansion at the appointed time. He sealed it in an envelope, stamping the wax with his rat king sigil, and marked it urgent. Chemp took the proffered message and, with a servile nod, backed out of the room. Let her take the risk. She was living on borrowed time already.

7

The parlor's walls looked bare to Drinith now that the pictures of previous Hax meritocrats no longer dominated them. Only the portrait of her immediate predecessor, her friend and benefactor Epmar, remained, taking pride of place above the mantelpiece. The others had been banished to haunt less frequented corners of the mansion so that Drinith might avoid their condemnatory glares.

Jarma sat on the couch across from her. In times past, they might, at first glance, have been mistaken for each other, but Jarma now accented her appearance to distinguish herself from her friend. The regal burst of lime curls covering her pate reminded Drinith of a lion's mane. The only jewelry she ever wore was the brooch Drinith had given her. It bore the Hax emblem, an alerion taking flight.

Ensconced beside her was Quiescat, the Oracle of Godsdoor, dressed in his white cowl. His two crystal eyes might regard Drinith with enigmatic impassivity, but the blue-black face in which they were set squirmed with disquiet and uncertainty.

"I don't like it," he said, waving the letter up and down in front of him. "Not one little bit. Why can't Greny Scylax go himself? He must suspect some kind of trap. You can't go to Osro Onez's mansion on your own. You simply can't." He let Jarma gently pry the missive from his hand. "She has despised you since your first encounter at Elca Trajar's ducal reception. If the Veiled Meritocrat hadn't wrested you from her clutches, you might be still rotting in a cell in Inkeep. Or worse."

"Greny's instructions are specific. I must go alone," Drinith said. "I wasn't even supposed to tell you."

Jarma's lips moved as she read the letter. Glancing up, she noticed Drinith watching her and blushed. She pressed her mouth shut, her gaze continuing to dart back and forth down the sheet. Drinith repressed the urge to assure Jarma that her embarrassment was unnecessary. She didn't want to deepen her friend's discomfiture by acknowledging its existence.

"And we both know why," Quiescat said. "Because I'd see it for what it is—a trap. Feign illness and decline. Let him mire some other poor fool in this dubious business."

"But Magian might be at the root of this threat," Drinith said. "If we found proof implicating him, we could break the impasse in Parliament in our favor."

"We don't even know the nature of the danger the Ducal Steward has uncovered. Greny himself could be behind it! That would explain his reluctance to go." Quiescat shook his head. "We have no idea of the power struggles within the Iron Circle. Greny has always struck me as someone out of place and unpopular in the meritocrat class. This invitation might be a pretext to isolate him from his rodent bodyguards so that he can be arrested. And in you blunder, at his behest, marking yourself as his trusted associate."

Jarma looked up from the letter. "Another possibility is that Osro and Greny have discovered your network of sympathizers in the Blue Quarter. This meeting could be a ruse to facilitate *your* arrest."

Quiescat rubbed the back of his neck. "Jarma makes an excellent point."

"Either scenario is possible," Drinith conceded. "But if it was Greny's intention to arrest me, surely he could have summoned me to his tower using any one of countless pretexts that would arouse less suspicion. If he had simply invited me to dinner, I would have probably accepted without a second thought. I'm sure the same applies to him with respect to Osro. Greny's unpopularity is why he was made a cordent general in the first place. He poses no threat to the Meritocracy because of it."

"No threat to the Meritocracy, true, but to individual meritocrats?" Quiescat shook his head again. "You mustn't go. You simply mustn't."

"But I have to," Drinith said gently. "Don't you see? I can't turn my back on Greny—"

"Because he'd happily stab you in it." Quiescat threw up his hands in frustration. "Don't tell me that you've begun to trust the Rat King."

"Of course not," Drinith said. "But I must maintain the impression that I do."

"Even at the risk of your life?"

"I'm going," Drinith declared. She couldn't sit about waiting for the Parliament to decide their response to Magian's offer. She needed to do something.

"Quiescat is correct," Jarma said. "You're too vital to risk on such a potentially dangerous venture. But you're right as well. We need to know about this threat, whatever it is. Let me go in your stead. I'll play Meritocrat Hax for the night."

"Absolutely not."

"Drinith," Quiescat said. "You're key to Rhumgad's liberation. Jarma..." Turning the inhuman gaze of his crystal eyes toward the girl, he fell into an awkward silence.

"I'm expendable," Jarma stated.

"I didn't mean—"

Jarma straightened, looking every bit a meritorian, betraying no hint of the diffident maid she had once been. "It's the truth. I'm sure Drinith would expect nothing less than the truth from either of us."

"I'll not risk your life," Drinith said with a firmness that she hoped might avoid further argument.

"You're letting your attachment to me overrule your good sense," Jarma said. Quiescat gave an emphatic nod.

"My objections are entirely practical," Drinith lied. "Jarma, you are quite capable of convincing servants that you are me, but other meritocrats are a different matter entirely."

Jarma pursed her lips, clearly stung.

"I'm not in any way implying you're unsuited to be a meritocrat," Drinith hastened to explain. "Over the last two years, I've chatted with nearly every meritocrat at some point, oft in intimate circumstances. Even Osro Onez, despite her distaste for me. An idle question might expose you as an impostor."

"If so, what of it?" Jarma scoffed.

"You said yourself that you're expendable. You're not to me, but to the likes of Osro Onez or Greny Scylax in a tight corner...." Drinith shrugged. "The Meritocracy would never countenance my inexplicable disappearance. That's not down to the value they put on me personally, you understand. It's the threat such a vanishment might pose to the stability of their regime. It gives me some protection among them and that is why I, not you, should go."

Her advisers admitted defeat with glum silence.

"I survived cannibals and monsters on Ophigee," she said. "I think I can manage a nighttime excursion to Osro Onez's mansion."

"Then at least take Woad or his wife Tazran with you, if not into the mansion itself, then to its gates," Quiescat pleaded.

"Very well," Drinith said. It seemed a sensible compromise. "And, of course, I'll be armed." She patted the secret pocket that contained her knife, the deep black of her dress concealing the little bulge it made.

"I still don't like it," Quiescat said, rubbing the back of his neck. "You saw what this false princess of Kaplar brought—an assassin's tool. That was meant as a threat. But if you must go, then so be it. You are not a child any longer. I cannot stop you. Just...just be careful. I feared you were lost on Ophigee. I have no wish to repeat that experience."

"If our nerve fails now, Kaplar is lost forever."

Quiescat sighed. "True. Go now before I change my mind."

8

Ngry shouts outside drew Drinith to lift the corner of the curtain and peer out of the palanquin at the milling crowds. Two cordents wearing black and blue check brigantines roughly dragged a ragged Nosteran along the street in the opposite direction to her palanquin. A third cordent wearing the same colors strolled after them, cradling a pile of bread rolls in her arms. The three were bluechecks, reporting to Greny's rival cordent general, Posaleum Minol. Around them, hawkers accosted passersby, exhorting them to examine their wares. A stooped man waved his fist at urchins scampering away with some of the spilled bread rolls he was trying to gather onto a wooden tray. Incessantly suffused in the inner sun's light, Gyre never slept.

"At least there are plenty of people about," Drinith murmured, mostly to herself.

Tazran, sitting across from her, fingered the pommel of her dagger. A sliver of chain mail peeped above the shallow V-shaped neckline of her tunic. The ex-mercenary was nicknamed the Widow on account of having buried three husbands before she married Woad. Though she hadn't a gray hair on her head, her haggard face told the tale of a life hard lived. Drinith often sensed a sadness behind her fierce demeanor, but tonight she was as taut as the mechanism within the springbow, cocked and ready on her lap.

She ventured the opposite opinion, apparently just to make conversation. "I'd prefer fewer people. It would be easier to see a foe coming at you. Not that it'll matter in Woodshard. Always quiet there, quiet as a grave."

Drinith had visited Woodshard before to call on some of its resident meritocrats. Day or night, the park had always offered a pleasant respite from the din of the city. "I suppose you agree with Quiescat and Jarma that this visit isn't a good idea."

"Young Nosdan and I will be close by and alert for the first hint of trouble, but we can't see what awaits you in Meritocrat Onez's mansion. You'll be on your own in there. You'll have to deal with any threat you encounter by yourself."

Drinith slipped her hand into her secret pocket and touched the slender hilt of her knife. She also wore her mail shirt beneath her dress and her alicorn bracelet on her wrist to test any food or drink her host might offer for poison.

The gentle sway of the palanquin came to a stuttering halt. The front of the palanquin dropped suddenly, almost throwing Drinith on top of her companion. Outside, Nosdan snarled, "Get away or I'll call the cordents! This palanquin belongs to a meritocrat. Have you no respect?" The bright giggles of children taunted him. The rear of the palanquin fell so the cab became level again.

"Wait here," Tazran muttered, scrambling out the door. Shrieks of laughter greeted her threatening barks, only to fade away amidst the general hubbub. She stuck her head back into the cab. "The front casquar stepped on a crude caltrop, possibly thrown by one of those kids pestering us. The bird's too lame to carry us further. It might be a coincidence. I've heard of a few incidents like this recently. I'll go see if I can hire a replacement."

"We haven't time," Drinith said, rising to exit the palanquin. "We'll be quicker on foot."

"I'm not sure it's such a good idea," Tazran said, but she dutifully helped Drinith out of the cab.

Three men garbed in bright colors tottered on high-heeled shoes toward them. Peacock feathers jutted from the rear of their bird-shaped tricornes, a hat currently considered the height of fashion among courtesars. The leader's gilded feathers were particularly striking. Red eyes decorated the scalloped hem of his emerald cape. His doublet bore the whorl-shelled wyrm of House Orom. His black hair was adorned with silk flowers and braided into two fat dragon tails that hung over his shoulders. He had an impossibly smooth and youthful face, like red porcelain, but powder couldn't entirely conceal the score on his left cheek and a neat notch on the side of his nose. His rose eyes glowed with mirthful arrogance. Drinith had seen him about before, but she knew little about him other than he was a son of Ecethor Orom.

Off to the side Nosdan held nervous sentry, clenching and unclenching his fists. Drinith warned him not to do anything rash with a subtle shake of her head.

"Does the meritocrat require an escort?" the courtesar asked, doffing his hat and bowing deeply. "I am Rosel of Orom. My two brothers-in-arms are Ticen of Sonet and Cofran of Ozenlor."

Ecethor was a close friend of Elca and a committed member of the New War Faction. Cofran's meritocrat was lukewarm in her support while Ticen's mother maintained a stubborn neutrality. Courtesars, of course, were bound by their code to not meddle in Gyran politics, but the political and the personal converged in their duels with surprising frequency.

"The trouble with these courtesars is, if you accept their help, it will be impossible to be rid of them," Tazran muttered under her breath.

Rosel flashed a menacing grin at her. "You need not fear us," he promised Drinith. "For us, your word is law."

Drinith didn't bother to point it out a meritocrat's word was law to everyone in Gyre. Rosel's smile was too stiff and practiced, and an unsettling lascivious glint lurked in his lingering gaze. She should be wary of this peacock and his friends. But the Courtesar Code protected her, and who knew what dangers lurked between here and

Osro's home? She looked to Tazran to confirm her urge to accept his help. The Widow conceded defeat with a reluctant nod.

"I am on my way to the Woodshard district," Drinith said. "Would you mind escorting me as far as Diadem Bridge?"

"We would be honored," Rosel declared, smiling up at her from the depths of another bow.

Nosdan remained behind to tend to the injured casquar. The giant black bird jerked its hooked yellow beak at its caretaker just once, but was too much in pain to further rebuff his ministrations. "That'll take some time to heal," Nosdan murmured, gingerly probing the massive taloned foot. "If I ever find the scoundrels who did this, they'll be sorry."

The three courtesars, taking the lead, plowed through the crowds with embarrassing arrogance, while Tazran trailed behind Drinith far less conspicuously. Drinith greeted with relief her first glimpse of Diadem Bridge, an elegant curve across a large chasm, burnished by the inner sun far below. As soon as she stepped onto its stone deck, she took a deep breath and said, "Good courtesars, thank you for your help. I have no further need for your protection."

Rosel studied the dark woods on the far side of the bridge, then returned his gaze to her. "Are you certain, Meritocrat?" He glanced dismissively at Tazran who glared back with fierce disdain. "I'm sure I speak for my companions when I say we would be delighted to accompany you the rest of the way to your destination. There's no telling what danger may lurk in that park at night."

"I'll be fine," Drinith said firmly.

Rosel bowed. "Of course, Meritocrat. But at least allow me the pleasure of calling to your mansion tomorrow to put my mind at ease that you finished your journey without mishap." Ticen and Cofran frowned behind him.

"Very well," Drinith sighed.

"Then I will bid you farewell for now. I will know no sleep this night in anticipation of seeing you again." With a parting bow, he flounced away, followed by his muttering companions.

Tazran grinned. "Quiescat won't be too happy when Rosel of

Orom turns up at your door. Unless his two friends slay him for usurping your attention." A guffaw burst from her. "He comes across as more turkey than peacock, to be honest."

"If he becomes a nuisance, I'll pluck his feathers." Drinith was a meritocrat, after all.

Tazran's face stretched with dismay. "But you'll break his heart."

Drinith stared at her in disbelief. She couldn't be suggesting there was some romantic spark between them.

Tazran burst out laughing again, so loud it echoed across the chasm. "You should see your face." Sobered by Drinith's ill-concealed annoyance, her hilarity quickly faded. "We had better press on or you'll be late. Once we've passed the cordent checkpoint on the far side of the bridge, I'll drop some distance behind you, near enough to step in if something happens, but not so close as to be noticed. And I won't be merrily meandering along the path either. I'll be moving under the cover of trees and hedgerows as much as possible, so don't panic if you can't see me." She hesitated a moment, then asked: "May I speak freely?"

"Go right ahead."

"Don't mind my teasing about that silly courtesar. It's just I worry sometimes you show no interest in boys. I wouldn't want you to end up alone and crabby like your friend, the Oracle."

"I've a shard to free," Drinith said, flushing. "And anyway, it seems that every man I take an interest in ends up dying."

"It's not you. It's this life. I've lost three husbands and several lovers down through the years. Some I regret, others I don't. One was so bad, I had to kill him myself."

Drinith's heart skipped a beat at this unexpected and unsettling disclosure. She knew little of Tazran and Woad's mercenary past, aside from vague allusions and the occasional revelatory morsel such as this. She was probably better off not knowing. Their former lives didn't matter. They were her friends now.

"Best not to plan too far ahead," Tazran said. "Take your comfort where you can find it. As long as it's not some painted turkey. The difference between a courtesar and a turkey is the turkey will probably live longer. Find a real man."

"That's sage advice," Drinith said, hoping to finish the conversation before it became even more awkward. Warning her off courtesars was pointless. The Meritocracy wouldn't tolerate her taking a lover who wasn't one, particularly given the unusual circumstances of her elevation to a meritocrat, and she found courtesars as a general class irritating. She'd find no man in Gyre with whom she could share her life. That was a certainty.

"We had best focus on the matter at hand," Tazran said. They crossed the bridge in silence. Between the balustrades, their detail smothered in countless layers of white paint, the inner sun could be glimpsed far below as a smudged flare in the sepia cloud.

Recognizing Drinith as a meritocrat, three surprised cordents at the checkpoint stood to attention. Their black and red brigantines identified them as redchecks, members of Opriet Braesum's division. It would have been a comfort, however illusory, if some of Greny's yellow checks had been stationed there instead.

"Begging your pardon, Meritocrat," the sergeant said, stepping forward. "The park is a lonely place at night. I can spare a cordent to accompany you wherever you're going."

"There's no need," Drinith said, pointing to Tazran behind her. "My servant is more than capable of protecting me, I assure you."

"If you're certain, Meritocrat." Stepping out of her way, he bowed. The two younger cordents hesitantly followed his example.

Tazran stayed close until hedges and trees swallowed the checkpoint. She drifted behind, then melted into the blind darkness untouched by the squat lampstone pillars illuminating the path.

Drinith encountered nobody else as she hastened along majestic tree-lined thoroughfares crisscrossing the shardlet. Except for the persistent din of the city, reduced to a barely perceptible hum by distance, she might have been wandering through the heart of the countryside on Noster. Hulking manses protruded over the tops of trees like long-forgotten temples. She recognized the entrance to Osro's mansion by the reliefs of winged sirens on the gate piers.

She rang the bell at the gate and waited in vain for one of Osro's servants to answer. A second ring also drew no response. Perhaps Osro had dismissed her staff for the night. Or the servant on duty might have fallen asleep. Drinith reached through the gate and pulled down the handle. The gate squealed as she pushed it open.

She crunched down the gravel path toward the great house, expecting to be challenged at any moment. Plinthed statues of women loomed above her, the nameless wives and lovers of forgotten emperors plundered from their ruined palaces.

Trembling candlelight shone through the half-open doorway. Had the door been left ajar for her? She crept up the steps to the entrance, determined to make as little sound as possible. The door creaked open to her gentle push.

She glanced over her shoulder. Where was Tazran? Perhaps it would be wise to leave.

A low moan from within the mansion made Drinith shiver. She drew her knife—it felt so slight in her hand—and entered. A man, a servant judging by his dark blue livery, lay tucked behind a couch. Blood matted the back of his head. His upturned earthen green eyes opened. He stared up at Drinith a moment in utter confusion, then passed out.

The sound of creaking floorboards came from the parlor. Something hard clattered against the floor, followed by a frightened squeak.

Drinith took a deep breath, tiptoed over to the door and threw it open. So contorted by panic was the meritocrat's face, it took Drinith a moment to recognize one of the leaders of the Short War Faction, Cenmis Velso.

"It's not what it looks like." She held a bloody dagger in her hand. At her feet lay a crumpled body. Osro's bloodied siren medallion rested alongside it.

9

"I didn't kill her!" Cenmis squealed, the bloody dagger trembling in her hand.

Drinith's swallow hurt her dry throat. "Then you won't mind letting go of the knife."

The dagger dropped as if forgotten and stabbed the wooden floor.

"I found her like this," Cenmis said, clasping her hands. "She invited me here."

"I was invited here too, in a fashion," Drinith said. "Do you know why she asked you to come?"

Cenmis opened her hands in a gesture of bewilderment and despair. She looked around as if searching for an answer.

Drinith pointed to the pile of scrolls and books beneath an emptied bureau. "Did you do that or...?" Drinith asked.

Cenmis nodded. "I rifled through the desk, too, hoping to find some clue what her real purpose was in inviting me here, but I discovered nothing strange except the sunfinch." She directed a quivering finger at a dead bird on the low table in the center of the room. "Perhaps we should—"

"What's going on here?"

They both jumped at the thunderclap of Thaxen's voice. She

stood in the doorway, fixing her malevolent gaze first on Drinith and then on the body. Shifting shadows behind her alerted Drinith to the presence of two men in dark gray uniforms, armed with springbows.

"It's not what it looks like," Cenmis said.

"So you say," Thaxen said with daunting fierceness. Her black eyes narrowed as she stared at Cenmis's bloody hands.

"I didn't kill her," Cenmis bleated.

Drinith's hand trembled with the sudden remembrance that she held her own knife. As she edged it toward its secret pocket, Thaxen waggled one regal finger scoldingly.

"Ah ah ah! Slide it along the floor to me, please."

Drinith stooped to place the knife on the wooden floor, then kicked it over to Thaxen, who stopped it with her foot. One of her henchmen retrieved the weapon and held it before Thaxen so she could examine it. She studied the blade intently. Drinith hoped that she might return it to her after finding no blood, but Thaxen left it with her flunkey.

"Drinith, what do you say happened here?" Thaxen asked as she approached Osro's body.

"I found the servant in the reception hall, clubbed senseless." Drinith had forgotten him. She repressed the impulse to rush to the poor man's aid. This wasn't the time for abrupt movements. "Cenmis arrived just before me, I think."

Cenmis gratefully pounced on Drinith's statement. "Yes, yes. I found poor Osro lying here, already dead. Perhaps the preservators could treat her?"

Thaxen crouched beside the corpse and examined it. "She's too long dead." She yanked the bloody dagger free. "The handle bears the Onez siren." She touched the blade and rubbed a little of the blood between her finger with her thumb. "How long ago did you find her?"

"Moments ago," Cenmis insisted. "Just before Drinith arrived."

That couldn't be true given her rummage of the bureau and the desk, but Drinith let her claim go unchallenged.

"I'll return in a moment." Thaxen left the room. One of her guards drew the doors almost shut.

"Can we trust her?" Cenmis whispered. "She could accuse both of us of the murder."

Drinith left her question unanswered. *I'm not even sure I can trust you.*

Heavy boots tramped about the reception hall beyond. Drinith and Cenmis heard Thaxen bellow, "Take care of the servant and search the rest of the mansion!" The Intelligencer General reentered the room without her bodyguards, carefully closing the doors behind her. "Where are your palanquins?"

"I walked here," Cenmis said. "I live only a short distance away and Osro was emphatic that I should come alone."

"I had to abandon my palanquin," Drinith said. "One of the casquars went lame."

"So you came alone too?"

"Yes," Drinith lied.

Cenmis's face lit up with sudden inspiration. "If we testified before a pair of truthscryers, I'm sure we'd be able to prove our innocence."

Drinith had not forgotten the painful lesson of her trial on Ophigee. Her fate must never depend on truthscryers again. "No!" she and Thaxen declared in unison.

"You know how such testimony can be twisted," Thaxen said. "There's no guarantee that the questions wouldn't stray into uncomfortable topics. I'll only submit to truthscryers as an absolute last resort. My people will find any remaining traces of Osro's killer. I'm puzzled why Osro summoned us here. Cenmis, you and I belong to her circle of friends. But why would she invite you, Drinith? You've never been…a favorite of hers."

"Perhaps it had something to do with Magian's delegation." Cenmis suggested.

"Perhaps," Thaxen said. "But why would the Rhumgadians kill Osro?"

In other circumstances, Drinith would have vehemently protested such loose language. It was improper to cast Magian's minions as Rhumgadians. They were something else entirely. They didn't represent her people. But she daren't say anything that might antagonize Thaxen and remind her of their mutual antipathy.

"Osro was a member of the faction working to end the blockade," Thaxen continued. "Unless..." Her eyes fixed on the dead bird.

"Unless?" Drinith prompted, after a long silence.

Thaxen pursed her lips and nodded to herself.

"Well?" Drinith demanded.

"Unless they intended to pin this murder on you. We must leave at once." She shot out the door and yelled to her servants to prepare to leave.

"What about Osro?" Cenmis pleaded, chasing her. Drinith hastened after them.

"What about her?" Thaxen muttered as she charged out the front door, down the steps. "There's nothing we can do for her. This whole meeting has to be a trap. Osro mightn't have even written those invitations."

She halted abruptly and peered back into the mansion. "You two, head to your homes. We'll meet in the morning. Talk to nobody else about this until then." At her nod, the guard carrying Drinith's knife threw it on the gravel.

Drinith hesitated.

"Go!" Thaxen leapt into her palanquin. "Hurry!"

Drinith snatched up the blade and dashed after Cenmis. They raced by Thaxen's palanquin, into which her driver and one of her guards were loading the insensate servant, proceeded down the gravel path and through the open gate.

"You can spend the night in my mansion, if you wish," Cenmis said between gasps when Drinith caught up with her.

Drinith didn't dare trust her. "I had better head home, thanks."

"Osro's killer might be still lurking about. Wait here. I'll get one of my servants to accompany you to Hax Mansion."

"No need, no need," Drinith said, stalking away. "I'll be fine, I promise." As soon as she had slipped out of Cenmis's sight, she broke into a run.

Cenmis couldn't be trusted, and neither could Thaxen. As for Greny, he had sent Drinith to Osro's mansion in his stead. He must have had some inkling of the peril that awaited her there. He might have even murdered Osro and sent Drinith to take the blame.

No, she mustn't give in to paranoia. Panicking would only make this situation worse. Greny wasn't well liked, but he had a reputation for being incorruptible to a fault. He knew she was innocent. He'd protect her. Hopefully.

Unlike Osro and her other guests, he wasn't aligned with the Short War Faction. Whoever had instigated this murder might have invited him in the hope he would discover Thaxen and Cenmis standing over Osro's corpse. A denouncement from him would be enough to secure their conviction.

That suggested somebody in the New War Faction, probably Elca or Okia, had set this up to discredit their rivals. It would make sense given the damage Magian's offer had done to their cause. Or Cenmis had murdered Osro for some unrelated reason. Or Thaxen had killed her and returned to the mansion, so Cenmis and Drinith would presume her innocent. Or Magian's agents had simply slain Osro to throw suspicion on the New War Faction. In which case, Greny had been invited not to denounce Thaxen and Cenmis but to absolve them.

Drinith had been too long in this accursed city. Its pervading sense of threat had seeped like damp into her bones. When she first arrived in Gyre, the Meritocracy had been daunting, but at least there had appeared to be some order to its structure. As time passed, it became increasingly clear that it was in actuality a patchwork of ambitions and rivalries threaded together by the veneration of tradition and the fear that its hegemony might collapse. Maybe, she resigned herself with a sigh, it was the natural order of life to be always besieged by fear.

Part of her longed to flee the city and its dark machinations, but leaving Gyre would be an admission of guilt and any hope of liberating her homeland would be gone. She was also tired of running. Drinith had spent most of her childhood wandering from one shard to the next, begging for help from its rulers. She couldn't return to that vagabond existence. She had worked so hard to establish herself in Gyre, and the local Rhumgadian exiles relied upon her.

"Drinith, wait," someone croaked.

Whipping her knife from its pocket, Drinith turned to face the speaker. Tazran staggered from the darkness of the forest and leaned against a tree. She raised her bowed head, revealing one eye swollen and bruised, her lip cut. She spat into the grass. "A bunch of thugs jumped me, then disappeared with my knife, springbow, money pouch, and boots." Gritting her teeth, she limped toward Drinith. "I don't think it was a robbery, though. The theft seemed like an afterthought. They must have noticed I was wearing mail, but they did not try to strip me of it."

She threw her arm over Drinith's shoulder. Dragging her along, Drinith recounted what happened in Osro's mansion.

"Nasty business. Scylax has put you in great danger." Tazran halted, gently pushed Drinith away. She hobbled over to the nearest tree and propped herself with one hand against its trunk. "You need to leave me here. You can't wait for me. Either Thaxen Savarel or Cenmis Velso might send killers in their pay to hunt you down."

Drinith looked around in desperation. There had to be some way to convince Tazran to come with her. "I'm staying if you are."

Tazran rolled her eyes. "Great idea! Get us both killed to salve your conscience. Has it not occurred to you that I might be safer on my own? Those thugs would have already killed me if that was their intention, and your meritocrat friends are likely unaware I am here."

"You're right," Drinith admitted. "I'll go."

The crunch of feet along the path spurred both of them to retreat into the forest's shadows. Thaxen's palanquin sped by, accompanied by four jogging guards.

"Go now, before you're discovered," Tazran whispered. "I'll call to your mansion as soon as I can."

Drinith ran toward Diadem Bridge. A babel of voices ahead made her take cover in the foliage again. She watched cordents race by in the direction of Osro's mansion. They must know about her murder. Perhaps Thaxen had reevaluated the situation and decided the safer course was to turn Cenmis and Drinith in.

Smoke scented the air with an ominous sourness. A gate creaked open behind Drinith, and servants, many still in their nightclothes, bolted in the same direction as the cordents. How had word traveled so fast?

Drinith tucked her golden emblem of merit under her cloak. Her pursuers, if they existed, would be looking for a meritocrat. She hastened to the bridge. The checkpoint was abandoned. The cordents on duty must have headed to the mansion. As she crossed the bridge, she glanced back to confirm nobody had followed her. Something caught her eye, a thick column of black smoke rising against a flickery glow from the park. She guessed what was burning: Orso's mansion. Thaxen certainly was making a determined effort to obliterate any evidence of her involvement. Could that resolve extend to murder? Thaxen was certainly callous enough to kill, and she detested Drinith.

A redcheck cordent led a large crowd of men and women carrying buckets across the bridge in the opposite direction. Drinith froze as the cordent waved at her furiously. Was he ordering her back?

"Out of the way!" he yelled. "Bucket brigade passing through!"

She pressed against the parapet as faces flushed with excitement flooded by. She continued across the bridge as soon as the stream of people sufficiently thinned. A crowd had coalesced at the far end to stare across the chasm. She pushed by them, ignoring their eager questions, and fled down the street. Here, the habitual clamor of the city continued, oblivious to the drama in Woodshard. She was safe, or at least as safe as anyone wandering the streets at night alone could be. She avoided eye contact as much as possible as she hurried along. Every face she glimpsed, no matter its demeanor, posed a potential threat.

Her visit to Greny could wait. She needed to get back to her mansion first, warn Quiescat and Jarma, and get help for Tazran. The meritocrats had proved their ruthlessness before, arresting Drinith's friends while she was trapped in Ophigee. Now, one of their own had been murdered, a crime tantamount to treason.

A chattering mob clogged the bridge over the canal ahead. They were staring and pointing at something floating in the dark water. Drinith didn't feel safe pushing her way through them, so she headed along the canal to the next bridge.

Some spectators at the rear, having the same idea, broke from the back of the crowd and dashed past her. Determined not to be blocked again, Drinith ran with them. She wormed halfway across the bridge before becoming trapped in the press of excited gawkers. They surged forward, jostling her, pushing her against the parapet as the object in the water floated nearer. It looked... It couldn't be... As it drifted on, there could be no doubt. It was the side of a palanquin, and over the rectangular door was a mandrake, Thaxen's emblem.

10

Greny sipped his lukewarm tea and poured his restless gaze over the nightly reports. They contained the usual litany of luncheons and dinners, inconsequential affairs, open and illicit, business deals, duels, petty spats, suspected pregnancies, mysterious letters, overheard whispers. Ordinarily he loved puzzling over them, piecing them together into revealing sequences. But he couldn't concentrate. His thoughts kept drifting to what might be happening at Osro's mansion.

He pushed the stack of reports away, and rising stiffly from his desk perused his shelves for something to read. He enjoyed histories of the Nosteran Imperial Court, not from the grubby age of Mock Emperors with their tarnishing crowns and shrinking territories, but from when the Empire was at its height of its strength, to all appearances indefatigable and insuperable. They were always packed with politics, intrigue, and betrayal, while the passage of time had rendered the violent passions and rivalries that shaped them into nonthreatening curiosities. The books were entertaining, sometimes titillating, and, he fancied, educational. What was the Meritocracy but a court without a monarch?

He picked out Scavar Teram's weighty biography of the emperor Hevis IV and settled into his chair, but the text proved too turgid to keep his attention. He slapped the tome shut and tossed it onto the desk. It landed with a loud thump, blowing the topmost parchments off the stack and sending them gliding onto the floor.

Unable to think of any other distraction, Greny rose from his seat again and paced the room.

For a man who had been accused by more than one of his prisoners of having no conscience, regrets often nagged him. Of course, he never slid into contrition. He did what was expected of a cordent general. Someone had to protect the Halcyon Republic from those who would pick it apart. They were always lurking in the shadows—fools and philosophers, tyrants and would-be saviors, idealists and cynics, the selfish and the self-denying—an endless deluge of threats with nothing in common but their hatred of Gyre and its institutions. The meritocrats themselves sometimes posed the greatest danger. He didn't trust ambition, not even his own.

His mother's imperious visage glared down on him from her portrait. She would have preferred his brother, Erphel, to succeed her, but he had loved the sword too much to become a meritocrat. Erphel was the lucky one. A courtesar's enemies never hid behind smiles and lies. They acted with honor. And if a courtesar avoided a hero's death, he could end his career by simply putting aside his sword and his name and live out his days in comfortable anonymity, free from threat. Erphel probably slept soundly in a warm bed every night, dreaming of past duels and romances.

A sudden urge to summon Thean made him feel foolish. She was dead, of course. Despite her faults, or perhaps because of them, she had relieved a little of the tedium that often beset him, and the tower felt emptier without her. He should have been kinder the night he sent her to the Plank. Someone with her qualities rarely fell into his hands.

Did he send Drinith to her death tonight? Or set in motion his own?

A knock on the door. News of Drinith perhaps. "Come in."

Deetch's gray muzzle peeped through the opening door. He entered, bowed, and presented Greny with a sealed note from his second-in-command, Nayz. After Deetch had sniffed it, Greny sliced the seal open with his knife, and unfolded the message. Thaxen Savarel's palanquin had been dumped in the canal, along with several corpses. Thaxen was among the dead and Osro's mansion in Woodshard was on fire!

"Prepare my palanquin," Greny ordered, adding the note to the heap. "I must leave as soon as it's ready."

Drinith, too, might be a victim. Or, worse, the perpetrator. Greny slipped on his conical helmet and his emblem of merit, then hurried out the door, throwing on his coat as he took the winding stairs two at a time. His legs ached by the time he reached the bottom. He once had an engineer examine the possibility of installing an elevator in the tower, but in the end, Greny couldn't bring himself to trust such a contraption. He'd have to move to one of the lower chambers when he was too old and frail to make the climb to the top, but that hopefully wouldn't be for a long time yet.

A kerfuffle greeted him in the reception hall. Quiescat of Godsdoor remonstrated with Chemp and Deetch. Glimpsing Greny, he tried to push by the two giant rodents.

"Let our guest through," Greny said.

Quiescat squeezed past the parting ratchers with a wary glance. He stood before Greny brushing the coarse bits of brown and gray fur from the sleeves of his cowl with clear distaste. "Drinith hasn't returned home. The city is full of rumors about meritocrats being murdered. I'm worried."

"So am I," Greny said. *Though probably not quite for the same reasons.* "If I'm to help her, I need to know exactly what has happened."

Quiescat gaped at him. "How am I supposed to know? You sent her to Osro Onez's mansion."

So Drinith had confided to Quiescat about the meeting against Greny's strict instructions. She no doubt told the Oracle everything. "Don't waste time telling me what I already know. Did she go to

Osro's mansion alone?" Greny made a subtle gesture with his hand, significant only to him and his rodent servants. Deetch scurried into the guardroom.

"She went by palanquin," Quiescat said. "The driver accompanied her and one of our most trustworthy friends, Tazran Glastum. The palanquin returned early. Apparently, one of the casquars went lame. Drinith and Tazran continued on foot."

"Did the driver know the details of her mission?"

"*Details?*" Sarcasm inflected Quiescat's voice. "No, only the destination." He apparently didn't notice Deetch returning with two other ratchers, Zetch and Queek. The latter, with the impatience of youth, closed on the Oracle, but a sharp flick of Greny's hand stalled him. The Oracle made a puzzled frown at the gesture but didn't comment.

"This is very important," Greny said. "Only you, Drinith, and Tazran Glastum knew the purpose of her journey?"

"Yes," Quiescat said after a moment of hesitation, "but Tazran would never betray her."

"Comforting to know."

Quiescat's frown deepened as Greny struck his fingers repeatedly against the palm of his hand to make a soft clapping sound. The ratchers surged around the Oracle. Quiescat tried in vain to pull free of the claw-like hands seizing him.

"Take him to the Yellow Section at Inkeep. He's not to be harmed," Greny commanded. It would have been a pleasure to hold such a learned man like Quiescat here in the tower. The conversation certainly would have been stimulating. But the possibility remained that Greny might have to release him.

Greny met Quiescat's stare. Horror and incredulity imbued those two glittering spheres with such peculiar humanity that Greny chuckled. "I would have thought that an oracle would have seen this coming. While I possess you, I have Drinith where I want her. She would never put your life in danger."

"You detestable traitor!" Quiescat cried as they bundled him out the door. "Trai—!" A gag choked off the word. The ratchers' sensitive hearing didn't appreciate screaming.

Deetch approached Greny and signed that his palanquin was ready. Greny followed the ratcher outside, ignoring the bound Oracle's condemnatory mumbles as he hurried past. *If I am a traitor, whom or what do I betray? Certainly not the Halcyon Republic.*

11

—————

Greny drummed his fingers against the half door of the palanquin, fighting the impulse to spring through it and run to the canal. What was taking so long? If he had gone to Osro's mansion, cordents might be now fishing out his corpse, but, as the import of the murders sank in, he could draw little comfort from his lucky escape. They were an attack on the Meritocracy, and the Meritocracy was at its most dangerous when threatened.

The palanquin halted. Lifting the curtain, Greny peered out the window. Alongside the canal stood a large metal crane, its chugging engine lost in belches of steam. Its arm gracefully plucked Thaxen's palanquin from the waterway. Black water spilled from the vehicle's windows and doors and splashed against the cobbles. A dozen cordents in yellow and black stood in a rough semicircle beyond the falling streams in expectation of the palanquin's descent. As Greny exited his palanquin, Nayz detached from the group. He was a weedy little Nosteran with a long, sharp nose and a weak chin. Greny had overheard his subordinates refer to Nayz as the Rat Prince on occasions, but the implied intimacy between the yellowcheck colonel and his general was illusory. Greny had never warmed to the man, much less trusted him. If only Nayz was as reliable as Greny's ratcher servants.

"Is Thaxen in there?" Greny asked, pointing to her palanquin.

Nayz's curt bow extended no farther than his shoulders. "No, Meritocrat. We found her body floating in the water. The witnesses who came forward so far claim a half-dozen hooded and masked assailants armed with springbows ambushed Meritocrat Savarel's party on a bridge across the canal. Her guards had no time to react before they were struck down. The attackers toppled her palanquin off the bridge and then scattered. Of course, we're offering coin for more useful witnesses, and I've told everyone to squeeze their informants for information. Perhaps you might like to examine Meritocrat Savarel's corpse?" Assuming it was an excuse to converse in private, Greny agreed.

A shivering family huddled outside the crooked hovel where Thaxen's body had been stored. The father shushed a protest from his son as Greny and Nayz passed them and entered. Cold blue light from lampstone fragments embedded like stars in the ceiling illuminated the kitchen. The chill air smelled of staling blood. Black rivulets extended across the wooden floor from the doused fire. Thaxen lay on the table, covered in a sheet.

A clot of dried blood on the gray cloth made Greny queasy, so he looked around, fixed his gaze on the dirty crockery piled in one corner. No doubt, they had been hastily moved there to make room for the corpse. Crushed fragments of a broken bowl lay scattered on the floor.

"You removed the springbow bolts?" Greny asked, feeling his throat tighten.

"Meritocrat Savarel was stabbed to death." Nayz shut the door. "The redcheck cordent checkpoint at Diadem Bridge reported that Meritocrat Hax entered Woodshard not long before midnight, accompanied by the so-called Widow, Tazran Glastum," he whispered, glancing at the corpse as if afraid Thaxen might be listening. "A redcheck spotted her alone on Diadem Bridge again, not long after the Ducal Steward's mansion was discovered ablaze. She wasn't wearing her emblem of merit, but he still recognized her from their earlier encounter."

If Opriet's redchecks caught Drinith, Greny's part in this fiasco would be exposed. He might lose his command. Worse, truthscryers might pry into his private life. "Our yellowchecks had better find her before the redchecks. It's a matter of cordent honor."

Nayz's eyes narrowed with appraisal, probably attempting to work out the true motive behind Greny's instruction. Mysteries intrigued him, which made him a good investigator, but also posed a potential threat should his curiosity turn toward his superior.

Greny scrabbled for a more satisfying reason. "If the redchecks discover her first, their cordent general will use her arrest as leverage to take over the investigation of both murders. The yellowchecks must be the first to locate her. Not the redchecks or the bluechecks."

Nayz smirked. "I've some good news on that score. The yellowcheck squad I sent to help the redchecks secure the area around the mansion discovered the Widow injured and hiding in the forest. I took her into custody. She is already on her way to the Yellow Section at Inkeep."

"Well done," Greny said. Loyal ratchers staffed his wing of the prison. His involvement would remain a secret. Unless... "Did she say anything?"

"She claimed unknown assailants ambushed her earlier, but she didn't mention Meritocrat Hax. She said she had a fight with her husband and went for a walk to cool her temper. Liked the forest at night."

Greny chuckled with relief. "I'm sure she does. Good work." His secret was safe for now unless... Drinith's meritorian, Jarma—he had forgotten her. She must know as much as Quiescat. "Place the meritorian Jarma Hax under protective custody. Bring her to my tower. Detain Drinith's staff, too, and send them to Inkeep. But be discreet. These arrests mustn't become common knowledge. And be gentle. Nothing broken, nobody hurt."

"Of course," Nayz said slowly. "I'll warn everyone to take care, but Meritocrat Hax's associates have a history of resisting arrest."

"Our cordents have every right to defend themselves," Greny said, "but I'm sure our agent in her household will help you manage the situation peaceably."

"Do you think Meritocrat Hax killed Meritocrat Savarel and the Ducal Steward?"

"Throwing Thaxen's palanquin into the canal has a certain theatricality, as has burning Osro's mansion," Greny said. "The perpetrators could have ambushed Thaxen in Woodshard and tossed their victims into the Crevast, but no, they wanted us to know they had struck. It's a declaration of war. Drinith's interest lies in waging war in Rhumgad, not here." Unless she had been indoctrinated or enslaved in Ophigee and now served its Diarchy, but that seemed improbable. Surely Quiescat would have noticed any change in her personality. It might be worth questioning him on the matter, just to be sure. "Nevertheless, it's critical we find her."

"Meritocrat Hax may attempt to hide with her own kind in the Blue Quarter," Nayz said. "It currently falls in the bluechecks' sector...."

"Remember, Drinith's a meritocrat. *Her people* rule this city."

"My apologies, Meritocrat." Nayz gave a proper bow this time.

"Don't worry about the Blue Quarter for now. Concentrate on the Hax Mansion."

The door creaked open. Greny's irritation at the interruption quickly turned to alarm as the long, skewed face of Opriet Braesum, cordent general of the redchecks, entered. Her emblem of merit, the knotted asp, rested on her forehead at the center of a burst of black coils. She always had a sickly gray pallor, but her eyes had the luster of polished amber. Behind her followed the other cordent general, Posaleum Minol, to all appearances dressed for a ball instead of a crime scene. Even the blue bar on her dress was embroidered and inlaid with gemstones. Despite her youth, it was rumored that she had already visited the Grand Preservatory on numerous occasions to tweak her appearance. Greny could well believe it, given her frown left no hint of a line on her oval face. She wore her emblem of merit, a hercinia, on a small black fur hat.

Nayz fled the room as soon as they had cleared the doorway.

Opriet stalked over to the corpse, lifted a corner of the sheet, winced, lowered it again. "At least her killers left us a body. Poor Thaxen. Dear me. So cruelly slain." She puckered her lips, broke into a smirk. "I suppose Elca Trajar is her natural successor. She and Thaxen split the role of intelligencer general. Mere happenstance? I wonder..."

"You think Elca might be behind these attacks?" Posaleum asked, stricken. She was a fervid disciple of the New War Faction.

"I merely think...it's convenient for her that two leaders of the Short War Faction are dead. Though I must admit neither Osro nor Thaxen was very popular. Thespenilea would make a more obvious target."

"Maybe Thespenilea murdered them to consolidate her leadership," Posaleum offered eagerly.

Opriet shrugged. "Hardly seems her style."

"Shouldn't you be in Woodshard?" Greny asked.

Opriet licked her lips, tilted her head to straighten her gaze. "We're due to swap sectors two days from now. Posie and I think the exchange should be postponed for now."

"I concur," Greny said.

"Given the sensitivity of this matter, we also think only one cordent general should take charge of the investigation." Posaleum nodded along as Opriet spoke.

Greny's chest tightened. "And which of us—?"

"You, of course," Opriet said.

Posaleum's jaw dropped. "That wasn't my understanding...."

"That's why the three of us are here discussing it," Opriet said with a crooked grin. "So that there's no confusion."

"But Greny..."

"Is it his integrity or his ability with which you have a problem?" Opriet asked.

"Neither, of course," Posaleum said. "I...I think this should be decided by the Vicenary Jury."

"The Ducal Steward generally convenes it, remember.

Unfortunately, it is likely she is dead, so the honor falls to her deputy, the Justiciar General Devaner Tiranicon. I'm sure she, like most of the other jurists, slumbers in her bed, oblivious to this calamity. I'm sure she'll issue those all-important black envelopes first thing in the morning. But until then, we three must make do without the Jury's guidance and make the best decisions we can. It falls to us to manage civil emergencies."

"This isn't a fire or a riot," Posaleum said.

Greny shook his head at his colleague's naivety. "It's much worse. It's a strike at our Meritocracy, carefully planned and executed. It's liable to embolden every malcontent in the city to cause trouble."

"Greny knows what he's talking about," Opriet said. "He was a cordent general during the Silverfish Revolt."

Greny squirmed at its mention. He preferred not to be reminded of what he did during that fraught time, the sacrifices he made. "If you want me to head the investigation, I would be more than happy to do so."

"I see," Posaleum said icily. "You invited me here merely to bear witness to your decision."

"I didn't invite you," Greny said.

With an exasperated huff, Posaleum strutted out the door. Opriet shut it after her.

"Hopefully, when she calms down, Posie will come to realize I did her a favor," she said. "She is better off sticking to skimming her bluechecks' bribes."

"I'm surprised she was so in favor of you taking over," Greny said.

"I'm sure she wasn't. She hoped we'd deadlock and be forced to choose her as a compromise. Posie is as ambitious as she is vain, and avaricious. She hasn't learned that if you follow ambition too far in Gyre, you'll end up dropping into the inner sun."

"Is that why you handed this investigation to me?"

"I'm sympathetic to the Short War Faction because Cenmis is my close friend. And Posie curries favor with Elca at every opportunity. You're the only true neutral among us. You're beyond reproach. And you appear to be already making progress."

"What do you mean?"

"I understand you already have a prisoner."

The redchecks must have spotted the Widow being taken into custody. "I wasn't aware I had one."

Opriet's slanted grin called him a liar. "Drinith has probably left my sector, but if my people detain her, I'll make sure she's handed over to you. I can't say the same for Posie."

Opriet is afraid. Two meritocrats are dead, a third is wanted for questioning. There's no telling where the investigation might lead or how the likes of Elca, Okia, or Thespenilea might interfere with it. The Meritocracy has no patience with failure. It will want the culprits swiftly caught and brought to justice. Opriet views the investigation rightly as a trap, but I'm already caught in it thanks to Drinith.

He could smell the metallic scent of blood again. He could taste it on his tongue.

He left the house with Opriet. Thaxen's palanquin still bled rivulets of brown canal water across the cobbles. It looked like a misshapen severed head, pocked with springbow bolts, the windows and door gaping in horror. Greny bid Opriet farewell, then climbed into his own vehicle. Hopefully, he wouldn't share Thaxen's fate by the time this was over.

As Greny traveled through the city, he mulled over the murders. Who could be behind them? What did their perpetrators hope to gain? Almost any meritocrat might muster a force of comparable size to the one that ambushed Thaxen.

A hooded figure burst into the cab, taking Greny unawares. The ratchers Deetch and Zueel daggers drawn, attempted to climb in after him. "Call off your little mice," the stranger rasped, pressing a knife against Greny's throat, "before one of us gets hurt."

"Get back!" Greny said, halting his servants with an outstretched hand. "I'm fine." If it was the stranger's intention to kill him, he'd already be dead.

"I suggest you continue on your way," the stranger said. "A moving target is harder to hit."

"Do what he says," Greny croaked. Alarmed at the ratchers' hesitation, he added in his most authoritative voice. "That's an order!"

The ratchers reluctantly obeyed, and the palanquin moved on. Releasing Greny, the man plopped down on the opposite seat and removed his hood. His lank, shoulder-length gray hair and silver-blue eyes were immediately familiar, but it took Greny a moment to put a name to Thaxen's spy master. "Gartson, what is the meaning of this outrage?"

The question drew a cutting smile. "You need to be more careful. You should travel with more than two mice. Poor Meritocrat Savarel..." The smile faltered as he put away his dagger. "Four bodyguards and a driver couldn't save her tonight."

"Were you with her when the attack happened?"

"No. I met her on her way back from setting fire to the Ducal Steward's home in Woodshard. She had made every effort to hide her trip there from me. Not unreasonably, I was aggrieved by her lack of trust and intensely curious as to why she was being so secretive. She always had been a very private person, but I had assumed I was the one person she could be frank with. When I saw one of Meritocrat Onez's servants slumped unconscious across from her, I was forthright in my curiosity, asking for, no, demanding an explanation, but she ignored me. I'm not sure if she even heard me. She just stared at a dead bird on her lap, lost in her own musings." Gartson kept glancing out the windows with irritating frequency.

"A dead bird?"

"A sunfinch. When I finally pierced the meritocrat's daze, she ordered me to hasten back to her mansion to bolster the guards there and to prepare this for you." Gartson drew from the folds of his cloak a square envelope and waved it. "It's simply an invitation to visit her. She wouldn't tell me why, but I presume it's connected to tonight's events. You can have it if you want. It seems kind of pointless now."

Greny took it and tucked it away inside his shirt.

"I just don't understand it," Gartson said, peering out the window yet again. "I've never seen her so rattled before, so broken."

"I could do with someone of your immense talent," Greny said. "Help me find her killer."

"I'm leaving Gyre. Thaxen's gone; I, too, must take my leave." Gartson's casual mention of her first name took Greny by surprise. "My immense talent, as you call it, couldn't protect her. The rules of the game have suddenly changed, and I have no appetite for learning the new ones."

"So you'll leave your meritocrat unavenged?"

Gartson smirked. "She plainly didn't want me involved. I plan to honor her wishes. Maybe if you die, your mice might think differently. They seem a devoted lot." He peered out the window again, but this time he flung open the door and leapt from the cab.

"Wait!" Greny cried, but Gartson had already hopped over the parapet of the bridge the palanquin was crossing and raced along the canal.

"Let him go!" Greny ordered as the ratchers primed their springbows. "We need to return to Scylax Tower with all haste." *Before we're ambushed by someone who wants to do more than talk.*

12

────────

Jarma paced the parlor, sat, paced some more. This seemingly endless wait for news was intolerable. With no sign of Drinith and no word from Quiescat, all she could do was stew in her apprehension. Every sound, every footstep, every creak made her pause to listen in vain for her friends. She emitted a pained sigh as the clock rang the second bell of the ebbnight hour. How much longer must she wait?

Desperate to do something, anything, she hastened to Drinith's office and, sitting at her desk, removed Versifer's notebook and thumbed through it until she found the poet's prophesies. The first two had already come to pass, so the third must very likely be next.

"I write gibberish symbols in red on an endless scroll. My quill runs dry. I use the wound in my chest to refill it. The sound of tearing paper makes me look up..."

The passage daunted her and left her feeling a little foolish. Why did she dare to imagine she could decode this passage when it had confounded Quiescat? Already an oracle long before she was born, he had devoted his entire life to understand the subtleties of dreams and portents. She had been an illiterate maid two years ago. These images would remain impenetrable gibberish to her no matter how many times she read them.

The door swinging open made Jarma gasp and press the notebook to her bosom. Nosdan, wide-eyed, burst into the room. "You have to get out of here. The house is being raided."

Jumping to her feet, she turned toward the secret door.

"No," Nosdan warned. "There are cordents already waiting for you at the secret exits."

"Then what do I do?" Jarma asked. If Drinith had been here, she'd have known.

Nosdan touched his forehead. His face lit up with inspiration. "Follow me."

As they hastened along the corridor, a scream came from somewhere behind them. They dashed into the nearest servant staircase. Jarma often used it as a shortcut from her room to Drinith's office.

"Where are we going?" Jarma asked as she trundled after Nosdan up the steep steps.

"Cordents are watching the garden," he said. "And the windows on the ground floor have fortified glass and bars. Your best chance is to climb out of one of the bedroom windows on the next floor and make a run for it across the plaza."

In no position to quibble, she took the lead after they emerged from the stairs and headed to her room, the farthest on that wing from the grand staircase at the center of the mansion.

"We need to make a rope," Nosdan said as she locked them in. He interrupted her as she pulled a sheet off her bed. "Black would be better."

Jarma threw open her closets, packed with a monotony of black dresses. She twisted each one in turn into a rope, while Nosdan tied them together. Wringing the fabric comforted her a little. Part of her envisioned the dresses as the necks of phantom meritocrats. She loathed the whole contemptible lot, their plotting and scheming, the power they held over the lives of her and her friends.

"Cordents! Come out now!" a voice bellowed somewhere down the corridor. There followed a muffled bang, then the sharp crack of splintering wood. Not every bedroom door was locked. It wouldn't take the cordents long to reach Jarma's door.

Nosdan tied the makeshift rope to a metal curtain tieback. Jarma wasn't convinced the black stud would hold her weight, but there was no time to test it.

"You ready?" Nosdan asked.

Jarma kicked off her shoes. They were too clunky to run in. She removed her brooch; its glimmer in the night's dull light might betray her. She placed it on her nightstand, but her hand lingered indecisively over it. Leaving it behind would be a disavowal of her rank. She picked it up and slipped it into her pocket.

Another bang, much louder, much nearer.

Nosdan threw clothes over the lampstone candles, plunging the room into darkness. The curtains opened, and the nighttime city carved a latticed wedge of dull light across the room. The window squealed treacherously as Nosdan opened it.

The slit of light beneath the door flickered. The handle rattled.

Nosdan tossed the rope down from the narrow metal balcony and helped Jarma climb over the rail.

Bang! A figure extracted its booted foot from the shattered door, teetering by one hinge.

"Go!" Nosdan cried as he charged toward the silhouettes spilling inside. Jarma started sliding down the rope. The fabric ripped, and she fell.

Somehow, she found herself rolling across the plaza. As shouts filled the night, she sprang to her feet and dashed like the wind across the cobbles, barely sensible in her panic to the pain the uneven stones inflicted on her bare feet.

She quickly cleared the plaza and raced down Chandler Street. Being residential, it was eerily quiet at this time of night. Nobody appeared to be following, but she couldn't help repeatedly glancing over her shoulder. She was so distracted, she almost rushed straight into the silhouette blocking her path. As she attempted to veer around the stranger, something stung her side. A numbness shivered through her. Her limbs went limp, and she dropped onto the cobbles. Her attacker lifted her up and dragged her into an alleyway. She managed a plaintive moan before a sweet-smelling rag covered her mouth, and passed out.

13

———

Drinith paused at a stall and ordered its strongest tea, as much to gather her nerves as to relieve the dryness of her mouth. Its owner, a sturdy, middle-aged Nosteran woman, gave her a suspicious frown as she filled a bowl on the counter from a steaming spout. Drinith's hand trembled as she picked it up and gulped down a mouthful. The burning hot liquid stung her throat so badly she almost choked on it.

"Be careful," the vendor said. "You'll do yourself damage drinking tea that hot. Here, give it to me. I'll add a little cold water."

With a nod of gratitude, Drinith returned the bowl. The tea could have been water for all the interest she took in the taste. Osro and Thaxen were dead. Her relations with either had never been cordial, but their murder shook Drinith to her core. Cenmis might be also dead, or she might be behind the murders. Drinith needed to get to Hax Mansion.

"You haven't paid!" the vendor yelled.

Drinith halted. Turning, she placed the bowl, forgotten in her hand, on the counter, and flashed her emblem of merit. "Come to my residence later and I will ensure you are recompensed."

The vendor opened her mouth, shut it again. It would take a

foolhardy person to challenge an emblem of merit. "Of course, Meritocrat. I should have recognized you. My apologies."

"That's all right," Drinith said, stalking away. A creeping sense of her vulnerability quickened her steps. The vendor hadn't recognized her, but others might.

It was dawn by the time she reached her home. She pulled the cord of the doorbell with relief and then with increasing irritation when nobody answered. Had everyone fallen asleep within? Surely Fenvar should have remained alert for her meritocrat's return.

Drinith failed to notice three courtesars swaggering up to her until they had encircled her. Rosel doffed his hat and swept it to his chest as he bowed so low he nearly kissed the cobbles. He and his companions must have been lurking nearby, waiting to pounce on her. "We meet again, Meritocrat. The morning sun rises early, it seems. You promised me I could call on you today."

Hadn't she suffered enough trials this night already? She rang the doorbell a third time. Why did nobody answer? She would have to speak to Fenvar about this unacceptable delay. If these courtesars had been assassins...

"It is still night for me," Drinith said, banging a fist on the door. "My bed awaits." Blushing at her unfortunate turn of phrase, she hastily added, "I will host no visitors until well into the afternoon."

"Then I must wait here until the time comes for you to honor your solemn vow," Rosel declared. Ticen and Cofran exchanged rueful glances. They had little to gain from such a vigil.

"Mind you don't get in anybody's way," Drinith muttered.

The emergence of a mandolin from under Rosel's cloak spurred his companions to produce flutes. "We shall play here to soothe you to sleep."

Another time, Drinith might have appreciated their tune, even enjoyed it, but here and now, every note grated on her. She pounded on the door with greater vigor until it finally swung open.

"Apologies for the delay." Fenvar looked flustered, and so she should for leaving her meritocrat stranded on the doorstep with these pestering fops.

Drinith entered the reception hall. Why was it so dark?

"Meritocrat, please take this as a token of my affection." Rosel lunged through the shutting door and offered Drinith a butter-colored rose. Sighing, Drinith took it. One of its thorns dug into her thumb. Fenvar pressed her back against the door to close it as, retreating outside, Rosel strummed his mandolin to the flutists' shrill accompaniment.

Hooded silhouettes stirred from the shadows. Dropping the rose, Drinith reached for her knife, but Fenvar pushed her hand away from the secret pocket and encircled her in a bear hug.

"What are you doing?" Drinith demanded as she tried to break free of the butler's steely embrace.

"Quick! I can't hold her for long!" Fenvar pleaded.

As the hooded figures closed, Drinith wrested free of Fenvar's grip and slammed her elbow into the butler's chin, sending her sprawling backwards. Drinith reached again for her knife, but bodies slammed into her.

"Help!" she screamed as she toppled over.

"You mustn't hurt the meritocrat," a male voice rasped. Something heavy banged against the outside of the door.

"There's a knife hidden in her dress," Fenvar blurted.

Drinith strained against the tightening grip of her captors, but her secret pocket remained stubbornly beyond her dancing fingers. Her attackers wrenched her arms behind her back and bound her wrists. The black and yellow brigantines glimpsed beneath their cloaks identified them as members of Greny's cordent division. Hands patted down her body. The knife tugged her dress as it slipped from its hiding place.

"My apologies, Meritocrat." The nasal voice of Greny's favorite human toady, Nayz, was unmistakable. "Don't worry about your friends and staff. They're all safe."

"What is the meaning of this?" Drinith demanded as she was hauled to her feet.

Nayz removed his hood to reveal his blushing face. "I have orders from my cordent general to detain you in connection with the deaths of Meritocrat Thaxen Saveral and the Ducal Steward."

Another bang against the door.

"They're wasting their time," Fenvar said. "The door is built to withstand a battering ram."

As Drinith craned her neck to peer at her, Fenvar sneered, her normally calm demeanor warped by malicious glee.

"Why?" Drinith asked. "Why did you betray me?"

"You weren't supposed to reveal that you were in our employ, butler," Nayz groused.

"Have the decency to answer me at least, Fenvar," Drinith demanded. "How could you betray the Hax name after so many years of service?"

Bang.

Fenvar lifted her chin to look down on her mistress. "I served the Hax family, not some foreign usurper. You replaced decent, hardworking Gyran servants with Gadflies at every opportunity."

"You encouraged me to dismiss Perian."

"I did the girl a favor," Fenvar said. "Being part of this Gadfly household would taint her more than an accusation of spying from you ever could."

"Traitor!" Drinith roared.

Bang.

"Are they ever going to stop?" a cordent whined.

A splodge of spittle struck Drinith's cheek.

"That's all your opinion is worth to me," Fenvar said.

"Arrest her." Nayz thrust a finger at the butler. Approaching Drinith, he gently dabbed her wet cheek with a handkerchief. "My apologies, Meritocrat." Even now, bound and helpless, she inspired fear in her captors.

Bang.

Fenvar's jubilation shifted to fright in an instant. "What? Why?"

"Do you really have to ask? You just assaulted a meritocrat," Nayz said. "Bag her and put her with the other prisoners."

Fenvar blinked woundedly, like a chastened child. "But...but I'm on your side." She backed up against the door and reached for the handle. "I have been absolutely loyal."

"Like you were to Meritocrat Hax?" Nayz asked, shaking his head. "You could have played along as instructed, but you couldn't help meddling in her detainment. Now you're worthless to us."

Fenvar twisted the handle as she turned to run. Rosel careered through the door, sword drawn, his two companions close behind. Fenvar stumbled by them and bolted down the steps.

"Unhand her, you devils!" Rosel thundered. Somebody shoved Drinith to the floor. As grunts and groans and the clangor of metal filled the room, she crawled on her knees toward the door. A dead weight fell across her legs. The wounded cordent fumbled to grab her, but she kicked him off her. Glass shattered. Something made a heavy thump.

"We're cordents, you fools!" Nayz cried, but the battle raged on.

Rosel hauled Drinith to her feet. "Run, Meritocrat!" The scent of blood assailed her nostrils as he bundled her out the door.

While he cut her bonds, she hazarded a glance back into the house. Ticen and Cofran fended off a half-dozen cordents or more. Wounded yellowchecks littered the floor. In their midst lay the rose, unsullied and incongruous. One man clutched a rag to the bloody stump at the end of his arm. More cordents poured out the entrance to the servant stairs. *Gods, Rosel and his friends mustn't die on my behalf.* Before she could protest, Rosel plunged back into the mansion, his command ringing in her ears: "Run!"

She leapt down the stairs and raced across the plaza. The clatter of boots echoed behind her—pursuing cordents from the mansion. The slowest listed to one side, his hand pressed to his shoulder, but the other two, their arms pumping fast, were doing their utmost to catch her. A familiar face waved at her from the start of Thunderclap Street—Woad, thank the gods. She veered leftward toward him.

Between them stood Fenvar, arms open, ready to grab her former mistress.

Drinith swerved to avoid her, but the butler lunged at her.

"Gadfly!" Fenvar cried as she swung her fist. Drinith dodged it, pushed her back so hard she landed on her buttocks.

Woad started running down the street before Drinith reached him. No time for explanations while cordents pursued them. They raced down busy streets, weaving through the crowds, across narrow bridges, and through dingy alleyways.

"Where are we going?" Drinith asked between pants when they stopped to catch their breath.

"Wealgiver Street," Woad said. "Cordents have checkpoints on the bridges to the Blue Quarter."

It was only when they were inside the safe house that the full import of what had happened struck Drinith.

"I can't believe Fenvar betrayed me," she said. "I dismissed Perian on her word." That really stung.

"If you hadn't, Perian might be right now in a restraining coffin on the way to Inkeep," Woad said. "This city teems with traitors and turncoats. You would do well to remember that."

"At least I can depend on you," Drinith said.

Woad's face squirmed. "Tazran and the Oracle are under arrest. I think Jarma might have escaped. Any idea where she might go?"

"To your inn, maybe."

"The Blue Quarter is cut off. So are the Perches and the dirigible port. We won't be safe here for long. It's only a matter of time before they discover this place."

"Any word of Cenmis Velso?"

Woad looked askance at her. "What has she to do with this business?"

"She was at Osro's mansion last night. I need to get to Woodshard and talk to her," Drinith said. "She will be able to clear my name." *Unless she was behind the murders.*

14

G reny leaned forward in his chair, slapped both hands on his desk. Nayz sat hunched on the same seat Thean had been bound to the previous night. He blushed beneath Greny's glare like a chastened child as he stole glances at the scratches worn by chains in the armrests. And well he should! He was lucky Greny hadn't also clapped him in chains for this calamity.

"Arresting a meritocrat is a matter of the utmost delicacy," Greny said, absently rubbing the polished wood. "It requires a surgeon's grace. You let Drinith escape. People passing through Hax Plaza witnessed the spectacle of cordents chasing a meritocrat."

"The cordents were wearing hooded cloaks," Nayz said lamely as he peeked back at Chemp and Queek standing behind him.

"Oh, that's so much better," Greny said. "Why didn't you tell me that at the start? A meritocrat being chased by random people through the streets. A good example to set for the common folk."

"She wasn't wearing her emblem of merit...." Nayz said.

"A meritocrat is a meritocrat whether or not she wears her emblem. And Drinith is very...conspicuous."

"Of course," Nayz said in a placatory tone.

"The entire city now knows we intend to take her into custody, and everyone with half a wit will presume her arrest is connected to the murders of Thaxen and Osro." Greny sighed. "Worse, her meritorian is at large. You let her slip away, too."

"She can't get far," Nayz said, blushing. "I'll find her and Meritocrat Hax. I'll find them both. I promise."

"You also wounded three courtesars. Their mothers and sisters have demanded recompense for their injuries."

"They attacked us," Nayz said, lurching forward in his seat. "If they hadn't got in the way..." He threw up his hands.

"They claim you failed to identify yourselves as cordents."

"I..." Nayz hung his head. "It doesn't matter what I say."

"That's the first sensible thing you've said since you arrived. Thanks to your incompetence, I'll soon have the entire Vicenary Jury prying into this investigation. Elca, Okia, Thespenilea, and the rest will stick their snouts into my business, asking awkward questions, giving *helpful* advice, casting aspersions at each other, and generally adding to my problems. You might as well have the entire Parliament sitting on my shoulders, yanking my reins. This case could very well be taken away from me."

Nayz looked up, unspoken hope on his face. He wanted nothing more than to be rid of this case.

"Don't worry, you won't escape so easily," Greny said. "You'll just end up reporting to my successor. Posaleum Minol would likely take charge. You'll find her not so lenient to those who embarrass her."

"I'm sorry," Nayz said. "What else would you have me say?"

"I warned you to be careful. Perhaps you've grown too complacent in your position."

"I have served you well for many years."

"So did the casquar I had put down last week."

"I forgot you're only sentimental about your rats," Nayz snapped.

Greny burst out laughing. Nayz's mute rage made him guffaw all the harder. Perhaps Greny was being too hard on him. He had proved a reliable servant in the past, and who could Greny trust to replace him? "I'm only giving you a taste of what I expect to receive from the Vicenary Jury."

"Of which you're a member," Nayz said, still annoyed.

"Meritocrats share one thing in common with rats. They are dangerous when cornered. These murders threaten the state's stability. The culprits must walk the Plank before they wreak greater damage." A morsel of honesty to salve Nayz' hurt feelings. Too much, perhaps. It was not something Greny generally did: badmouth his own class to inferiors.

"We found the sunfinch. It was on Meritocrat Savarel's person." Nayz approached with the nervous jerkiness of someone who was trying to remember how to walk, all the while keeping a nervous eye on Chemp and Queek. He placed the dead bird on the desk and retreated back to his chair. Its damp plumage was ruffled and broken. "There's a ring on one leg."

"You haven't examined it?" Greny asked.

Nayz shook his head. "I thought it best to leave that to you." An eager smile spread across his narrow face. He was like a cat leaving a gift for his owner. Greny never liked cats. Detestable, untrustworthy creatures, prone to attack his servants.

Greny pulled the band off the leg and studied it with a magnifying glass. It was made of horn or some similar material. A tiny folded piece of translucent parchment was stuck to the inside. It tore as Greny pried it free with a tweezer. He opened out the tiny fragments, but they were blank. The canal must have washed away whatever had been written on it.

Nayz, perhaps alert to his master's disappointment, said, "I will find Meritocrat Hax and her meritorian."

Greny leaned back in his seat. "Don't worry about Drinith. Finding Jarma is your priority for now."

Nayz gave him a venomous scowl. "Do I understand right that you want me to call off the search for Drinith? After berating me for fumbling her arrest?"

Greny couldn't help smiling. "That's right. Leave her to me."

Nayz's eyebrows arched, furrowing his forehead. "And how do you intend to find her?"

"Never you mind." Greny blew his silent whistle and two burly brown ratchers entered. Nayz's eyes popped open with panic. His knuckles paled as his hands squeezed on the armrests.

"No need to be afraid," Greny sneered. "I'm not sending you to Inkeep just yet. I'm assigning two of my ratchers, Zetch and Treek, to assist you."

"To watch me, you mean."

Greny tapped the side of his nose. "Exactly so, but that's our little secret. I promise they won't embarrass you in front of your peers. They'll even zealously follow your instructions unless, of course, they conflict with my interests." He gestured to Nayz that he could leave.

As the cordent colonel followed the two ratchers out the door, he muttered, "After all these years, you still don't trust me." Greny made no answer.

If only life were so simple. It would be good to consider Nayz a friend, but Greny had witnessed too many examples of treachery down through the years to trust anyone who wasn't a ratcher. He had engineered more than a few betrayals himself. For example, he knew exactly where Drinith was at this very moment and who was with her. Little could she guess that her good friend Woad Glastum, on whom she so relied, was another of Greny's spies.

15

———

rinith glanced up and down the canal as Woad helped her onto the flat-bottomed boat. Thankfully, nobody was around to witness this theft. Stealing didn't sit well with Drinith, but using the canal as a walkway was frowned upon and they would attract less attention traveling on water. The public bridges to Woodshard were too heavily guarded. The canal offered their best opportunity to access the shardlet.

After Woad had piled a half-dozen bundles of bedding onto the boat, he cut the mooring and punted with unnerving leisure down the canal. Drinith relaxed a fraction only after they had put a good distance between them and the scene of their crime. She shied from the bargemen passing in the opposite direction, though they surely wouldn't recognize her. Her hair braids were stuffed inside a large peaked cap that shaded her face, and she wore loose-fitting men's clothing.

"Are you sure you don't know where Jarma is hiding?" Woad asked for the third time. "There's no way she could have sneaked inside the Blue Quarter. It's completely cut off by cordent checkpoints. I can't even get a message in or out, much less a person. We have to find her before she's caught."

"If I had any idea where she was, we'd be going there instead," Drinith snapped.

"I know. I'm sorry."

"I'm sorry, too, for being so testy. I'm worried about her and Quiescat, and Tazran, of course. Not to mention my servants, who have been dragged into this mess through no fault of their own." If Drinith had heeded Quiescat's advice and ignored Greny's summons, they would have never become mired in this sinister affair. Where could Jarma be? Drinith had lost enough friends to this dangerous city already.

A surprising number of punts and barges were moored by the access well to Woodshard. Cordents in black and yellow wandered among the workers, busily offloading their goods. Woad moored in the first available berth and Drinith helped him toss the bundles onto the bank. Carrying two bundles in her hands and one under her arm, she followed him toward the access well. She craned her head to peer over the parapet at the parkland below. The charred wreck of Osro's home stood out as a scorch mark amidst the patchwork of mansions, tidy forests, and manicured gardens.

A cordent blocked their path and gestured to them to stop. Drinith's stomach fluttered with apprehension as the man's eyes expanded with a hint of recognition, but they quickly shrank to disapproving slits. "Where do you think you're going? I thought your kind were all penned in the Blue Quarter."

"We work for the Clean Well Laundry," Woad explained. "Our employer took us in after the Blue Quarter was sealed off."

"Lucky you," the cordent sneered.

"We have a delivery of bedding for Meritocrat Velso's residence," Woad said casually. "Here's my employer's authorization."

The cordent studied the letter. "Appears in order," he said with reluctance. "But it doesn't take two of you to deliver that bedding."

"They're too bulky for one person to carry," Woad said.

"You both could comfortably carry half the load." The cordent shrugged. "Better yet, one of you can make two trips. That way the other can wait at your punt in case it needs to be moved."

"That will take all day," Woad whined.

"And how is that my problem?" The cordent thrust the letter out over the parapet. It fluttered in the breeze as he waved it about. "Maybe this letter might fly away, and I'm so forgetful. Why did you Gadflies come here again?"

Drinith gazed back down the canal to hide her disgust. Suddenly realizing that her fist had balled with the urge to punch this scoundrel in the jaw, she forced it open.

"Hey, look at me when I'm talking to you!" the cordent yelled.

Drinith acquiesced, doing her best to swallow her anger. The other cordents fixed stares on them. Even some of the delivery people stopped work to watch the unfolding scene.

Woad raised a placatory hand. "My son meant no disrespect. He's only a stupid boy. He can deliver the bedding as punishment. I'll wait on the punt." He rummaged under his coat and drew out three blackened coins. "Here are a couple of copper dragons to recompense you for my boy's tomfoolery."

The cordent scrunched up his nose at the pittance.

"Please," Woad said. "I can't afford to lose this job. It's hard for our kind to get decent work." He rummaged in his coat again and drew out an empty money pouch. To Drinith's surprise, when he shook it over his palm, a dull silver finch tumbled out. He offered it to the cordent with the coppers. "Please take them."

The cordent's mouth shifted from side to side. He reached for the coins. "If you insist."

"Thank you," Woad said.

The cordent licked his lips as his hand hovered over Woad's palm. He plucked the silver coin and balled his fist around it. "You can keep the coppers. They'd only dirty my hand, and fair is fair."

"Very generous of you," Woad said, without a hint of sarcasm.

The cordent handed back the letter. "Be on your way."

"I thought for a moment, he was going to throw those coppers in your face," Drinith whispered to Woad as they proceeded to the access well.

"I had to take the risk," Woad said. "Offering too much would make him suspicious. We're dirt poor Gadflies, remember."

After they had deposited the bedding on the goods lift, Woad handed her the letter. "You'll need this in case you run into any patrols." He passed her the copper dragons. "And take those in case they look for money. Don't offer them a bribe. Hand the coppers over only if they demand payment. Good luck down there."

The noise in the stairwell threatened to give Drinith a headache —the urgent stamp of boots up and down it, the hiss and chug of the steam engine at the bottom for the lift. She bolted out the ground door, through the hot, wet breath of the engine. The bedding had already been removed by two workers at the bottom and thrown to one side in a heap. She grabbed the bundle containing her black dress and another at random, and headed for Cenmis's house.

The noise from the engine quickly faded, and the warble of sunfinches filled the air. Drinith passed several park workers raking away cart tracks from the gravel path, and cutting lawns and weeding flower beds, in keeping with local meritocrats' fastidious wishes. A cordent patrol strolled by her as if she were invisible. Presumably they didn't consider a Rhumgadian boy carrying blankets and sheets a worthy target of their avarice. She had heard plenty of stories of the petty corruption rife among the cordents, but it didn't feel so petty after experiencing it firsthand. If Drinith was ever in a position of authority in Gyre again, she would work to change that. Surely Greny Scylax would help. He would never condone such larceny. Everyone exalted him as incorruptible. But first, Drinith had to clear her name and save her friends.

Nearing Cenmis's home, Drinith ducked into a copse and changed her clothes. She knew she must look a state in her crumpled black dress, but that couldn't be helped.

She approached the gate, took a deep breath, and pulled the bell cord. Two scowling guards exited the mansion and trudged over to her. The ill-fitting mermaid surcoats over their worn armor suggested that they must have been recent hires. The scent of stale drink wafted from them. Judging from their violent glowers, if Drinith hadn't turned up in her urchin rags, they would have chased her from the gates.

"The meritocrat is currently mourning her dead friends and accepting no visitors," the bigger guard said irritably. Thick red bristles covered his heavy jowls and red ringed his rheumy eyes. "And even if she was, she wouldn't let a ragamuffin like you darken her door. She holds client courts twice a week in Bath Lane. That's where your sort get their opportunity to plead—"

She flashed her emblem of merit. "She'll meet me. Tell her Meritocrat Hax has called to see her on an urgent matter of mutual importance."

The heavyset guard looked her up and down. "If you don't mind me saying so, *Meritocrat*, begging your pardon, but you're not exactly accoutered in a manner befitting your rank." His comrade's gaze nervously flicked back and forth between them.

"I will dress how I please," Drinith said. "Mark my words. Cenmis will be furious when she learns of your impertinence."

"But, but—"

"To impersonate a meritocrat is a crime punishable by death, so if I prove to be a liar, you can have the pleasure of watching me walk the Plank."

The guards looked at one another as if trying to push each other with their stares. The shorter one sighed and trudged back to the mansion.

"We meant no offense, Meritocrat," his colleague croaked, evidently determined to hedge his bets. His diffidence would evaporate instantly if Cenmis refused her entry.

"It's unusual for guards such as yourself to answer the gate," Drinith observed.

"These are unusual times. I was celebrating my sister's wedding when Meritocrat Velso summoned me here. I'd say every blade in the city has been hired by one meritocrat or another."

The second guard glowered as he stomped back down the gravel path from the mansion. "The meritocrat will see you."

Drinith exhaled a forgotten breath as she stepped through the opening gate. The two guards flanked her up to the mansion. Two of their comrades stood, weapons drawn, inside the reception hall. The butler's fretful stare briefly held her gaze before Drinith asked, "Where is your mistress? I'm here to see her."

The parlor door swung open and Cenmis emerged, looking fierce. "Seize her!"

The four guards pounced on Drinith before she could react.

16

———

As his palanquin wound its way through clogged, sluggish streets to Woodshard, Greny strummed his fingers against the windowsill in vexation. Chemp was sitting across from him, his springbow primed for the next assailant who tried to invade the cab. Greny had also doubled the complement guarding the palanquin outside to four, not including the driver, Zueel. If six alert ratchers couldn't protect Greny, nothing could save him.

Having nobody else to whom he could vent his simmering frustration, he muttered to Chemp, "This is a mistake. Simply arresting Drinith at Glastum's hideaway would have avoided this convoluted subterfuge." Aside from a brief twitch of Chemp's whiskers, he did not respond. One of ratchers' greatest virtues was they knew their place.

The plan had seemed foolproof when Greny conceived it. First, encircle Cenmis's estate with his ratchers to prevent Drinith from escaping again. Then enter the mansion on the pretext of interviewing Cenmis and her staff. Discovering Drinith in her home would point suspicion at Cenmis and impel her to cooperate. At the same time, this apparent stroke of luck would conceal from Drinith Woad's part in her capture. She had confided only to him about

Cenmis. As long as Drinith trusted the ex-mercenary, Greny controlled her clandestine organization through him. But now, as Greny's scheme approached its culmination, doubts beset him, particularly about Drinith. Could he be wrong about her? Could she actually be the murderer?

Greny had compelled her to go to Osro's mansion in his stead, and it was hard to see how she would have been otherwise drawn into this mess. Her captured friends, and Woad Glastum, were certainly convinced of her innocence. And yet Greny couldn't entirely share their conviction. Other factors were at play here, forces as yet hidden. Who knew where the truth might lie?

A squeak from Chemp interrupted his musings. The ratcher signed to him to listen.

Greny concentrated on the hubbub beyond the palanquin—the usual babel of the crowds, the trundle of carts, the screeches of casquars, yelled promises of bargains in a dozen languages, the distant roar of a dragon, the faint peal of a bell. And then the entire city hushed and the distant bell alone filled the attentive silence. It had to be an alarm in some other part of the city.

Greny leapt from the palanquin and dashed into the nearest block of flats, Chemp and the other ratchers following close behind. Bounding up the stairs to the top floor, Greny pounded on the first door he came across. "Let me in!"

He didn't wait for an answer. As he struggled to catch his breath, he signaled Chemp and Queek to break down the door. Nobody was in the flat, but several people must have lived there judging from the rolled up sleeping mats, blankets, and pillows piled neatly by the wall. Greny hastened to the nearest window and threw open the shutters. The distant bell still sounded, summoning cordents from across the city. A flashing signal light blinked above the roofs of the Diplomatic District. What in Empyrosis's blazing bowels was happening over there to warrant a blanket call out?

Returning to the street, he left Zueel with the palanquin and made his way on foot, accompanied by the other five ratchers. Fretful cordents who happened across his party—yellowchecks and redchecks mostly, but also a smattering of bluechecks—joined him until their group swelled to thirty or so.

The shouts and cheers of the rioters echoed in the empty streets long before Greny reached them.

"Gadflies out! Gadflies out!" they chanted.

A sizeable crowd had gathered in Accord Avenue, armed with crude cudgels and missiles. They bayed at a multicolored line of cordents blocking their access to the Rhumgadian Embassy, a grand building in the early Restoration style marred by various gaudy flourishes to cater to its current residents' vulgar taste.

Greny formed his party into a wedge and, with truncheons at the ready, they pushed and jostled their way through the crowd toward the line. The mob turned their anger at these intruders, flinging missiles at them, hitting them with their fists and even makeshift clubs. Greny, in the center of the wedge, could do little but cringe as stones flew above him. Spittle wet his face. The crowd swallowed up a brown ratcher, Sneeth or Dweed, Greny couldn't be sure which. The poor devil would never survive the mob's unbridled wrath.

"Somebody, help him!" Greny cried, but he doubted anyone heard; Greny couldn't even hear himself over the mob's screams as the wedge's momentum carried him forward. Bodies pressed so tightly around him he couldn't move his arms. Was he going to be crushed?

The group finally reached the line of cordents and spilled beyond it. From seemingly out of nowhere Nayz grabbed Greny, and together they pushed their way through the dispersing group.

Greny looked around in vain for Treek and Zetch. "Where are the two ratchers I assigned to you?"

"I sent them to find you! You need to stop Meritocrat Minol now!" Nayz roared, pointing at a second line behind the first. Posaleum strutted in front of it, barking at the cordents to ready their springbows.

Greny tripped on a prostrate cordent, but Nayz held him upright. Clear of the crush, Greny batted Nayz's hand off him and staggered over to Posaleum. "What in Empyrosis do you think you're doing?"

Posaleum jerked her head toward him. "What do you think? Readying to scatter that crowd." Her nose wrinkled in disgust as the surviving ratchers, their musky odor made rank by sweat, gathered around Greny. Chemp, Queek, Dweed, and Kleest were accounted for. So it had been poor Sneeth who had been swallowed up by the crowd. A terrible shame, but there was no time to mourn his passing.

"You can't shoot at that mob," Greny argued. "Dragons, we didn't even do that during the Silverfish Revolt! The mob obviously blames the Rhumgadians for the murders of Thaxen and Osro. Are you really going to shoot at them and turn that anger against us? That would spread this riot throughout the whole city!"

"So what do we do?" Posaleum asked, part in anger, part in desperation.

Greny glanced at the injured cordents lying and sitting between the two lines, the missiles raining down on them. "Merge the two lines. Switch out the injured and exhausted if you can spare them. If it looks like you're going to be overwhelmed, retreat toward the embassy in good order. Are the Rhumgadian delegation in there?"

"Yes," Posaleum said.

"I'll evacuate them."

"I tried already. That ox, Moylar, won't budge. He just stood in the lobby, arms folded, spitting insults at me, stupid with delight, as though this attack is exactly what he hoped for. There's nothing but a steep drop to the inner sun on the far side of the embassy garden and the street is completely blocked. No sign of Opriet, of course, when we need her."

A cordent general should rely on herself, not others. Greny bit back his retort. Posaleum was unreliable as it was. Insult her and there was no telling how she might react. "Leave the ambassador to me. I'll figure something out. As soon as I have his retinue safely away, we'll let the mob take out their righteous fury on the property. Hopefully, that will sate their hunger for vengeance."

"And if it doesn't?"

"One step at a time," Greny said, indicating to the ratchers to follow him as he pushed through the second line and ascended the steps to the door of the embassy.

The lobby was tiled with an enormous mosaic of the Rhumgadian Bone Tree. A chandelier of three spheres, red, white, and clear, reached down from a bright blue vault. Ancient tapestries, worn and faded with age, adorned the smooth pink walls. A large group of worried Rhumgadians huddled together in one corner. Lysan Moylar stood alone, staring out of a long window, looking every bit as delighted as Posaleum had described.

His smile curdled as he waved a finger at the ratchers. "I want those misbegotten creatures out of this building immediately."

Greny ignored the remark. "Your safety is of paramount importance. Have you any secret exit from the embassy that you can use? An access door to the sewers, perhaps?"

Moylar answered with a beefy sneer. "I'm sure you know much more about the sewers than I, Rat King."

Did he know about the Holver Dronan incident? Could that thug have been working for Magian after all? If Greny had taken Holver prisoner and had a truthscryer interrogate him, what might have he uncovered? Damn Ecethor and that pathetic urge to protect her daughter that moved Greny to toss the Gadfly into the inner sun. The security of Gyre should have come before all other considerations.

Moylar blinked, his grin flattening. "Did you come here merely to stare at me?"

"We won't be able to hold back the protesters for long," Greny said. "I cannot guarantee your safety when they force their way in."

"Pfft. This type of open revolt would never be tolerated in Rhumgad. That mob would have been doused in dragon flame by now."

"Thanks for your insight," Greny said acidly, "but you're not in Rhumgad and we prefer not to burn our own city." He turned to his ratcher companions. "Find a ladder or rope or anything else that will help us get over the garden walls."

Moylar puffed out his chest and looked down on Greny with

violent disdain. "You cannot seriously expect us to abandon our embassy to those ruffians! I'd rather die."

Greny shrugged. "If that's your choice, who am I to argue? I'll just pop out and tell my colleague not to waste her time holding back the rioters." Judging from the alarmed faces of the other Rhumgadians who had drifted from the group in the corner to listen in, they didn't share the ambassador's sentiment.

A brick smashed through a window and slid across the floor.

"They are getting nearer," Greny said with a nonchalant grin. He headed for the door.

"Wait," Moylar said.

Greny turned his best smile on him.

The ambassador bowed his head, his face squirming with anger. "Very well. Since you admit to being incapable of controlling your people, I suppose I must leave." A wicked smile burgeoned. "There's little of value here in any case."

Queek returned and signed that the ratchers had found ladders.

"Everyone, follow me to the garden," Greny said. Queek raced at his heels down the hall, Moylar striding beside him. They passed through a large reception room into the garden. The four wooden ladders propped against the boundary wall stretched a good distance over it. Chemp, Kleest, and Dweed stood atop of three of them, working with stones to bend back the green bronze spikes, designed to repel trespassers, along the top of the wall. Snatching a largish rock, Queek scurried up another ladder and worked on the spikes within his reach.

The other Rhumgadians' delay in following struck Greny as odd until the first of them appeared, lugging heavy cases. He hadn't the time or the inclination to argue with them. If their possessions got them killed, so be it.

The Rhumgadians lingered some distance from the ladders, watching while the ratchers, who repulsed them, worked on the top of the wall. The ingrates approached only after the last spike was impaired. What harm did the superstitious fools think the ratchers might do to them? Give them fleas?

Filling the ladders, the Rhumgadians passed their baggage up for those at the top to throw it over the wall.

"Leave that until last." Moylar pointed to a slim oblong incindar box. "It can't be simply tossed over. The item it contains is delicate."

A vexed head rose from above the other side of the wall. The man with a large, forked silver mustache and coiled eyebrows glared at the invaders of his garden. A gilded track covered the slender tonsure across the center of his pate. It was Byun Kran, the Maxthez Ambassador.

"What is the meaning of this?" the ambassador demanded. "You can't just throw this junk into our property!"

"The Rhumgadian embassy is about to be stormed," Greny said. "I need to get these people out of here."

"So the crowd will turn on us!" Byun Kran thundered.

"The crowd will never know unless you delay us," Greny said.

The ambassador's head trembled for a moment with mute exasperation. "Then be quick about it."

Greny addressed the ratchers. "Slide two of the ladders over the wall and prop them on the far side so our Rhumgadian friends can safely descend into the Ambassador's residence."

Much to his satisfaction, as the ratchers neared the ladders, the Rhumgadians on them dropped their goods and either jumped off and scurried away, or else leaped down into the Maxthez garden. As soon as the ratchers withdrew, the Rhumgadians scrambled back onto the ladders again and the evacuation resumed with greater haste than before.

The operation was again briefly interrupted when Moylar himself decided to follow his precious case over the wall, and the remaining Rhumgadians cleared a path for him and patiently waited for him to cross. Despite this delay, it wouldn't be long before everyone would be safely out of danger.

"The princesses will burn if you don't save them."

Greny turned to the whisperer, but the scrawny man in a servant's livery behind him stared back at him with mild bafflement. Had Greny imagined it?

"Where are the princesses?" he demanded.

The man didn't speak. His guilty expression answered for him.

Greny grabbed his lapel, but the man wrenched free of his grip and, glancing angrily at his assailant, stalked toward the ladders.

"Ratchers with me!" Greny cried, racing back into the building. "We have to find those girls." Dragons, could they be dead? Could Moylar have slaughtered them so he could blame the Gyran mob for their deaths, and by extension the Meritocracy? That would explain Moylar's initial refusal to leave. He wanted to make sure the embassy would fall before he departed.

"Chemp and I will take the top floor," Greny said to the ratchers as they entered the reception hall. Glass and missiles littered the floor. The backs of cordents were visible through the broken windows. It wouldn't be long before they either retreated into the building or let the mob through. "Queek and Kleest, take the next floor down. Dweed, the floor below that." A group of injured cordents lay huddled against one wall. "If you can stand, get up!" Greny yelled at them. "There is a group of girls locked up somewhere in this building. We need to find them."

By the time he reached the top of the stairs, every breath hurt and his lungs felt on fire. Why had he chosen the top floor? He and Chemp rushed along the corridor, trying each door in turn, knocking urgently on them when they were locked. The princesses might lie dead behind any of them, but he must hang on to the hope they yet lived.

An acrid scent assailed him. A white haze hung over the next corridor he turned down. Smoke spilled from under one door. Greny pounded on it, to no avail. He listened, but the only sound coming from inside was the crackle of burning wood. He reached for the handle, flinching at the sting of its intense heat.

"Chemp, can you hear anyone inside?"

The ratcher, endowed with preternatural hearing, shook his head. The Rhumgadians must have deliberately started this fire. There could be others elsewhere throughout the building.

A chorus of shrieks came from downstairs. Led by Chemp, Greny rushed down two flights to where Dweed stood outside a busted door. Greny pushed past him and frowned at the trembling scissors and hairpins arrayed against him. The terrified girls were all dressed in plain white smocks. Their fine clothes and jewelry were probably already in the Maxthez Embassy.

"We're here to evacuate you," Greny said, glancing at the ratchers behind him. Queek and Kleest had just arrived.

"Ambassador Moylar told us to wait here," one girl said in heavily accented pyratic.

He left you here to die. "He sent us to collect you," Greny lied. "Follow me."

"The other princesses are in the next room," the girl said.

"What's your name?" Greny asked.

She raised her chin imperiously. "Princess Eslaf of House Sathbad." She was the one who claimed Drinith's throne.

"Well, Your Highness, I'll need you to assure your friends in the other room we're no threat."

Eslaf looked dubious, but she complied. With a wary glance at Dweed, she cupped her mouth to the door to the other room, explaining to the princesses that Greny had come to rescue them before the ratchers battered it open. As Greny led them through the foyer, Posaleum stumbled into the building.

"How much longer?" she barked, coughing. The smoky haze had filled the entire embassy.

"Not long now," Greny promised, racing toward the garden. Two ladders lay on the ground by the wall.

"Quick! Get over the wall! Jump if you must!" Greny commanded the ratchers as soon as they had propped them back up. To the girls, he said, "You follow them. They'll help you down."

As the girls climbed up, Moylar's head rose above the wall. "I see you found our missing princesses."

"No thanks to you," Greny growled.

Moylar made a play of counting them with a finger. "All sixteen, I see. You have stolen none for your tower."

"What is that supposed to mean?"

Moylar laughed. "I assumed your habit of imprisoning pretty girls was common knowledge, but perhaps I'm ill-informed?"

A few of the girls gazed down at Greny with such tremulous fear, it turned his stomach. "You're ill all right—in the head," he muttered, hoping the ambassador wouldn't notice the blush heating his cheeks.

As soon as the two ladders were clear, he grabbed the nearest one and started pushing it into the Maxthez garden. "Help me! These ladders mustn't remain on this side of the wall." It lifted out of his hands, and the other two tilted upward as they slid across the coping and disappeared.

Greny raced back into the building. "Let them in! Let them in!"

Rioters poured through the front door and then the windows. Greny sat beside the group of wounded cordents. Taking no notice of them, the mob ripped the tapestries off the walls, pulled down the statues, even stripped the gilded wood off the stair's banister and tried to pry the golden tesserae from the mosaic. A woman planted herself on the stairs and shouted not to damage its runner as her friends tried to cut a section free. All the while, the relentless stream of rioters rushed by them. Greny spotted a couple of guilty-looking cordents skulking amid the crowd, no doubt looking for a share of the loot.

"We had better get out of here," Greny said, rising. "Before the fire spreads."

The cordents had formed a new line on the far side of the littered, bloodstained street. A dead ratcher lay forgotten in the detritus of the riot, its fur matted with black gore. Poor Sneeth was unrecognizable except for the familiar sharp kink in his tail.

Greny pulled two yellowchecks out of the line and thrust a finger at the corpse. "Bring him to my tower now!"

His violent glare quickly dispelled their hesitancy, and they hastened to collect the corpse.

Posaleum and Opriet paused their whispered conversation as he approached. Of course, they wouldn't apologize for this grievous oversight, nor would he upbraid them for it. They had more pressing matters to discuss.

"Were you and the ratcher close?" Posaleum sneered. Offended by the reek of carnage and rubbish, she held a sachet underneath her flaring nostrils.

"He deserved better than being left like rubbish in the streets," Greny groused. "Where were you, Opriet?" *Leaving me with this smirking fool.*

"Organizing the defense of the Blue Quarter," Opriet said with a lopsided smile. "I figured that if the crowd couldn't take the embassy, they'd turn on any Rhumgadians they could find, no matter what side they were on. Once I had bolstered the cordents at the bridges to the Blue Quarter, I gathered any who could be spared and came here to relieve you. Unfortunately, the embassy had been stormed by the time we arrived."

"Greny told me to let the rioters in," Posaleum said.

"I'm sure there was no other choice. Better the Rhumgadian Embassy burns than the city." Opriet nodded at the first wispy tendrils of white smoke creeping from a top-floor window. Already, a few rioters exited the building carrying chairs, books, a chamber pot, a bust of some anonymous Rhumgadian, and other random objects.

"We must stop them and confiscate those stolen goods," Posaleum blurted.

"And ignite another riot? Let them keep their trophies," Opriet said. "They'll go home satisfied that they have avenged their murdered meritocrats and struck a blow against Gyre's enemies." She acknowledged with a nod a passing man robed in a fine tapestry. "Let them through!" she yelled. "They have struck a blow for Gyre's honor this day!" Several of the looters cheered.

Opriet leaned close to Posaleum. "The ones with no loot are the greater danger. They'll go home, envying their more fortunate companions and looking out for something to rob."

"What about our injured cordents?" Posaleum said. "We can't let their assailants escape justice."

"I must admit I am impressed by this concern you exhibit for your subordinates," Greny said.

"I was injured myself." Posaleum pointed to a cut on her forehead. "Do you know how much it will cost to remove the scar?" She threw up her arms and looked down at her dirty dress. "And my clothes are ruined."

Opriet made a dismissive gesture. "We'll mete out justice for your suffering all in good time when the crowd has dispersed and the culprits have no mob to protect them."

"What do we tell the Vicenary Jury?" Posaleum asked. "They'll be looking for someone to blame."

"We'll tell them it was either let the embassy burn or call the Dragon Keeper in," Greny said. "Everything will be reduced to ash and rubble if we let dragons run wild in the city."

"But we need to find who initiated this attack," Opriet said. "This wasn't a spontaneous outbreak of anger. Osro or Thaxen weren't that popular with the common folk. Somebody encouraged them to riot."

"But who?" Posaleum asked.

Opriet tilted her head so she could look Posaleum straight in the eyes. "Somebody from the New War Faction, maybe. This attack might be sufficient provocation for Magian to withdraw his offer."

"Or somebody in the Short War camp blames Magian for the deaths of Thaxen and Osro," Posaleum said.

"Or Magian's agents stirred this up themselves," Greny said, remembering the princesses.

Someone cleared his throat beside Greny. The yellowcheck shied away from his stare. "Begging your pardon, Cordent General. I was dispatched from Woodshard with urgent news."

What could be more pressing than this riot? "What is it?"

"Meritocrat Velso is dead," the yellowcheck said with a trembling voice. "She has been murdered."

17

———————

Drinith kicked helplessly as two of Cenmis's guards forced her arms behind her back. A third guard, a hefty giant with a spiral silver goatee reminiscent of a unicorn horn, patted her down. His striking appearance had caused Drinith to notice him in Cenmis's company before. He must be her regular bodyguard. For such a big man, his hands moved with surprising nimbleness and speed. She bristled at the intimate liberties he slyly took in his search but held her tongue. He quickly found her blade and removed it from its secret pocket. He also took her precious emblem of merit.

"This is not the sort of the behavior I would expect of a meritocrat," Cenmis sneered as he offered her the gold disc. She gave a sharp nod to the female butler sweating profusely to her left. "Take it, Jelsan." The butler, a fretful middle-aged woman hunched as though carrying an invisible weight, reverently took the emblem and polished it with a piece of velvet.

"Are you sure she has no more concealed weapons, Grivel?" Cenmis asked the big guard.

He leered knowingly at Drinith. "My search was thorough, Meritocrat."

"Then let her go."

The two guards did so.

"I had hoped for a more hospitable welcome," Drinith groused, attempting in vain to smooth the wrinkles from her clothes. The butler approached, and holding the disc by its edge, offered it to her. She snatched it from the woman's hand and placed it on her head. She felt vulnerable, robbed of her blade.

"Be glad I haven't handed you over to Greny *yet*," Cenmis said. "Come."

Drinith followed her into the parlor. It was like stepping into a riotous flower garden. The furnishings were patterned with a red orchid motif. Orchids in fine porcelain pots on pedestals lined the wall opposite to the windows, their cloying incense heavy on the air. The glittering red flower in the center of the row outshone the others. At first glance, it looked as though it had been wrought from jewels, but it was in fact a living plant from the shard of Magmel, a fabled scarlet crownmaker.

Cenmis seated herself on a couch and, picking up a silver bell, cradled it in her hands. Drinith moved to take the armchair beside her.

"I'd prefer if you sit over there," Cenmis said, pointing to a more distant seat. Despite her irritation at being ordered about, Drinith complied without protest.

"You can close the door. I'll call if I need you," Cenmis said to Grivel, who hovered by the threshold. He looked dubious but withdrew. The door shut with a sharp click. "My apologies for your rough treatment under my roof, but two meritocrats are already dead and I plan to not be a third."

"You can't seriously think I murdered them."

"I must defer to Greny's judgment. He raided your home. Every cordent, red, yellow and blue, is hunting you."

"He might be knocking down your door, too, if he had gone himself to Osro's residence and discovered you standing over her body. Osro invited him, not me."

Cenmis blanched. The bell tinkled gently as she sat forward. "If he knows...? Of course. He's hunting you to conceal his own involvement. He's afraid suspicion will fall on him. They say a rat is most dangerous when cornered. You haven't told anybody of my involvement, have you?"

"Only somebody on whose discretion I can absolutely rely."

Cenmis scowled. "I hope you're right, for both our sakes. Thanks to the murders of our dear colleagues, the entire Meritocracy is fevered with fear and suspicion. You gave me the benefit of the doubt over poor Osro's death. I'm willing to extend you the same courtesy. By corroborating each other's innocence, we can extricate ourselves from this dreadful mess."

Eying Drinith intently, Cenmis placed the bell on the low table in front of her. "I never liked Greny, to be honest. There are too many dark rumors about what happens in his tower. And then there are those appalling rodents who serve him. Greny has developed a somewhat sinister obsession for them. Trusts them more than humans. He even changed his family emblem of merit from a dragon scale axe to a wheel of rats. His colleague, Opriet Braesum, is a dear friend. She'll protect us from the Rat King."

Drinith agreed with a nod, despite her misgivings. She couldn't be certain that Cenmis wasn't the murderer, but she needed to clear her name and free her friends. "Who do you think killed Osro and Thaxen?"

"I've been wracking my brain trying to answer that very question," Cenmis said. "Thaxen likely burned Osro's mansion to hide her involvement. She would have probably packed Osro's servant off on a dragon to some distant shard with a sizable fortune had they both lived. As a meritocrat with a lot of enemies, Thaxen feared scrutiny. We all have secrets and peccadilloes that we'd rather not become common knowledge."

Cenmis rubbed the corners of her mouth. "Everything between finding Osro's corpse and your arrival last night is a blur. The only thing I remember is the dead bird. That struck me as odd. As for the documents on her desk, in my frantic state, I couldn't take anything in. I could have read the killer's confession and not absorbed a word.

"Orso, Thaxen, and I used to be great friends in our youth, but we fell out over a courtesar. It was quite a scandal at the time. My mother nearly disinherited me. It's one thing for courtesars to fight for the favor of meritorians. It's quite another for meritorians to claw each other in the street over some peacock who took their fancy. Later dalliances cooled my passion, and I saw our feud for the inconsequential nonsense it truly was. It wasn't worth remembering, much less maintaining a lifelong feud. Of course, one of the regrettable inconveniences of our rank is we can't simply apologize. Healing old wounds requires subtlety and patience. In truth, I originally joined the Short War Faction to heal our rift."

Drinith winced in disgust that a decades-old romantic squabble potentially shaped the fate of countless innocent lives. How many times had she witnessed the personal caprices of meritocrats impacting the Meritocracy's polices?

"My efforts met with mixed success," Cenmis said wistfully. "Much to my surprise, Thaxen proved the easier to befriend again. Perhaps she sensed that my desire for reconciliation was genuine, or she succumbed to nostalgia or loneliness. We did share a keen interest in horticulture." She waved vaguely at her orchids. "Thaxen loved her garden a little too much for her station. She often worked there like a common laborer. That's why her hands were so calloused, even as a young girl. I would sometimes come away from her mansion burdened with an armful of dirty vegetables, my dress covered with clay and bits of leaves. Breeding flowers is a fitting pursuit for meritorians, fruticulture is a forgivable diversion, but no member of our class has any business debasing themselves with the tending of vegetables. I often told Thaxen that, much to her amusement, until I realized it only spurred her generosity with her cabbages." Moved by the memory, she dabbed her eyes with a handkerchief.

It was hard to square this homely recollection of Thaxen with the daunting meritocrat Drinith had known. Part of her wished she had been acquainted with this other Thaxen. Another part struggled to accept her existence. "And Osro?"

"Osro kept her distance, but of course, that was nothing new. She was a bit of an outsider even in her own faction," Cenmis said. "Being Ducal Steward, she had to maintain a certain decorous detachment from the rest of the Meritocracy. Her sudden invitation to visit her took me by complete surprise. It was a long missive full of shared reminiscences from our youth. She gave the strong impression that she wanted to rekindle our friendship properly and expunge the last embers of our former enmity. I never for a moment imagined accepting her invite would embroil me in this dark intrigue."

Her eyes popped open. She slapped her thighs. "Tea! I have been a terrible host, but I'll rectify my oversight immediately."

Drinith inhaled to protest. Such courtesies could wait until she had cleared her name. But Cenmis leapt to her feet, cutting Drinith short with a grin. "Don't you dare refuse. I won't hear of it."

As her host stepped out of the room to arrange some refreshments, Drinith mulled over her account of Osro's letter. It made no sense. Why invite Thaxen and Greny to expose a sinister plot while encouraging Cenmis to visit on the pretext of cementing their reconciliation? What could Osro hope to achieve with such subterfuge? Unless Cenmis was part of the conspiracy that the Ducal Steward had intended to expose. Had Orso planned to catch her unawares? Did Cenmis murder Orso to protect herself? If that was the case, Drinith had walked into a trap.

Drinith essayed a smile as Cenmis reentered. Behind her, Jelsan carried a large silver tray laden with a large pot of tea and enough scones and cakes to feed a dozen hungry people. As Cenmis took her seat, the butler laid the tray on a low table.

"Jelsan, you can go. I'll serve." Cenmis poured a drop into her bowl and stared at the faint color of the water with dissatisfaction. "I might let it draw a while. My serving etiquette needs improving, it seems. I don't know why I was so hasty to pour."

"Your secret is safe with me," Drinith murmured as the butler closed the door behind her. "But tell me, what do you think was Orso's real reason for inviting you to last night's gathering?"

"Honestly, I have no idea. Perhaps she believed it was the only means by which she could convince me to come. Frankly, I would have never crossed her threshold if I had any inkling of this sinister business."

Cenmis poured the tea, spilling a drop on the tray. She emitted a playful tut. "Of course, your question presumes she wrote that invitation. I've reread that letter a dozen times. It contained little that wasn't common knowledge among meritocrats of my generation. The rest might easily be gleaned from a night swapping stories over a few bowls of hard tea. A close friend of Osro's or me, or even a heedful servant, might easily cobble it together."

After a moment's reflection, she added, "I'm not denying Osro wrote it. I'm just saying you can't assume anything. A lot of people stood to gain from her death—whoever succeeds her as the Ducal Steward for a start; her heir, her enemies, political and personal. You, for instance, had a reason to take comfort in her demise."

Drinith nearly choked on her tea. "Pardon?"

"She accused you in the wrong of attempting to kill the Ducalion. But for the intervention of your notorious Veiled Meritocrat, Osro would have locked you away in Inkeep. Had Magian's Crevastival attack succeeded, you might have even been executed as one of his agents in the fevered aftermath. Yes, you had ample reason to hate her." Cenmis's smile turned brittle; her gaze intensely scrutinizing. Her hand rested on the butter knife on her plate.

"That was all in the past, forgotten," Drinith said. A lifetime ago, before she went to Ophigee.

Cenmis picked up the knife and casually stabbed the air in front of Drinith. "You could have arranged this whole thing to unite the Meritocracy against Rhumgad. All that is needed now is some evidence Magian is behind the killings. You manage to get entangled in his plots with surprising frequency."

"No, you're wrong," Drinith said firmly. "I had no hand in the plot."

Cenmis stopped smiling. "Or perhaps you work for Ophigee. Perhaps you're their agent."

Drinith returned her host's glare. "If I had wanted to kill you," she said evenly, "I could have easily done it the night when we left Osro's mansion." The dull blade her host held wasn't the real threat, but at one cry from her, her bodyguards would swarm the room. "I thought we agreed we're not enemies."

"You're right," Cenmis said, a wan smile bending her lips a fraction. After cutting open her scone and buttering it, she placed her knife on her plate. "I'll invite Opriet over after we've had our tea. For all we know, Greny is the true villain. I'm at a loss why Osro dragged me into this mess, but I'm determined—" Her eyes bulged. Shooting to her feet, she clutched her throat whilst making gagging sounds.

"Is something lodged in your throat?" Drinith asked in alarm, glancing at the uneaten scone. What could Cenmis be choking on?

Drinith knocked over the service tray as she lunged to catch the toppling woman. At the crash of the tea service, the doors flew open. Grivel and his three colleagues entered, swords drawn. Cenmis slipped through Drinith's arms and flopped onto the tea-soaked rug. She stared up at Drinith amidst the broken crockery and scones, her face swollen and darkening, her eyes wide with fright.

"Get her to the Grand Preservatory quick!" Drinith yelled. "She's been poisoned!" Drinith had also drunk the tea but appeared to be fine; the toxin must have been dispensed in some other manner. But the mystery of how Cenmis ingested poison would have to wait. The immediate priority was to save her life.

"The palanquin, now!" Grivel roared. He pushed past Drinith and scooped up Cenmis's limp body in massive arms. "No time. We'll carry her." He rushed out the door, two of his compatriots on his heels.

Drinith moved to follow, but the fourth guard blocked her with his sword. "Begging your pardon, Meritocrat, but it's in your interest to stay here until this matter is resolved."

She would be tested before truthscryers for certain. Even though her testimony would prove her innocence of the murders, her foes in the Parliament of Merit would expand the interrogation to include her imprisonment on Ophigee and the foiled Crevastival attack.

Concealing Gelasin's involvement in the plot would be enough to send her to the Plank. She had to get out of here!

Her gaze swept the room for something heavy—yes, the vase on the pedestal beside her chair would suffice. The guard's eyes narrowed suspiciously. "I suppose you're right," she said, smiling. "I should be safe enough here with you here to protect me." She brushed her hand across her forehead, dislodging her emblem of merit, letting it drop to the ground. As he bowed to retrieve it, she seized the vessel and brought it down on his bowed head. The blow smashed the bottom of the vase, spilling rich black soil on the groaning man. Drinith grabbed her emblem of merit and the man's dagger and dashed for the door. Jelsan filled the threshold, wide-eyed with shock. Drinith pushed by her, raced through the reception hall and out the front door.

As she dashed down the gravel path, heavy boots crunched behind her. Slipping through the slightly open gate, she glanced back at the now recovered guard, transformed by her ruse into a bloodied, enraged monster, chasing her with sword in hand.

Even if she could give him the slip in the forest, he would raise the alarm with the cordents at the bridges, ending any hope of escape. Surely she could outrun him, half-dazed as he was and weighed down with cumbrous armor. But the glances she cast over her shoulder confirmed he slowly gained on her, his sword pumping up and down. She had little chance of beating him in a fight. But she had one thing going for her—she was a meritocrat.

She cut across a bend, trampling a flower bed, to see Diadem Bridge ahead. The three cordents at the checkpoint lurched from their casual poses and drew their batons. The grunted breaths of the guard grew louder behind her.

She threw up her hands. "Help! Help! I'm being attacked!" As she hurtled by the cordents, she flashed her emblem of merit too fast for anyone to recognize the Hax alerion, and added breathlessly, "Take him alive! Your cordent general will want to speak to him."

Voices rose in anger behind her, but she kept running. As she crossed the high point of the arch, she threw a glance back at the checkpoint. Cenmis's guard was pinned face down on the path, his hands manacled behind his back. The gazes of the cordents standing over him swiveled in unison from their captive to the bridge. One hastened after Drinith, but she was well ahead of him. She crossed the rest of the bridge and plunged down streets at random until she was certain she had lost them. She'd head back to Wealgiver Street and wait there for Woad. If Cenmis was dead, so was any obvious chance of clearing her name.

18

———————

Standing in Cenmis's parlor, Greny buried his face in his sweaty palms and took a couple of deep breaths. He threw up his hands. "Why didn't the cordents at the bridge arrest Drinith?"

Nayz met his stare with resolute unrepentance from the far side of the mess on the floor—the spilled tea service and a smashed flowerpot still littered the stained carpet. "You instructed them not to accost the meritocrat. They simply followed your orders."

"They should have acted on their own initiative. They knew Cenmis Velso had been poisoned."

"The captain took half of his contingent to the riot. His sergeant accompanied Meritocrat Velso to the Grand Preservatory, leaving three relatively inexperienced cordents behind."

"The sergeant should have stayed."

"Her priority was to save the meritocrat's life."

"Which she failed to do," Greny pointed out.

"The poison was too potent, yes. Meritocrat Velso died before she reached the Grand Preservatory."

"I would have thought, given the utmost importance and delicacy of this investigation, you would have assigned more experienced cordents to Woodshard. I shouldn't have to fret about these organizational minutiae. It's up to you to manage the deployment of my cordents."

"I had every experienced yellowcheck scouring the city for information about the murders. Then the riot started."

Nayz's arrogant smirk as he shrugged filled Greny with rage. *Rat Prince indeed! No doubt he's proud to be called that. Probably named himself that in his arrogance. Too stupid to appreciate that my nickname is a jibe, combining two things the Meritocracy despises—rats and monarchs. I have endured being called Rat King by my peers for so long I have become too inured to it, but I won't put up with being mocked by the likes of this arrogant whelp!*

"Are you aware," Greny said, "that your men call you the Rat Prince behind your back?"

Nayz blinked uselessly, struck momentarily speechlessness. Recovering, he said, somewhat haltingly, "I cannot see how that figures into the matter at hand."

So he did know! What else is he hiding from me? "Are you deliberately trying to stymie this investigation?" Greny demanded point-blank.

"Of course, not. Are you?"

"What is that supposed to mean?"

"You're being less than frank. Your inspired hunch that Meritocrat Hax would visit Meritocrat Velso's home wasn't anything of the sort. You *knew* she'd go. You have an informer among her followers, somebody very close to her, and for some reason, you don't want me to know their identity. I must say, it shows a singular lack of trust on your part."

The muscles in Greny's forehead strained so much they hurt. Part of him would dearly love to send Nayz in a restraining coffin to Inkeep, but the sudden incarceration of his deputy would draw too many awkward questions from the Vicenary Jury. "You seem a trifle confused as to which of us is the meritocrat. You answer to me, not the other way around."

There had been a time when such a barb would have floored Nayz, but his brazen grin didn't falter. "I am well aware that you are in charge, Cordent General. I meant no offense." The tang of arrogance in his tone hinted otherwise. "I always understood you preferred the warty truth. It would be better if—"

"Get out!" Greny's roar burned his throat. Queek and Chemp stumbled through the door, swords drawn.

Nayz gave them a nonchalant glance over his shoulder. "I already have a lead on how Meritocrat Cenmis was poisoned."

Greny dismissed the ratchers with a brusque wave of his hand. "Go on."

Nayz drew a scroll from the inside of his coat and unfolded it. The drawing of a woman's right hand, palm upward, was covered with black blobs. "The burns on Meritocrat Velso's hand appear to indicate that she had absorbed the poison by holding an object." He crouched down and pointed vaguely at the mess of sodden buns and broken crockery on the floor. "From careful study of their pattern, I have determined it must have been one of the butter knives lying on the floor."

"So Drinith didn't murder Cenmis." Relief flooded Greny. He might yet extricate Drinith, and by extension himself, from this mess.

Nayz scratched his pointed chin. "True, she's unlikely to have poisoned the knife herself, but she may have ordered it."

"To what possible end?" Greny blurted, his temper getting the better of him again. "She hoped Cenmis could clear her name."

Nayz cocked his head and grinned. "Is that so? How could you possibly know that?"

"I'm warning you: don't push me too far or your excessive prying into my business will prove your undoing," Greny growled.

Nayz was undaunted by the threat. "Maybe Meritocrat Velso proved less helpful than she expected." He seemed to particularly relish in this speculation. Of course, bad servants always took perverse pleasure in their employers' calamities.

Greny shook his head. "This poisoning took planning. It's not the sort of thing that could be done on the spur of the moment."

"It might have been a contingency in case Meritocrat Velso proved uncooperative."

"Drinith is cut off from her supporters."

"The ones you know of, maybe. This source you won't divulge—can you really trust them?"

"I hold someone dear to him in Inkeep," Greny said.

"Ah, so it's Woad Glastum," Nayz said gleefully.

"That's right," Greny said. There was no further point in denying it. "And he knows the price of crossing me." *And if you're not careful, you'll learn the same lesson the hard way.* Had Nayz any family? Greny had never asked. It probably would be too obvious to inquire about their well-being right now. Another time. Nobody would take much notice of Nayz's kin being whisked off to Inkeep.

Nayz straightened and eyed Greny with a hint of alarm. "There is a way we might catch the murderer," he said, adopting his most ingratiating tone. "We let the staff return and watch for whoever proves eager to clean up this mess. As far as the culprit is concerned, we're in the dark as to how Meritocrat Velso died, and they'll want to keep us that way."

"Unless they know the poison has lost its potency by now."

"True," Nayz conceded. "But it's still our best hope of catching them."

"Very well," Greny said wearily.

As Nayz scurried away to set his plan in motion, a vase of red flowers drew Greny's gaze. They glittered in the sunlight passing through the windows. Greny approached them, realized the petals were delicate, curved wafers of crystal. This must be Cenmis's renowned scarlet crownmaker. Greny had never seen it before. The flower looked like the work of a master jeweler. Every petal was perfect. Even the delicate gilded stems showed nary a blemish. He found it hard to believe that anything so perfect could be alive.

It was a shame that his first viewing of such a wonder was under these tragic circumstances. Cenmis had never invited him to her home. No, she had once, a halfhearted gesture that he had spurned out of hand. She had been looking for something from him. He could tell from her demeanor. A favor of some kind. But even as she asked, it was plain that she already assumed her ploy was bound to fail. She made it against her better judgment on the off chance she might be mistaken.

His hand trembled as he reached toward the glistening blossoms. Their petals felt smooth and brittle, like wafer-thin glass, and clinked against each other as he stroked them. Suddenly, afraid his touch might shatter the delicate crystals, he tucked both hands behind his back.

He leaned close to the plant and sniffed. The crownmaker's fragrance wasn't particularly alluring or strong. In fact, it was quite muted, but the plant was famed for its crystalline beauty, not its scent.

Nayz announced his reentry with a cough. He approached, his gaze admiring the scarlet crownmaker. "Is that really a plant?"

"It is—a living plant worth more than a thousand times its weight in gold." How could any meritocrat squander precious ducats on such an extravagance? Even Okia, the richest meritocrat in Gyre, would never be so profligate. To think Cenmis had kept it here unguarded in her parlor, where a light-fingered servant might steal a blossom. Obviously, she had trusted her staff with it and her life, but her confidence had proved to be misplaced. One of them had betrayed her.

"It certainly catches the eye," Nayz observed.

A maid entered and, whispering a breathless apology, knelt down and began to tidy up the mess on the carpet. Greny rolled his eyes. This slip of a girl was hardly Nayz's assassin. She had just set about gathering the fragments of porcelain and lumps of sodden cake and placing them on the tray when a voice rang out.

"Wait!" Everyone turned to face the flustered butler standing in the doorway. "I'll take care of that, Deryn. You're needed in the kitchen."

The maid nodded, reached for the silver tray.

"I said leave it!" the butler shrilled. She glanced guiltily at Greny, her servile stoop deepening. "Begging your pardon, Meritocrat."

"And your name is?" Greny asked the butler as the maid fled the room.

The butler stiffened to attention. "Jelsan, Meritocrat."

"Have you butlered here for long?"

"Ten years," Jelsan said with a proud lift of her chin. "I started out in the scullery and worked myself up to butler."

"Impressive, wouldn't you say, Nayz?" Greny said. The cordent nodded. "Surely cleaning the carpet is beneath you."

Jelsan's top lip twitched infinitesimally. "If you want a job done right, do it yourself, I always say." The butler donned a pair of gloves, then gestured at the dirty carpet. "May I, Meritocrat?"

"By all means." Greny masked his growing anger with what he hoped was a convincing smile. To think this wretch might have murdered the woman who had raised her up from nothing!

As the butler hunkered down on the soiled carpet, Nayz strolled over to the door. Panic clenched Greny's heart. Was the fool about to abandon him, leaving him alone with this potential killer?

Nayz peered out the door, and after muttering something crept up quietly beside the butler so that his shadow crossed her back. Nayz drew his dagger and watched the butler work. She mopped up the tea soaked into the carpet, cleaning around the knives, leaving them until last.

"You forgot the knives," Nayz observed.

The butler froze a couple of heartbeats, then, with mute annoyance, slipped off her gloves and pocketed them. She picked up the knives in quick succession and threw them onto the tray. After rising off the floor using the low table as support, she stooped and lifted the silver tray in both hands. Greny spotted too late that the two knives nestled in one of her palms.

Swinging around, she flung the tray and its contents at Nayz. In the instant he raised his hands to shield himself, she attacked Greny with the butter knives. Greny backed away from her as he drew his dagger and stumbled into two potted plants, which crashed to the floor. Jelsan bounded over a third pot Greny deliberately threw in her path. Chemp and Queek burst into the room, swords at the ready. Greny grabbed the vase of the scarlet crownmaker to throw at her, but he could barely lift it. The butler, possibly swayed by years of Cenmis's injunctions to mind the priceless plant, looked on with horror. Her momentary hesitation gave the ratchers enough time to reach her.

"Don't kill her!" Nayz cried, staying their swords. "We need her alive!"

Queek emitted a pained squeal as Jelsan slashed his muzzle with one of her knives, the force of the blow ripping the blade from its handle. The butler thrust the other knife at Greny. He blocked the blow with the flowerpot, but it slipped from his hands, petals snapping off the blossoms as the pot landed at his feet.

The ratchers finally seized the butler, forced the remaining butter knife from her grip and pinned her hands behind her back.

"Queek, are you okay?" Greny cried, brittle petals crunching underfoot as he rushed to his servant and offered him a handkerchief to press to his bloody muzzle. "Nayz, call a healer quickly! The wound might be poisoned." Greny had already lost one ratcher today.

"It's likely the handle rather than the blade that's poisoned," Nayz muttered.

"Have one of your men escort Queek to the Grand Preservatory," Greny commanded. "Tell the preservators I'll pay whatever his treatment costs."

Scowling, Nayz obeyed.

"You don't approve of the beneficence I show my servants," Greny observed as soon as Queek had departed with his escort.

"I just think it's a pity that you don't apply the same benevolence to your cordents," Nayz groused.

"Your resentment be damned!" Greny snarled. "My ratchers have earned my generosity countless times over. And they aren't as insolent."

"I spoke in anger, Meritocrat. I beg your forgiveness," Nayz said, realizing he had gone too far.

The apology didn't even merit acknowledgement. Instead, Greny bent down and recovered the crownmaker. The base of the vase had cracked and only two flower heads remained intact, but hopefully, the plant would survive. Should it die, recompensing Cenmis's heir for its loss might bankrupt him.

A choking sound drew his attention to the butler. Jelsan's face had darkened and her bulging eyes filled with blood as if she was hanging from an invisible noose, but the most horrible part of her death was her ugly sneer of triumph. She had cheated her captors, or at least thought she had.

"Take her to the Grand Preservatory," Greny said, but Jelsan had already slumped in Chemp's arms.

"I had hoped the butler might lead us to whoever is behind the attacks," Nayz said.

"Too late now," Greny muttered. He lifted Jelsan by the hair to stare into her dead eyes. Her frozen smile mocked him. A snap beneath his foot reminded him of the crownmaker.

"While you were worrying about your injured ratcher, the butler was biding her time for the poison she had absorbed to kill her," Nayz said. "That was why she removed her gloves, in order to contaminate her bare skin with the poison. She knew we were on to her."

"She knew because you as good as told her," Greny groused. "And you delayed the ratchers arresting her."

"She wouldn't tell us much after being hacked to death by their swords."

Greny dropped Jelsan's head. "She won't tell us anything now, either." He watched Chemp lay the corpse on a couch. Nayz might have tipped her off deliberately. He might have called out to the ratchers to give the butler enough time to kill Greny.

"I'll have the house searched thoroughly," Nayz said. "If there's any evidence here, I'll find it."

And my ratchers will watch your every move. If you're part of this conspiracy, I promise you'll think the butler's death gentle.

19

Greny brooded on Cenmis's murder all the way back to his tower. As far as he knew, with her death, he had become the sole survivor of the group who was supposed to gather at Osro's mansion that night. Thanks to Nayz's incompetence or deliberate betrayal, Greny had lost his best lead. The butler's death wouldn't impress the Iron Circle. It would want whatever conspiracy she served destroyed root and branch.

Mocking laughter erupted from within the parlor as Greny entered the reception hall of his tower. Deetch signed that two meritocrats awaited him. Greny approached the parlor door, listened.

"I hope sitting in this dreary place doesn't give me fleas," a woman said, bursting into a high-pitched titter. A second woman chuckled appreciatively.

The laughter trailed off as Greny entered. Elca smiled slyly, but Ecethor beamed with triumph. She was dressed in a most ridiculous cascade of black silk. On her red hair, she wore a tiny boat-shaped hat.

"To what do I owe this pleasure?" Greny asked as he sat across from them. The tray of tea and cakes that Deetch had provided remained untouched. Did they already know about Cenmis's death, or did they simply turn up their noses at food prepared by ratcher hands?

Greny had no appetite, but he forced himself to eat. The tepid tea suggested that his guests had been ensconced in the parlor for a while.

"I heard about Cenmis. Tragic, simply tragic," Elca said, Ecethor nodding along. "I understand you apprehended the assassin."

"It was the butler," Greny said. "She's dead. Poisoned herself." He shared nothing that Elca wouldn't soon know if she didn't already.

"Was Cenmis's murder connected to the others?" Elca asked.

"I'm sure you understand I can't discuss the details of my investigation while it is ongoing." He directed a sidelong glance at Ecethor. Elca might be entitled to have her question answered by virtue of her membership of the Vicenary Jury, but Ecethor certainly wasn't.

"Of course," Elca said with a knowing grin. "I wouldn't want to undermine your investigation in any way. I came here on a different matter. Apparently, Ecethor erroneously left you with the impression that her brineflower smuggling operation was a private, and therefore illegal, enterprise. It's actually part of our preparation for a possible invasion of Rhumgad. Useful intelligence travels with the brineflowers, while the operation helps us develop relationships with various potential allies."

"Ecethor may have mentioned to me such an arrangement before as a vague potentiality, but not an actuality," Greny said. *Ecethor, what price did you pay to secure Elca's help? Do you not realize that the Iron Circle's wrath would be gentler than Elca's friendship?*

Elca patted her companion's arm. "You know her—she is the epitome of discretion."

Greny arched his brows in surprise. "No offense to Ecethor, but she has the reputation of being the exact opposite."

It was clear from the clench of Ecethor's jaw that the observation stung.

"I'm shocked that you let yourself be seduced by such tittle-tattle," Elca said. "I always presumed you to be very perceptive. The best person to keep a secret is not she who never opens her mouth, but she who superficially appears incapable of such a feat." She added with a crafty smile, "And sometimes silence speaks louder than any words. I'm sure you had no inkling of Ecethor's operation until she told you."

"She did tell me, though."

"Because she holds you in such high esteem. She trusts you. Isn't that right, Ecethor?"

Ecethor nodded. She hadn't said one word since Greny arrived. Her uncharacteristic muteness, Greny thought sardonically, must be a type of reverse ventriloquism, given she was behaving like Elca's puppet.

"It should be a relief to you," Elca said, "given all events of the last few days that demand your attention, that you needn't take any further interest in Ecethor and her silly brineflowers."

"So, to be clear, you sanctioned Ecethor's operation."

"I did. You have the word of one member of"—she made a circular motion in the air, the symbol of the Iron Circle, with her finger—"to another."

"Then, I'll not call you a liar." *However much I might want to.*

"Very good," Elca said. She patted Ecethor's lap. "I have some other business to discuss with Greny. Would you mind waiting for me in the reception hall?"

"Of course, Elca," Ecethor said, grinning like an exuberant child. Her silk dress rustled crisply as she strode from the room. At Greny's signal, Deetch, who peeped his muzzle across the threshold, shut the door.

"And what would this business be?" Greny asked.

"You have something I want, or rather someone—the Oracle. He's key to our conquest of Rhumgad. If the Parliament agrees to it, of course."

"I'm afraid I can't just hand him over. He's material to my investigation."

"Of course. I just want to make sure he stays safe in your care and nothing unfortunate happens to him."

Could the rumor that Elca had a tryst with Quiescat be connected to her peculiar interest in his fate? She never struck Greny as particularly sentimental about her lovers. On the contrary, she often took a malicious pleasure in those who sacrificed their lives to win her favor. Her explanation seemed plausible enough, but still... Quiescat knew that Greny sent Drinith to Osro's house. If that became common knowledge, Greny himself might quickly fall under suspicion.

"You don't seem so concerned about Drinith," he remarked casually.

A teasing grin formed beneath Elca's ghostly pale eyes. "I'm not. She is the rightful ruler of only one of Rhumgad's many realms, and she hasn't put a foot in it since the day she fled it as a baby. It's doubtful she could command the loyalty of even a significant fraction of Kaplar's populace. Her femininity puts her at a disadvantage among a people used to male rulers."

Why hadn't Greny thought of something so obvious before? He had never considered how thoroughly primitive Rhumgad was. The frisson of excitement that shot through his surprise discomfited him. "But the Oracle is a different matter, yes?"

"Yes, his reputation, despite the best efforts of Magian to tarnish it, has grown since he fled his temple at Godsdoor. He's not an unproven stripling. His roots sink deep into Rhumgadian soil. And he is touched by the divine. And, frankly, beneath his hard, prickly demeanor is a soft, malleable nature that would be easier to control. He would make a much better figurehead for our invasion."

"That's, of course, if it goes ahead."

"Indeed."

"It's fortunate for your faction that so many of the Short War leaders have died."

Elca's grin only grew slyer. "You're looking in the wrong direction. The Short War Faction is in the ascendant thanks to Magian's offer and Drinith's involvement in these murders will no doubt only add to the prevailing mood to accept it. It will make some of her steadfast supporters in Parliament waver, and those already wavering will turn against her. If I had been the mastermind of this conspiracy, I would have made sure no suspicion would fall on one of my closest allies. And I would have targeted Thespenilea. She was already the most popular and charismatic of the Short War Faction's leaders. The deaths of her rivals within her own faction have strengthened her position."

"You think Thespenilea is behind these murders?"

"She has benefited the most, has she not? In one fell swoop, she has been elevated to the uncrowned queen of her faction and the most powerful meritocrat in Gyre. She'll soon be Ducal Steward. You had better be careful. Your impartiality will make you a threat in her eyes. Tyrants hate those they can't bend to their will. Unless you can deliver a knockout blow to her ambitions, my advice is to think seriously about retiring. Maybe marry and pass your emblem of merit on to your wife."

"I hope that's not an offer. I have no intention of stepping down, thank you," Greny said firmly. The prospect of being a meritocrat's husband, bound to her will, voiceless and helpless, filled him with revulsion.

"Then you must prove what we both suspect," Elca murmured, "before it's too late. We both know Drinith is innocent."

Greny's heart beat a frantic tattoo. "We do?" he asked with what he hoped would pass as nonchalance.

"If I can see that plainly, then you must too, being generally an excellent judge of character."

"You certainly are complimentary today," Greny observed sharply.

"I know you don't like me. You suspect my motives. Many people do. I've never seen the need to apologize for my ambition or my ruthlessness toward my enemies. I would certainly benefit from Drinith's exoneration and Thespenilea's ruin. But put that all aside a moment and focus on the hard logic of my theory instead and try to find a flaw in it."

"Here's one—lack of evidence."

"That's something that you can rectify," Elca said. "I'm sure you'll follow the evidence wherever it leads without fear or favor."

"And what about the storming of Magian's embassy? How does that fit into your theory about Thespenilea?"

Elca's pale eyes expanded as she pressed a hand to her bosom. "Surely you don't think I had anything to do with that?"

"It certainly would benefit you if its sacking infuriated Magian sufficiently to withdraw his offer."

Elca's wicked smile declared Greny a fool. "He won't withdraw it. Magian made it from a position of weakness in the first place. He hasn't the dragons to take us on. Besides, haven't you heard? Lysan Moylar has packed up his circus and departed for his home shard, giving us a red month to make our decision. Thespenilea negotiated with him personally, I understand. Epitan Griman is most aggrieved at the usurpation of her role as Ambassador General, but she's pretending she was privy to the agreement so as not to appear feeble."

"I have always admired how you're always so well informed," Greny said.

"I must admit I am sometimes taken by surprise by the gaps in your knowledge given all the resources you, a cordent general, have at your disposal."

"Quite," Greny grunted.

Elca sauntered over to the door. She pushed it open, paused. "You won't find Thespenilea ringing your doorbell any time soon. These murders have put everything she craves within her grasp. Be careful. Remember, you're a nuisance to her ambition. Goodbye, Greny. I'll show myself out. I wish you well with your investigation."

Greny drummed his fingers against the leather armrests. The seductive persuasiveness of Elca's argument lingered like the sweet and salty tang of her perfume. Greny must watch Thespenilea carefully.

The sound of Elca and Ecethor exiting the tower was followed by another door opening. Woad entered the parlor between Kleest and Queek, his hands bound behind his back.

"Is tying me up every time I visit this place really necessary?" he grumbled.

"Think of it as a compliment to your combat skills," Greny said. "I'm assigning you a team of ratchers to help you bring Drinith to me."

"You promised she'd never know about our arrangement." He winced as he strained against his bindings.

Woad would happily kill me, even at the cost of his own life. He'd rather die a hero than have his friends know him as a traitor. "Think of it as doing Drinith a favor. She'd be safer in my custody." Greny smirked. "She trusts you. She'll accept any excuse you offer for your betrayal. Tell her your wife's life depends on successfully bringing her to me. Drinith will understand, I'm sure."

"You're enjoying this!"

Greny shrugged one shoulder. "A mite, I admit. It relieves a little of my considerable stress. I know Drinith didn't murder Cenmis and the others. She has nothing to fear from me. Unlike your wife, who nobody other than you cares about."

Woad stumbled forward, his bald head down in the manner of a charging bull, but the two ratchers held him back. He stared at Greny with teary eyes. It took a lot to make a man like him betray his emotions.

"Don't dare play the innocent victim with me," Greny said. "I don't even have to hurt Tazran. All I have to do is tell her the truth about you and free her. Let her moral outrage do the rest. Then you'll have a moral dilemma like no other when she comes looking to kill you for what you did."

Woad ceased to squirm. "I'll do what you ask."

"I know." Greny had given him no other choice.

20

───────

Drinith's distinctive appearance—a green-black Rhumgadian in a meritocratic black dress—made her uncomfortable. She was drawing too many curious glances from passersby on the streets. It was only a matter of time before she was spotted by cordents or one of their many informants. Ducking down an alleyway, she found a faded cloak hanging on a stick from an open window to dry. Its hem was still a little damp, but not so much that it couldn't be worn. She yanked it free and ran.

"Dirty Gadfly!" a woman bawled out the window at her, but Drinith already dashed back into the street and threw the cloak over her. The theft of such a garment wouldn't inspire much interest from cordents, but, judging from its countless mends, it had been a prized possession of its owner. Drinith would return it when she could, if she could, but this cloak might be all that kept her from arrest for now.

She hastened to Wealgiver street, her only remaining haven in this hostile city. She approached the door of the safe house and knocked. No answer. Woad probably still waited for her where they had moored their stolen boat, but she dared not return to the canal. She had to hope that he would eventually return. She idly browsed the stalls, fending off offers of bargains with promises to come back another day. The unnerving mixture of suspicion and expectation in the gazes of the vendors made her reluctant to touch anything. All the while, she scanned the crowd for any telltale signs of recognition, any lingering stares or furtive glances.

It was late in the evening when Woad finally came down the street. He wasn't alone. The tip of a furry snout protruded from beneath his companion's hood—it had to be one of Greny's ratchers. What in the fiery bowels of Empyrosis was going on? Woad muttered something to the creature. With a nod, it veered away from him and melted into the crowd. Woad looked grim as he stalked toward the safe house.

She pretended to examine a trinket until he passed her, unmindful of her presence. As he opened the door, she crept up behind him and pressed her dagger against the small of his back.

"I saw you with a ratcher," she whispered.

"It approached me with an offer from Greny Scylax," Woad said. "He'll free Tazran if I sell you out. Of course, I won't. I don't blame you for being suspicious, particularly after Fenvar's betrayal. But remember, I pledged you my loyalty after you saved my life." At her prompting, he unlocked the door and slowly entered. She followed, pulling the door closed behind her with one hand.

The instant it clicked shut, Woad's elbow slammed into her face, slapping her against the door. Before she could recover, Woad's punch to her stomach doubled her over. A blow to the back of her head knocked her to the floor, and she fell unconscious.

INSISTENT SLAPS to her cheeks brought Drinith around. She was tied to the very same post to which Gelasin had once bound her. She gasped for a moment as two years melted in an instant, and she saw his cratered grin again hovering above her. But it was Woad sitting on a chair before her, and he wasn't smiling.

Leaning forward, he folded his hands together and fixed a dead-eyed stare on her. "I'm sorry. I had no choice."

"If I can prove my innocence," Drinith said, "then this nightmare will be over. Tazran and the others will be released."

"It's not that easy," Woad said. "Meritocrat Velso is dead. And even if you could prove you're not the murderer... The Rat King knows about our network of sympathizers. Cordents arrested me as I helped Quiescat raise money for your rescue from Ophigee. I was Scylax's prisoner all during my disappearance. He is very persuasive at making his prisoners talk. He forced the truth out of me. I told him everything in the end. I had no choice."

"Why didn't you warn me of this when I returned to Gyre? We could have avoided this."

Woad rose stiffly from his seat. Strolling over to the window, he opened the shutters and peered out. "I should have, perhaps, but it's too late now. The damage is done." He rubbed the sill. "Scylax promised Tazran's freedom if I hand you over to him. He says you've nothing to fear from him."

"And you believe him?"

No answer.

"You can't trust him," Drinith said. "Look at what happened to Fenvar. As soon as she had no further use, Greny's lickspittle, Nayz, had her arrested. The Rat King's word means nothing, and you mean nothing to him."

"What choice have I?" The question wasn't rhetorical. His pained gaze pleaded for an answer.

What could she say? She had put her faith in him, and now he had turned out to be yet another traitor. "Greny isn't the only meritocrat in the city. He's not even the only cordent general. I'm certain Elca would help us if I could talk to her, explain what has happened. She has invested a lot of political capital in an invasion of Rhumgad. She'd use every tool at her disposal to protect us." Of course, no *us* existed. His treachery had made sure of that.

Woad swiped an errant tear from underneath one eye. "It's too late."

"And whose fault is that? Why didn't you tell me?"

He was about to say something, but shook his head. "It doesn't matter." He looked in pain, as though whatever he was holding back repeatedly stabbed him in the gut.

"Greny already knows, so you might as well tell me," Drinith said. "You owe me the truth, at the very least."

Woad's chin dropped to his chest. After an interval he lifted his head to meet Drinith's unblinking stare. "I was part of Gelasin's plot to attack the crowds at Crevastival."

"No!" Even after his betrayal of her, Drinith couldn't believe it.

"Tazran didn't know. She wouldn't have approved. That first night you and I met, my intention in bringing you to this house was to hand you over to Gelasin. Obviously, that plan fell through thanks to the pentacular poisoning me. I would never have asked the preservators to bring you here if I had known that wretch Zin awaited you."

"I saved your life that night and this is how you repay me."

"If Tazran wasn't in Inkeep…" He shied from her glare. "The Rat King says he won't harm you. Handing you over is my only chance of freeing her."

"The moment you give me to Greny, your value to him will cease and any chance of Tazran escaping the Plank will vanish. Surely you realize that. You're not a fool."

"I wish I could share your faith in my intelligence. A day hasn't gone by since Gelasin recruited me to his conspiracy that I haven't regretted accepting. So what are you suggesting? I let you escape?"

"Come with me," Drinith said. "Help me."

"Tazran will be executed. Scylax made that clear. There remains a slim chance he might keep his promise to release her. And you'd have to defeat the whole Meritocracy to succeed."

A fist pounded on the front door.

"He might even spare Quiescat and the others," Woad said. "Without you, our organization isn't a threat." He yelled through the window at whoever was banging on the door. "I'm coming!"

"You've made your choice, it seems," Drinith said. "I suppose this betrayal is minor compared to the cold-blooded murder of innocent people."

Woad offered no rejoinder as he stomped by her out of the room. Returning with three ratchers, he pointed at Drinith. "There she is." He stared out of the window as they loosened the rope wrapped around Drinith and hoisted her to her feet.

"You can't even look at me," Drinith sneered as she vainly tested the cord wrapped around her wrist.

Woad turned and frowned at her, as if this was her fault. She took some comfort in his flinch as she spat, though the spittle fell short of its target.

The anger slid from his face, leaving only shame and contrition. "I'm sorry. I know that's little consolation."

"Traitor!" Drinith cried before the ratchers gagged her. They dragged her from the room and down the stairs. Outside, an open restraining coffin waited, its sun-grayed black silk lining tattered and stained. A brown ratcher held the reins of the casquars destined to carry it. A sizeable crowd watched. They knew this contraption was used only for important prisoners.

"No, please no," Drinith begged, but her gag contorted her words into a hopeless moan as her captors hauled her nearer the vessel.

A loud bang made Drinith shudder. Smoke and flame rose from a shattered stall. A second explosion filled the air with screams. While the majority of the crowd stampeded away from the blast, a half-dozen hooded figures stood their ground. In the brief moment it took their springbows to fell the four ratchers, one of them had leaped over the restraining coffin to Drinith and cut her bindings. A glimpse beneath his hood revealed green eyes above a thick cloth mask. Despite their uncanny familiarity, Drinith couldn't place who they reminded her of.

"Follow me," he rasped.

Her gaze swept the dead and dying ratchers strewn at her feet as she pulled down her gag. "Who are you?"

He and his companions didn't bother to answer as they raced toward the fires. Drinith followed.

She almost lost them in the thick smoke, but one of them, a heavyset man, grabbed her arm and pulled her into a narrow lane. She followed the line of hooded figures down it, keenly aware of the man breathing heavily right behind her, denying her any opportunity to slip away. Had the Veiled Meritocrat again intervened to save her, or did her rescuers work for someone else? Could they be behind the meritocrat murders?

A wet grunt suddenly cut off the rhythmic pants behind her. The man clutched his bleeding throat as he toppled. Woad leaped over him, holding a bloody dagger.

Drinith clutched the empty pocket where her knife should have been and cursed. All she could do was run.

"You can't trust them." Woad reached out a hand to her. "I can help you."

Two of her rescuers pushed by her and attacked him with knives. The group's leader grabbed her by the hand and dragged her down the lane. A feminine shriek echoed through the lane. Woad had felled one of his attackers.

Another member of the group turned and rushed back down toward him. As the man passed Drinith, he drew a springbow from beneath his cloak. She caught her breath on the urge to plead for him not to kill Woad. Her sense of obligation to the traitor made her feel foolish.

Hazarding a glance over her shoulder, she glimpsed Woad taking cover behind the body of his second attacker as he closed on the retreating springbowman. As the man slowed to reload, Woad tossed aside his bolt-bristled corpse-shield and charged, slamming into him before he could lift his weapon.

"Stop him!" the leader yelled to his remaining comrade.

"You must think I'm an id—" the other man began. A springbow bolt struck his eye, slapping his head against the wall.

"Wait for me outside the lane," the leader growled to Drinith as he primed his springbow again and trained it on Woad.

Drinith fled the alleyway and plunged through the milling crowd to the far side of the street. From there, she kept expectant watch on the lane's shadowy mouth. Would her chief rescuer emerge from it, or Woad, or neither? The callousness with which the masked man had dispatched one of his own had left her deeply shocked. How could she entrust her life to such a killer? The surprised face of the boy she had slain on Ophigee flashed unbidden in her memory. How well did the masked man know the comrade he had killed? She doubted his victim's face would haunt him; his cold-bloodedness would allow no such sentimentality.

Her chest tightened as her rescuer—she grudgingly granted him that distinction, despite his utter callousness—emerged from the lane. Removing his hood and mask, he looked around, obviously searching for her, but she remained hidden by the passing traffic. The young man appeared from this distance to be a typical maroon-skinned Nosteran. There was definitely something familiar about his silver eyes. She had seen him before, but she couldn't place him. If he was still alive, then Woad must be dead.

A mournful hollowness gripped her, immediately followed by a surge of anger. She resented Woad's death. He might have been a traitor, but he had once been a good friend. Or perhaps she still hadn't yet emotionally accepted his betrayal. In any case, she had a choice to make—should she alert Woad's killer to her presence, or should she slip away?

21

———

In one of the ground floor rooms of Woad Glastum's so-called safe house, Greny shook his head in disbelief over the shrouded ratchers lying in a row on a floor. Feerth's death stung in particular, given that he had served Greny for many years. The others—Qweelch, Sheeg, and Eedee—were relatively new arrivals, but Greny grieved for them too. Chemp and Queek also looked mournfully down at their dead comrades.

Dragons! Greny swore to himself. *Queek might have died too if the blade and not the handle of the butter knife had been poisoned.*

Although the wound had been treated, thanks to the incompetence of the cordents who accompanied him to the Grand Preservatory, an ugly scar remained on the right side of his muzzle. Greny resolved to see to its removal as soon as possible. His bond with his servants was almost familial—nay, stronger. Unlike their human counterparts, their loyalty was unquestioning and unquestionable. He certainly felt their loss keener than that of the three dead meritocrats.

Nayz's face, Greny decided, was built for contempt. The little man couldn't hide his glee. No doubt, he wished his cordent general lay alongside them. He hated Greny almost as much as he despised ratchers.

"At least someone has finally foiled one of these attacks." Greny nodded toward Woad Glastum, who grimaced in pain in the corner of the room as a cordent healer tended to his wounds. A bolt was lodged in his shoulder. A second had shattered his left shinbone. "Will he live?"

"It'll be red months before he'll be fully healed," the healer said.

"Then send him to the Grand Preservatory. I want him back on his feet as soon as possible."

A spasm of indignation flashed on the man's face, but he knew better than to question Greny's order. "Of course, Cordent General." He kept nodding obsequiously as he hastened out of the room.

"If you had involved me in this operation, we might have caught the attackers' leader, and Meritocrat Hax," Nayz muttered under his breath.

Ignoring him, Greny attracted Woad Glastum's attention with a curt wave and pointed to the line of dead Gadflies staring up at the ceiling. "Do you recognize any of them?"

"No," Glastum said. "And I make it my business to know every Rhumgadian who frequents the Blue Quarter. They're not from there."

Greny rubbed his jaw. "If you say so."

"My guess is that they are agents of Magian recently arrived in the city."

"They have been incredibly effective for newcomers," Greny said. Cenmis's butler, Jelsan, wasn't Rhumgadian. Neither were any of Osro's staff. Greny had made sure to check. "Whoever is directing them must be already well-established in the city."

"This was in the restraining coffin." Nayz produced a small golden feather and twirled it between his thumb and forefinger. "We found another in Jelsan's room. It may be intended as some kind of signature for the group behind these attacks."

Greny plucked the feather from Nayz and waved it at Woad Glastum. "Does a sunfinch feather mean anything to you?"

"Why would Rhumgadians adopt such an unambiguously Gyran symbol?" the ex-mercenary scoffed. "It makes no sense."

"Whoever is behind these attacks might want the general assumption to be that their organization is Gyran," Nayz said. "It would make it more attractive to local malcontents."

"These assassins must work for Magian," Glastum said. "They might receive their orders from his ambassador, Lysan Moylar, perhaps, or another member of his delegation."

"As we speak," Greny put in, "the Rhumgadian Ambassador and his retinue are already winging their way back to their home shard."

"Perhaps their contact is some other clandestine agent," Glastum suggested.

"Why would Magian's agents seek to help Meritocrat Hax?" Nayz asked.

"To discredit her," Glastum said. "After rescuing her, he could kill her and dispose of the body over any of a hundred precipices."

Nayz sneered. "If that's the case, she's already dead."

A look of mingled regret and chagrin clouded Glastum's face.

The healer reentered in stoic silence with two other cordents bearing a stretcher.

"You don't seriously intend to carry me on the same stretcher you used to gather the corpses!" Glastum barked.

"You're strangely squeamish for an ex-mercenary," Nayz observed.

Woad Glastum wrinkled his nose. "Human blood wouldn't bother me, but it carried ratcher corpses, too. It's covered with their blood and fur. It puts my teeth on edge just thinking about it. I might get some disease."

"Get on it or stay here until your wounds fester and kill you!" Greny snapped. "Be thankful I mustn't choose between saving the life of one of my servants and your treatment. The lowest ratcher is worth a dozen treacherous Gadflies like you!"

A wry smile played upon Nayz's tight lips, betraying his delight at his superior's anger.

Glastum's eyes rounded. "I meant no offense."

"You offended nonetheless," Greny said. "Remember, the

continued well-being of your wife depends on you remaining in my good graces. Insult my servants again and I'll have her flogged!"

A spasm of violent hate contorted Woad Glastum's face. Smothering it with an expression approximating submissiveness, he bowed his head. "I'm sorry. Of course, I'll do whatever you want."

Nayz snickered. "I understand the Widow has quite a few scars on her back already."

It was Woad Glastum's turn to sneer. "The men who made them died painfully, I assure you." He looked up at the healer standing over him. "Get me out of here, please. The smell of blood is making me nauseous."

Greny quickly dabbed on more ointment under his nostrils. He and Nayz watched Woad being carried from the room.

"Why is that stinking Gadfly getting such special treatment?" Nayz demanded rudely. At least he had the tact to wait until they were alone to question Greny's judgment.

"You don't approve?"

"*Your* cordents are injured doing their duty every day and you send none of them to the *Grand Preservatory*. I understand you have a soft spot for your ratchers, but this Gadfly…"

"I assure you, his special treatment, as you call it, will last only as long as his usefulness. And he has secured our best lead so far."

"I discovered Meritocrat Velso's murderer."

"And then managed to let her kill herself and prevent her interrogation."

"To save your life."

"Which you put in danger in the first place."

"I identified the significance of the sunfinch feather."

"But not its meaning. For all we know, it might be intended to distract us. As soon as Woad Glastum is healed, I intend to make him a temporary cordent colonel."

"That's my rank!" Nayz fumed.

"He'll report directly to me," Greny said.

"The lower ranks won't be happy," Nayz whispered, glancing at Greny's bodyguards. "First, ratchers are formally made cordents. Now, a Gadfly is promoted to a colonel. I'll have to explain this to the other cordents."

"If you feel you must provide explanations, so be it. One advantage of being a meritocrat is I don't have to explain myself to anyone." It wasn't true. A black letter had arrived summoning him to the Vicenary Jury. His fellow jurors would demand answers. And results.

"Can you really trust Woad Glastum?" Nayz persisted.

"As long as his wife is secure in Inkeep, yes. My ratchers will watch him carefully, in any case." *Just as they keep an eye on you.*

"Are you certain you can control him? Meritocrat Hax's escape was awfully convenient, don't you think? Woad could have been in on it."

"It wasn't very convenient for the five thugs lying over there. Drinith would never countenance such slaughter simply to add authenticity to her escape."

"We only have Woad's word that Drinith was here. He could be lying."

"You yourself turned up several witnesses who saw a Rhumgadian woman with the ratchers."

Nayz shrugged. "That doesn't mean the woman was Meritocrat Hax. It could be her meritorian, for example."

"The trouble with you, Nayz, is, though you're excellent at coming up with questions, but you're not so good at answering them. When next we meet, I expect you to have answers."

Greny stormed from the room, followed by his two bodyguards.

22

———

Jarma awoke, her head wrapped in a suffocating velvet darkness. She reached up to remove the bag, but manacles arrested them, biting into the backs of her wrists. Her mouth had an unpleasant tarry aftertaste. So, she had been captured after all and now she was a prisoner in Inkeep, or worse, Greny Scylax's tower.

"You're awake at long last." The voice wasn't Greny's. It was gravelly, but unmistakably female.

The bag slid upward and cold air slapped her sweaty cheeks. She blinked away the sting of the cold-blue light from a three-legged lampstone stand. Beyond it, against a curtain of shadow, sat a woman dressed as a meritocrat or a meritorian. She wore no telltale emblem. A square black hat covered her head and a thick veil obscured her face. *Could this be the same Veiled Meritocrat...?*

"Yes," the woman said. "I'm the same woman who rescued Drinith from the Ducal Steward's restraining coffin."

Can she read my mind?

"And no, I can't read your thoughts. I'm just very good at guessing what you might think next."

She moved a red disc on a circular game board. Concentric circles and lines partitioned the board in a manner reminiscent of a spiderweb. Jarma had learned the rules of Demons and Angels as part of her education to be a meritorian, but she wasn't particularly adept at it. Judging from the positions of the yellow and red pieces, the game was quite far along.

"What do you want from me, Meritocrat?" Jarma asked.

"There's no need to be so formal, Jarma. I'm a friend."

Jarma lifted her arms to display her chains. "If you're a friend, why did you clap me in irons?"

"That is merely a precaution. If your hands were free, you might be tempted to lift my veil and if you glimpsed my face, I'd have to kill you."

Icy fear shot up Jarma's spine.

"Come now," the Veiled Meritocrat said. "Don't be naive. This isn't some childish game. You're lucky I rescued you before you blundered into a cordent patrol. Your meritocrat has landed herself in a spot of bother thanks to the Rat King. She's the prime suspect in the murders—"

"She would never murder anyone," Jarma blurted.

The Veiled Meritocrat, apparently playing against herself, moved a yellow counter. "I know she is innocent of the deaths of Osro and Thaxen, but innocence alone isn't enough to protect her. Or you either. In this city, the truth is whatever is convenient for the Meritocracy. I fear that Greny's investigation may lead to someone whom the Iron Circle would never dare to try. They'll need someone else to walk the Plank, and Drinith and you are an expedient sacrifice. You are foreigners, after all. Titles and an emblem of merit don't alter the blood in your veins. Gyre's invasion of Rhumgad may never happen and if it does, it's unclear that Drinith is critical to its success."

"So Drinith and I are doomed."

The Veiled Meritocrat drew her thumb and forefinger together, leaving a barely perceptible gap. "Not quite. There's still hope you might yet escape the Void." Her hand hovered over the board like a hawk searching for prey. "My agents are working hard to expose the mastermind behind these murders. Already they've made substantial progress." She replaced a yellow counter with a red one. "But Greny is a problem not so easily solved. He would prefer a thousand Driniths fell into the inner sun than risk his seat in the Iron Circle."

"I thought he had a reputation for incorruptibility."

The Meritocrat slid the yellow counter near the center of the board. "He is impossible to bribe, it is true, but for him, self-preservation outweighs his vaunted scruples. Fear keeps him a lonely prisoner in his tower." She snorted. "He is even guarded by ratchers, like those unfortunates incarcerated in his section of Inkeep." Her fingers danced over one red counter and then another. "Greny has no friends, trusts nobody other than his ratchers." Choosing the second, she used it to take a yellow counter. "I'm sure you're aware of the rumors about the guests he sometimes entertains."

"I've heard...passing references."

"Sometimes a prisoner sentenced to death piques his interest." The Veiled Meritocrat rubbed the yellow counter between her fingers. "Occasionally, it might be a sage or a philosopher. Greny fancies he's an intellectual. Most often, it is an attractive young woman. He keeps her in Scylax Tower until he grows weary of her company or the delay in her execution draws attention. Then..." She flicked her wrist, tossing the disc onto the floor. It rolled in a broad arc into the darkness.

"And you think Greny would make Drinith one of his guests?"

The Veiled Meritocrat shook her head. "That would bring too much scrutiny. Like all rats, Greny prefers to dwell in the shadows. On the other hand, you're an ideal candidate. He has a soft spot for you. And, frankly, your humble background is a bit of an embarrassment to many meritocrats. Nobody would care what he did to you."

"It's a good thing I'm your prisoner instead of his," Jarma said bitterly.

The Veiled Meritocrat picked up a discarded red piece and tapped its side against the board. She stroked it against her veil, approximately where her chin or mouth might have been. "As I said,

Greny poses the greatest immediate danger to Drinith." She shoved a red counter to the center of the board—an illegal move. The meritocrat placed the piece in her hand on the outermost ring on the board. "And I fear he can be only stopped with your help."

"Tell me what I must do," Jarma said.

"Do I really have to explain?" the Veiled Meritocrat asked with weary dismay. "I always thought you were quite a bright girl, despite the belatedness of your education. Can you not guess? Greny is inclined to be woefully indiscreet with the pretty, young girls he imprisons in his tower, divulging his darkest secrets in the certainty that they'll be safely swallowed by the Void."

"You want me to be the bait in a trap for him," Jarma said, bristling at the gibe about her intelligence. She remembered how Drinith had echoed her own fatalistic words: "I'm expendable."

"I can't guarantee your safety," the Veiled Meritocrat admitted. "I might have overestimated his attraction to you, or he may be too preoccupied with solving the murders to bother with a guest at his tower. Events may overtake our plan, and he may dispose of you before I can mount a rescue." Everything she said had a bleak ring of truth.

"And if I refuse?" Jarma asked.

The Veiled Meritocrat placed a phial of black liquid on the game board as if it was just another piece. "Immemoreal. You'll wake up safe in an alley, but you'll have no recollection of our conversation and you'll have to survive on your own. And you won't be able to save Drinith from the Rat King."

"Then it seems I have no choice," Jarma said. Doubtless she, too, was just another counter on the Veiled Meritocrat's board.

23

Greny's gaze wandered about the Vicenary Chamber as he entered. No expense had been spared to lend it the false impression of austerity. The finest lampstone sheets paned the long windows to give the impression of natural light, here, deep beneath the Parliament of Merit. The severe high-backed chairs encircling the black table were deliberately designed to look uncomfortable when in fact, sitting in them was like lounging on a cloud. According to tradition, the table itself was older than Gyre, a relic of its founder's conquests in her beloved emperor's name. The ancient language inscribed on its warped and cracked surface was doubtless long extinct and forgotten. A single slab of dull red marble from distant Magmel covered the floor. He often wondered who was the intended audience for this faux asceticism. Only the jurists ever entered this chamber.

Almost swallowed by the vaulted darkness above, the marble heads of the queens of Gyre formed a watchful circle. The Wealgiver looked down disdainfully on the Ducal Steward's chair. The base of her neck was crooked where it had been crudely severed from a statue during the bloody birth of the Meritocracy. To her left was the Hoarder, then the Plunderer, the Sunfinch, and the Great; next the

Architect, the Iron, and the Silver; followed by the Golden, the Dreamer, and the Storm. The blindfolded bust of the infamous final queen, Karis the First and Last, completed the ring. Her presence was a reminder to those who sat below her of the gravity of their mission —to protect their republic from enemies, foreign or domestic.

It came as some relief to find Justiciar General Devaner Tiranicon seated by herself. A worse fate could have been waiting for Greny.

"Did you have much difficulty securing a key to the chamber?" Greny asked to pierce the oppressive silence as he sat across from her.

"I had my own copy. Remember, I am Osro's deputy."

"You wouldn't be interested in becoming the Ducal Steward yourself?"

Devaner shook her head emphatically. "Why would I throw away my life's work to become the jailer of a single pampered prisoner?" After a sudden sneeze, she rubbed a finger on the table's black surface and studied the dirt collected on its tip. Scrunching up her nose, she rubbed the smudge off with her thumb. "Whose turn was it to clean the chamber?"

"If memory serves," Greny said, "it was Drona Torn's, but the conflagration marshal and her colleague Egava Sipian are away on Noster."

"Not good enough," Devaner huffed. "Drona should have swapped with someone else. The dust in here plays havoc with my nose." She tapped the table. "This upstart generation of meritocrats wants to rule Gyre, but even a little light dusting is too much effort for them. The discipline that served our republic so well is flagging. The sumptuary laws are flouted—dresses cut in all sorts of revealing ways, occasionally not even true black, coiffures shaped into crowns and bedecked with gems and strands of precious metal. Some even wear makeup like a courtesar. Foreign music. Foreign dancing. Even foreign meritocrats."

"We all began here as foreigners," Greny said amicably, just happy for the distraction.

"After nearly a thousand years, I think we have earned the right to call ourselves natives. Our ancestors were the first to settle here, the

Nosteran landlubbers being too stupid and insular to cross the gap from their shard. But we forget our roots. Mark my words, flouting tradition will unravel everything we have built here. Terrible business, these murders. And the riot! A blot on the Meritocracy."

"I hope you're not implying that three of our colleagues died due to lower necklines," Nacyn Revistan said, announcing her arrival. The Dragon Keeper was a short woman with a handsome face and an intense, deep-set stare. Her emblem of merit, the knotted serpopard, rested on her cyan halo braid. She was as dangerous as she was patient, slow to strike against those who crossed her, but devastating when she did.

"Of course not," Devaner said with disgust. "I'm simply saying that when one rule is not followed, people start to question everything. Ronel Olapsin understood that. When she was Ducal Steward, she—"

"You voted to expel her from this chamber as I recall," Nacyn said as she took her seat.

"I'm talking about Ronel in her prime, not as she was near the end," Devaner said. "Obviously, she couldn't continue any longer as Ducal Steward. She had become autocratic and capricious. But we owe her a debt of gratitude for restoring order after the Silverfish Revolt. And Greny, you too, of course."

A pang of shame. The utter contempt in his brother's eyes... Greny had had no other choice. Dragons, he had saved Erphel's life! He had saved many lives.

"Greny?" Nacyn said, gently calling him back to the present. "Speaking of Ronel, I assume Elca will take over Thaxen's portfolio and become our sole intelligencer general."

"Indeed," Devaner said sourly, folding her hands together. "Quite a comeback for someone who previously departed this chamber in disgrace."

"You know the proverb," Nacyn said. "Ability can be rewarded once ambition's been thwarted. Elca is a reformed character."

Devaner stretched her neck from side to side, bending her high collar. "Tell that to the mothers and sisters of the courtesars she destroyed." Glancing at the open door, she leaned forward and whispered, "These murders certainly come at an opportune time for her."

Nacyn snorted. "You cannot seriously believe she contrived such carnage?"

"Of course not," Devaner said with a bitter smile. "I'm merely observing that she benefits from her rivals' deaths. Her influence expands while the Short War faction is plunged into disarray due to the loss of so many prominent members."

With her fingertip, Nacyn made a little circle in the dust on the table. "I appreciate the logic of your observation, but I'm sure if Greny had any reason to suspect Elca, he'd be interrogating her in Inkeep. Is that not the case, Greny?"

Greny nodded, nervous to say anything that might inadvertently commit him in their eyes to one faction or the other.

"Matters are fraught enough without letting unbridled speculation deepen our divisions," Nacyn said. "I have never witnessed Thespenilea so emotional, so prone to violent outbursts. There is no telling what she may do if she comes to suspect Elca had a hand in her friends' deaths. Unless, Devaner, you possess incontrovertible proof of her guilt, it's best to keep your conjectures to yourself."

Greny surmised from Devaner's knowing sneer that Thespenilea already knew her opinion and most likely had shaped it.

The three of them nodded to Opriet Braesum as she strolled into the chamber. Greny shied from her sympathetic, slanted smile as she took her seat beside Nacyn. Opriet knew he would face hard questions from the other jurists about his failure to prevent Cenmis's murder.

Posaleum Minol, looking uncharacteristically pale, arrived soon after. The wound remained on her forehead. The four crude stitches looked more severe that the slender cut they closed.

She was accompanied by her close friend, the jurist Ederion Visentar. Delicate gold fretwork encased the latter's bald head down to her nose and cheeks, her eyes shining like sapphires. On her forehead, at the center of this web of gold, lay her emblem of merit, a winged spider. The Parliament recently increased the fine for violating the sumptuary laws specifically to curb her flouting of them, but if anything, it only emboldened her inclination for ostentation.

Posaleum nervously rubbed her hands together as she sat down. In a preemptive display of contrition for her failures at the riot, she wore a drab black dress with a plain blue bar extending down the right shoulder. "It's always as cold as a crypt down here," she said, shivering.

"If you wore heavier clothing, you wouldn't notice it," Devaner said.

Posaleum straightened in her chair, pursed her mouth.

The leaders of the New War Faction arrived together. Okia Vavar looked every bit of her prodigious age. Aretro Falier appeared physically ill. Even Elca had lost her swagger.

Thespenilea Reiner entered next, her jaw set, her eyes smoldering with quiet anger. She sat down without a word and glared at everyone.

The remaining jurists followed in quick succession. Griman Epitan, the raven-haired ambassador general, stalked into the chamber, her shoulders hunched as though a dragon sat upon them. The pregnant conflagration marshal Anyrim Norcaro entered in loose fitting maternity clothes. The portly censor general, Inamyr Minan, hobbled slowly over to her place with slow, heaving breaths. She struck her alicorn cane against the floor with the care of a mountaineer scaling a cliff until she reached her seat and collapsed onto it with a sigh of relief.

Zizor Findel arrived last, looking even more wide-eyed than usual. Halting by the door, she surveyed the room. "Is the governor general coming?" she whispered.

"Leca's away on a tour of the provinces," Griman said. "No point waiting for Egava and Drona either. They're on Noster paying our mercenaries."

Zizor barred the door and took her seat. The meritocrats removed their emblems of merit and placed them on the table. The ritual was supposed to remind them all that their paramount focus was the welfare of their state, not their own. But the emblems left indentations on several foreheads, and the kissing tingle of the metal lingered on Greny's skin. Ederion looked strangely naked without hers.

"Dragons, the chamber is so empty!" Inamyr observed. A third of the seats were vacant.

"Not so long ago, twenty meritocrats had the privilege to sit at this table. Now, our full complement is only seventeen," Thespenilea observed. "Thaxen and Osro aren't even interred on Mount Riddle yet, and now Cenmis has been murdered. And there have been riots in the Diplomatic District and Wealgiver Street."

"The incident on Wealgiver Street wasn't a riot," Greny corrected. "It was an attack similar to the ambush of Thaxen's palanquin. I eliminated five of the assailants." And four ratchers died, but he didn't dare mention them. The other jurists would only laugh at him.

"The leader escaped," Thespenilea said. "As did Drinith Hax, whose rescue was the attack's main purpose."

"For all we know, it was just as likely to be a kidnapping," Aretro said.

The black tufts of hair shaped into dorsal spines above Thespenilea's eyes climbed her forehead. "Really?" she questioned, her gaze falling on Greny.

"It's a possibility," Greny allowed. "We're still investigating." It sounded weak even to him. Why should he protect Drinith? These Meritocrats would pounce on any hint that he wasn't up to bringing the culprits to justice. They'd remove him from the Jury and diminish him to a has-been, insubstantial and ignored, vulnerable to his many enemies in Parliament.

"I must offer my heartfelt condolences on the death of your friends, Thespenilea," Elca said. "Though we may be rivals, we are first and foremost meritocrats. An attack against one of us is an attack against us all."

Everyone clapped the table, rattling their emblems. The dust they raised set Devaner sneezing uncontrollably. Thespenilea didn't clap with the rest. She sneered at Elca and nodded at the Ducal Steward's empty seat. "Who is chairing this meeting?"

"I suppose that honor falls to me," Devaner said with grim resignation. "I was Osro's deputy."

"Forgive me," Elca said. "I propose Thespenilea should take the chair. The three dead meritocrats were her friends. Unless you object, Devaner."

Greny exchanged confused glances with his neighbors. Why would Elca concede such an honor to her bitterest rival? She had enough votes around the table to wrest the position for herself.

Devaner broke into a sheepish grin, eager to be relieved of the burden. "If it is the will of Jury…"

Thespenilea leaned forward, rested her chin on her hand, and studied Elca. "That's generous of you," she said at last.

Elca shrugged, a crafty smile stretching below those liquid pearl eyes. "Under the circumstances…"

"If it is the will of the Jury," Thespenilea said bleakly.

No objecting voice cut through the whispery assents fluttering around the table.

"Very well." Thespenilea leaned back in her seat and folded her arms. "Let's review those circumstances you mentioned, Elca. Three meritocrats have been murdered and the prime suspect is *your* friend, Drinith."

Elca smirked. "The Rhumgadian isn't my friend, and my interest in her home shard is absolutely not for her benefit." She made a vague circular motion with her forefinger toward the table. "Remember, this jury entrusted Thaxen and me with her management. When she was imprisoned in Ophigee, we moved to disinherit the lowborn girl she designated as her successor to the Hax Alerion. And, may I point out, this jury admonished us for our actions."

"It was a question of timing," Inamyr said. "That's all. You should have waited until we were certain Drinith would never return."

"The consensus at the time was that she wouldn't," Elca said.

Inamyr responded with a shrug. "But she did."

"I think the point Elca is making is that nobody could have predicted that turn of events," Nacyn said.

"This isn't the topic we gathered here to discuss," Devaner said.

Elca ignored her. "The incident proved such a great embarrassment for Thaxen that it turned her against good sense and she joined the Short War faction."

"The Short War has benefited our republic for generations," Thespenilea said. "It has kept Noster pliant and trade flowing. Our wealth is built on commerce, not conquest. The Short War became intractable because neither Gyre nor any of its rivals had the capability of conquering Noster outright. Yet you seem to imagine we would have no difficulty in conquering a foreign shard thousands of leagues across the Void."

"We digress," Devaner said timidly. "Such debates are best suited to Parliament. We need to stick to the matter at hand."

"Devaner, you should chair," Thespenilea said. "My temper's too hot."

Devaner hid her consternation behind her handkerchief, honking her nose, snorting and snuffling. "But it is the Jury's will that you should preside. Besides, the dust here! I can hardly breathe, much less speak...." Her voice withered to a rasp.

Thespenilea's mouth compressed into a slim, bitter line. "If it is the Jury's will, then so be it. Greny, update us on the current state of your investigation."

Mesmerized by her glare, Greny hesitated long enough for Posaleum to chip in with a razor-sharp smile. "He might explain why he facilitated Drinith's return to Woodshard to assassinate poor Cenmis." Was her intention simply to embarrass Greny and distract from her own failings during the riot, or had she some deeper motive? She must feel Elca's declared ambivalence to Drinith's fate gave her license to turn on the Rhumgadian.

"Cenmis's butler murdered her," Greny said flatly. "When the culprit realized I was about to arrest her, she orchestrated her death with the same poisoned knife she used to kill her meritocrat."

"But the butler was clearly part of a greater conspiracy," Posaleum said. "And Drinith had a strong motive to kill Cenmis and the others. The three meritocrats belonged to the Short War Faction. They stood in her way to retake her *birthright*." The word reverberated in the chamber like thunder. Everyone knew the birthright to which Posaleum referred—Drinith's claim to the Blood Crown of Kaplar. It had been something that made her foreign and untrustworthy even before the current crisis.

"But surely if Drinith had engineered these murders, she'd have been careful to be nowhere near their occurrence," Aretro said. "She'd have made sure to eliminate herself as an obvious suspect. Does she really possess the resources to ambush Thaxen's palanquin, burn Osro's house, and rile the common folk to riot?"

"Her servants," somebody murmured. Greny didn't catch who.

"I incarcerated them in Inkeep," he said, uncertain if the speaker had intended her comment as a statement or a question.

Posaleum's pale face swelled with a triumphant grin. Greny didn't like the way she stared at the palms of her knitted hands as though they hid some secret object visible only to her. "I have suspected for some time that her charitable works in the Blue Quarter were a cover for a network of Gadfly sympathizers. This organization doubtless played a part in the murders of Osro and Thaxen." So she had found a thread of the truth. Did she know Greny held the other end?

24

Should Drinith reveal herself to Woad's killer? Her fate hanging on a knife-edge of indecision, she watched him search for her. As he moved slowly down the street, peering into shop windows and alleyways, she headed in the opposite direction. However isolated and desperate she might be, however great her curiosity about her rescuer, Drinith daren't entrust her life to someone who slew his own comrade so wantonly.

Drinith couldn't keep wandering aimlessly about the city until a cordent patrol or a random checkpoint caught her. She needed a plan, and she needed help. But Quiescat and Tazran were imprisoned in Inkeep, Jarma was missing, the Blue Quarter was cut off, and Woad knew the sympathizers living in other parts of the city better than her.

She still had her emblem of merit, but she couldn't sell or hock it. Everyone in Gyre would recognize it on sight, and the price on her head doubtless exceeded its value many times over. No doubt the deaths of her ratcher captors and even her rescuers would be added to the tally of her crimes by Greny and the other meritocrats, driving up her bounty.

A commotion ahead snapped her from her musings.

"She's too old. Let her go." A courtesar bowed to a plump, older Highlander—a Rhumgadian exile. Around him, his brightly garbed companions followed his example. The woman ran off, wide-eyed with fright. The courtesars were hunting Drinith, no doubt to avenge the dead meritocrats.

As they moved down the street toward her, Drinith swerved into the nearest alley. It reeked of rot, stale beer, and urine. A grubby stone wall blocked the far end. There were no windows by which she might escape. And the doors were locked. A beggar lay asleep in one corner. A rat scurried out from behind him. Drinith's insistent tap on the man's shoulder failed to stir him. Even as she gently turned the man's head, she could feel an empty coldness beneath his waxy flesh. His dull, uncomprehending stare proclaimed him beyond her help. *Poor old fellow. This city, teeming with people and abounding with wealth, is blind to misfortunates like him, but will happily sell his corpse on to the Butchers of Laxur to make their abominable automatons.*

The clack of high-heeled boots echoed down the alley.

"It's dark down here. Get out your torch."

Drinith turned the corpse back on its side and nestled close against it. With any luck, the courtesars would think they were just a pair of paupers, living rough.

The footsteps drew closer. The light of the torch shone through the hood of her cloak. She could feel its hot breath against her back. Movement shivered through the dead man. There must be a rat stirring on the far side. She gritted her teeth to stifle a scream.

Something prodded her shoulder. "Hey, wake up. Did you see a pretty Rhumgadian woman around here? Green-black skin. Black hair."

Drinith didn't dare look around. The slightest glimpse of her face would betray her.

"You're wasting time, Timpel. Those layabouts know nothing. Do you really think you'd find a meritocrat here in the midst of this excrement? The only thing this pair of drunkards have seen is the inside of a cask. Leave them be."

A rattish squeak from the far side of the corpse made Drinith's stomach roil. She began to gag.

"You're right," a second man sighed. "It wouldn't surprise me if we got fleas hanging around here."

"Fleas is the least of our worries. She sounds like she could get sick at any moment. She could have anything. *Anything.*"

She imagined them standing behind her, their lace handkerchiefs pressed disdainfully over their mouths.

"Let's go," the first voice said. "It's a hot bath for me tonight. And a tonic from my healer first thing in the morning."

The clack of their heels drifted into the distance. Drinith pushed herself away from the corpse. In the corner of her eye, she could see it juddering, shifting. A rat's head, big as her fist, emerged from the dead beggar's threadbare coat. In its jaws it held a bloody chunk of flesh. She sprayed the ground with vomit as she fled. She needed air, sweet air, free of such macabre spectacles.

Drinith stumbled into the street. *I must look a sight. I could be easily arrested as a vagrant if I stray into the wrong area.* Jarma had to be in similar straits unless she had found aid from someone. But who?

Perian! Greny and Woad would have discounted her as a potential helper given her acrimonious dismissal from Drinith's household. Jarma might have turned to her for assistance, and the former maid was the sort to give it. Even if Jarma hadn't, Perian might offer Drinith at least a temporary refuge. If, of course, she could forgive her former mistress for her sacking.

Perian's mother lived in the Red Quarter, close to Orphan Gate, but Drinith didn't know the exact location of her home.

In the early years of Gyre, the Red Quarter had been the exclusive preserve of hired laborers from the mainland. The Nosteran character of many of the faces Drinith encountered there was indisputable, but its denizens hailed from across the Crevast. Even a smattering of Rhumgadians, presumably descended from earlier generations of immigrants predating Magian's rise, wandered its streets.

The buildings were mostly six-floor tenements. The newer ones appeared to have been built of imported stone, but the older ones were daubed pink. Damaged plaster and peeling paint revealed the ancient yellow stone beneath. The quarter lacked the usual statues and artworks, and massive mansions and other fine architecture, that enlivened much of the city. The fountains, all the same plain design, were often clogged with steeping garments as men and women battered wet clothes on their broad rims.

Beginning to feel lost in the eerie uniformity of the streets, Drinith welcomed her first sight of the Orphan Gate. It was the last fragment of the wall that had once girted the quarter before it burst beyond it. Now doorless and unguarded, the gatehouse was little more than a monument to a time when Gyre treated Nosterans with suspicion, a premises for a coterie of hairdressers working under its imposing archway, and a convenient post for countless washing lines.

As Drinith scanned the passersby for someone vaguely friendly to ask directions, she met Perian's stern glare. The girl pressed a huge basket of laundry against her hip with a chapped hand.

"I was wrong," Drinith said, approaching her. "I'm sorry."

Breaking into a grin, Perian nervously glanced around. "Follow me."

They entered a nearby tenement. Drinith walked slowly behind the huffing girl as she laboriously carried her basket up three flights of worn stairs.

"It's me, Ma," Perian said as she knocked on a weathered wooden door.

The door parted a sliver, then jerked open. A hunched, gray-haired woman filled the threshold and scowled at Drinith. "*She's* not coming in here!"

Perian deftly pushed by her. "Don't be ridiculous, Ma."

Drinith nervously followed, but the Perian's mother made no attempt to bar her.

"Meritocrat, this is my mother Colyan." Perian said, but the old woman ignored her attempt at introductions as she looked up and down the hall and shut the door. Lines of wet clothes festooned the room. Laundry in mounds and overfull baskets smothered the sparse furniture.

"I'm afraid, Meritocrat, our home is not as grand as you're used to," Perian said with embarrassment. "We work as washerwomen to make ends meet."

Colyan stood with her beefy arms folded across her chest, regarding Drinith as if she were a roach. "A fine turn of events!" she spat. "The meritocrat who ruined your good name and with it any prospect of a comfortable life—a guest in my home? I'll not have it, I tell you!"

"She said she was sorry," Perian said.

"Well, that's nice of her and all," her mother clucked, "but since every blade in the city is hunting her, she's not exactly in a position to restore your job or your reputation. Everyone knows she's a fugitive. *Everyone*. The entire city talks about nothing else."

"I am innocent," Drinith said.

Perian's mother frowned. "Then I hope when the meritocrats catch you, they treat you fairer than you did my daughter."

Perian planted her hands on her hips. "Enough, Ma."

Colyan shook her head. "Your meritocrat's only here because she has nowhere else to go."

Drinith couldn't bring herself to deny the truth.

"Ma, you're giving me a headache," Perian said.

"Bah! If you think you've a headache now, wait until the cordents find her here. It's only a matter of time before they batter down our door. Half of the quarter must have seen you with her. You know what happened to Vinsin on the fifth floor. She was arrested simply because of the color of her skin, despite her being twenty years the meritocrat's senior and living in the Red Quarter all her life. Everywhere, palms itch for the bounty on your meritocrat."

"My mother makes a good point, Meritocrat," Perian said, hastening to the door. "I need to find a better hiding place for you. I'll be back soon." The door slammed behind her.

Her mother shook her head. "There she goes, running off on another fool's errand. All my life, I've warned her not to waste her loyalty on anyone who held her in contempt, but she can't help herself. First, Meritocrat Orom docked her wages on account of another servant's error. Then you ruin her entirely, leaving her with nothing but a paddle and a mound of dirty clothes between her and penury."

"I was lied to by somebody I trusted implicitly," Drinith said, blushing. "I was fooled by her slander."

"You obviously didn't trust my daughter *implicitly*. You took the other woman's word over hers."

"To my shame."

"Absolutely. The sad thing is that Pery would do anything for you. She accompanied you to Ophigee despite her terror of dragons because you needed her. For weeks, I've had to listen to her weep at night as if somebody died, because you cast her out and stripped her of her good name. For a long time, she blamed herself, you know. And now you turn up at her door and she forgets it all like *that*." She snapped her fingers. "She's so joyous at your crumb of vindication, she can't see you're just using her."

"I'm not," Drinith protested, blushing. She wanted to believe it was true.

"Would you have come here today if you had anywhere else to go?"

Drinith headed toward the door.

"Where are you going?" Colyan demanded.

"Away from here. You are right. It was selfish of me to put the safety of both of you at risk." Drinith opened the door. "Tell Perian I am truly sorry, and if I manage to extricate myself from my current difficulties, I'll make proper amends for the wrong I did her."

"Wait."

Drinith paused on the threshold.

"Have you any money?"

Was she really trying to exploit Drinith's guilt to extort her? Drinith would dearly love to give her emblem of merit to Perian, *not her money-grubbing mother*. But, despite its enormous value, its possession would pose an unacceptable peril to the ex-maid. Drinith glared back at the woman. "I have nothing except a couple of coppers."

Grinning, Perian's mother reached under a mound of clothes on a dresser. A small, dented metal box rattled as she pulled it free. Opening it, she approached Drinith and offered a battered silver finch and four copper dragons. "It's all I can spare."

Drinith hesitated.

"Go on," the old woman said.

Drinith took the coins. "Thank you."

"No, *thank you*," the old woman said warmly, her demeanor transformed by the knowledge that this threat to her daughter was about to leave.

Drinith hastened down the stairs from Perian's apartment. She had to be well gone by the time Perian returned.

As she exited the building, pulling her hood over her head, a blood-curdling scream came from the Orphan Gate. Perian kicked and twisted as two ratchers bound and gagged her. Woad, flanked by two more ratchers, watched them deposit the wriggling girl into a restraining coffin.

Weaponless and outnumbered, Drinith could do nothing to help her. As she considered warning Perian's mother, two of the ratchers bolted by her into the tenement, undoubtedly heading to the apartment.

Gods, had Drinith brought them here? Or had Woad guessed she'd be desperate enough to beg for help from the girl she had wronged? Any rescue effort Drinith could attempt would be futile against Woad and his minions. Drinith needed to strike at the root of her troubles—the Rat King himself, Greny Scylax.

25

Greny could feel the other jurists' gazes fall upon him, weighing his reaction to Posaleum's revelation.

"But is Drinith's organization responsible for the murders?" Okia Vavar asked.

"The assassinations of Osro Onez and Thaxen Savarel almost certainly," Posaleum Minol declared with insufferable smugness. "The closure of the bridges to the Blue Quarter cut Drinith off from her supporters. She had to murder Cenmis with the sole sympathizer available, the butler."

"The butler, I understand, was a Gyran through and through," Aretro Falier said. "Why would she help Drinith?"

"Coin," Posaleum said.

"You must be careful," Zizor Findel said breathlessly to Thespenilea, her enormous eyes exaggerated with fear. "You're likely to be her next target."

"To what end?" Aretro interjected. "Any hope that we might invade Rhumgad is surely gone." She glanced irritably at Elca Trajar and Okia Vavar, neither of whom had made the slightest effort to defend their apparently former ally.

"Vengeance," Thespenilea Reiner said. "She spent her life

plotting Magian's dethronement. Now no other purpose remains to her but to take revenge on those who frustrated her dreams of becoming an empress."

"Speculation," Okia murmured, no doubt merely to assuage Aretro's anger.

"If Drinith's the murderer, she's very helpful indeed, turning up at key moments to confirm her villainy," Opriet Braesum said. "It's more likely somebody else is coordinating these attacks to point suspicion at her."

She dismissed Thespenilea's violent scowl with a shrug. "Thespie, you know I have always leaned toward the Short War Faction. However, it would be remiss of a cordent general to ignore the facts, no matter how counter they run to her natural sympathies. Posie's support of the New War Faction hasn't dissuaded her from doing her duty and sharing her suspicions about Drinith." She turned to Posaleum. "Have you any proof that this network of sympathizers exists?"

"*I* have," Greny said. His seizing the initiative from his rival drew surprised and bemused stares from around the table. "Not only have I proof, but I have infiltrated the organization at the highest level. I possess the name of every member. Her organization had nothing to do with the murders. Of that, I am certain. Drinith had a very good reason to keep Cenmis alive. They met at Osro's mansion the same night as the murders. Cenmis could have corroborated Drinith's innocence."

"Why didn't you tell us this before?" Thespenilea demanded.

"I'm telling you all now. In the current circumstances, it's the safest course. For all I know, one of you might have orchestrated these murders." Greny cast what he hoped was a meaningful glance around the assembly. "I can give an absolute guarantee that Drinith's organization had no involvement in these attacks. The man who managed it on her behalf is one of my agents."

"That doesn't mean she's not behind the murders," Thespenilea said. "She might work for Ophigee, our state's bitterest rival. It's naive to assume they made her one of their benefactors simply based on the technicality that she survived the Ascent. For all we know, the real Drinith is dead and the woman we presumed to be her is an impostor."

"To what purpose?" Okia asked with genuine curiosity.

"To draw us into invading Rhumgad, so the Shopkeepers can exploit our distraction to seize the initiative on Noster."

"The plot you outline is remarkably subtle for somebody who has so easily incriminated herself," Aretro observed.

"A double bluff perhaps," Anyrim Norcaro said.

Inamyr Minan planted both elbows on the table, rubbed her hands down her face and sighed loudly. "We can spend the day constructing all manner of plot and conspiracy. All we have so far are three dead meritocrats and a fourth suspected of killing them. Whether Drinith is innocent or guilty, she must be apprehended as soon as possible."

"That member list of her organization—I want it," Posaleum said, tapping the table. "It's time that we purged the Blue Quarter of subversive elements."

"Send them all to Beamstone," Thespenilea muttered, her face ugly with rage.

"We need to be careful," Opriet said. "There's bound to be many sympathizers beyond the formal membership of the organization. Turning its members into martyrs will incite some of our other Rhumgadian guests to violence against us."

"I'm not just talking about Drinith's network," Thespenilea said. "I mean every ungrateful Gadfly in the city. Toss the lot of them off the Plank."

Aretro blinked owlishly. "Thespenilea, I cannot believe you're seriously suggesting that."

Thespenilea sneered back at her. "Load them onto dragons and dump them into the inner sun."

Aretro shook her head. "Surely there must be a better solution than mass murder."

"That's easy to say when you're unlikely to be their next victim."

Thespenilea was afraid. All the meritocrats were to a greater or lesser degree.

"The primary focus of Drinith's network was Magian's overthrow," Greny said, doing his best to sound matter of fact. "Its secondary purpose was to counteract the tyrant's efforts to destabilize our state."

Thespenilea threw up her hands. "Drinith's no fool. She must guess our ultimate ambitions for her home shard. She might have created her private army primarily to help her pry Rhumgad from Magian, but she also knows she'll have to fight us or become our puppet."

Aretro gave an uncharacteristic sneer. "I thought she was an agent of Ophigee."

"She could be both," Devaner Tiranicon said glumly as she wiped her nose with a handkerchief. "She has displayed a remarkable capacity for defying our expectations in the past."

"If her organization posed an immediate security risk," Greny insisted, "I would have eliminated it already."

"Moving against the Rhumgadians in part or as a whole will cause major ructions in the other minority communities living in our city," Opriet said. "And there are other malcontents who seek to exploit any general strife. Frankly, we struggled to contain the incident in the Diplomatic District. Have we really enough cordents to deal with more widespread rioting throughout the city?"

"Don't look at me," the Dragonkeeper Nacyn Revistan said, raising her hands. "Dragons aren't much good for street fighting unless you want to reduce the city to rubble and cinders."

"Our army—" Ederion Visentar blurted.

"No!" Anyrim Norcaro, the sole conflagration marshal in attendance, thundered. "Have you learned nothing from history? Inviting soldiers, whether they're mercenaries or levies, into Gyre is a recipe for anarchy. We'd be better off taking our chances with Nacyn's dragons."

Devaner nodded. "Agreed. Letting mercenaries loose in Gyre would not be appropriate."

"The vast majority of our people hate the Gadflies." It was the first time Greny had heard Elca Trajar utter the term. "They would love a chance to drive the scourge from our city. We can rely on them in a fight against the Rhumgadians."

"Why wait for the Gadflies to riot?" Zizor Findel asked. "The incident in the Diplomatic District proves our common folk are hungry for vengeance. Turn them loose on the Blue Quarter. We can clear out whatever's left after they've wrecked it."

"No no no," Elca said. "We must avoid conflict in the city, if at all possible." She leaned forward and chopped the air with one hand. "So, this is my suggestion: we keep the Rhumgadians bottled up on the Blue Quarter for now. Greny controls Drinith's second-in-command and through him her entire network. If she is behind these murders, we should have her executed quietly and pretend that she is just another victim of this conspiracy. We can blame Magian—"

"Even now you're plotting to invade Rhumgad," Thespenilea grumbled.

"The Gadflies will trust us like never before," Elca said. "If Parliament chooses to invade Rhumgad, they'll be willing allies."

"And if the Parliament ultimately decides otherwise...?"

"We return the Gadflies to their home shard. Magian can deal with them. Let the Rhumgadians fight their own wars."

"Sounds like a fair compromise," Aretro said nervously.

Thespenilea shrugged. "Is it? Drinith's a traitor no matter how you look at it. She's not one of us. She has never been. The safest course is to cast her into the Void as soon as she's caught."

"You would pass a death sentence on her without giving her a chance to defend herself," Aretro said, aghast.

"Greny's word is all the evidence I require. Do you need more?"

Greny's heart sank. This was, in part, his fault. If he hadn't obliged Drinith to go in his stead to Osro's meeting... Of course, he'd be likely dead now and in no position to feel guilty.

"We all took an oath, Aretro, to defend Gyre, no matter the personal cost," Thespenilea said. "It's our duty to root out any threat to the Halcyon Republic and eliminate it. She was a useful instrument for furthering our interests, nothing more. Now, not even

Elca needs her." She craned her elegant neck to look upon her rival. "Is that not correct?"

"What happens to her is inconsequential to me," Elca said. "I want the Oracle."

Thespenilea smirked. "You can have him, to do with as you please."

"And what of Drinith's meritorian?" Aretro asked softly.

"She is Drinith's creature and should share her mistress's fate."

Too bad. Greny always had a soft spot for Jarma, but speaking up on her behalf would achieve nothing except give the impression of sentimental weakness.

"Let us vote," Thespenilea said. "I'll vote first. I vote for death."

Devaner cleared her throat. "Death."

"Death," Opriet said.

"Death," Elca confirmed.

"With regret, I can see no other sensible option," Okia said. "Death."

"Death."

"Death."

"Death."

"Death."

The word echoed quickly around the table until it reached Aretro. She hesitated a moment, hung her head. "Death." Greny couldn't help but feel a little aggrieved. So much for her vaunted conscience. In the end, she was a coward.

It was Greny's turn. He could demur, but if he did, he would draw the ire of the other jurists. And their suspicion.

He searched the circle of somber marble faces above him in vain for inspiration. How many death sentences had the queens above them witnessed over the centuries? How many heated debates, how many decisions, good and bad, had they looked down upon? Yet, the Halcyon Republic endured.

"Well?" Thespenilea asked.

"Death," he said, sealing the two girls' doom.

26

───────

As the jurists filed out of the chamber, Opriet Braesum gently grasped Greny's forearm and whispered in his ear, "Let's watch the executions a while."

Greny's impulse was to refuse. He had so much to do. And yet this invitation was so out of character for Opriet, it intrigued him. She must want to talk in private.

"Very well," he said.

Slipping down a side corridor, they climbed the stairs to the largest of the semicircular balconies on the fourth floor, the so-called Gallery of Veils. It had once been the tradition for the Vicenary Jury to gather here, their faces concealed behind thick black veils, to watch a particularly notorious enemy of the state walk the Plank.

Opriet leaned over the balustrade and peered down. "The best view in the house."

A sizable crowd had gathered at the slender red promontory jutting into the Void. A narrow channel cutting the mob in two stretched from the Plank to the Mortuary of Sin, an ugly, squat building nestled beside the Dragon Church. Along it, ratchers in black clothing led bound and gagged criminals. A heavyset man suddenly lurched to one side to break free of his captor, but the ratcher held him fast. One of the creature's comrades helped him roughly drag his reluctant prisoner onward, to a ragged chorus of boos and jeers. At the end of the line, four ratchers waited with spears to drive the condemned off the Plank, should their courage fail them.

Greny had witnessed this scene too many times for it to hold his interest. His gaze drifted to the steps of the Dragon Church. Three brightly clad youths tottered down them like newborn deer taking their first artless steps. The Courtesar Code would protect them on their so-called Sword Day, but how long would these new courtesars survive on the streets of Gyre before that same code got them killed? The families followed at a discreet distance, a handful of gaudy courtesars in the midst of the drab meritocrats and meritorians. At the bottom of the steps, the newly fledged courtesars turned and waved enthusiastically to them. They waved, too, at Greny's balcony, likely assuming him to be a woman. He nodded in appreciation. In Gyran society, such a presumption was a high compliment.

The sweeping of the cries and jeers from the crowd into a single, soaring *ooh* drew his attention to the Plank. The heavy man advanced hesitantly along it. He made a sudden move to charge back along the promontory, but the ratchers' spears left him nowhere to run. He gingerly backed away before their thrusts, glancing behind him to confirm he had still somewhere to retreat to until there loomed only empty sky. The spears' last coordinated lunge drove him back that last fatal step, and he fell. The crowd exploded in cheers.

"It's a terrible way to kill someone," Opriet observed as she leaned on the balustrade. "The axe would be gentler, swifter."

"If it cuts cleanly," Greny said. "You were the one who suggested this spectacle."

"After our recent misfortunes, it's wise to remind our people that we still control the city, that the wicked will be punished, and all will be made right with the world. And our people love a good execution. It will put them in good humor and cool their tempers. I have no doubt of its necessity, though I take no pleasure in it. It feels wrong to turn death into an entertainment."

"That's an unusual sentiment coming from a cordent general," Greny said tartly.

"It's not one that would ever stop me from doing my duty," Opriet said. "A farmer may love her cattle, but that won't stop her slaughtering them when she must."

Another long *ooh* accompanied the next prisoner striding resolutely toward the end of the Plank. He stepped into the Void without any resistance whatsoever, his bravery—or was it just resignation?—earning deafening applause and cheers as he plummeted.

"You didn't ask me to come here simply for philosophical discourse," Greny remarked.

"Posaleum is determined to destroy you," Opriet bluntly replied.

Greny snorted. "You dragged me up here to tell me that?"

"I don't think you are aware of the true extent of her animosity towards you. She doesn't merely want to force you from the"—Opriet made the euphemistic circular motion indicating the Iron Circle with her finger—"or take your emblem of merit. Posie wants you down there." She pointed at the Plank.

"What have I ever done to her to provoke such violent hatred?" Greny asked. "Aside from a few minor quips at her expense."

Opriet's crooked grin turned grim. "They weren't a few and, to her, they weren't minor. But no, I don't believe they're at the root of her hostility. You sent a favorite cousin, Ondra Taspinet, to Beamstone."

"The girl was a traitor," Greny growled. "Her own mother and sisters denounced her. The entire Vicenary Jury sentenced her."

"That's true, of course, but you were the one who arrested her. Posie blames you personally for her death. Until now, she's been too wary of taking you on because of your formidable reputation, but she senses in the current crisis an opportunity to topple you. If she finds any excuse to destroy you, she will take full advantage of it. And she has allies. There are others who harbor grudges against you for one reason or another."

To think all his years of selfless dedication to Gyre should be repaid with such ingratitude. All the while he had strove to protect the Halcyon Republic, he had unwittingly spun this web of grievance that now threatened to ensnare him. No, this enmity began before he even wore an emblem of merit. Some simply could not forgive him for not taking up the sword like his brother. In his own way, Greny was as much an outsider as Drinith or Jarma.

"You have friends too," Opriet added hastily. "Even admirers. Your service during the Silverfish Revolt, your sacrifice, is not forgotten."

"What would you have me do?" Greny demanded. "Surrender my emblem of merit? Marry and become my wife's shadow?"

"I'm not saying that. And, frankly, I don't believe you would ever heed such advice. Take this simply as a warning of danger ahead." Opriet touched her emblem of merit. "I'm thinking of stepping down as meritocrat and retiring to my estate in Cheor."

"You would retire now?" Greny asked in disbelief. "At this critical juncture?"

"Is there any moment in the last ten years which hasn't been? At any instant, the entire city might plummet into the Void. If it happened, would my presence prevent it?"

"So, you would hand your emblem of merit to your daughter and thrust her into the midst of this crisis."

"She'd sit safely in the back rows of the Parliament of Merit, studiously neutral and a threat to nobody."

"That's no guarantee of safety," Greny said sourly. "I always sit in the very back row."

"You're a cordent general and a jurist," Opriet said. "Such power draws envious gazes no matter where it sits."

"What is this vaunted power that I possess? The power to be hated. Like the daredevils who occasionally cross between Gyre's shardlets on tightropes, I must balance every step with utmost care. And now you tell me that Posaleum and others are intent on cutting the rope beneath me."

"You don't think I have accumulated my share of enemies? I prefer to bow with grace now than end up pushed out like Ronel

Olapsin. Or worse." Opriet paused, then added soberly: "You should consider the same course."

"Your daughter won't have you by her side to guide her."

"I've been preparing Hestis all her life to take my place. If I didn't think her capable, I'd have made one of her sisters my successor."

"You are lucky to have a clutch of daughters to choose from." Greny couldn't help but sneer. Opriet had six daughters, but it was rumored she hadn't given birth to two of them. She had swapped two sons for them to ensure the boys never became courtesars. He didn't know for certain it was true, but it fitted with her sentimental nature. So did her warning him about Posaleum and her intention to step down.

"My second eldest, Etapion, is a fine, sweet-tempered girl," Opriet said. "I know you said you have no interest in marriage—"

"I will not marry." *I will not be an outcast in my own house. You come to me pretending to be my friend, all the while plotting to diminish me.*

The clearing of a throat announced Ecethor's presence. How long had she been there? How much had she heard?

"What do you want?" Greny asked.

The question drew a sheepish smile. "I just wanted to thank you personally for your help on that certain matter I recently brought to your attention."

"There's no need."

"Of course there is," Ecethor said, grabbing his hand. As she shook it, something scratched his palm. "I'm in your debt." As she released it, the tiny piece of folded parchment almost slipped from his grip.

"You're welcome," Greny said.

"What was that about?" Opriet asked after Ecethor left.

"I don't know," Greny admitted, his fist wrapped around the parchment.

As soon as he could, he excused himself. Retreating to a quiet corner of the building, he unfolded the message and examined it.

Meet me where we entered the sewers tonight at the second bell of evenight.

What was Ecethor up to? What information could she possibly impart that would require such secrecy? Perhaps Ecethor didn't entirely trust Elca's intervention to save her. Or the price of her help might be too much. But this invitation had very much the smell of a trap. In the current chaos, what was one more dead meritocrat?

Not feeling safe alone, even within the parliament building, he hurried to the side exit and had a valet summon his palanquin. A familiar whistle alerted him to Deetch's approach. What was he doing here? He should be back at the tower.

The ratcher bowed and signaled—*three moon woman tower.*

Greny gasped. He glanced around guiltily, but nobody had seen, and even if anyone had, they wouldn't understand. Could Drinith have really delivered herself to him?

27

───────

The soot black tower had been built for war. Its bottom three stories were windowless. The six floors above them, banded with jutting spikes, battlements, and bartizans, looked like boxy forts stacked on top of each other. The structure had started leaning precariously soon after its construction, owing to unstable soil at its foundation, and the condition had only worsened over time; despite the persistent threat of imminent collapse, it had stood for hundreds of years. Rectangular holes above the entrance hinted at a drawbridge and moat long since removed. Ratchers, armed with pikes, stood guard on either side of the studded door. The passage of time had worn the reliefs of double-headed axes on the walls to invisibility. They must have been the emblem of whatever family had owned it before the Scylaxes. On the brattice above the door, a gilded plaque bore Greny's wheel of rats.

Drinith took it all in from under her hood as she strolled by the building. Wandering the cold streets of Gyre through the night and into the early morning had not dulled her enthusiasm to face Greny, but she couldn't walk up to the door and demand an audience. She couldn't trust any agreement he might offer about her safety.

She must catch him while he traveled the city. The street Scylax

Tower stood on ended in a precipice, so he would have to enter or leave it by Plume Bridge. She hurried there. She kept a wide berth from the beggar woman already sitting against its parapet, pleading for coins from passersby.

Drinith stared out over the parapet and pretended to watch the punts move up and down the smooth gray surface of the canal beneath. She palmed the knife she had bought with the pittance Perian's mother had given her. The gnarled wooden handle felt as though an animal had gnawed on it. The blade, dull both in finish and edge, leaned slightly to one side and looked likely to snap off at the slightest impact. It would be useless in a fight, but Greny wouldn't realize that if it was pressed to his neck.

"The rain's coming soon," the beggar said. "I can feel it in my bones. A red month of rains." Her cough sounded fake. "Might wash me away this time, I think. This city is no home for the old and frail."

A glance confirmed the woman was neither. A creeping dread gripped Drinith that the woman was speaking to her. The last thing she needed was to draw attention. Pretending not to hear, she casually moved further along the parapet, away from the beggar.

"Any spare change? I'm talking to you, lady." The beggar mumbled something under her breath. "Deaf, are we?"

Drinith stalked over to her, dropped in the woman's lap her sole remaining coin, a worn serpent. "It's all I have."

"I'm sure," the beggar said with a snicker, returning her attention to the passersby.

She made an audible spit. "Dirty rats!"

Drinith followed her gaze to a palanquin bearing Greny's badge approaching the bridge, heading toward the tower. Already clutching her knife in her dominant hand, Drinith slipped her emblem of merit into her free hand. She'd make a dash for the door as it passed, holding the emblem of merit aloft so the beggar woman and plenty of other witnesses would know who she was. It would make it harder for Greny to make her disappear, if that was his inclination.

Drinith turned around, hiding her hands behind her back. A woman scolded her petulant child as she dragged him along. Two other women carried trays of dragon-shaped turnovers on their heads. Three boys played with small stone marbles, clapping and cheering as they tossed them against the parapet. A tall, pot-bellied man propped himself against the opposite parapet by the elbows and watched them. A drunk man staggered along, lurching wildly as he droned an off-key ditty. He bowed to the beggar woman as if she was royalty, plowed into the children's game, earning several punches for his trouble.

Drinith glanced again at the palanquin, willing it to hurry. The wrinkled purple marrows on the cart ahead of it toppled off. A small crowd quickly gathered around the spill only to have the ratchers to drive them back. The cart's owner started remonstrating with the creatures as they started to pick up the vegetables. Drinith's nerve stretched to breaking. If only she could come up with a better plan...

GRENY PEERED through the curtain of his cab and tapped Ecethor's note against the sill of the window. This delay was intolerable. What was taking so long to clear this obstruction? He resisted the impulse to hop out of the palanquin and help to pick up the spilled vegetables himself. Not only would it be unseemly for a meritocrat to stoop to such menial labor, but it would also give any lurking assassin a perfect opportunity to strike.

An urgent squeak from Chemp gave him a start. The ratcher pointed to the window and waved his claw from side to side to indicate *no*. Of course, the curtain wouldn't protect Greny from a crossbow bolt. He leaned back in his seat and drew the folded shutter, plunging the palanquin into darkness. He might as well be sitting in a restraining coffin.

He shifted in his seat and cleared his throat. The smothering gloom of the vehicle became so impressive he could no longer stand it. Ignoring Chemp's plaintive squeak, he opened the door and stepped out. The owner of the cart argued with the ratchers as they picked up his fallen produce and packed it back onto his vehicle. The man fell silent as soon as he saw Greny.

"What is the problem?" Greny asked.

The man tucked his hands behind his back and twisted on the spot like a boy caught shooting his slingshot at passing palanquins. "Begging your pardon, Meritocrat. People won't buy my vegetables now that your servants have handled them because..." He gave the nearest ratcher, Kleest, a venomous glance. "Because of their resemblance to giant rats. No offense intended."

"I understand." *Superstitious backward fool.* "I will buy everything on the cart."

The man bowed. "Thank you, Meritocrat! Thank you!"

"Would five gold ducats suffice?"

"You're too generous, Meritocrat."

I know. "Chemp, pay the man." *It might at least buy some respect in this city, maybe even a little love. I already inspire fear aplenty.*

The man's smile never wavered as he took the money from the ratcher, Greny noted with disgust. He had no qualms about taking money from a rattish hand. To think grubby wastrels like him called ratchers vermin! This city would be far better off if this rabble was replaced by Chemp's exemplary race.

Commotion ahead. Armed men and women ran toward the palanquin. The ratchers drew their weapons and formed a protective circle around Greny as the vegetable seller and the other human cowards fled. Greny might crouch behind his servants, but at least he didn't run.

TWO WOMEN STRODE BY, chatting and laughing, completely engrossed in their conversation. A young man and woman sauntered along the bridge, a courting couple clinging close to each other and whispering. As they drew near Drinith, their eyes slid in her direction in unison, and she knew they were not lovers. She slashed at the hand attempting to grab her arm, causing her attacker to free her with a high-pitched yelp. The flimsy knife had come apart; she tossed away the bladeless handle.

The pot-bellied man blocked her path. "Cordents! Surrender!"

She tried to swerve around him, but he shoved her against the parapet. He and the other male cordent grabbed her. Her emblem of merit fell, flipped, and rolled away.

"She cut me!" the female cordent huffed.

One of the cordents holding Drinith roared in pain and let her go. A cracking punch sent the other sprawling across the bridge.

It took her a moment to recognize the drunkard from the earlier episode at the bridge, when he blundered into the children's game of marbles—his face now tense and full of urgency. She remembered those upturned green eyes. He was her rescuer in Wealgiver Street and, she now realized, the injured servant in Osro's mansion. He grabbed her hand and dragged her in the opposite direction to the palanquin. "Run or we're both dead!"

The female cordent tried to block their escape, stretching out her uninjured arm to latch on to them. Drinith's rescuer made to go around her, but changing course at the last moment he barreled into her, knocking her to the ground, and leaped over her.

Following, Drinith glanced back at the palanquin sinking below the hump of the bridge. As the three injured cordents clambered to their feet, a half-dozen others gave chase.

"Quick, through here!" her rescuer urged. He grabbed her arm, nearly wrenching her shoulder out of place, and pulled her like a limp rag doll through a crowded tavern.

He flung an open pouch at the ceiling, causing a rain of coins behind them. As the patrons scrambled to collect the windfall, he dragged her out the back exit. They raced along the canal to the next bridge, crossed back onto the far side, and turned into an alley on the next street. There appeared to be no sign of their pursuers.

"Who are you?" Drinith asked between pants.

"My name doesn't matter," he said. "I represent your only hope of escaping the Plank. This is the second time I've saved you from the

Rat King's clutches, and the last. If you run off this time, I'll not help you again."

Greny's palanquin couldn't be too far away. She could reach it provided she could get past the swarming cordents and Greny's rodent bodyguards....

"I'm leaving," her mysterious companion said as he headed toward the mouth of the alley. "The choice is yours to follow me or not, but this is the last time I'll offer my help." At least he had aided her. Greny, on the other hand...

Drinith hastened after him.

"Wise move," he muttered as they plunged into the crowd.

Drinith shook her head. Was this wisdom or folly? Only time would tell.

THE LEADER of the approaching mob hailed Greny. "Have no fear! We're bluecheck cordents on the hunt for the Meritocrat Hax."

Greny peered over Chemp's shoulder at the mob of excited faces. "Do I look like Drinith?" he sneered.

"Of course not," the cordent said after a pause, as if he had to think about it. He blushed. "We spotted her in the vicinity. We gave chase, but she has escaped for the moment."

What were a group of Posaleum's minions doing here out of uniform? "What's your name and rank?"

The man stood to attention. "Dignet Arunsor, Captain."

"Are you sure it was Drinith?"

"Absolutely, Meritocrat," Captain Arunsor insisted.

Greny couldn't resist a smile. Drinith already waited for him in his tower. The woman hunted by Posaleum's minions was probably some Rhumgadian stray trapped outside the Blue Quarter. "And how did you happen to be here to find her? This street is currently in the yellowcheck sector."

The captain sheepishly studied his boots. "You'll have to talk to Cordent General Minol about that. I'm just following her orders."

So Posaleum had the impudence to have me watched, by at least a dozen cordents, no less. She must have hoped to find me consorting with Drinith. "I will ask your meritocrat, as you suggest."

Captain Arunsor blanched, but at least he had the good sense not to answer back. Clearing his throat, he produced a gold disk. "We found this." Holding it by the edge, he offered it to Greny. Chemp took it, and after a careful sniff gave it to Greny. It bore an alerion taking flight—Drinith's emblem of merit.

"I'm surprised Drinith escaped so many pursuers," Greny observed. "Particularly given that the street on the far side of the bridge is a dead end."

The captain looked sick, his eyes dead with resignation. "She had help. A drunkard. At least, he pretended to be."

This drunkard could be the same man who helped Drinith escape Woad Glastum at Wealgiver's Street. "Tell me this. If she's not here now, why are you standing here?"

Captain Arunsor straightened. "I thought you might need assistance."

"As you can see, my servants have things well in hand. I suggest you focus your efforts on capturing Drinith."

The captain gave a solemn nod. "Thank you, Cordent General." He turned smartly on his heel and joined his fellow bluechecks.

Greny watched them scurry away until, suddenly realizing the nakedness of his position, he returned to his palanquin. If the Rhumgadian woman at his tower wasn't Drinith, then it must surely be Jarma.

28

As Greny entered the parlor, Jarma shot to her feet. Her relieved smile looked genuine enough, but she held her hands in a clasp. No hint of dishevelment marred her lime green coif or her prim black dress. She looked every bit a meritorian on a social call to another household. In point of fact, she had a more noble bearing than her former mistress.

"Dragons, I was worried!" Greny said. "It's been days since you were last seen. Where you have been? Sit, please." Taking a seat across from her, he slipped his bone-white chrysanth-shaped truthstone from his pocket into his gloved hand.

Her gaze fixed on it. "I see. My word isn't good enough?"

"A truthstone isn't just for testing the veracity of a statement," he said, pleased by the steadiness of the stone's weight. Of course, he wasn't lying. He just wasn't telling the full truth. "It can sometimes pick up subtle inconsistencies in a story. By pointing them out, it can help stimulate the memory and maybe discover details that might otherwise be missed."

Jarma looked unconvinced. "Why did your cordents raid the Hax Mansion? Why have you been hunting Drinith and me? You sent her to Meritocrat Onez's home."

"I'll explain all, of course," Greny assured her. He gave a brief and carefully edited summary of what had happened since her disappearance. Every time he skipped awkward aspects like Woad Glastum's betrayal or the Vicenary Jury's plan to execute Drinith, the stone weighed heavier in his sweaty palm. Focused on his face, Jarma didn't appear to notice the momentary spasms of his hand caused by these fluctuations of weight.

But then her gaze suddenly fell upon his hand. He casually laid it flat on the padded leather armrest to hide any telltale tremors.

"How did you evade us so long after you escaped your mansion?" he asked.

"A man attacked me. He injected me with some drug to knock me unconscious." She reached toward her mouth, paused. "I can still remember the sweet smell of the rag he used to stifle my cries for help as I passed out."

The truthstone's weight remained steady. She spoke the truth. "Describe the scent."

"It was sweet and salty," Jarma said. Her eyes opened. "It was some sort of brineflower perfume."

Greny stroked his chin. "And after that?"

"I can remember nothing before I awoke in the cab that brought me here." She produced a glass phial stained with a black residue. "This was in my hand when I woke. I had a sour, tarry taste in my mouth."

Greny bid Chemp take the phial and sniff its contents. As soon as he removed the stopper, Greny thought he detected a faint whiff of immemoreal. The ratcher's hand signals confirmed his suspicion.

"What did your...servant say?" Jarma asked.

"The phial contains an amnesia-inducing drug."

"Immemoreal," Jarma said, aghast. So she had heard of it. "Can the memories be recovered?"

"I'm afraid not," Greny said. "Its effect is irreversible."

"So, I may never know what happened to me during my abduction." Jarma rubbed her lips with trembling fingers. The truthstone confirmed her candor, but Greny didn't need it. Her dismay was obviously genuine. "I'm to be left with this hole in my memory, this gaping nothing."

He wrapped his fist tightly around the truthstone, felt its petals press into his fingers, and cleared his throat. "No need to worry. You're safe now," he said, ignoring the change in its weight. He wished it was true, but the Vicenary Jury had sentenced her to death.

He pitied her. It was partly his fault her life now hung in the balance. She had started out as a simple maid, after all, and though she carried herself with a grace and dignity far exceeding what her background might have promised, she must be hopelessly out of her depth in this intrigue.

He'd make sure she wasn't hurt or frightened. Greny liked her, preferred her to Drinith. He knew the poisons for a gentle death. She'd simply go to bed and fall into a peaceful slumber from which she'd never wake. He'd have Chemp dispose of her body in the sewers afterward. No, she deserved better than that. He could sneak her into his family mausoleum. She could sleep forever in one of tombs as a meritorian, his secret wife, a future mystery for his successors to the Scylax name.

"My escape from Hax Mansion left me quite disheveled," Jarma said, examining herself curiously. "Yet my hair and clothes are immaculate. For example, I tore a sleeve, but it has been expertly repaired. And though I fled the house barefoot, I now wear a fine new pair of shoes. What do you think this all means?"

"I don't know," Greny said. Thanks to Deetch's quick thinking, the driver who brought her to the tower was under arrest. He claimed that Jarma herself had hired him with the instruction not to disturb her on the journey. An unimportant nobody, he was already on his way to Inkeep.

"Oh, and I had this." She lurched toward him and proffered a golden feather.

Deetch stepped between them, his hand on the hilt of his dagger, and indicated with a wave that she should draw no nearer.

Her eyes rounded with fear as Greny stared open-mouthed at it. "Are you all right? Did I do something wrong?"

"Of course not. There's no need to be afraid," he said, forcing a smile. The feather might be treated with poison, or her clothes, or her cloying perfume. Dragons, Jarma herself might even be poisoned! Her every breath might be filling the room with death. "Deetch, take Jarma to her room. Arrange a bath and new clothes for her. She must be tired after her ordeal."

Still wide-eyed, she hesitantly followed the ratcher out of the parlor.

Greny rubbed a palm against his forehead, pressing his emblem of merit against the cushion of skin between it and his skull. Jarma took immemoreal with no sign of coercion. She must have been a willing accomplice to whoever had sent her to Scylax Tower. By the same token, her rescuer may have manipulated her with lies and left her ignorant of the true purpose of sending her to Scylax Tower. If she came here as an unwitting assassin, Deetch would soon find any poison hidden in her possessions or on her person. Why give her the golden feather, though? Its discovery could only arouse suspicion. Jarma's delivery into his hands felt like a taunt.

It was as if he was blindfolded, and he kept stumbling forward, reaching out into the darkness. All the while, his tormentor silently laughed as she dodged his probing hands and kept one step ahead of him. He wouldn't be mocked! She wouldn't be laughing at him anymore after he caught her.

Jarma sat on the corner of the bed trying to make herself look small as a procession of ratchers filled the large, ornate brass bathtub with buckets of steaming water. The stench of damp fur made her queasy until one of them poured a fragrant oil into the water. The ratcher who seemed to be in charge drew a faded screen around the tub, hung two towels on it, and indicated that she should undress.

She obeyed, fearful of what these creatures might do if she refused. She fled behind the screen and removed her clothes, draping them over the frame. The chill, dank air against her skin made her shiver. Wincing with disgust, she scooped off a few floating hairs before stepping into the warm, milky water. As she sank into the bath, her clothes slid away from their resting pace. She covered her breasts with her arms as a hairy hand reached around the bottom of the screen and snatched her boots and underclothes.

"What am I to wear?" she pleaded, but the only answer was the patter of the creatures' feet across the carpet and the slamming of the door. She stood in the bath and craned her neck above the screen to make sure she was alone. Fresh clothes had been left on the bed. The ratchers had taken her jewelry.

The dew of cooling bathwater clinging to her naked body made her shudder, and she sank back into the bath's warmth. She was trapped, isolated, her life at the mercy of Greny's whim. Whatever possessed her to come here? Imprisoned in this tower, Jarma couldn't help herself, much less Drinith.

Worse was this alarming void in her memory stretching from her kidnapping to her arrival here. It felt like a physical part of her was missing. Anything might have happened to her in that period. For all she knew, Greny himself could have administered the immemoreal as part of some grandiose scheme to extract information from her. She was little more than a counter on an Angels and Demons board.

She gasped as she remembered the veiled woman moving red and yellowed counters around the grid.

"Take this," the Veiled Meritocrat said, placing the phial on the table. It had contained the same residue of black immemoreal it held when Jarma gave it to Greny. "You'll carry this on your trip to Greny's tower. The drug it contains is potent enough to wipe away a couple of hours of memory for good, at least. But you won't drink it. Oh, no. Not a drop. You'll drink this instead." Beside the first phial, she placed a second containing a dull green liquid. "It's another amnesic called slipwell. It, too, makes its imbiber forget, but its effect is transitory. It hides rather than destroys memories. They return once the drug wears off."

A connected image of a physical object could accelerate the process. For example, the Angels and Demons board the Veiled

Meritocrat had played upon. She had hoped that Jarma's first game with Greny would stimulate her recollection, but the very thought of the game counters had spurred Jarma to remember early.

"Your sudden arrival at Scylax Tower will make Greny suspicious. He'll test you with a truthstone. The slipwell will help you to convince him that you are as much at a loss as he about what happened to you."

"And the feather?" Jarma remembered twirling the hollow tubular stem between her fingers.

"A distraction. A mystery for Greny to puzzle over."

Jarma didn't believe her, particularly given Greny's reaction when he first saw it. To the Veiled Meritocrat, Jarma was merely bait in her trap. And the terrible secrets the Veiled Meritocrat shared, including Woad Glastum's treachery, was the poison.

29

Drinith's companion led her through a series of taverns and teahouses, mostly in the front door and out the back. He sometimes circled back to check the front of the building from a safe vantage to confirm they weren't being followed. He kept glancing over his shoulder, too much for Drinith's liking.

As evening closed, their meander continued across the city. Drinith almost stumbled into him when he came to an abrupt halt outside a rundown shop near a decrepit fountain. Above the door was a blackened open book, barely visible in the dim twilight. The premises certainly had seen better days.

"This is as far as I go," he whispered, handing her a black copper coin. A crude bird shape had been scored onto one side. "Give it to the shopkeeper. Good luck." As he dashed away, she repressed an urge to call out to him. She didn't even know his name.

Nobody else was about except for a sleeping beggar nestled under the broad lip of the fountain's basin. Bracing herself for the squalor she might find within, Drinith pushed it open. The tinkle of a bell made her shiver. The shop, to her surprise, was clean and imbued with a subtle florid scent. The old books packed on the shelves showed signs of wear, but no hint of dustiness tickled her nose.

A gray-haired man smiled at her from behind the counter. His sunlight-yellow face retained a youthful handsomeness despite his advanced age. He had a striking gray-blue birthmark on his neck. His eyes were an early morning blue. She closed the door and dropped the black coin on the counter. "I believe I'm to give you this."

He picked it up and tossed into a drawer under the counter. "Welcome, Meritocrat Hax, to both my shop and my abode." He gracefully bowed his head. "Or should I refer to you as Your Imperial Majesty?"

Such a formal salutation felt odd and more than a little alarming coming from this stranger. Nobody outside her closest friends referred to her by that title and then only in whispers.

"My name is Qilin Pine, humble shopkeeper, and your honored host until your current difficulties are resolved." Rounding the counter, he locked the door. She followed him upstairs. The furniture in the room at the top, like the books, was worn but well-kept. Her mouth watered at the smell of stew wafting from a bubbling pot on the stove. By the window stood a gilded cage taller than her, containing a dozen twittering sunfinches.

"I keep them as a hobby," he said. "I love the sheen of their golden plumage and their chirping brightens the evenings. Would you care for something to eat?"

"I weary of these idle pleasantries," Drinith said plainly. "Who are you really?"

For a long moment, Qilin took her measure. He cleared his throat, glanced at the cage. "You might say I represent your last hope." He added with a bleak smirk, "A little bird has told me that the Vicenary Jury has sentenced you to death."

Drinith gasped. "My friends! What—"

"They are still imprisoned in Inkeep for now, and presumably safe until you are caught, and the Meritocracy has no further use for them. Everyone from the cordent generals to the brightest plumed peacock to the lowest gutter spy hunts you."

"So, what are you offering? Escape?" She couldn't leave Gyre, not without her friends. She couldn't abandon the exiles of the Blue Quarter either.

Qilin shook his head. "I could smuggle you out of the city, but what good would that do you? Magian will hunt you wherever you go and all your ambition to free your homeland, the quest that has shaped your life from your birth, would shrivel and die."

She found his description of her solemn mission to free Kaplar a little distasteful, but she let it slide. She was in no position to pick a fight with her host.

"I offer something much better than mere survival," he said, "a chance to help your beleaguered people."

Drinith pretended to look about the room. "Have you really got that many dragons hidden away here?"

"No. I'm not talking about Rhumgad. For now, at least. The exiles from your homeland who live here are your people, too. You can make a real difference to them and the common folk native to this city. And you can help the Halcyon Republic's own banished children, dispossessed and dispersed across the Crevast. You could even bring a lasting peace to the Noster's beleaguered inhabitants. Gyre could become a beacon of hope across the Crevast."

She could feel the weight of a thousand grubby compromises, great and small, lifting away. She'd be finally free. The prospect dazzled too much for her to trust it. "Forgive me for being cynical, Qilin, but what do you get out of this?"

"The same as you—the liberty to live and love, the knowledge that I leave this world in a better place than I found it."

He approached the cage and fed the birds seeds through the bars. "Our group is not strong enough to overthrow the Meritocracy alone, but with your people's help we could succeed. Your suspicion is understandable, even laudable, but we have no such doubts about you. We've been studying you for some time. You might be a meritocrat in name, but you haven't become one in nature. Nor could you, for the Meritocracy's hatred of royalty meant it could never truly accept you. They'd never give you back your beloved Kaplar. Magian's offer of spice monopolies already has brought them very close to ending their campaign against him. Your current fugitive status will give them the perfect excuse to make peace with him. His reputation will be rehabilitated in Gyre, while you'll be vilified in every way imaginable."

"So, what do you want me to do, exactly?"

"Be a bridge between your people and ours."

"Were you responsible for the murders of Orso, Thaxen, and Cenmis?"

"Please don't mourn for them. They wouldn't have given your death a second thought. As members of the Iron Circle, they handed out death sentences to countless innocents whose only crime was to question their tyranny. As meritocrats, they ordered cities razed and countries ravaged, the wealth of nations plundered. They fattened their fortunes upon the endless misery of the Short War, while treating it as an entertainment. They peppered the prattle at their dinners and balls with idle discussions about its twists and turns."

Drinith's face burned. She had listened to those discussions many times and even partaken in them occasionally. She couldn't deny Qilin spoke the truth, but an instinctive wariness gnawed at her. Who was this "humble shopkeeper" really? "You sound like a foreign agent," she couldn't resist saying.

"I might say the same of you, Benefactor," he said with a grin. "Have no fear. I'm Gyran through and through. We both fight against tyranny. Is that not enough? Or have I misjudged you? Do you prefer the empty promises of those who hate everything you stand for?" He spoke lightly, as if in jest, but there was an edge to his questions. She shied from his probing gaze.

"I appreciate that this is a lot to take in," he said amicably. "Only two days ago, you imagined yourself as one of the rulers of this city. Now, you're its most notorious criminal."

She couldn't help smiling. He was wrong about that, at least. She had always felt an interloper in the exalted company of meritocrats. Over the last two years, she had never imagined her emblem of merit truly hers. And she could remember no day in her life that she had felt safe.

"You must be tired and hungry," Qilin said abruptly. "I imagine being hunted gives one quite the appetite."

She nodded. It was the first thing he had asked that didn't leave her conflicted. After bidding her to sit at the table, he poured two bowls of stew and passed one bowl and a bread roll to her. She didn't recognize the dark-gray meat floating in the bright yellow gravy, but it was tasty enough and quite tender. It was bulked with pearl beans, onions, and peppers, and seasoned with Nemon spices.

"Hopefully, the casquar meat is to your liking," he said, slightly embarrassed. "It is a cheap meat, but I'm rather partial to it. I would have had prepared something more sumptuous if I had known earlier I'd have such an important guest."

This culinary revelation—she'd never before consumed the meat of a casquar—gave her pause, but only for a moment. Hunger overwhelmed any reservations. "I'm grateful for any fare," she said, "however modest."

Drinith ate the stew and bread ravenously, oblivious to the admiring gaze of her host. The casquar meat, despite having a somewhat gamy quality, was actually quite tasty. The roll was a bit stale, but she soaked it in the soup to soften it. She polished off both with surprising speed, leaving her bowl as clean as a dragon's tooth.

"Well, I shan't have to wash that one, eh?" Qilin said impishly. Drinith felt her cheeks burning.

As Qilin made tea, the licorice smell of a hard variety filled the kitchen. She took the bowl with an appreciative nod but hesitated to sip it. She needed to keep her head clear. Qilin watched her as he drank his tea. "It's not poisoned, you know. It helps me sleep at night."

She smiled, lifted the bowl to her lips and pretended to sip it. "How did you become involved in this...?" *Conspiracy? Rebellion?*

"I'll tell you another time. I don't enjoy dwelling on the past over hard tea." After taking another sip, he raised his bowl in a salute. "To the future and freedom."

Smiling, Drinith again raised her bowl to her lips and again pretended to drink. They sat in melancholic silence, both staring into their drinks. Neither remarked on the rain pattering against the building's exterior.

She felt drained to the bone, her heavy eyelids yearning to draw down on an exhausting day. Almost nodding off with the bowl in her hand, she put it on the table.

"Tired?" he asked.

Her nod spurred him to walk over to a wall, press one section of wood and then another. A panel slipped out of position. He lifted it away, revealing a small alcove. The shelves on the far wall were neatly stacked with hefty tomes, ancient and expensive, judging from their ornate, scuffed spines. A narrow, dented mattress covered most of the floor. "That's where you'll sleep tonight. I trust you won't find it too uncomfortable."

Entering the secret alcove, she lay down on the mat. The tickle of airborne dust made her nose twitch. She could feel the hard floor through the meager stuffing, but she had slept on worse.

"Thank you," she said.

"See you in the morning," Qilin said as he slid the panel back in place. A slim candle lampstone on the bookshelf provided the only light.

The onset of this overwhelming fatigue had been so sudden. Had the stew been drugged? But it was too late to do anything if it had. The thought slipped away from her like flotsam on an ebbing tide into black oblivion.

30

As soon as the palanquin halted, Greny climbed out of the cab into the night's ocher gloom. The house's yellow facade made it stand out from its dull neighbors in the terrace. A previous owner must have done a great service for some meritocrat to be permitted to strip away the pink render. Greny smiled as he approached the door, accompanied by Chemp and Queek. This excursion would surely confuse any spies who saw Greny arrive here. What possible reason could bring him to this hovel? they would ask each other. Who had he come here to meet?

Queek knocked on the door for him. It swung open to reveal a frightened middle-aged man wearing a nightshirt. He bowed repeatedly as he retreated before his guest. "Welcome, Meritocrat."

Greny strode inside. A woman and a young girl in nightdresses clutched each other in quiet terror in one corner. Dweed, one of the advance party, kept a springbow trained on them.

"You've nothing to worry about," Greny said breezily as he strode past them, down the hall and into the kitchen.

A crude hole had been smashed through the back wall. Greny noted with some irritation that he had to stoop to pass through it. In the cobbler's workshop, another family stood against a wall—a stooped old man, a young woman, and four whimpering children, the youngest, Greny guessed, not older than five. While Geekel kept watch on them, Kleest drew back a shutter to reveal a fogged section of window. He quickly rubbed a patch of glass for Greny to peer through. Ecethor's mansion stood across the road—an ugly, overwrought monstrosity covered with lewd reliefs of entwined lovers and courtesars engaged in battle. Ecethor's preference in architecture was much like her taste in fashion—far too flashy and prone to extravagance. It was said that her mother had been a miser. Ecethor certainly had made up for that.

Greny glanced at the stack of ducats on the workbench, catching the dull light of the draped lampstone in the center of the room. Recompense for the disruption of this invasion that the cobbler and his family had suffered. All five coins he had stipulated lay there. If human cordents had secured the two properties, they would have stolen the sunfinches and left their owners with a few copper serpents. And yet everyone looked down on ratchers. Look at the children—so frightened, already turned against that which they don't understand.

Kleest emitted a soft squeak and pointed out the window. A palanquin had halted outside Ecethor's mansion. Greny rubbed another circular patch in the fogged-over glass to get a better view, but he couldn't make sense of the blurry knot of shadow around it.

"How many guards?" he asked.

Chemp, peering beside him through the window, signaled eight. Greny hadn't expected so many. The main door of the mansion opened and Ecethor exited, flanked by two more guards.

"I'll go out and meet her by myself," Greny said.

Chemp shook his head and signed *young*.

"What do you mean?" Greny demanded irritably.

Chemp's furry fingers signed rapidly: *Young girl in the palanquin. Daughter, not mother.*

Clearly, Cibiela's ostentatious departure was intended to distract anyone from keeping watch on her mother's movements. The ratchers' keen eyesight had once again proved invaluable. Ecethor was certainly more cunning than Greny had ever credited.

As the palanquin and its escort moved down the street, Greny pulled up his hood. "Wait for me here," he ordered. Ignoring Chemp's protesting squeaks, he exited the shop, strode across the street and up the steps to Ecethor's front door.

The maid who answered his tug on the doorbell stared at him in a paroxysm of blinking bewilderment. "Meritocrat, I'm very sorry. Meritocrat Orom has just departed the mansion."

"I think you might be mistaken," Greny said, craning his neck to peer beyond the girl. "If you look around, I'm sure you'll find her."

A frowning butler stalked out of the shadows between the curving arms of the bifurcated staircase and shoved the servant to one side. "Cordent General, I'm afraid Meritocrat Orom isn't home," she said, her bulk filling the threshold. "I will, of course, tell her you called as soon as she returns. Is there a message you would like me to give her?"

Greny should have brought a couple of ratchers to sweep these fools out of his way. "Stand aside or feel my wrath!"

The cowed maid trembled with terror, but the butler was made of sterner stuff. "No offense is intended," she said, "but Meritocrat Orom gave me strict instructions to permit nobody to enter."

"Get out of my way!" Greny tried to push by her, but the butler stood her ground and would not shift.

"What is the meaning of this?"

Greny and the two servants looked at the speaker, already halfway down the left arm of the stairs. Ecethor, her face livid with indignation, flounced down the steps and waved the surprised butler and maid out of her way as she strode to the door. She halted within slapping distance of Greny.

"You agreed not to bother me," she growled, "and yet here you are threatening my staff in my own mansion."

"You invited me, remember?" Greny whispered.

"Not here. Never here. Why did you come here, dooming both of us? The doors of this mansion, both public and private, are closed to you. Understand?"

"Tell me what's going on."

"It's too late." She slammed the door shut.

He pounded against the door until the fists of both hands bled. He'd make her talk tomorrow. He'd stand her before the Iron Circle, Elca be damned.

He crossed the street back to the shop, where the ratchers patiently awaited him.

"Fetch my palanquin!" Greny told them. "I'm going home!"

Greny brooded all the way back to Scylax Tower. He had been undone by his own cleverness. No, not cleverness—suspicion. If he had trusted Ecethor, if he had met her in the sewers as she had asked, he'd probably possess whatever terrible secret she had promised to share. For now, at least, he was left to wonder what it was. Asking for the Vicenary Jury's authorization to interrogate her would bring him into direct conflict with Elca. Worse, this pressing secret might have nothing to do with the murders of Osro and the others. It could be an entirely unrelated matter, adding to his problems instead of solving them. It might have no import at all—Cibiela might have landed herself in trouble again, or the two sons.

He was sorely tempted to turn the palanquin around and head back to Ecethor's home, but she'd certainly refuse to speak to him again and he couldn't arrest her on a vague suspicion. He couldn't afford further humiliation at her hands. His authority depended on his perceived invulnerability. If that slipped away, his many enemies would pounce. Writing to Ecethor would only provide her with physical proof of his embarrassment. Even using fading ink might not protect him. She could open his letter in front of a dozen witnesses, all of whom could testify to its contents. He'd have to wait for a chance to confront her in Parliament or at some public event where decorum would limit her opportunity to shun him. Greny mustn't grovel. He had to be patient. But patience was so hard....

Arriving back in his tower, he couldn't face the long, winding stairs to his quarters, so he plunked himself on a couch in the parlor and ordered a pot of hard tea. He drank it to the dregs quickly and ordered a second. Tonight, of all nights, he longed to sleep, to close his eyes for a few hours and awake from dreamless slumber refreshed and resolute.

His head swam, his brain softened and pickled in the cheering haze of the tea's intoxication. The sudden remembrance of the other Jurists' condemnatory stares sobered him a little. No matter how much he sacrificed, it was never enough. The Meritocracy was an insatiable monster. Its hunger to survive had consumed generations of meritocrats. Like desperate lovers, they courted its favor until old age or misfortune cast them into the political void. Then, their friends and even their families deserted them. Despite its precarious nature, many meritocrats still craved high office. How many coveted his position even now amid this crisis? How many whispered prayers for his fall?

Elca Trajar was an extraordinary woman indeed to claw her way back to the top after her expulsion from the Iron Circle. Her detractors had cited a plethora of reasons at the time—her unbridled ambition, her avarice, her love of the foreign, her tendency to meddle in matters best left to others. She had been even accused of turning courtesars against their houses, though at that time, she had been a plain, flat-chested woman, ill-suited to such seduction. In the wake of her expulsion, she had refashioned herself, body and soul, into someone far more formidable, terrible even. If only he could similarly reinvent himself. He should have been a courtesar like Erphel. It must be so sweet to lead such an innocent, uncomplicated life.

He fancied Elca's heavy perfume still clung to the air from her previous visit. His hand reached out to touch her invisible form, but he'd never possess a goddess like her. To him, love was a trap, a murder of self, the surrender of everything that made him who he was. As much as he despised this lonely life, Greny was rooted in it, and it was rooted in him. He was its prisoner as much as Jarma was his.... Poor Jarma, banished to his mother's room, alone and lonely like him. He began to weep, whimpering to himself like a child. A ratcher entered, but Greny barked at him to leave. The ratcher hesitated a moment, then obeyed.

Greny had always admired Jarma. Such a sweet girl. He had quietly reveled in the disgust of his sister meritocrats at her elevation to meritorian. Jarma and he were of a kind, after all—outsiders, anomalies, unfortunate flaws.

He wiped the wet from his face. His melancholy was a stain no deluge of hard tea could wash away. It was like a birthmark, as much a part of him as his eyes or the heart beating under his rib cage.

He should check on his guest. Jarma might be lonely too. He rose from his seat and wobbled out of the room. A ratcher by the door reached to grab him with a squeak of alarm, but Greny waved him off. "I'll have no need of your help tonight, Kleest, Queek, whatever your name is. I am going to call on my guest and then head to my bed. Or *some* bed, if I'm lucky." Chuckling, he winked at the ratcher and gave it a companionable jab in the ribs. A guarded twitching of its whiskers was the creature's only response.

Pairs of starry eyes appeared in the darkness beyond them. Greny waved an arm at them with such force, he almost fell forward. "Go to bed, all of you. Nothing to see here." He hiccupped. "I give you all the night off."

He headed up the spiral staircase that wound up the tower. After the second time he stumbled into the lampstone banister, he reluctantly held on to it. His head was so light. He must be near the top of the tower. How had he missed Jarma's room? The shadow behind him, he realized with a start, wasn't his. A ratcher had followed him all the way up the tower.

"Go away," Greny said. "I don't need you."

The ratcher, like a shadow, didn't budge until Greny restarted his climb. The creature maintained the same respectful distance throughout his master's meandering ascent.

Greny finally arrived at Jarma's door, easily identified by the forked crack in one of the stone jambs. Nostalgia stirred as he ran a numb finger along it. As a child, he had known every fissure and fault in the building, and feared them, convinced that one day they would cause the tower to collapse. He couldn't feel the familiar crack. It might as well be smooth.

The dark varnish couldn't conceal the lighter-colored section of wood in the door around the lock, the color of bone under stretched skin, a scar left after Greny's mother died locked within the room. She had become mistrustful of her servants as her health deteriorated, even suspecting them of poisoning her.

Pressing his forehead against the door, he knocked. "Jarma, are you asleep?"

No answer.

He knocked again and tried the handle, but it was locked. He slumped into a heap, his back pressed against the wood. "I hope you like the room. It was my mother's." True, but only when she became too old and feeble to climb the tower, and it finally became her prison. "Did I tell you there's spare clothes in the wardrobe if you need them?" His mother's clothes. "Jarma, are you all right? Answer me please, so I know you're safe."

The silence from the room was stubborn and loud.

"Jarma, you're being very rude," Greny said. He looked up at his shadow looming above him. "Open the door." But the ratcher didn't move, didn't even squeak in acknowledgment. Perhaps he really was a shadow molded into a ratcher by Greny's tea-soaked imagination.

"We should be friends, you and I," he said to Jarma. "We're both prisoners in this tower. We're both something we were never supposed to be. Those we love have betrayed us." He buried his face in his hands and burst into tears. Not a sound came from Jarma's room, not the slightest consoling murmur, only heartless silence.

Inflamed with indignation, he twisted around and pounded on the door. "How dare you ignore me! I promise, Jarma, you'll pay for this cruelty. Yes, you'll pay!"

31

———————

rinith started. Looking up at the low planked roof above her, she clutched at her blanket like a panicky child seeking solace in a favorite doll. Had she been spirited into a restraining coffin during the night? No, she lay on the same worn-out mattress in the same cramped little room. The lampstone candle on the bookshelves still shone to her right. Someone, presumably Qilin, had thrown this blanket over her during the night.

Movement on the other side of the panel—footsteps across the wooden floor and carpet accompanied by a soft, rhythmic squeak. Water plunged into water. A metal bucket handle squealed to the rhythm of more steps. Qilin must be out there.

Drinith threw off the blanket and examined the two curved brass handles on the inside of the panel. They were spaced asymmetrically, located approximately where Qilin had pressed to dislodge the panel the previous night. She took hold of them and pressed down the little catches on them with her thumbs. The panel shifted loose with a click. As she struggled to keep it upright, footsteps approached. She nearly toppled forward as the panel pulled away from her, forcing her to release it. It slid to one side, revealing Qilin's smiling face. His sunlight-yellow complexion retained a youthful handsomeness despite his advanced age. His eyes were an early morning blue.

"I've prepared a bath for you," he said gesturing toward the steaming brass tub in the corner.

She gave him a dubious look. Did he really expect her—

"Don't worry. You'll have complete privacy," he assured her. "I'll be downstairs in the shop. Your breakfast is on the table, and I've left fresh clothes on the chair. My apologies again that your quarters are so cramped. I hope the mattress wasn't too uncomfortable."

"I slept well," she said, though it was probably mostly due to exhaustion rather than the comfort of her bed.

She listened to him thump down the stairs, then stripped off and dipped herself in the steaming bath. The warm water invited her to wallow in its embrace, but she forced herself out of it and quickly dried and dressed. While she had the place to herself, she should find out what she could about her host.

Most of the furniture was foreign and far too ornate to belong to a simple shopkeeper. Accounting ledgers lay neatly stacked on the desk. A pile of receipts was impaled on a brass spike. Neatly arranged quills shared a silver tray with an ornate silver ink pot. If Qilin wasn't wealthy, he certainly had expensive taste in furnishings.

The edge of a wooden box was visible under his bed. Her snooping instinct got the better of her. Dust tickled her nose as she dragged the box into the open, and made her sneeze. She glanced at the door and listened. No telltale thumps on the stairs suggested he had heard her. She undid the clasp and opened it. It contained carefully folded piles of gaudy clothes—the sort a courtesar might wear. She lifted the topmost tunic to the light. Dark brown patches of dried blood marked several rips and punctures. Beneath the garments, she found an ornate dueling blade, about a third of its blade shorn off, and a dagger.

Footsteps at the door. How had she not heard him climb the stairs? She started stuffing the clothes into the chest—too late. The door swung open. Drinith still grasped the tattered tunic; a shamefaced smile twitched upon her lips.

"I see you've found my old gear." Qilin looked amused, even a little flattered at her curiosity. "I was a courtesar long ago, but it's a young man's game. My meritocrat urged me to quit after a particularly bloody duel, so I took up an honest trade instead." A wistful gleam in his eyes tarnished his smile. "I have lived here ever since, forgotten."

"What happened to her?"

He winced. "I'd rather not talk about it."

A sunfinch fluttered down onto the windowsill.

Qilin clasped his hands together. "Thank all dragons, she's back! I always worry about my birds when I grant them liberty."

She thought this an odd practice and remarked: "Then why take such a risk?"

His reply, long in coming, had a note of caginess. "They deserve their freedom now and then, like their wild kin. They almost always return, to my great relief." He walked over to the window and rested a finger on the sill. The bird hopped over and, with a flutter of its wings, alighted on it. He carried her over to the cage, opened it just a fraction, and let her fly inside. "Such intelligent, loyal creatures. Courtesars are often dismissed as peacocks, but male sunfinches would better represent them."

"Sunfinches don't look much like fighters."

"You should see them in springtime. Males would happily peck their rivals to death with all the ferocity of lions. I have to be careful of my birds in the spring. Funny you should say that. You don't look like much of a fighter either, but by all accounts, such impressions are wrong. Breakfast?"

"Please."

He rummaged around a press and placed a kettle of water and a frying pan on the little stove. Drinith sat down at the table while he prepared their meal. As soon as he finished, he joined her, and they tucked into a soft morning tea and sliced yellow tea eggs on fat pancakes.

"I'm sure the fare isn't as good as you might find in your own mansion," he said. "Cooking was never my strength."

"They're very good," she assured him.

His delicate eyebrows curved upward. "Thank you. They're an old family recipe. At least, they're a recipe from my family's kitchen, supposedly passed from one cook to the next in an unbroken line stretching back to the Wealgiver's arrival on Gyre. It's one of the few mementos I retain from my past life. Courtesars aren't supposed to keep any possessions as such beyond their sword and the love of their sweetheart. Of course, it's nonsense really. We keep our allowance from our family—our so-called sword dowry. And, unless they're determined to end their lives on some rival's blade, most courtesars squirrel away a little something extra for when they put aside their bright plumage."

"Is that why you're part of this insurgency? Because the courtesars are treated unfairly?"

"I hated the meritocracy long before I quit being a courtesar. My meritocrat educated me. You must surely see the oppression in Gyran society. You view it from a stranger's perspective."

Drinith gave a polite nod. What government in this region of the Crevast wasn't oppressive? Qilin wasn't the fatherly sage he had appeared last night. He mightn't be a courtesar anymore, but the old idealism of his code remained, transformed, bent to the political ideals of his lost beloved. It was hard to put faith into such a quixotic character.

At the same time, Qilin wasn't a delusional madman. His colleagues had rescued Drinith. He was part of an organization, a senior member, if not its leader. And he might be very well her last hope.

His eyes narrowed. "Something wrong?"

"I'm just thinking about what you said last night," she said. The irony of her situation was not lost on her. Qilin's bloody campaign against the Meritocracy had made Drinith a renegade in the city she supposedly in part ruled. But her former meritocrat allies had cast her aside and, in the end, they never loved her. She was only a convenient instrument to further their ambitions, nothing more. She owed them no loyalty. Nonetheless, her stomach knotted at the significance of what she was about to say. "I'll help your insurrection, but I have one condition. You must help me rescue my friends from Inkeep. If you truly want to liberate Gyre, then start with them."

He pulled a face. "What you are asking for is next to impossible. Inkeep is built like four fortresses in one, making a direct assault utter folly. In the past, it has even withstood dragon attacks.

"And trying to gain entry through trickery is fraught with risk. A proscribed cult attempted to spring their leader from it a few months ago. The only survivor told me they tried to pass themselves off as cordents delivering a prisoner to gain entry. He stayed with the palanquin to mind the casquars while his comrades entered. The doors shut, and he never saw them again. They gave themselves away somehow." He shrugged. "They might have simply smelled wrong to the ratchers. Only they know for certain."

"I can't abandon my friends," Drinith insisted.

"I have friends I care about, too. You're asking me to risk their lives away on a fool's errand."

She slapped both hands on the table. She trembled with the urge to storm from the shop. Apparently, she had reached another dead end. "So that's it? You just abandon them to the Plank?"

Qilin spread his hands, palms upturned, in a helpless gesture. Drinith hadn't noticed until now that the third and fourth digits on his right hand were missing above their knuckles. Judging by how well the injury had healed, it hadn't been recent. "If you have a better plan..."

"Greny's the key," Drinith said. "If we could take him captive, we might be able to barter his freedom in exchange for my friends' release."

"It might work," Qilin conceded reluctantly. "At heart, he's always been a coward and the ratchers wouldn't dare risk his life. They'd release your friends to save him. We might secure the whole section. What an embarrassment that would be for the Meritocracy if Greny ended up as an inmate in his own prison!"

She caught a sudden spasm of discomfiture on his face before he turned toward the cage. He strolled over to it and tapped it gently, sending the birds within it aflutter.

"I will see what I can do," he said at length. "It may take...some time, but, yes, I can liberate your friends. And secure their escape from Gyre. But I expect something in return. I need proof of your dedication to our cause."

"You didn't appear to be in any doubt last night," Drinith observed sharply.

"I believe you are on our side, of course," Qilin said. "But more lives than mine depend on your good faith. I need you to do something that commits you to our cause, which puts you beyond any mercy the meritocrats might deign to grant."

This might be the only chance to free her friends, and the meritocrats had damned her already. But she hesitated. "What would this proof involve?" *Who do I have to kill?*

Qilin fed seeds to the birds through the bars. "I don't know exactly, yet. You must be patient."

Patient? She bowed her head to conceal a bitter smirk. Her friends' lives might depend on that irrevocable commitment, that covenant sealed in meritocratic blood.

Drinith tensed at the sudden tinkle of the shop doorbell, but Qilin looked unworried. "Relax, please. If our visitor posed any threat, the lookout outside would have burst into song. I'll go down and see who it is."

Despite his reassurance, she was on tenterhooks until he returned, grinning broadly. "Fantastic news! The meritocrats are turning on each other exactly as she predicted."

"Who is she?" Drinith asked.

"Doesn't matter," Qilin said. "For now, at least. The important thing is that another meritocrat was killed with no effort on our part! Ecethor Orom is dead."

Ecethor? Ecethor was so innocuous.... Yet Qilin looked so gleeful. Gods!

Reading Drinith's dismay, he instantly sobered; embarrassment colored his face. His hand jerked a fraction as if he might try to reach for her in a conciliatory gesture but thought better of it. His face hardened. He didn't like being judged, but Drinith couldn't hide her disgust.

"Don't feel sorry for Ecethor," he said. "Beneath her guise of frivolity, she was just as cutthroat as any other meritocrat. If you want to ever win your kingdom back, you'll need to toughen up. You'll have to make some unpleasant choices, sometimes against your moral inclinations."

Who was this has-been courtesar to lecture Drinith? She had spent her own life being hunted, forced into one terrible compromise after another to simply survive. She had been impelled to lie. She had killed. "I'm fully prepared to do what I must, thank you, but I won't take any pleasure in it. I thought you courtesars loved honor."

"There's nothing honorable about living a lie," Qilin said.

As if by unspoken agreement, they dropped the conversation and Qilin went about cleaning the birdcage.

They stewed in brooding silence until that evening. Even over their evening meal, they hardly exchanged a word aside from the occasional whispered thanks when a dish was passed.

Drinith rose from her chair as soon as she finished and announced, "I'm going to bed." She carried her plate and bowl over to the basin on a wooden table beside the stove and cleaned them in some water from the kettle.

"You can leave them," Qilin murmured. "I'll clean them afterward."

"It's all right," Drinith said, picking the plate out of the basin and drying it with a cloth. "They're nearly done."

"How did you sleep last night?"

"Fine, I suppose. I found it a little claustrophobic, to be honest."

"There's no need to shut yourself into the alcove," Qilin said. "Just leave the panel leaning against the hole. I'll click it in place if there's trouble. I always have a lookout stationed nearby. They'll start singing 'The Dragon's Call' if they spot any imminent threat."

No doubt, they'd also alert him if Drinith tried to leave, but for now, that didn't matter. She had no other place to go.

That night, when she finally fell asleep, she returned to Ophigee, the gloomy tunnels of the Whetstone. The boy, his face already livid with shock and terror at his own death, leaped out of the sepulchral gloom. Drinith stabbed him again as she had done in countless other dreams before. But this time, he emerged a second time, a third, and then a fourth. He poured toward her from the darkness, only to taste her pitiless spear again and again. Bodies piled like a wall around Drinith until she could no longer hold back the deluge of terrified faces, and it engulfed her.

She awoke with a start. At the creak of a floorboard, she peered out through the narrow gap between the panel and the wall. Qilin sat hunched over his desk. She couldn't tell what he was doing, but it involved precision, delicacy, and immense concentration. He leaned back and breathed deeply, resting from his labor, then hunched down again in perfect, intense silence. After some time, he took another gasping breath and stretched. After this cycle repeated twice, he rose and, holding a ring in one hand, opened the door of the cage, grabbed one of the fluttering birds within. Shutting the cage again, he manipulated the bird with both hands. *Obviously he had been composing a message—a miniscule one the ring could accommodate. What an extraordinary practice!* He kissed it, released it out the window, and it flapped away into the morning gloom. He must be using the birds to communicate with someone. But who?

32

An urgent squeak woke Greny. The hard tea he'd drunk the previous night had left him nursing a gnawing headache and a mouth that tasted like sewage. With bleary eyes, he looked about. Daylight streaming through the windows stabbed his eyeballs. He lay fully dressed in his own bed. A ratcher loomed over him—Deetch.

"What time is it?" Greny muttered, wincing as he attempted to rise. His innards felt packed with sludge.

Deetch signed that it was the second dayrise hour. So early. Greny rose and tried in vain to stretch away the stiffness wracking his body. That was the problem with hard tea. When it wore off, it left Greny feeling decrepit.

His hands still hurt from battering Ecethor's door. And Jarma's. Begging. Cajoling. Threatening. Memories flooded back unbidden, more stinging than the morning light. Thank all dragons, he had been so out of it he had forgotten that her door was locked from the outside. All he needed to do was to ask his ratcher companion for the key. Imagine if he had gained entry. Overcome by the hazy thinking and erratic passions brought on by too much hard tea, he'd have been helpless to her wiles. She could have made him her prisoner, or worse. In his befuddled state, he wouldn't even feel his throat being slit.

It doesn't matter, he assured himself, to quell the burning shame in his chest, *nobody outside the tower will ever know. The ratchers will tell no one, and as for poor Jarma, the Void swallows all secrets.*

He rubbed his hands down his face. His next meeting with her would be...awkward. He must be more careful around her. His attraction to her gave her a power over him. He mustn't yield to it. She would have to walk the Plank soon. It was an inevitability that she'd die.

Deetch signed that Nayz waited for him in the parlor. Having slept in his clothes and in no mood to expose himself to the dank air of the tower, Greny didn't bother to change and followed the ratcher downstairs.

Zetch and Treek loitered sheepishly outside the parlor. Greny acknowledged their timid chirps of salutation with a curt wave. As he entered the room, Nayz glared contemptuously at him.

"I hope you've come with some good news," Greny snarled.

"Meritocrat Ecethor is dead."

Greny collapsed into an armchair and stared dumbfounded at him. "I called to her home last night."

"I know," Nayz said severely. "*Everyone* knows. The gossipmongers' tongues have been flapping in earnest. You two had an altercation, they say."

"It was a matter between two meritocrats. It had nothing to do with the other murders, and it's none of your concern."

"You need to start telling me the truth, the whole truth, if you want to escape the Plank."

Greny leapt to his feet. "What's that supposed to mean?"

"You didn't tell me that Meritocrat Velso's butler, Jelsan Estin, had been a servant in your household."

"What sort of jest is this? The butler didn't much look like a ratcher to me."

"Jelsan was a servant girl in Scylax Tower in your mother's time."

Greny didn't remember her. "My mother had a lot of servants. So?"

"Some may say that you fired her and the other human servants so that they could enter other meritocratic households and act as your spies."

"What utter balderdash!" Greny exclaimed.

"It might be," Nayz conceded, "but there are those who are more than willing to believe it."

"You've been in my service for many years. You're intimate with my actual network of agents. Dragons, you help build it!"

"I know you have secrets, too," Nayz said. "Matters that you decline to share with me. You even conceal agents from me—the Gadfly Woad Glastum, for example."

Greny's hands hurt as he squeezed them into tight fists. "I should send you to Inkeep for this insubordination!"

The threat drew only a brazen smile from Nayz. "And draw unwelcome scrutiny from an already paranoid Meritocracy? I doubt it. If I were you, I'd be more worried about Cordent General Minol. She has already uncovered your connection to the butler."

"You told her."

Nayz shook his head. "I found out about Jelsan from her. She invited me to betray you. According to her, it was my duty as a loyal son of Gyre to testify against you."

"Why didn't you then?"

"Habit, I guess. I have served you faithfully for many years, despite your open contempt towards me. And I'm unconvinced of your guilt."

"That's generous of you," Greny said sarcastically.

"You can depend on me," Nayz said stiffly. "But Woad Glastum's elevation to cordent colonel has caused a lot of anger in the lower ranks. There's plenty who would happily take up Meritocrat Minol's offer."

That's exactly what a traitor would say. That's how he'd try to inveigle his way into his victim's confidence. Greny would have loved nothing better than to call Nayz a turncoat to his face, but he had to be cleverer than that. Let that ungrateful wretch think he had won him over. Greny made a nod that he hoped would appear grateful. "How did Ecethor die?"

"The rumor is she poisoned herself. I can't say for sure. The bluechecks have secured the mansion and they are keeping tight-lipped about the details."

Greny would have to talk to Posaleum directly. That meant pleading with her for information, humiliating himself before her. No doubt, she'd tell anyone who would listen that he had come to her like a beggar. All because Nayz hadn't the wit or initiative to beat the bluechecks to Ecethor's home. Or he had both, but chose not to use them to undermine his superior.

"Get out of my sight!" Greny snapped.

Nayz's shudder lasted the briefest instant. Staring at Greny in mute defiance, he saluted and stalked out of the room.

Greny massaged his scalp to relieve his growing tension headache.

"Deetch, fetch me tea!" he barked. "The strongest stuff we have." Even as he said it, he changed his mind. As much as he craved the consoling dreaminess of hard tea, he needed to keep his wits sharp. Opriet would help him. She was on his side, or at least claimed to be.

Deetch soon returned, but on his tray lay a black envelope. Greny groaned. It could only be a summons from the Iron Circle.

HE HURRIED through the paneled meeting rooms of the Parliament, the places where lesser committees carried out their business, each one indistinguishable from its neighbors except for the meritocrats who happened to loiter there. In one, three sat in a semicircle, examining a parchment. In another, two stood in a dark corner, exchanging whispers. Both groups fell silent and stared at Greny as he hurried past. Two more rooms were empty, while in the fifth, ancient Tival Ronad purred softly like a sleeping cat on one of the benches along the walls. Her eyelids lifted a fraction as he breezed past.

He hastened down the spiral staircase to the Chamber of Whispers. Inside, most of the other jurists were already seated around the table. Leca Monem, Drona Torn, and Egava Sipian had returned in haste from their missions. The two meritocrats who had been chosen to replace Thaxen and Osro also attended. The silver-haired Cicer Ziter, an ardent New War Factioneer, had planted herself in Greny's favored chair, much to his annoyance. The Short War Faction's most recent addition, Gafyso Olapsin, despite only receiving her emblem of merit the previous day, regarded him as if he was the newcomer. Dragons, she was so young! True, Greny had been her age when he had become a jurist, but he had done something to be worthy of joining the Jury. Gafyso owed her promotion to grubby compromises. Thespenilea was ensconced in the Steward's seat. Devaner, crumpled in the neighboring chair, looked sweaty and relieved.

He was so focused on the others' fearful and angry stares that Elca's fingernail, as sharp and strong as any knife, stabbing his chest took him by complete surprise.

"What is the meaning—" Greny spluttered.

"You gave me your word, Greny," Elca declared, her starry face severe with indignation. "You promised you would leave poor Ecethor alone, but you couldn't help yourself. I warned you she was as fragile as porcelain."

Surely Greny would remember if Elca had said that. Ecethor hadn't looked ready to take her own life. On the contrary, she had been afraid for it. Elca's violent anger must be for the benefit of their audience. She never let her emotions get the better of her. She had even inured herself to her previous banishment from the Iron Circle with superficial good grace.

"Have you nothing to say?" Elca demanded. "By all accounts, you were most talkative last night."

"Elca, sit down and let him speak," Thespenilea said coldly.

Greny grabbed the nearest free seat like a drowning man

clutching at a drifting log. Emotions ran so high, one misstep by him would be enough to turn this meeting into a trial.

Only Posaleum looked unconcerned as she twirled a golden feather.

"Was that found in Ecethor's house?" Greny asked.

Posaleum nodded with an infuriating, wry grin. "It was found in her hand."

"Then, her death wasn't an accident," Greny said, doing his best to throttle down his anger and sound reasonable. "She was assassinated like Cenmis and the others. Her murder should be part of my investigation."

Posaleum's slender eyebrows arched higher on her smooth forehead. "Why did you call on her last night?" She added conceitedly: "You were certainly determined to avoid being followed, all for naught. My spies tracked your every move."

"She asked me to visit. Then she changed her mind."

"That's not what her daughter said." Leaning back in her seat, Posaleum stroked the feather's vane with the tip of her finger. "According to her, Ecethor intended to go out that night."

"I'm sure she did." He shouldn't have misstated the nature of Ecethor's invitation. If the Jurists had him tested by truthscryers, that lie might well prove to be his undoing. "Ecethor might have told her that, but she asked me to call." He could feel himself being dragged toward the brink of self-incrimination. "A pair of truthscryers can easily corroborate that."

Panicked nays rippled around the table. Most of the Jurists were afraid of what he might say, what secrets his interrogation might reveal. They were like a pack of dogs encircling a bear, afraid to be the first to attack.

"That won't be necessary," Thespenilea said. Greny heard a phantom *yet*.

How much longer would his reputation for secrets protect him? "Then Posaleum can hand over whatever evidence she has gathered—"

"No," Posaleum snapped.

"That won't be necessary," Thespenilea said. "We've decided it would be better to run parallel investigations. You will continue to probe Drinith's connection to the murders, while Posaleum will explore other lines of inquiry. Hopefully, it will lead to more transparency in the investigation."

Greny should have been relieved at this reprieve, but he could only feel anger as he escaped the chamber. He couldn't endure this insult for long. He needed to find Drinith, put his loyalty beyond question. But how? Quiescat must know where she was hiding. If necessary, Greny would torture the Oracle to extract her location.

33

Drinith sat at the table, her chin resting on her palm. The bright chirping of Qilin's sunfinches chipped away at her patience. She was just as trapped in this city as these birds in their gilded prison. If only she could escape, leave all this behind. The exiled Rhumgadians in the city might be a lot safer if she left Gyre. The meritocrats would no longer regard them as an immediate threat. But she couldn't forsake Jarma or Quiescat or Perian or... Woad would have been the list had he not betrayed her. His treachery called into question Tazran's loyalty, too. She had been bound to Drinith by Woad's solemn promise to serve her.

She seemed beset by traitors—Fenvar, the odious Zin, and, of course, the greatest betrayer, Gelasin. Even Zoen had turned her back on Drinith after she had carried the girl out of the bowels of the Whetstone.

I need to stop dwelling on things I can't change! She picked up the slim booklet that Qilin had encouraged her to read, an anonymous manifesto perhaps fifty pages long. The gentle depressions in the soft leather cover reminded her of fingerprints. It opened naturally midway through. To her surprise, the text was not professionally printed, but rather handwritten scrawl. She read a passage to herself:

"The story of Gyre is not one of destiny but of happenstance. Had the Emperor of the Crevast not disappeared, Olmpeda Wealgiver might have never sought a new home for the crews of her seven dragons. Had a storm not forced them to shelter on the archipelago, she might have never settled here. If she and her descendants been less prone to bear daughters, and her only three male successors had not been ineffective, reckless, and short-lived, the custom of female primogeniture might never have become established. If Karis the First and Last had been less of a tyrannical monster, if she had not convinced herself of her immortality and murdered her own children to prevent them threatening her eternal reign, the institution of monarchy might have never plummeted with her into the Void.

"Fear held the nascent republic together—at first, of would-be tyrants among the meritocrats themselves and later, of the Emperors of Noster. Had Hevis V not fallen for the then Ducalion, Emenis Braesum, and replaced her with a Nosteran governor, Gyre might've become merely a regular province in his empire. The republic might have never had the opportunity to experience its second flowering of independence.

"Many assert as axiomatic that the Nosteran Empire's decline and the rise of Gyre were bound to happen. However, the meritocrats of the period we remember as the Vassalage never contemplated such a dramatic change in fortunes. They believed the Nosteran Empire to be as permanent as the suns and moons. None of them could have conceived the sequence of events that led to its contraction into a single city ruled by emperors only in name. They never imagined that one bloody day their descendants would conquer that city and slay the last Mock Emperor.

"The hegemony of Gyre and its four rival republics over Noster now appears as unassailable as that of the empire they destroyed. Gyre's institutions and traditions, too, look as impregnable as the stout yellow walls of the Ducal Palace. They have become in the minds of Gyrans a self-evident natural order. In truth, they are no stronger than a thought. They are as ephemeral as a dream that evaporates on waking. Don't surrender to despair! If you have already read this far, if you have heeded my message, you have woken. Others will wake too."

Drinith drew comfort from the passage, but she was thinking of her own struggle with Magian. His invincibility might yet prove equally illusory.

"I see you're reading the book."

Drinith jerked, catching the booklet before it fell from her fingers. *Damn his feline stealth! I must be more alert in the future.*

"Who wrote this?" Drinith asked, brandishing the book.

Hesitation again, a reflexive doubt about his guest. "The leader of the Silverfish Revolt, Ricoen Zurin."

"Never heard of her."

"Of course you haven't." He sauntered over to the stove. "One of the Meritocracy's greatest tools is silence. They plaster over the cracks in their granitic edifice with it. Ricoen came the closest since Hevis V to tearing the Meritocracy down. She woke up the common folk and led them to Crimson Plaza to demand a better government." He placed a bowl of yellow tea in front of Drinith; she glanced at it disinterestedly. Sitting across from her, he held his own bowl with both hands, studying the yellow pool as though he was about to jump into it.

"I remember that day so well." He sipped the tea. "A rumor spread that the Dragon Keeper was about to release her dragons on us, but Ricoen's soaring voice held the crowd and calmed them. Cordents attempted to encircle us, but it quickly became apparent they hadn't the numbers to do so. Many of them ignored their superiors' orders or even openly joined us. The Parliament was like an oyster, and Ricoen was the knife jammed between its valves, ready to pry it open. Yes, it was quite a day."

He inhaled a deep, nasal breath. "We were so close to succeeding, you could smell victory, you could taste it on the air. And then it all fell apart. I was tricked into betraying her."

With misting eyes, he took another gulp and winced. "I was a fool, a damned fool, a naive courtesar, too trusting, too besotted with honor. By convincing her to negotiate, I put her into the hands of our enemies. I didn't realize it at the time. None of us did. We thought we had won. We ended up celebrating our defeat, our utter vanquishment, singing and chanting through the night and into the next day. All the while, the meritocrats held Ricoen as their prisoner, no doubt laughing at our folly while they waited for us to exhaust ourselves and disperse."

"And what happened to Ricoen?" Drinith asked gently, despite guessing the answer. The Void had probably swallowed her.

Qilin expanded his chest and tensed as if about to leap from a great height. "They made her Ducalion."

34

With the scroll clutched tightly in his hand, Greny entered the cell after the screaming stopped. The Oracle lay insensate on the floor, black drool trickling from the corner of his mouth. Greny knelt beside him and wiped it away.

"I hope you didn't kill him," Greny said nervously, bending his ear close to Quiescat's mouth to listen for breath. The ratchers exchanged nervous glances. "If he's dead, there'll be Empyrosis to pay."

A faint movement of air tickled his earlobe. Needing further proof Quiescat yet lived, he pressed his ear against the Oracle's chest. Yes, there was a heartbeat, strong and slow. Greny struggled to rise to his feet. "Help me up," he said, reaching out to the warden, Mileek, who quickly obliged. Another ratcher, Riskeel, was trying to rub off black spatters on the floor and walls with a dirty rag.

"I hope you haven't given him too much immemorial." Frowning in disgust, Greny unfurled his handkerchief and dabbed the tarry black residue from his knees. Force-feeding prisoners the amnesiac was a messy and dangerous business.

While the ratchers carried the insensate man from the cell, Greny grabbed the black stool in the corner and sat down. The round seat was hard and tilted to one side. A stained pillow jutted from the mess of filthy blankets on the bed like a stuck-out tongue. How many prisoners had passed through this cell since the bedclothes had been changed last? Ratchers were prone to slovenliness about such matters.

Greny retrieved the stick of chalk off the floor. He had been wise to agree to the Quiescat's pleas for a writing instrument. Lines of symbolic characters tattooed the shadowy back wall.

"Mileek, bring a light," Greny yelled.

With a squeak of acknowledgment, the warden carried in a torch. Its light filled the cell, revealing the white writing scrawled on the wall. The pyratic glyphs were shakily drawn but still readable. Greny unrolled the scroll and used the fresh version of the prophecy to amend the errors in his transcription from the previous cell Quiescat had been incarcerated in.

I write gibberish symbols in red on an endless scroll. My quill runs dry. I use the wound in my chest to refill it. The sound of tearing paper makes me look up. The scroll festoons the sky, forming a gigantic web. Three shadows move across it like a three-legged spider until they settle around Drinith. Dressed as a bride, she struggles against invisible bonds. I move toward her on unseen wings. Gold symbols run down her face like tears. I rub one away, and it burns my fingers. I look around and the whole web is aflame. I turn back to Drinith, but she's gone. Everything has disappeared and the Crevast stretches before me in all directions. I spot a glinting object hurtling downward. Distance makes me mistake a screaming woman for a twittering bird at first. Massive black dragon jaws emerge from the clouds and swallow her.

QUIESCAT WAS OBVIOUSLY OBSESSED with this passage. Not only had he written it twice, but he had stared at it both times for hours as a mathematician might puzzle over an intriguing equation. Greny could not deny a creeping dread. He had already wasted two days on this enigmatic message. If the Oracle of Godsdoor could not divine its meaning, what chance had Greny of doing so? And yet the prophecy consumed him, too. He hadn't been able to think of anything else since he first read it.

What could the endless scroll represent, or the three-legged spider? Could the latter be him? He was hunting Drinith. But why was she dressed as a bride? Quiescat flew toward her on wings, and he mistook the cries of the falling woman for birdsong. Could these images be connected to the dead sunfinch, and the gold feathers left to taunt the cordents?

This perplexing parade of images might be simply a clever ruse on Quiescat's part to drive Greny to distraction. The Oracle might be toying with his captor. And yet, if this was some sort of trick, how had his scheme survived his memory wipe?

Rolling up his parchment, Greny exited the cell and entered the neighboring one where Quiescat had been rehoused. Mileek provided a stool for Greny to sit on while he waited for the Oracle to regain consciousness. It amused Greny that the ratcher stood behind him, cudgel in hand to ward off the Oracle should he attack. The thought of this wizened stick of a man resorting to physical violence was ludicrous. *I could best the old seer with ease,* Greny flattered himself.

Quiescat spluttered awake. He blinked, revealing his peculiar crystal eyes. He looked about, fixed a confused gaze on Greny. "Where am I? What am I doing here?"

"Do you remember what day it is?" Greny asked.

Quiescat paused mid-rise, his eyebrows flexing upward in confusion, then sank back down on the bed. "I'm not sure."

"What was the last thing you remember?"

Quiescat scowled. "Being dragged into this infernal prison. Why did you arrest me? Where's Drinith?"

"Drinith has been kidnapped," Greny said.

"Gods! Why? How?" The Oracle's stricken look shifted again to anger. "This is your doing. You sent her to visit Osro Onez. You're involved in this mess somehow. That's why you arrested me."

"You were in danger. I took you into protective custody. That is all. We don't know who kidnapped Drinith or why yet, but she gave me this before she disappeared. Do you know what it means?"

As Quiescat examined the parchment, his eyes rounded. He clutched it in both hands. "How did you get this?"

"Like I said, she gave it to me. She said it was important."

"It's the third prophetic vision of my...predecessor, Versifer. His two earlier prophesies came to pass, so this one is likely to be fulfilled next. As for its meaning, your guess is as good as mine. I only deciphered the previous visions in retrospect. I fear this one might be the same."

"Well, you must decode it as soon as possible. Drinith's life may depend on it."

"It's not that simple!" Quiescat shouted, springing to his feet. His outburst prompted Mileek to draw a fraction closer to Greny. Quiescat sat again, and after composing himself continued in a softer tone: "I partially decoded a previous prophesy predicting Drinith's visit to Ophigee only by observing the Halo Sea's similarity to a cauldron. Frankly, I doubt it's possible to unravel the third prophesy from the words alone. I need clues, prompts if you will, to work with."

This might be a clever trick to access information about the world beyond his cell, Greny mused. *Still, no harm in playing along.* Greny outlined almost everything that had happened, changing only details that might portray him in a bad light, like the raid of Hax Mansion and the attempted arrest of Drinith in Wealgiver Street.

Quiescat rubbed the back of his neck. "The dead sunfinch and the feathers chime with parts of the vision. I know they're the only birds native to the Gyran archipelago, and for that reason are Gyre's emblem. But do sunfinches have any symbolic significance I'm not aware of?"

"Well, they are considered the Ducalion's property," Greny replied. "Injuring them or disturbing their nests during the mating season without the Ducal Steward's permission is a crime punishable by ten lashes, but a few meritocratic families and individuals quietly keep them as pets."

Greny had an epiphany: *like my brother!*

No no no. The idea is preposterous. Erphel couldn't have had a part in these murders. He's much too honorable, too much in love with the Courtesar Code and all that nonsense. And he would never put his beloved in danger. He has lived as an anonymous recluse for years, cut off from meritocratic politics to protect her.

Greny sprang to his feet and rushed toward the door. "I must go."

"Why?" Quiescat's eyes widened with sudden comprehension. "You've realized something, haven't you? *Haven't you?*"

Suddenly the Oracle leapt up and, seizing Greny's arm with both hands, swung him around so they faced each other. Shying from Quiescat's desperate, inhuman stare, Greny wrenched his arm free as Mileek attempted to force the Oracle back down on the bed.

Greny dashed out the door and barred it shut just as Quiescat tore free of the ratcher. Grabbing the grilled hatch in the door, he pressed his face against the bars, his crystal eyes aglitter in the torchlight. "What do you know?"

Greny slapped the cover over the hatch. In truth, he knew nothing, and he felt embarrassed even suspecting his brother.

"Tell me!" The hatch failed to muffle Quiescat's plea.

Even the thought felt like a slight on Erphel's character. The brothers had never been close, and after the incarceration of Erphel's lover in the Ducal Palace, Greny had been warned to avoid him. Nonetheless, some strange yearning gripped to visit him now—guilt perhaps, or loneliness, Greny couldn't tell.

35

Something was wrong. Qilin remained as pleasant as ever, but a twitchiness had crept into his manner. At every flutter of wings outside, his eyes fixed on the window only to turn away again, downcast with worry and disappointment.

Around noon, he sent Drinith back to her secret room, sealing her inside this time. When he finally released her, she noticed there was one less bird in the cage.

His mood deteriorated throughout the afternoon. He couldn't stay still for long. Conversation quickly faltered owing to his distraction. His unease turned to dread. She felt powerless to help him, given she wasn't supposed to know the birds' purpose.

It was a relief when he disappeared downstairs. As a diversion, she dug out a book of Rhumgadian history from the shelf in the alcove. The leather-bound cover was old and battered, the pages dusty, their edges foxed. It creaked as she opened it. A giddy excitement gripped her as she recognized the script—not Pyratic, but High Dremic, the language of her homeland, Kaplar.

She turned a couple of stiff pages. Almost lost in the ornamentation at the top was a name—Dreneth—the masculine version of hers. Dreneth Skycarver was her direct ancestor, the founder of her dynasty. Here it was, his story, and the history of his successors. With a trembling hand, she turned to the back. It ended at the succession of her great-grandfather, Hemrath Bastion. She turned back to Dreneth Skycarver's chapter.

She knew this story, or at least its bones. Quiescat had taught her. And yet as she read, a queasy horror gripped her. Of course, Kaplar had been an empire once, and even claimed the title when it had shrunken to a small kingdom. She knew of its conquests, but the brutality of them had never been laid bare to her before. What was the difference between her ancestors and the usurper she sought to overthrow?

A great weight of dismay and shame pressed down on her chest. Reading the book was like wading across of a mire of gore and corpses. She forced herself to finish Dreneth Skycarver's chapter, but the cruelties of his successor, Kelneth Godly, proved to be even harder to stomach.

The triumphalism with which all these barbarities were recounted sickened her. She tried to convince herself this book must be propaganda written to discredit the House of Kaplar. But turning to the foreword, she realized this was idle fancy. The author proclaimed he had written the tome to honor her great-grandfather. Imagine Hemrath Bastion or his successors, Drinith's grandfather and father, taking pride in this vile butchery. Did her people even notice a difference between Magian and her father?

She slammed it shut in disgust and pressed her hands to her cheeks. If there had been an open fire nearby, she would have gladly burned it. Why hadn't Quiescat told her? He had raised her on half-truths and lies. He had prettied and simplified her family's history. Even he had betrayed her.

She opened the book again, desperate to find some glint of redemption amid the horror.

"Something not your liking?"

She jumped. Qilin was standing at the far side of the table. Again, to her great irritation, his featherlight steps had taken her by surprise.

"This book," she said, a mite breathlessly. "It horrifies me. The Blood Crown of Kaplar was bloodier than I ever imagined."

"It's no more terrible than the history of Gyre," he said.

"It is to me." *Because it is my history. To think I've idolized these tyrants and murderers!*

"No sign of any sunfinches?" he asked casually.

She shook her head.

He stole a glance at the window, then rubbed his careworn face. "You mustn't blame yourself for your ancestors' sins."

"But it's been my mission to perpetuate their legacy."

"You are your own person. Never forget that. You're not obliged to be like them. You don't owe them anything. You don't have to be a princess, or a meritocrat, for that matter."

"And if I was neither, what use would I be to your revolution?" *I am used by everyone for their own ends—Qilin, Greny, Gelasin, the Meritocracy, and even Quiescat.*

He hesitated, unsure how to answer. "It is true that your unique position provides some advantages. Without them, you'd still have a role—less exalted perhaps. Or maybe you think that's beneath you?"

"I've made a lot of sacrifices to be here," she said.

"So have I. Your ancestors might have said the same."

They both turned toward a flutter at the window, but the sill was empty. Qilin tapped the table with his fist.

Since they both appeared to be in the mood for hard truths... "Have your messenger birds gone missing before?" she asked.

His face jolted with surprise. "So you know?"

Drinith raised one eyebrow. "You are not the only master of stealth."

Qilin allowed himself a chuckle, the first token of mirth she'd heard. It had a musical ring she appreciated. "It has happened a few times, but never to consecutive birds. I've never gone so long without one of them returning."

He glanced at the cage. "I'm nervous about sending another. If I lose them all, I'll be effectively cut off from *her*." His beloved was

Ricoen Zurin, the Ducalion, trapped in the Ducal Palace, under constant surveillance by those who purported to serve her.

He strode over to the window and, planting both fists on the sill, bowed his head. "It's been so long since I spoke to her, since I held her in my arms. The birds feel like prayers to the land of the dead. If I ever truly lost her…"

"There must be some other way to communicate," Drinith said.

His fingers quivered as he stroked his jaw. "There's a route by which she sends me replacement birds, but it's somewhat precarious and only works in one direction." A bleak smile briefly curled his lips. "Usually, I use a bird to request them." He shrugged. "This delay is probably not as sinister as it seems. She could be busy. I'll be patient a little longer. If no bird arrives by eventide, I'll send another. I'll prepare the message now, just in case."

He strode over to his desk and, with a tweezer, removed a tiny square of translucent parchment from a small pot and fixed it on a sticky pad. "I'll write the message in code on this and attach it to the inside of the bird's leg ring. Should the bird come to some tragic end, the message is liable to come unstuck and go unnoticed by third parties." He swung his magnifying glass over it and readied a fine brush. "Apologies in advance. I won't be able to talk while I am writing, or breathe for that matter. I ask that you do nothing to distract me. It's an arduous process to write one of these messages. It's fortunate that my training as a courtesar has given me a steady hand."

His hand wasn't so steady earlier. "I won't disturb you."

He gave a nod in thanks, then sucked in a breath. She sat completely still, wary that the slightest movement might distract him. She might as well be sitting for a portrait, though the artist in this case had no thought of her. His attention was focused on his love imprisoned in the Ducal Palace.

The first bell of eventide rang, but no bird returned. Qilin carefully folded the paper in four, brushed it in a clear resin, and attached it to the inside of a bone-white ring. After waiting a while for the resin to dry, he took a bird from the cage, its head peeping with apparent indifference from between his fingers, and put the ring on its leg. With a kiss on its head, he released it out the window. Drinith watched it fly over the rooftops until it faded into the evening gloom.

"It must work this time," Qilin murmured.

"Why do you have a history of the Kaplar Empire?" Drinith asked.

"You intrigued me from when you first arrived in the city. I wanted to understand you through your ancestors, but I was wrong. They are nothing like you."

Thank the gods! To think she had always put them on a pedestal.

"I discovered a passion for reading histories," Qilin said. "Courtesars generally frown upon reading. It's not considered a masculine pursuit. Of course, any member of a meritocratic house must be able to read. And it's important to take pride in your family history. But reading for simple pleasure seemed a waste of time in those fervid days of my youth. Time, past or future, only extended as far as the reach of your blade. Every day throbbed with violent passion because it could be your last."

"You sound like you miss it."

"I miss the simplicity, the sense of bold purpose, the camaraderie. I miss *her*." He glanced at the window. "It's going to be a long night."

36

The last time Greny had smelled anything so foul, he had been down in the sewers. How could people live in these cramped, crud-caked lanes? The Crannies were worse than the Blue Quarter! The Gadflies had it good in comparison. Might as well make a home in a chamber pot as this filthy place! He shielded his emblem of merit with one hand, lest it be stained by the fat water drops raining down from the clothes hanging like dead men from a web of lines high above him. It was like living in the bowels of a cave in this perpetual gloom.

A clutch of men and women paddled clothes around a fountain in a small open space. A seedy character, shabbily dressed and badly in need of a bath, sitting on the rim impetuously decided to entertain them with an irritating shanty, the sort drakers sing when drink makes them boisterous or melancholy. This one—called "The Dragon's Call," if Greny weren't mistaken—had the traditional call-and-response structure, but the vocalist had to sing the refrain alone a couple of times before his audience joined in.

> *The land's dead beneath my feet*
> *Its air's as sour as a corpse's fart*
> I was born for scales and sails
> This land's no place for me!
> *The Crevast's sweet, sweet winds call*
> *Dragons' roars quicken my heart*
> I was born for scales and sails
> This land's no place for me!

GRENY FOUGHT the strong urge to shove the instigator of this caterwauling into the fountain. If there had been any cordents around, he would have had him arrested for disturbing the peace.

The vaguely feminine statue gushing water into the dirty pool must have been impressive long ago, but much of its detail had worn away. The figure's lower jaw was gone, and a red stain descended from what was left of its mouth down its front. It might have represented a hero of the republic or someone simply popular among her peers, or it could have been an act of self-aggrandizement. Now it was just an anonymous lump of stone.

A shop front faced it, its red paint cracked and peeling, the open book above its door stripped by the elements of most of its gilding. As Greny approached the shop, some washers paused to watch him. No, it was his ratcher escorts that drew their gaze. Doubtless, they probably had never seen ratchers around here before.

Greny placed his hand against the door, hesitated as he braced for his brother's contempt. "Kleest and Dweed, wait here," he said as he pushed it open. "Chemp, Queek, come with me."

SOMEWHERE OUTSIDE, several voices sang a familiar and rousing ditty.

They say the world's an egg
And the inner sun's a yolk
I was born for scales and sails
The land's no place for me!
If I'm not on the wing soon
I'll have drunk myself stony broke
I was born for scales and sails
The land's no place for me!

"'IT'S 'THE DRAGON'S CALL'!" Qilin rushed to the window and peered out. "He's here, he's here!" He turned toward her, his face drained of color. "Into the alcove, quickly!"

The pressure of Qilin's hand against Drinith's back hastened her into the compartment. Qilin grasped the panel to slide it into position, changed his mind. Rushing over to his bed, he threw open his case and rummaged through it. Drinith didn't see what he removed until he thrust it into her hand—the sheathed dagger.

"Your test may have arrived much sooner than either of us expected," he said, his voice trembling with panic.

"What's happened?" she asked, but he slammed the panel in place without answering.

BOOKS PACKED EVERY SHELF INSIDE. The shop was imbued with a florid scent reminiscent of a courtesar perfume popular in Greny's youth. His brother, Erphel, on the far side of the counter, looked up from a tome and regarded him with distaste. Like his premises, he had seen better days. The years had taken their toll on the former courtesar. His fiery red hair had grayed and thinned. Lines fissured his once smooth face and even his formerly bright yellow complexion had dull, custardy pallor. The famed "love spot" on his neck that had attracted such attention from his female admirers had turned ashen. In his dowdy clothes, he looked every bit a shopkeep.

"They are not allowed in here," Erphel said darkly, slapping his book shut and pointing at Chemp and Queek.

"In different circumstances, I might have agreed to your preferences, but..."

Erphel sighed in resignation. "Very well, they can stay. What in Empyrosis's fiery bowels do you want?"

"I thought I'd drop by and see how you're doing, Erphel."

"I'm not named that anymore."

"I forgot you put away your name when you put away your sword. What's the name you go by now? Kiln? Kelen?"

"Qilin Pine."

"Pine, eh? Very apt." Greny brushed his hand against the spines on the nearest shelf. He rubbed the tips of his fingers with his thumb though no dust clung to them, smiling at the thought of Erphel exchanging his sword for a duster. "You'd sell more books if your shop was in a better location."

"This area suits me fine. I have enough customers to get by."

And a generous sword dowry, guaranteed for your lifetime by our mother. "I'm glad to hear you're doing so well."

Erphel folded his arms below his scowl. "Why did you come here really? It must be nearly twenty years since we last spoke."

"I had a hankering to visit my elder brother. Is that so wrong?"

"You never attend our sister's anniversary prayer at the crypt."

"No, but I paid for it," Greny said. No doubt Erphel had fond memories of his twin, but to Greny she had always been just a name on a plaque. "And you never attend Mother's." It was a calculated guess. Greny didn't either. He had spent more than enough time as a child in that miserable place, listening to her mother's sobbing echo through the vault.

"Do you know why our mother picked you to succeed her?" Erphel taunted. "She knew you wouldn't survive for a day as a courtesar."

"And you'd make a terrible meritocrat." *Too besotted with your honor.*

"I think we're both even on that score. Don't you?"

"I don't know about your sword, but your tongue is as sharp as ever," Greny said. "At any rate, I didn't come here to bandy insults and open up old wounds. I need your help. Thaxen, Osro, and Cenmis are dead." He paused for effect. "You don't look very surprised."

Erphel sneered. "Everyone in the city knows. The crowd washing their clothes in the fountain have been chatting about that and the riot for days. Do you really think nobody but your meritocratic friends would take notice of such events?"

"You don't seem too upset about their deaths, either."

"Why should I? They turned their backs on me when I needed them. You all did."

"That's the problem with you courtesars. You imagine everything is so simple. You very nearly lost her, you know."

The surprise on Erphel's face quickly turned to anger. "I did lose her. She's locked up in that gilded prison."

"I mean, you could have lost her to the Void. Osro, in particular, did her best to save her." *As did I, for all the thanks I got.*

"I'm sure she did," Erphel muttered. "So much so that Osro devoted her life to being Ricoen's jailer. I'm sure you all had a good laugh at the irony of tricking her into taking the Ducal Crown. Don't deny it! Don't pretend you acted out of compassion, either. Ricoen's popularity among the commoners saved her. You were afraid of them."

"After your beloved entered the Ducal Palace, they soon forgot her, and she forgot you."

Erphel's lips twisted into a contemptuous smirk. "If only I could do the same to you. You hardly came here to reminisce about this ancient history."

"I'm trying to find their murderer."

"I thought it was Drinith Hax."

"She's a suspect, yes, but she's not my sole line of inquiry. The clues I have so far are a dead sunfinch and a couple of golden feathers. I remembered you used to keep them as pets."

"You think I'm the murderer?"

"Of course not. I just thought if you still kept them, you might know others with the same interest."

"Was the bird male or female?"

Greny blushed. "I didn't think to look."

"If it has a crest, it's a male. They're more flamboyant than the female."

"Then it was a female."

"Any other distinguishing features?"

"Not really. Can they be trained to send messages?"

"They are a bit small to carry letters," Erphel said with a derisive chuckle. "Why do you ask? Did you find a message on one?"

"A ring made of bone. It has been suggested that a message might have been attached to it."

"What a fanciful notion! I don't know anyone else who keeps them. They are the legal property of the Ducalion, remember? I only got away with my pets because I didn't cage them. They just became attached to me. They're not particularly intelligent birds and struggle to learn the simplest tricks. The idea that someone could successfully train them to deliver messages is preposterous."

"Funny, I remember them being rather clever birds. At least you seemed to be able to make them obey your commands."

"Your memory is playing tricks on you, Greny. They landed in my hand or on my shoulder if I placed a treat on it. I'm sorry I couldn't be more help." Erphel cleared his throat. "There's a good teahouse nearby. Do you want to grab a bowl with me? My treat."

It was the first time Erphel had spoken to him like a brother since their mother made Greny her meritorian. But Greny didn't trust the strange, bright joy expanding in his chest. And there were murders to solve. He could feel the weight of the Meritocracy's expectation pushing him toward the exit. "Another time perhaps."

"Give me some warning, next time," Erphel said, "and I'll prepare a better welcome."

"I'll do that," Greny promised, heading out of the shop. Chemp exited ahead of him, Queek after.

As soon as Greny stepped outside, he changed his mind about the tea, but the door locked and Greny didn't fancy being seen pleading to re-enter. He resolved to call again another day when he hadn't four murders dangling over him.

37

Drinith held her breath as the panel clicked and slid away. Qilin looked so utterly downcast that she couldn't help but feel sorry for him. "Who was that?"

Qilin's thin smile only accented the bleakness of his demeanor. "A ghost from my past determined to haunt me." He hesitated. "The Rat King himself, no less."

Drinith gaped in astonishment. "Greny Scylax was here?" As she absorbed the revelation, her stupefaction turned to anger. "We could have grabbed him here and now, rescued my friends! Maybe ended this nightmare! Why did you not seize him?"

His placating gesture had the opposite effect. "A moment, please."

"I could have put your lingering doubts about me to rest," she said tartly.

"Let me explain," he said with vexing patience.

"Do you really trust me so little that you'd prefer to let him walk out your door than rely on my help?" She was trembling with anger.

"Of course I trust you, but he had two ratchers with him and another pair just outside. We couldn't possibly take on that number by ourselves." His gaze slid toward the cage. "And we had no plan—"

"We have a plan!" she insisted. "But you'd rather dither until your beloved gives her approval!"

"Please, Drinith, you're being too loud."

"And I shall only get louder! Don't you understand, my friends might be walking the Plank at this very moment! Coward!"

He ignored her invective, remained exasperatingly calm. "Please, someone outside might hear you. Some of the ratchers may be still nearby. They have incredibly sensitive hearing."

She threw up her hands in mute frustration. He gestured toward the table. They sat side by side, facing the birdcage. Qilin rested his clasped hands upon it and stared at them in abject silence. Drinith's gut hurt as though it had been physically kicked. Her cooling temper left her spent and deeply embarrassed by her outburst. "I am sorry," she said, and laid a gentle hand on Qilin's shoulder. She was apologizing as much to her friends in Inkeep as to her host.

"You really aren't one of them. A meritocrat, I mean," Qilin said. "I appreciate this situation has been very trying for you."

"You have a gift for understatement. Any day now, my friends might be executed and all I do is hide in the wall like a..." She was about to say *rat*. A sudden thought struck her, a question so obvious, she should have already asked it. "Why would Greny visit your shop, of all places?"

Qilin contemplated his hands as he fashioned them into a steeple. "He is my younger brother."

Drinith gasped. "And you don't bother to mention this vital information until now."

"He and I have been estranged for many years." Qilin's nostrils flared in disgust. "There's nobody in Gyre I despise more than Greny Scylax." He spat the name as he pulled back his shirt to reveal a double-headed axe tattooed on his chest. "This is the true emblem of our family, not his wheel of rats." Drinith glimpsed a second sigil, the Zurin spiral-horned lion beside the axe. "My mother foolishly made him her successor, and after she died, he trashed all that she had held dear. He banished servants who had faithfully served my family for generations and packed our tower with his disgusting man-rodents. He tricked me into helping him imprison the woman I loved."

"So why did he turn up in your shop today?"

Massaging his forehead, Qilin groaned. "A stupid error on my part. It appears that I was a little too clever in picking the symbol for our group. I never imagined my dear brother would remember I kept sunfinches. He never struck me as the sentimental sort." Qilin smirked. "Not to worry, he just dropped by to seek my expert advice. He doesn't suspect me. To him, I'm merely a ghost from his past."

"I hope you're right," Drinith said. She wasn't so sure that he was.

"Believe me, if he had even a scintilla of suspicion that I was in any way involved, he'd have turned up here not with just a few ratchers, but with every yellowcheck in Gyre."

"Nevertheless, he is groping in your direction. We can't simply sit here and wait for him to connect you to the feathers. Time may run out for both of us very soon. We need to strike now while we still can."

While she spoke, Qilin had strolled over to the open window. He peered outside, his hands on its sill. He made a little trilling sound of enticement. There was no answer.

"Some revolution indeed to be stymied by a missing bird," Drinith groused.

"More than one bird is missing," Qilin said. "I understand your impatience. I know only too well the fear you have for your friends. I have lived with it every day for twenty years. Ricoen wouldn't even receive a trial if the Iron Circle discovered her part in this plot. They can simply poison her at any time of their choosing. If a nameless Ducalion passed away in her sleep, what of it?"

> *"They say the world's an egg,*
> *And the inner sun's a yolk..."*

"Quick, hide!" Qilin said. Drinith raced for the alcove.

As she clicked the panel into place, the shop bell tinkled downstairs. Heavy tomes spilled thunderously from the shelves.

Boots stamped up the stairs. "Cordents! Don't resist! We're here to search the premises!" More noise of ransacking. Something heavy thudded against the floor, shattered.

"I hope you're going to pay for that," Qilin said calmly.

"Certainly. Send me the bill," said the captain. His remark fetched a few derisive snorts and titters. Drinith pressed her ear against the panel.

"What are you looking for?" Qilin asked, again calm.

"You'll know when we find it." The sunfinches burst into panicked twittering and flapping. "Pretty birds."

"Leave them alone. Please."

The cage crashed against the floor. The birds screeched in terror.

"You didn't have to do that." Qilin's voice trembled with panic. If those birds died—

A knock against the panel. Drinith staggered backward, spine tingling. She slipped her knife from its sheath. She dared not breathe.

Another knock, then another. Drinith shuddered. *They must surely hear the hollowness on the far side.* Somebody murmured. Drinith grabbed her bedding and pressed it against the panel. Exploratory raps on the panel and farther along the wall. *The cordents must be comparing the sound.*

"I don't want any trouble," Qilin said. "I'm just a humble shopkeeper these days."

"These days, you say? What were you before?"

"A courtesar of Scylax."

"It's a crime to falsely claim to belong to a meritocratic family."

"Indeed. I'll warn my brother, Greny Scylax."

The rapping ceased.

"W-we meant no offense, b-but we have our orders."

"Of course, Cordent." Qilin's tone dripped with contempt. "Did your orders include smashing up my shop and damaging gifts from my brother?"

A hesitant silence. "N-no."

"Then finish what you have been ordered to do and leave me be."

"Of course," the captain mumbled. He addressed his cordents.

"Pick up that cage and make sure everything is returned to its proper place."

The rapping continued, as did the searching, but without the same violent fervor.

"It's unusual for retired courtesars to become booksellers, isn't it?" the captain observed, his newfound amiability creaking with unease.

Flapping wings set off cries from the cordents and shifting furniture.

"No!" Qilin yelled.

"You fool!" the captain snapped. "Why did you do that?"

"It attacked me," a female cordent pleaded.

"Pick it up off the floor before it marks the carpet!" the captain commanded.

"Leave it!" Qilin snarled. "I'll take care of it myself."

"As you wish," the captain said. "Are we finished here?" His question drew affirmative grunts from his team. "We'll leave you in peace, then. My apologies about your pet."

Drinith listened to them trundle down the stairs. The tinkle of the shop bell announced their departure.

At Qilin's call, Drinith removed the panel and reemerged into the room. He was crawling on his hands and knees, his desperate gaze fixed searchingly on the floor. He pointed vaguely at the table without glancing up. A dead bird and a bone-white ring lay on it. "The cordents are gone. And so is the reply from my beloved. It must have been dislodged when the cordent swatted the bird. Help me find it."

Both of them crept across the floor, scrutinizing every inch for the missing note. As the search dragged on, Drinith watched Qilin's quiet desperation turn to despair. One of the cordents might have mashed it into the carpet or carried it out of the building on the sole of their boot, or it might have slipped through a gap in the floorboards.

"You got rid of the cordents easily enough in the end," Drinith offered as a consolation.

"Thank dragons, they were bluechecks," he said. "Greny hadn't sent them. These random raids happen from time to time." He stood, saying, "Keep looking, please. I must see about my birds."

As she searched, Drinith glanced up now and again. Qilin righted the cage and tried to soothe the flustered birds with soft cooing sounds. He replenished their water and gave them fresh treats. She watched as he scooped up the dead sunfinch, and kissed its broken wing. He walked over to the window, cradling it in his palm with loving-kindness.

"No time for a proper burial," he remarked, mostly to himself. He turned his palm over and let the dead bird fall. "A gift to some starving alley cat."

It's hard to dislike or distrust a man, Drinith mused, *who cares so much for his birds.*

Just then her gaze fell upon a tiny mottled square. "Here it is! I *think.*" She dared not touch it.

"Where?"

She pointed. He hastened to his desk, grabbed something off it. He knelt beside Drinith and, with reverent care, picked up the note with his tweezers. As he examined it with his magnifying glass, a grin spread across his face. "Well done. It's the message I've been waiting for." Qilin exhaled a deep breath, as though he had been holding it for days. He chuckled gently, but his eyes shone with the rapture of a man in love.

"What does it say?" Drinith asked.

His eyes narrowed. "I don't know. It will take me time to decode it." He blushed. "Would you mind sorting out the shop downstairs? I'll join you as soon as I'm finished."

Drinith glanced back at him with a vague unease as she stepped out of the room. At his desk, he was preparing to examine the message with an exuberance she could not help but envy.

Downstairs, the cordents had been thorough in their destruction. The shelves were bare, and books littered the floor. She picked her way across to the door, locked it, and began sorting the tomes.

She had finished ten shelves or so when Qilin joined her. His elation had guttered. The dark coat he wore matched his humor. He answered her curiosity with a wan, unconvincing smile. "Ricoen has agreed to make your friends' rescue a priority, but I must make some arrangements to set it in motion."

A chill gust swept inside as he opened the door, driving the warmth from the room.

Unable to rise to a smile, Drinith nodded.

"Lock the door after me," Qilin said. "I'll knock three times, pause, and knock a fourth time. Take a peek from behind the blinds to make absolutely sure it's me. And of course, hide if you hear 'The Dragon's Call.'"

As he stepped outside and slapped the door shut, Drinith's spine tingled with more than cold. Something must be wrong. After locking the door, she hastened upstairs to Qilin's desk. She rifled carefully through it, forcing herself, despite her urgency, not to leave it noticeably disturbed. Not finding the message, she repeated the search with even more care.

It was gone. He must have taken it with him or, more likely, destroyed it. He was hiding something from her, but what might it be?

38

───────

Greny nervously fidgeted with his empty tea bowl as he waited for his guest. This was going to be embarrassing.

Nobody else other than you and Jarma will ever know and, after the Void has swallowed her, your shame will fade until you won't even remember it. Perhaps he should have saved himself the agony of this encounter and send her to the Plank. Yet he was reluctant to dispose of her. She might yet have her uses. And he needed someone to talk to, a captive audience as it were.

Jarma entered, flanked by Queek and Chemp. She wore one of his mother's austere, high-collared dresses. She looked every bit a meritorian as her gaze swept the room. It fixed on the bath, still steaming in the corner. She crinkled her nose in disgust. "I may have once been a maid, but I assure you I have no intention of helping you wash."

"I already have," Greny said, his cheeks burning. "The ratchers helped me." Why had he said that? The utter disgust on her face tempted him again to send her to the Plank. "Sit down."

Her shudder at his command, and her passive compliance, was gratifying. She was in no position to look down on him. He didn't need to apologize for battering her door in the middle of the night. He was in control, in this tower at least.

"Why have you called me here?" she asked, hugging herself as she eyed him intently.

"Tea?"

Chemp stepped forward to serve, but Greny casually waved him away. Greny poured Jarma's bowl first and then his own. He noted with some amusement that Jarma didn't touch hers.

"Worried it's poisoned?" He sipped from his bowl. "See? There's no need to be afraid."

"My time as Drinith's maid taught me a lot about poisons. The bowl may be coated in poison, or you might be immune to whatever drug is in the tea."

"Quite an elaborate way to kill someone I could send to the Plank with but a word."

"It might be a sedative, a soporific or mesmeric agent, or some sort of love potion." She paused and, glaring back at his lingering gaze, folded her arms across her breasts. "I've heard rumors about what you do to the girls you imprison here."

"Lies!" Greny blustered. "Ridiculous slander. I would never...I would never take advantage like that."

Jarma smirked. "You depend on desperation to wear them down."

It took all Greny's self-control not to send this spiteful upstart, this jumped-up maid, to the Plank. Young Queek, sensing his master's anger, drew his baton a fraction from its loop.

"Why spurn my hospitality now?" Greny asked. "You've been eating my food for a few days already."

"Nothing has passed my lips since I entered your tower."

"But surely..." Greny looked at Chemp for confirmation. The ratcher nodded.

Greny rubbed his forehead. "You've surely drunk something. Water?"

"Absolutely nothing," Jarma assured him.

People usually lasted only three or four days without water. Greny knew that for certain, having had reason to test the theory a few times in the past. That much time had elapsed already, and yet she remained in rude health despite her self-imposed starvation. She must have a secret source of water. She might be catching rainwater through her window. Or was this apparent miracle because of some charm she carried on her person?

"If you keep that up, you'll soon think poison would be a mercy," Greny declared gruffly.

"You betrayed Drinith," Jarma said. "You sent her in your stead to Osro Onez's mansion the night the Ducal Steward and Thaxen Savarel were murdered."

"It was her illegal organization that condemned her."

"Its purpose was to facilitate the return of her people to Rhumgad and to root out Magian's spies in Gyre, two goals which didn't pose any threat to your precious Meritocracy. On the contrary, they both aligned with Gyre's interests. Besides, you controlled her network through Woad Glastum."

Greny clenched his jaw. He gulped some tea while he composed himself. He removed his truthstone from his pocket as discreetly as he could manage while keeping his gaze fixed on Jarma. "How did you know about Glastum?"

"Drinith knew."

Impossible! She couldn't have. And yet the truthstone remained light in Greny's palm. "How?"

After a noticeable pause, Jarma shrugged. "How she knew? I don't know. I only know she did."

Could that really be true? Drinith trusted Woad. She turned to him for help after she escaped from the cordents at her mansion. And yet the next time they met, she pressed a knife to his back, or so he claimed. Could she have always known? Could Woad be pretending to be under Greny's control, all the while serving Drinith, protecting her, exactly as Nayz had suspected?

Rising, Greny walked over to the window with his hands clasped behind his back, and looked down on the gray, rain-lashed city. His ghostly reflection smoothed out the lines of anxiety on his face. He turned toward Jarma and asked, "Is this some sort of trick?"

"I speak the truth," Jarma said, unflinching under his gaze.

"Are Drinith and Woad working together?"

"I can't tell you. I only know she knew Woad worked for you."

The weight of the truthstone never wavered throughout the interrogation as far as Greny could tell, not even slightly. If Drinith knew, she and Glastum might have been in cahoots all along. What had he achieved since Greny had charged him to capture the renegade meritocrat? Only a few dead non-entities and nearly as many dead ratchers, and the arrest of one of Drinith's ex-servants on the chance she might turn to her. Most of Drinith's agents had disappeared before they could be arrested. The rest were protected so far by the same checkpoints that hemmed them into the Blue Quarter. Glastum's failures were too convenient. He couldn't be trusted, not at least until he had been properly interrogated. *I should have planted more spies in Drinith's organization to corroborate Glastum's claims,* Greny fretted. He feared he had overestimated his influence over the ex-mercenary.

Putting the truthstone away, Greny sauntered over to his desk and scratched out two notes. One, recalling Glastum to the tower, he sealed in an envelope. On the other, he wrote instructions that as soon as Glastum arrived, he was to be arrested and dispatched to Inkeep, where Greny could interrogate him at his convenience. After reading the unsealed note, Chemp took both messages and hastened from the room to carry out Greny's orders.

Greny returned to the table. He took a gulp of lukewarm tea and, resting his chin on a hand, stared at Jarma's untouched bowl. "Are you sure you won't drink? A sip wouldn't hurt, surely."

Jarma shook her head. He didn't like the hint of a smile on her lips, as if she had gotten the better of him in some fashion. He was succumbing to paranoia. This girl had been a servant for most of her life. Until recently, she couldn't even read. She had always struck him as a simple, forthright girl, insecure about her elevation to meritorian and incapable of guile. It was ridiculous to imagine that she had the wit or the audacity to manipulate him. She simply mistook starving herself for some sort of small victory over her captor.

He rested his head on his hand and grinned at the ex-maid. "Do you know how I can find Drinith, hmm? She has proved frustratingly elusive." She didn't answer, and he didn't expect her to. He had said it partly to tease her, partly to vent his frustration. He was still blind, still groping helplessly in the darkness.

Kleest slipped into the room and stood alongside Queek. One ratcher could surely keep control of a slip of a girl like Jarma. Chemp had no doubt sent him out of an abundance of caution.

"Why did you say you hated the Meritocracy?" said Jarma.

Greny bolted upright in his chair. "I never did."

"Yes, you did. The night you came to my door addled on hard tea. You said you hated the Meritocracy and burst into tears."

"It was the hard tea speaking. Nothing more." He rubbed his eyes with the heels of his hands. "It's difficult sometimes in my position. Lonely." It didn't matter what he said to Jarma. The Void would swallow her and everything he told her, eventually. "When I was an ignorant child, I envied the Ducalion in her palace. I assumed, like so many commoners do, that her facade of authority had actual power behind it. Of course, I was wrong, as in so many things. When I became a meritorian, I longed to take my place in the Parliament, to become one of the co-equal true rulers of Gyre. But when I finally inherited my emblem of merit, I learned all meritocrats weren't as equal as I imagined. A hierarchy existed, and at the very top was the Vicenary Jury." He made the customary circle in the air, indicating the ineffable Iron Circle.

"When I became a cordent general and took a seat on the Vicenary Jury, I quickly discovered the power of each individual member is not as great as I supposed. Actual sovereignty rests in the majority's will. Not even the Ducal Steward would dare defy it. Likewise, the Iron Circle, despite the fear it engenders in meritocrats, remains merely a puppet of the Parliament. Every part of the Gyran government is beautifully checked and balanced. That is why it has survived for hundreds of years while the regimes of countless emperors and tyrants have fallen into the Void. The individual meritocrats do not matter, only the Meritocracy."

"But it nearly collapsed, didn't it, during the Silverfish Revolt?"

"It came perilously close, that is true."

"And you saved it."

"You flatter me, child," Greny said, with a modest wave of his hand. "I did my part, but to say I saved the Meritocracy is a gross exaggeration. When guile and steel fail, there's always dragon fire. I merely lessened the damage. By convincing the Silverfishes' leader to surrender herself to the Meritocracy, I saved a large part of Gyre's populace from being incinerated. And I ensured the wound she inflicted left less of a scar.

"Of course, there is a possibility that, if I had said some things and left others unsaid, the outcome might have been different. I hadn't been a meritocrat long back then. I was incapable of considering anything other than the best interest of the Meritocracy. Things were simpler, at least as I perceived them. Ambition wasn't entwined with fear as it is now."

"You must be tired of being afraid."

Greny snorted. *You're the one destined for the Plank.* "I have endured that fear so long, it has become part of me. I wouldn't be who I am without it. Fear is necessary. Without it, ambition would tear the Meritocracy apart."

"It strikes me," Jarma said, "that you don't fit into the Meritocracy. In a city ruled by women, you're an aberration, an embarrassment even. You're as much a captive in this tower as I am."

Greny inwardly heaved a sigh. The observation was doubtless the opening move in enticing him to turn his back on a lifetime of fidelity to the Meritocracy. "I've heard the sort of appeal you're about to make countless times before. They have never worked and never will." *If my brother couldn't convince me, nobody could.*

"You like to think yourself incorruptible, but you lied to your precious Iron Circle when it suited you. You're lying again right now to me and to yourself. Admit it, as much as you proclaim your love of the Gyre's government, you live in terror of it."

"I'd happily die for Gyre!"

"You might surrender your life, but your emblem of merit is a different story. You are such a hypocrite. You talk of the Meritocracy as indomitable in one breath, then speak of its frailty in the next."

Indomitable? How did a maid learn such a word? "It's both. It's as tough as steel and fragile as glass. It's complicated."

"You can't even be honest here in the safety of your own tower with a prisoner you can dispose of at your leisure. The least you could do for me, while I await my execution, is to be frank."

So, she knows she's doomed. That saves a hard conversation. He sipped his tea, cold now.

"Personal ambition is a necessary part of government but also its greatest threat," he said. "It's why the Nosteran Empire tore itself apart, for example. The Meritocracy is designed to check the ambitions of those among its rulers who might seek to dominate it. We've had uncrowned queens occasionally, women of exceptional talent, charm, and ruthlessness who might have carved out kingdoms and empires elsewhere. Our traditions have been constructed through careful experimentation and hotly debated compromise to ensure such would-be potentates can never achieve their ambitions here. I love the clockwork precision of it all.

"But it protects the institution, not the individual. And it depends on the good sense and selflessness of the majority of meritocrats. Obviously, they all have their own ambitions, but those aspirations should align with the greater good. Their primary desire must always be the preservation and prospering of the Halcyon Republic. It helps a great deal if the leading meritocrats understand that and, better yet, actively foster it. It was true of Osro Onez and Thaxen Savarel, and of Ronel Olapsin before them. But the same can't be said for their successors.

"Elca Trajar has enough neck for two heads, and I've long suspected Thespenilea sheathes in her velvet charm an ambition as sharp as any dagger point. They have split the Meritocracy down the middle. One claims to favor the preservation of the Halcyon Republic and the other its prosperity—though in truth, I suspect these lofty goals are merely pretexts for their own advancement."

It was good to talk this through. He had been so focused on

solving the murders, he hadn't given the bigger picture much thought. "The recent killings have strengthened their position immeasurably. One or the other of them could be behind them."

"If they are such an obvious threat to your republic—"

"It's your republic, too."

"Not once it condemned me to death."

"Fair point."

"Anyway, if you are convinced Elca and Thespenilea are such a threat, why don't you kill them?" Jarma asked.

"What!"

"You're happy to make me walk the Plank when any danger I pose to your republic is minuscule. Yet, you let these greater threats go about their business unmolested. You could invite both of them here and have your ratchers kill them."

Greny emitted a breathless chuckle. "You cannot seriously…" But it was obvious from her demeanor, Jarma meant every word. "They balance each other for now."

"But if one of them is the murderer and kills the other, then the survivor's ambition would no longer be checked. Would you strike her down then? What would it take for you to move against her?"

"Their factions are incompatible, so if one of them died, then somebody else would take her place and the balance would be maintained."

"So, your plan is just to sit idly and hope for the best."

He pounded the table. "To defend the republic, I'd massacre the Vicenary Jury if I had to." Jarma's smile broadened into a grin. A shiver of fear lanced through him. In a rage, he had spoken treason, and yet what harm could come of it? Destined for the Plank, she'd never be able to tell anyone.

He signaled to Queek and Kleest. Jarma yelped as the ratchers grabbed her arms, her irritating grin of triumph snuffed out in an instant.

"As much as I enjoyed our little chats," Greny said, "I'm afraid your stay has come to an end. Take her to the Plank!"

She left between the two ratchers as meekly as a lamb. Her lack of resistance surprised him, but behind her meritocratic facade she was at heart a servant. Her former life had made her more prone to compliance than he imagined. Too bad she had talked herself into the Void.

Chemp returned, carrying a letter on a silver tray. After sniffing for poison, he presented it to Greny. It was a black envelope, a summons from the Iron Circle. Greny groaned. They would expect an update on the investigation. What could he tell them? His scant leads had gone nowhere. He hadn't captured Drinith. He hadn't caught the murderer. The Iron Circle would dismiss Quiescat's prophesies as indecipherable ravings. Apprehending Jarma had been Greny's only notable success, but he had sent her to the Plank. The jurists' interrogation of her would have likely only added to his troubles.

As he opened the letter with trembling hands, Chemp emitted a warning squeak. Greny had forgotten to put on his gloves.

"It's from the Vicenary Jury," Greny said. "It's unlikely to be poisoned, and it's too late now if it was."

The envelope contained two letters. One summoned him to a meeting of the Vicenary Jury in the morning. The other held a note from Thespenilea, the words, written in quick-fade ink, already vanishing. "We need to meet tonight." Beside the terse message was a stick figure with a featureless circular head hanging from a gibbet.

39

––––––––––

As Greny made his way down the tower's spiral staircase, a shout reverberated up it, followed by a string of guttural curses. He couldn't help but smile. The ex-mercenary must have arrived.

"Let me go!" Woad thundered. "Rat King, what is the meaning of this? Don't touch me, you mangy—" Something choked him off.

Greny found the mercenary lying at the bottom of the stairs, trussed and gagged. Six ratchers encircled him, their shadows crisscrossing him like prison bars. Geekel held a rag to his muzzle, while Kleest bandaged his bleeding knuckles. Stout Steevig's grin revealed a missing tooth. Imagine the damage the ex-mercenary could have wrought if he had an inkling of his arrest.

"I've heard a disturbing rumor that you may not be as committed to furthering my interests as you profess," Greny said. "Rest assured, you'll have an opportunity to clear your name in due course. I'm afraid I have an urgent appointment I must attend first. Deetch, am I right in presuming that our other guest has already left?"

The ratcher nodded.

"Very good. You can stash Glastum in her room for now. Keep him bound and gagged and under close watch. A resourceful man like him will seize on any opportunity to free himself." Greny bent close to the ex-mercenary. "There's no need to worry if you adhered to our agreement."

He watched four ratchers drag Glastum up the stairs, then readied to leave. Accompanied by Deetch, Greny exited his tower through a secret passage to a nearby lane. Dressed in red and black, he looked at first glance as any well-to-do merchant might, his emblem of merit concealed beneath a bulbous red velvet hat. He carried a cane with a silver handle shaped like a double-headed axe, though he hoped he would never have to use it to defend himself. He strolled down the street to where a palanquin waited. As he neared, a muscular brute of a man and a ratcher, Evreet, emerged from the cab. Greny climbed inside to find Chemp already waiting for him.

The man, the driver of the vehicle, warily approached the open door. "Where do you want to go?" he rasped. If the night went well, he would be handsomely paid. However, Chemp had warned him, in vivid sign language, that if anything happened to Greny, he'd never see his family again.

"The Royal Library," Greny said.

The man drew the curtain across the door. The palanquin lifted and rocked gently as it moved quickly down the street. Dweed and Evreet followed at a discreet distance. As usual, Chemp sat across from him, but Greny still felt naked in this dingy little cab. As he mulled over Thespenilea's summons, he twirled his cane against the floor so much he threatened to bore a hole in it. The Royal Library, sometimes mocked as the Book Prison, was guarded zealously by its staff. Greny should be safe within its thick walls under the librarians' vigilant gaze. At the same time, Thespenilea, or more accurately whoever wrote the note, could be depending on that reputation to lure him into an ambush.

The palanquin halted. Chemp hopped out. After looking around, the ratcher signaled it was safe to exit. As Greny stepped out of the cab, he glanced up at the lampstone statue of the robed figure hanging by her neck from a stone rope over the entrance—the library's patron saint, Helos the Martyr. It was she who sacrificed herself to a mob to save the library from being burned in the heady days of the Great Revolution. The library had maintained its independence and royal title ever since, even during the Vassalage. The lambency of her face couldn't hide its perpetual disgust at those who would trespass on her preserve.

The great doors resembled a spread book cover, a thick bronze spine separating the two ornate boards. A metal knocker shaped like a tassel ran a third of the way down it, the surface behind it scored by the rapping of countless generations of visitors. At Greny's instruction, Chemp struck the spine with the knocker, eliciting a sonorous knell. It was in the middle of the night and most of the librarians were probably asleep, but the delay in answering vexed Greny, nonetheless. This was the most obvious place for any would-be assassin to strike. He rapidly tapped the head of his cane against the bronze. "Answer!"

From behind the doors came the muffled sound of jangling keys. Metal scraped against metal. A viewing slit in the left door slid back. "Speak your business."

"I am here on urgent business for the Meritocracy," Greny huffed, pushing back his hat to reveal his emblem of merit. "I was invited."

"Are you or have you ever been a servant of the demons of Empyrosis?"

"No."

"Are you or have you ever been an agent of the Panatheneum?"

"No." Every moment Greny's entry was delayed, the danger grew. "You ask me these questions every time I come here, and every time I give the same answer."

"Perhaps you might answer differently this time. Are you or have you ever been a member of the Amnesian Biblioclast Conspiracy? Are you or have you ever been a worshiper of Agnosyn God of Inscience?"

The doorkeeper continued to rattle off enemies of the library, some of which Greny knew of by reputation, others only from his previous visits. He wondered if they were all real, or some were mythical, or even just made up to annoy him.

At last, the doorkeeper ran out of questions, and the left door groaned open.

The loupes protruding from the spectacles resting atop the old lady's gray pate looked like horns. She slid them down to the bridge of her nose; her eyes behind the thick, grimy lenses were huge and hypnotic. "We don't allow animals on the premises," she sneered, regarding the ratchers with a crinkling of her nose before restoring her specs to their cranial perch.

Greny lifted his chin. "These are my servants. To snub them is to slight me personally."

"To bring those hairy brutes here is an affront to this institution, *Meritocrat*." She used his title as if it was an insult. She twisted an acorn-sized golden trinket between her thumb and fingers. The ratchers squealed and stumbled backward, covering their ears. Greny couldn't hear whatever sound was causing them such agony. Beyond, the palanquin's driver fled in panic. No matter, Greny would deal with that coward later. First, he must relieve his ratchers from their aural torture.

"Let them go!" he demanded, threatening her with his cane, only to watch it fly from his hand.

"You should know you're in no position to make demands on this side of the threshold, Cordent General," the old lady said venomously. "Nothing may enter the Royal Library without the permission of its staff. Nothing."

"Release them." Greny could hardly hear himself over the ratchers' unbearable shrieks. "Please."

With a sneer, she twisted the trinket again. The ratchers' squeals ceased, and they regained their composure, though Greny sensed a timidity in their gazes.

"Wait for me by the palanquin," he said.

The trinket crawled over the librarian's fingertips and disappeared down the back of her hand. She beckoned Greny inside. The great door rang like a bell as it slammed shut behind them. The librarian whispered to a young girl, unnoticed behind her until now.

"I came to meet someone here," Greny said. "A meritocrat."

The old woman smirked. "Then you should be doubly pleased. Two await you in one of the reading rooms, Cordent General. Young Salicila will take you there."

On the marble flagstones of the reception hall were inscribed Gyran pyratic symbols, every one of them according to what Greny had been told on a previous visit. Bookshelves wound up the massive columns reaching into the vaulted darkness. Bone white figures dotted the chamber, alone and in groups—marble representations of respected patrons of the library, long dead; some held actual books in their hands. Salicila led him through this vast bibliothecal forest, by the famous silver inkpot fountain, and up two flights of stairs into a long room. Greny recognized the alchemical section by its signature scent of solvent.

At the far end, the girl pointed to a door. "They're waiting in there."

Greny took a deep breath to steady his nerves and entered.

Thespenilea looked up at him from the circular table where she was sitting. Elca, standing by her side, twisted around to grin at him.

The door closed behind him. The girl must have shut it.

"Surprise!" Elca said. She grabbed a chair and sat down.

Greny reluctantly did the same. He knitted his trembling hands together and, trying his best to sound nonchalant, said: "So, you both wanted to see me."

Elca stretched out her open hand. On her palm rested a white chrysanthemum on a chain—a truthstone.

"You know how to use that?" Greny asked.

"If you don't mind, we'll ask the questions for now," Elca said. "Did Osro invite you to visit her on the night she was murdered?"

Lying or dissembling would only make him look guilty. "She did."

Elca put away the truthstone. "It appears you're telling the truth." She tossed a piece of parchment onto the table. Thespenilea did the same.

Greny examined both notes. "Aside from the personalized gibes, they match the one I received. But mine faded quickly."

"So did ours," Thespenilea said, "but Elca, resourceful as ever, found a means to reveal the hidden writing."

"In truth, I cannot take all the credit," Elca said. "An alchemist I know helped me. Don't worry. She took immemoreal after she finished."

The private use of immemoreal was illegal, but that was a mere trifle compared to the substantial matter at hand.

"Do you still have your note?" Elca asked.

"I thought it best to destroy it," Greny said.

"Pity."

"So, we three were meant to fall into the same trap that killed Osro and Thaxen," Thespenilea said.

"Why didn't you go?" Greny asked.

"I retired early that night with strict instructions to my servants not to disturb me. A little too strict, it seems. It was the next morning when I was alerted to the existence of the letter. By that time, the ink had already faded, and I found the parchment inside blank."

"And your story, Elca?" Greny prompted.

"After I had dinner with poor Ecethor, my courtesar, Redgis of Sorzan, and I spent the rest of the evening together. We wandered the markets in Gemgarden. I bought him quite a fetching jade necklace. Then we returned to my mansion—"

"Get to the point!" Greny snapped.

"My story is similar to Thespie's. I only opened the letter the next day, and it was blank." She flashed a triumphant grin at Greny. "Of course, you read your invitation on the night it arrived. Otherwise, you wouldn't have known its contents without an alchemist's help."

Greny's heart sank. *Stupid, stupid, stupid. I have given too much away so easily.*

Elca had one hand under the table. She probably still held the truthstone in it.

Greny told the truth or, at least, a crumb of it. "I smelled a trap. It turned out I was right. So, are you two friends now?" He asked as much to fend off follow-up questions as to satisfy his own curiosity.

A grin blossomed beneath Elca's pallid eyes.

Thespenilea shook her head, hid a lean smile behind her hand. "Friends, no. We simply recognize our mutual interest in dealing with a common threat."

And am I that threat? "And who might that be? Magian?"

"I had a chat with Aretro," Elca said. "She, of course, is beyond suspicion, or she has lived an astounding lie since her birth. Despite her considerable talents, she lacks the instinct for something like this. She's much too squeamish. In any case, after some gentle prompting from me, she found her invitation mislaid in her mansion. That leaves only one faction leader unaccounted for—Okia."

The richest meritocrat in Gyre, Okia Vavar had always been fastidious about avoiding the envy of her colleagues. Perhaps she had finally grown tired of false humility. "Sounds like conjecture," Greny said. "Have you any compelling evidence, Elca?"

"We were hoping you can find it. You *had* a reputation for being good at that sort of thing."

Greny noted with displeasure at the implied threat in her use of past tense. "You don't know for certain that Okia didn't receive an invitation."

"You need to confront her tonight in her home in Charway and find out," Thespenilea said, "before the Vicenary Jury convenes in the morning."

And if Okia turns out to have also been invited, what then? And even if she wasn't, it may be a ruse to cast suspicion on her. Any of the others might be guilty—Elca, Thespenilea, even Aretro. This errand is a distraction. But Greny could not refuse without incurring the wrath of these two powerful meritocrats, and as weak as it was, this was his best lead.

"I'll go," he said, rising.

Elca gestured for him to sit down again. "There's something else you should know. Posaleum has always been a dear friend of mine, but since this current crisis began, she had become rather unreliable. She means you harm."

"So I've heard," Greny said with a smirk. "Thanks for the warning," he added wearily, feeling lost in an interminable labyrinth of treachery, real or imagined.

40

After Drinith had tidied the shop, she lingered downstairs, sometimes sitting, sometimes pacing, her gaze rarely straying from the door in expectation of Qilin's imminent return. However, it was night when the telltale sequence of knocks on the door finally announced his arrival. He offered her a sickly and unconvincing smile as he stumbled inside, drawn and sweaty like a consumptive.

"We must go." He thrust a dark hooded cloak at her. "Put this on."

"Where are we going?" she asked, but he already plunged back into the darkness.

Nighttime Gyre felt cold and unfamiliar after days cooped up in Qilin's shop. Drinith kept close to Qilin, afraid to be swept away from him by the bustle as they weaved through clamorous streets. They slipped down a narrow alley and stopped before a door so pitted and worn it looked as if a mischief of rats had gnawed on it.

"The group who will help you capture Greny are waiting inside," Qilin said, turning to go. "Good luck."

"Are you not coming in?" Drinith asked with alarm.

"It's best I don't," Qilin said. "I'm not even a name to most of them, and it must stay that way for now. Good luck."

She watched him hasten back down the lane and melt into the crowded street. He had led her to this alleyway with hardly an explanation and now he had just abandoned her. What really awaited her on the other side of the door?

Resting one hand on her knife, she knocked. The door creaked open a fraction. A familiar face peeped through the gap—her rescuer from the ambush on the bridge. "It's you!" she gasped. He peered beyond her down the alley as he opened the door and beckoned her inside.

Four other young men stood in a loose circle within, all Rhumgadian Highlanders. They regarded her with cool contempt.

"So, Tamric, this is the princess," one of them observed. He looked her up and down until her indignant glare averted his lecherous smirk.

"That's right," Qilin's deputy said. *Tamric. So, I've finally got a name for him.* He introduced the man with the lewd gaze as Parval, and the others as Neron, Thealren, and Jazro. A more disreputable-looking lot she could not imagine. *Probably all sporting false names.*

"I've never visited Kaplar," Thealren said. "They say it was a mighty realm until Magian crushed it."

Leaning against a wall, Neron picked his teeth with his dagger. "They say a lot of things about Kaplar, not all of them good."

Drinith blushed. No point in demanding an explanation for his gibe—thanks to that damn history book, she already knew.

"Save your aggression for the mission," Tamric warned.

"I've spent some time in the Blue Quarter," Drinith said. "I don't think I've seen any of you about there."

"We're not long arrived here from Numenal. They don't like exiles there."

Parval loudly hoicked up a gob of phlegm and spat it on the floor. "They don't like us much here either."

"Cost us the last of our coin to get here," Jazro groused.

Drinith did her best to hide her dismay. These Rhumgadians weren't the committed revolutionaries she had expected. Their principles only extended to the bottom of their empty purses.

"Enough chat," Tamric said, cutting into the center of the circle. "We had better get going or the night will be gone, and our quarry will have gone to ground. Drinith, you're with me. The rest of you pair up. Better to travel in three pairs than a gang of six. I'll be moving fast, so stay alert and keep up."

Neron and Thealren paired up; Jazro partnered with Parval. As they moved through the city's streets and plazas, Tamric kept checking behind him, presumably to confirm he hadn't lost the others. When Drinith followed one of his glances, he grimaced. "Keep your eyes ahead. Both of us looking back will attract unnecessary attention."

A clump of plumes bobbed above the crowd ahead—courtesars, possibly hunting her. With a sudden horselaugh, Tamric slid an arm around Drinith's waist and pulled her to him. She instinctively attempted to push free, but his grip tightened.

"Don't be a fool," he whispered. "The peacocks will notice."

She stared straight ahead at Tamric's chest, afraid he might take advantage of her glance upward to kiss her. Her hand slipped onto the handle of her knife. His sour, clammy breath that tickled her forehead and teased at her hair, filled her with revulsion. All she could think of was Zin. Tamric was just as dangerous and cruel.

"Do you see them?" he asked.

She leaned to one side just enough to glimpse the powdered faces pushing through the crowd. Rosel, readily identified by the golden feathers in his hat, strutted amongst the men who hunted her. Evidently, his professed love for her had been only hot air. She leaned into Tamric's chest and nestled in his shadow until the courtesars swaggered by and disappeared into the shifting throngs.

"That was close," Drinith said, relieved to escape Tamric's embrace almost as much as the courtesars' attention.

He snickered. "The peacocks are searching for Meritocrat Hax, and she'd never let some ungallant scruff paw her. They can't see beyond their code."

As they walked on, a hooded figure sidled up to Tamric. "The Rat

King left the Royal Library, but he's not taking the direct route to Charway," the man whispered. "He's heading toward Spinshard."

"If we hurry, we might be able to strike as Scylax crosses Spinbridge," Tamric said.

They bolted through a labyrinth of narrow lanes, hardly wide enough for two people to pass each other, until they emerged onto a large street that sloped down to Southspoke Bridge, a broad spike jutting into the Void. On the far side, Spinshard rotated almost imperceptibly. A slender connecting arm stretched from it, the so-called Spinbridge, which would soon connect with Southspoke, forming a temporary bridge across the dividing chasm.

The informant pointed to a nondescript palanquin at the front of a line of waiting traffic. "He's in there. Only three ratchers accompany him."

"Perfect," Tamric said. "The bridge cordents look half asleep at their posts."

It didn't look so perfect to Drinith. "What about the crowd behind him?" she whispered to Tamric. "They might intervene. With them behind us and nothing ahead, we'll trap ourselves."

Ignoring her, Tamric dismissed the informant and signaled the four Highlanders to gather around him. "Neron and Thealren, create some sort of distraction—steal something or start a fight, anything to keep the traffic's focus off the bridge. Just don't get caught or you'll end up walking the Plank for your part in this. Head back to the rendezvous when done. Jazro and Parval, you'll help deal with the cordent general and his ratchers. With luck, we'll strike so fast, nobody else will have time to react, and we can simply cross with the palanquin as soon as the bridge connects."

They descended the hill in pairs to avoid attracting attention. Tamric leaned close to Drinith. "Don't worry. This will go a lot smoother than your first rescue."

"You intend to kill the ratchers?" she whispered. "I had hoped bloodshed could be kept to a minimum."

"Funny, I don't remember you had any qualms about me killing them at Wealgiver Street," Tamric said. "They're not human. They're worse than animals. Torturers and executioners, the lot of them."

Seizing her arm, he jerked her to a halt. Jazro and Parval stared at them with surprise as they strolled past. "You've a choice: kill a few rats or leave your friends to rot in Inkeep. And neither of us will take a step further until you've made it. I'd rather abandon this mission than run the risk of your scruples betraying us. Qilin didn't want to burden you, but we've had reports that Scylax has signed your friends' death warrants."

That explained Qilin's somber mood and his destruction of the message before Drinith could read it.

She shied from Tamric's intense gaze, but it followed her, forcing her to face it. "This might be the only chance to save them," he persisted. "Do we take it?"

"Yes."

"Remember, no hesitation. You must strike before the ratchers realize what is happening. Otherwise, they'll kill the four of us. And your friends."

"I'll do what must be done."

He took her arm in his. "Anybody watching will assume we had a lovers' tiff." She cringed as he leaned close, but he flashed a bemused grin and drew back. They continued downward.

Jazro and Parval loitered at the edge of the throng gathered at the bridge, looking tense and out of place. Drinith and Tamric didn't acknowledge them as they strolled by and plunged into the crowd. Tamric released Drinith's arm. They plowed their way through to indignant stares and the odd aggrieved mutter. Gradually the heads thinned, and she had a clear view of Greny's palanquin and its rodent escort at the tip of the bridge.

Tamric squeezed her arm again, this time so tightly it hurt. "Wait," he whispered. "We're walking into a trap."

"Are you sure?" Drinith asked.

"I've made it my business to know the face of every cordent in Gyre worth a damn. I've spotted a half-dozen yellowchecks in the crowd." He pulled her backward. "We need to get out of here."

Screams rose behind them. A burning cart trundled down the winding road at the back of the crowd, causing them to surge forward.

"Too late." Tamric said. "We're too late."

41

———

Greny sat in his palanquin, waiting for Spinbridge to connect across the chasm, mentally turning over the suspicion, sharp as any dagger, pointed at Okia. How would she react to him turning up to her mansion, casting aspersions with every question? Of course, either Elca or Thespenilea could just as easily be the culprits. Or even both. They could have been in league from the beginning, spinning this plot to bolster their power, to carve up Gyre between them. The republic had thwarted many would-be monarchs, but never had two rivals acted in concert. Greny shivered at the notion.

Panicked screams outside. Racing feet. He lifted the curtain and peered back down the deck to the bridge's approach. There, a wall of fire rose over the melting, shifting silhouettes of a frenzied crowd. A dragon's roar shivered in the air. A dragon attack, here in the city? There hadn't been one in three hundred years! No, the cry came from a dragon leaving the perches some distance away. It wouldn't reach the bridge for several minutes. Cordents formed a line before the surging crowd and tried to beat them back with truncheons.

Ahead, the connecting span on Spinshard swung ever closer, promising escape and safety. Greny willed it on.

From the opposite direction, hooded figures dashed toward the palanquin. A ratcher squealed. Chemp yanked Greny back onto his seat, signaled him not to move. Springbow in hand, the ratcher leapt out the door.

Greny grasped the edge of his seat with both hands as he listened intently, but all he could hear was the panicked cries of the mob. As he lifted the curtain to hazard a glance outside, a Rhumgadian face appeared in the window. Greny screamed and fell back against his seat. *Ping ping ping*! In his steel grip the curtain rings snapped off their track. Cowering, he clutched the fabric over his eyes.

Something heavy struck the side of the vehicle. The cab rocked as it lifted and inched forward. At any moment, the casquars might startle and carry the palanquin into the Void. Greny scrambled out of the cab, stumbling over a dead man lying just outside. A sickening crunch of bones accompanied his landing on the corpse's chest.

Thank dragons, Chemp still lived! His springbow juddered until, with a squeal of disgust, he threw it aside and drew his dagger. A Rhumgadian hurtled toward him. Chemp whipped his tail around and swept the astonished man's legs out from under him. His dagger went flying; Chemp moved in for the kill. A second ambusher closed in on him from behind. Greny managed a feeble *look out*! Chemp whirled around and buried his knife in the man's chest. He fell against the ratcher, flailing in his death throes.

Meanwhile the first Rhumgadian had snatched up his knife and rolled to his feet. Chemp pushed the dead man away from him. The dagger squirted out of his chest, Chemp's paw still gripping the hilt. As Greny watched in voiceless horror, the surviving assailant charged. Chemp side-stepped, but the man deftly flipped his dagger from one hand to the other. His thrust found Chemp's neck; he kept twisting the hilt until Chemp's head butt sent him sprawling.

Chemp's paws couldn't stem the gouts of blood bursting forth from the puncture. His squeals emerged as wet, croaking gasps. In a final act of loyalty to his master, he threw himself on the Rhumgadian, jaws snapping at the man's neck. The Rhumgadian's scream was cut short by Chemp's curved incisors rupturing his jugular. They toppled over, Chemp landing on top, a twitching mound of blood-matted hair. Shreds of flesh hung from his slavering jaws.

I should have helped him. Damn me for the coward that I am, but I couldn't. Greny buried his face in the torn curtain and wept.

Around Drinith, the crowd thrashed, a sea of violent faces and fists. Something blunt and heavy struck the back of her head, leaving her dazed and lost.

"Cordents! We're cordents!" Tamric cried, raising one hand as he dragged her along with the other. "Let us through!" Cordents pulled them through their line. They stumbled into the open space. Greny's palanquin lay ahead. Greny stood frozen by his palanquin, oblivious to the chaos further down the road or the opposite span of bridge on the far side of the Void, swinging ever nearer. They might, just might, yet spirit him across and save Drinith's friends.

"You check on our two comrades. I'll take care of the cordent general," Tamric said. He gave her a fearful glance. No, not fearful. Guilty. He was going to kill Greny.

"They're dead." She gestured toward Jazro and Parval's bodies among the ratcher corpses. "I'm coming with you."

"If you must," he said sharply.

Shouting for help was pointless given the clamor of the panicked crowd and the cordents who fought to contain it. Drinith would have to save Greny herself. She tensed, steeling herself for the courage needed to block Tamric's knife when it struck out to kill the Rat King. She begged the gods to prove her suspicion wrong, but the heart thumping in her chest screamed otherwise.

Greny gaped at them as they approached. A wadded-up piece of fabric fell from his hand. In his eyes, glassy with stupefaction, a twinkle of recognition stirred before they bulged with panic. He turned and ran toward the edge of the bridge. Tamric sped up, with no call to his quarry to stop, as if he hoped the Crevast might kill

Greny for him. Drinith did her best to keep pace with him, though he was faster and pulled ahead.

Reaching the edge, Greny sank to his knees, shaking, staring at his closing executioner. A pathetic plea dribbled from his lips. "Drinith, please..."

Tamric's knife flashed, but not toward Greny. Drinith blocked it as it swung at her, but the force of the impact knocked her sideways. She stumbled clear of its swipe. Tamric hesitated, glanced at the simpering, groveling Greny. "Stay out of this, Princess, and I'll let you live."

Drinith sneered, her blade at the ready. "We wouldn't be having this conversation if you had more skill with your knife. Why attack me?"

Tamric frowned. "The Rat King must die, and I know you'd try to stop me. You don't hate the meritocrats enough to be one of us." He leapt the gap between them in an instant.

∾

Move! Run! This is your chance! Your only chance! As though trapped in a nightmare, Greny couldn't force his numb body to move while Drinith and the assassin met, their arms weaving into a series of slapping knots until they locked. A dragon's roar swallowed Drinith's yell. They twisted one way and then whipped the other, flinging Drinith toward the edge. Her arms flailed as she fell over. This time she screamed so loud that not all the dragons in the Crevast could drown it out. Her cry followed her down into the Void. Tamric peered over to the edge after her, his shoulders hunched as a mourner's might.

Greny scrambled to his feet as the assassin bounded toward him. Too late! He tripped and fell, sprawled across the ground. As Greny lifted to his hands and knees, a shadow spread over him. He closed his eyes, held his last breath, his chest tightening as it waited for the knife to strike. Why did the assassin delay? Why did he prolong Greny's agony? Better a quick death than to suffer this dread of anticipation. A light touch against his side shot a shiver through him. He groped at the spot but found no wound. A boot had glanced off him. He looked up at the two men fighting above him.

"Run!" Nayz roared, barely audible over the screaming crowd.

Greny crawled until he had cleared the combatants. Rising to unsteady feet, he staggered forward. He glanced back at the two men knotted together in a murderous embrace, paused. Chemp had died because of his cowardice. He mustn't let the same happen to Nayz. But even as Greny looked around for something to use as a weapon, Nayz stumbled backward, his blade slipping from his hand. His foe arrested his fall only to deliver a quick succession of stabs, a dozen or more, to his neck. As Nayz toppled, the assassin limped after Greny, a manic smile stretching across his face.

"Help! Help!" Greny cried, reaching out to the distant line of cordents facing the riot, deaf and blind to his plight. He tripped and slapped the ground. His head rang, blood trickled down his forehead. Again he crawled, but his pursuer closed despite his lameness.

A hand clamped onto his forehead and yanked his head back. Its fingers dug into his skin as he tried in vain to twist free.

"Your turn to die, meritocrat." A bloody dagger swooped down on him.

He reached up to block it. It sliced across his arm, but he managed to hold it back. His head slipped free of the assassin's grip, and he nodded forward. A crushing weight slammed into him. Cordents shunted the assassin away from him.

"Take him alive," he croaked. His head and arm throbbed. Blood trickled down his forehead. He felt a teasing chill on his pate as though the skin had been ripped away.

"Meritocrat." One of his rescuers knelt before him and studied the top of his head. "You'll need a couple of stitches on that." He pressed a white cloth against the wound.

"A couple?" Greny asked in disbelief. It felt as though his head had been carved open.

"It probably feels a lot worse than it is. Please put your hand on the cloth. No, Meritocrat, the other hand. I'll bandage the wound on that arm." As the woman worked, Greny looked back at the assassin, very much alive, kicking and squirming in the vice-like grip of the other two cordents.

Greny smirked and pointed to him. "Take him to the Yellow Section of Inkeep."

"You're wasting your time," the man growled as they dragged him away. "I won't talk."

"A pleasure is never a waste," Greny said. "And you'll talk. They all do in the end."

As soon as his wounds had been bandaged, he hobbled over to Nayz's corpse. He knelt down beside the dead man. The cooling blood soaked through the knees of his breeches, but he no longer cared. He pressed a hand against Nayz's cold forehead. Nayz's eyes popped open. With a heaving breath, he seized Greny's forearm.

He grinned, his eyes wide with disbelief. "You're alive."

"Thanks to you," Greny said. "Cordents! To me! Over here!" He waved his hand over his head to attract their attention. He tried to rise, but Nayz's grip anchored him.

"Don't waste your breath or mine. They can't help," Nayz said. He took a heaving breath. "Meritocrat Minol wanted me to betray you. I said I would consider it to buy you some time."

"I've never questioned your loyalty." If only that lie had been true. Greny patted Nayz's hand. "I'll look after your family." If Nayz had any daughters, Greny would adopt one as his heir. That would be the least he could do. If one was suitable, of course.

"I don't have—" The word ended in a rattle. His grip slackened as he slipped away. With trembling fingers, Greny closed Nayz's dead eyes, then wiped a burning tear from his cheek. To think he had distrusted Nayz through all his years of devoted service. To think of all those years of isolation Greny had suffered, when all this time, mistrust had blinded him to the true friend by his side.

A squeak alerted him to the two ratchers looming over him—Zetch and Treek, who he had assigned to escort Nayz.

"You should have been with him!" Greny snapped.

Treek signed that Nayz had given them the slip.

Greny didn't say anything. Couldn't. In his death, Nayz had proved himself to be as devoted as any of any ratcher. So many of Greny's servants had been slain since this crisis began: Dweed, Evreet. Feerth, Qweelch, Sheeg, and Edee before them. And fearless Chemp, loyal to his dying breath. Such a terrible loss in only a few days.

A cordent approached warily and handed him something. It was so bloody, dented, and bent, he didn't immediately recognize his emblem of merit.

The spans of the bridge closed together. Clamps like giant brass claws dropped to hold them in position while the traffic crossed. Pedestrians and drivers passing both directions stared at him with a mixture of confusion, curiosity, and even fear as he sobbed. Posaleum would pay for her scheming, but first Greny must face Okia. He must know if she was the spider sitting at the heart of this web of deceit.

42

The whistling howl of the Crevast mocked Drinith's scream as she plummeted. Tamric stared down, aghast, as if he had never meant to shove her off. His hunched form bending over the edge of the bridge quickly shrank to a dot, then disappeared from her view.

Gods save me. But nothing could rescue her now from the yawning jaws of the eternal Void.

Something hard slapped against her back. *Praise the gods! I've landed on a passing dragon's wing!* But now she began to slip down it toward the Crevast once again. She twisted round, stabbed at the wing with the knife she still held, desperate to stick it into the leathery surface, but the force of the blow bounced the knife out of her hand. She clawed for a grip on the wing in vain as it steepened precipitously.

Her slide slowed and reversed as the wing began to rise. If she could make it to the dragon's scaly trunk, she just might be able climb up it to the saddledeck and raise help from its crew. She tucked her arms against her body and let herself roll toward the dark hump in the distance. As she neared, she readied to reach out her hands, to grab a scale or anything that might anchor her to the beast. Her momentum slowed as the wing leveled again. On hands and knees, she scurried across the drum-tight skin. So near, so near. She lunged at the scales, but the wing dipped downward, and they slipped beyond her reach.

She had nearly slid to the edge of the wing when it began to rise again. But this time, instead of hurtling backward, she was thrown forward into the Void. She closed her eyes and begged the gods to strike her dead rather than letting her suffer the prolonged fall into the inner sun, slowly cooking in its terrible heat until she combusted.

Something soft slapped against her to the sound of shredding fabric. A second slap struck her, and then a third in quick succession. She opened her eyes. Drinith was smashing through a series of canopies, each one slowing her descent a little more. She might yet sur—

She hit the ground with a terrible shuddering thud reverberating through every bone in her body, punching her in every organ. For some time—a moment, an hour, or even a day; she was too dazed to guess—she lay where she was. Murmuring voices cut through her screaming pain. Clutching the wall beside her, she rose unsteadily to her feet, soreness spreading like a fire across her body. One side of her face felt swollen and tender, like a giant bruise. At least she hadn't broken any bones as far as she could tell, though the sharp pain in her right hip made her list to one side. In other circumstances, preservators might have easily healed her injuries, but she dared not go to them. They'd hand her over to the Meritocracy. As angry and bemused voices chattered from the windows above her, she limped up the path, uncertain where she should go.

She had landed on a long balcony on a built-up cliff face. High above, two bright blades carved the night sky—Spinbridge gradually drifting away from Southspoke. She looked up at the steep road zigzagging up the curtain of rock with trepidation, but there was nowhere for her to hide down here. Word would soon spread of an injured woman limping about after falling out of the night sky like some kind of demon. The cityscape that fringed the summit promised a warren of alleyways and lanes for her to shelter in.

Every awkward, tottering step hurt. She warded off the curious and the concerned with a menacing scowl. If cordents spotted her, they'd arrest her as a vagrant, or worse, realize who she was and send her to Inkeep. She kept alert for them in the vicinity, but she could hardly walk, much less run.

Staring passersby gave her a wide berth as she climbed with aching slowness, gasping for air. Her breathlessness surprised and alarmed her. She soon needed to rest, but she feared if she sat down, she would be too weak to rise again, so she leaned against a low wall. It didn't help. She set off again, stiffer than before.

She paused again to take in her progress. The road continued to stretch a daunting distance ahead, and she hadn't even reached the first corner. Every step felt like it was straight up. How could she hope to scale this cliff in her condition? She gritted her teeth and hobbled on, hugging the parapet with one arm to keep from falling. *I've got to get to the top. I have to. Little by little, I'll make it. All I need is perseverance and patience, and a little luck.*

Sly banter and raucous laughter drew her attention to the mob of courtesars rounding the corner and spilling down the ramp. Rosel's gilded plumage danced at the back. Drinith's shoulder and arm hurt as she drew her hood over her head.

"I hope we find her soon," one of them muttered. "These heels are killing me."

She crouched against the parapet. Hopefully—

"Excuse me, good lady." She didn't dare face the speaker. "We've heard that there is an injured Rhumgadian down here. We would very much like to make her acquaintance. You see, we are pursuing a missing meritocrat, also from Rhumgad. We want to assure ourselves that the ladies are not one and the same."

She pressed tighter against the wall. *Leave me be!* she wanted to roar but dared not in case Rosel recognized her voice.

Her hood gently stirred. "Come now. No need to be shy."

She twisted around and glared at her tormentor. The painted face recoiled in shock, then erupted in laughter. "Gods! I'd rather face some monster from the underside."

"That's not a very gallant comparison, Exarl," a second courtesar opined.

"My apologies," Exarl said with a deep bow. "I meant no offense." He turned to his companions. "I was alluding to the fierceness of her visage, not her unfortunate injuries."

"Let Rosel have a look at her, just to be sure she's not our errant meritocrat," a third courtesar said.

Rosel wearily plodded through the parting group. He gave her a cursory glance, as if she wasn't worth his time. His eyes expanded with sudden recognition. Her stomach twisted.

He shook his head. "It's not her. I'm certain." A wry smile. "The meritocrat is better looking."

She stifled a laugh, coughed to cover it, hurting her ribs.

"How did you sustain such terrible injuries?" Exarl asked.

"I fell off a dragon." She emitted a wheezy laugh this time. They all did.

"Probably drunk or delirious on hard tea," an unfamiliar courtesar opined.

"I will take you to a healer," Rosel said.

"I'll be fine," she said. "You have your meritocrat to find."

"Nonsense." Rosel took her arm and turned to his companions. "I will rejoin you on the hunt as soon as I have escorted this lady to the nearest healer."

"Rosel, that's mighty magnanimous of you," one of them scoffed, "but if you do the same for every beggar you come across, you'll bankrupt yourself and possibly your family in the bargain."

"I won't abandon a lady in distress," Rosel said fiercely. "Rich or poor. Young or old. Beautiful or plain."

"Just mind your money pouch," Exarl said.

Rosel's grip on Drinith's arm tightened. "What's that supposed to mean?"

Five heartbeats measured the silence before Exarl timidly answered. "I just mean be careful of pickpockets."

"You had better get to looking for Meritocrat Hax," Rosel said, "before someone else beats you to her."

With parting nods, his courtesar friends hurtled down the stone road like a startled herd of deer. Rosel waited until they slipped out of sight, then helped Drinith to her feet.

"I must get you to a healer," he said.

"That's where I was headed." She gazed up the steep, zigzagging road. Even with his support, she felt weak and unsteady.

"Why are you helping me?" she asked.

"I need you to accept my pledge of devotion," he said.

"Gods! What—?" So, his gallantry was just an excuse to proposition her. She would have shoved him away if she had the strength to stand by herself.

"I am on shaky ground regarding the Code for not turning you in. My sister blames you for our mother's death, and insisted I should help find you after preventing your arrest at your mansion. Accepting my pledge of devotion would override that imperative."

"Why would you choose to help me? I'm a pariah."

"I must insist. Otherwise, I will have to turn you in as soon as your wounds are treated. The pledge places an obligation on me, not you."

"But it would force you to fight for me against the entire city. I will not condemn you to death."

"You can repudiate my fealty at any time. That would end my obligation to you, and I would become another of your hunters again."

"I accept your pledge," Drinith said, eying him for any hint of triumph, but his face only softened with relief. "I don't understand what attracted you to me in the first place. There must be plenty of other meritocrats and meritorians who would be better suited."

He shuddered, his pace briefly stuttering. "They would expect... What I am about to say puts my life in your hands..."

"As mine is already in yours."

"I, well, I... Given your reputation, you wouldn't demand the same intimacies they'd expect."

"And what reputation is that?"

"You've spurned the advances of many fine courtesars, and then there are the rumors that you and your meritorian are lovers."

"We most certainly aren't."

"I stand corrected." His grip loosened as if he was about to lurch away from her, but he quickly tightened his hold again. He had such an expression of defeat and grim determination, Drinith couldn't help but feel sorry for him.

"Your secret"—*if I understand what you're trying to say*—"is safe with me. Are there many like you?"

"The one or two I knew of are dead." He smirked. "It's not something I could ask another courtesar. To be honest, if one of my companions put the question to me, I would answer him with steel."

"Leave Gyre," Drinith said. "There are countless places across the Crevast where you could live your life as you wish, free from the shadow of the sword."

"I am where I want to be," Rosel said firmly. "From the time I could pick up a stick and sport about with my friends, I wanted to be a swordsman. An honorable death doesn't frighten me. Better to live a glorious day than a thousand empty years."

"Halyard of Kasjor would have shared that sentiment."

"I am honored and humbled that you associate my words with such a legend."

"I just don't understand why you courtesars risk your lives."

"We do it for the Code, for our honor, our family, our country. Why do you stay in Gyre?"

"My friends are trapped here. I won't forsake them."

"See, you are wedded to your code, too."

They finally reached the cliff top and hobbled through a bewildering series of cobbled lanes until they halted in front of a wooden door. A tiny bouquet of dried flowers hung on it. Rosel pounded the door with his fist. "Shelba, wake up! You have a patient to attend to."

An ancient, hunched Nosteran opened the door. The woman looked as faded and brittle as the crown of dried flowers that rested on her white hair. She regarded the visitors with bleary irritation and then surprise. "She's not a courtesar."

Rosel gently pushed the door open and brought Drinith inside.

He sat her on a bed in a shallow alcove and placed a stack of coins on the table. "I want her wounds treated."

"Of course," the woman said. She helped Drinith lie down and began examining her. Drinith winced as the old woman peeled blood-caked clothes off her to reveal purple swelling extending down one side of her body. Shelba's fingers were as steely and sharp as any blade as she prodded Drinith's injuries. Drinith had to stifle a cry a few times.

"You've cracked two ribs, damaged a couple of tendons, and bruised half your body," Shelba said.

"And nobody else must enter here until she leaves," Rosel said.

"If somebody injured turns up to the door, I'm treating them. This isn't the Grand Preservatory. My ethics can't be bought for coin."

"Is there a back room that you can hide her in?" Rosel asked.

Shelba spread her hands. "This is the only room I have." The room had three other beds tucked into similar alcoves.

"Then at least pull the curtain across, woman," Rosel huffed.

The healer did so. Then she brought a bowl and, propping Drinith's head up, encouraged her to sip from it. The tea tasted salty. "This will numb the pain and restore your strength."

Haunted by the memory of Doctor Aerwig's attempt to administer her the highly addictive pain medicine Devil's Dew, Drinith hesitated. If Rosel trusted Shelba, then why should Drinith demure? She gulped down the brackish liquid in a couple of mouthfuls, pulling a face on the last gritty drop.

"I must go," Rosel said. "I'll be back in the morning to check on her."

"Don't worry, I'll take good care of her," Shelba said.

With a nod, Rosel disappeared out the door, slamming it shut behind him.

"That young man has a good heart. You're not the first stray he has brought here. Some of them four-legged, believe it or not."

Drinith wallowed in the healer's soothing voice as her pain melted away. She was safe here.

"Move your hand," Shelba commanded.

Drinith couldn't feel her hand as she obeyed. It was as if her body had dissolved and all that was left was a loose affiliation of thoughts floating on nothing. Yes, she felt really safe here with this smiling woman.

"We'll have you fixed up in no time," Shelba assured her. The cheeriness had left her voice, replaced by a cold pragmatism. "And then I'm going to call the cordents."

Some part of Drinith vaguely suggested she should fight her way off her sickbed, but she couldn't muster enough energy, and her senses were muddled. Her thoughts seemed to unwind on an endless spool. The world was shrinking, diffusing into blackness.

"You're the one everyone's hunting, aren't you? You're Meritocrat Hax. I'm doing this as much for Rosel's good as Gyre's. That lad is too softhearted. Helping you would be the death of him. Sometimes, you have to be cruel to be kind."

It was the last thing Drinith heard as she slipped into oblivion.

43

———————

Okia may have hidden her wealth beneath a benign senescence and reserved attire, but there was nothing modest about her palatial mansion. Reputed to have a hundred rooms, it had a massive columned portico with a domed roof at its entrance. Reliefs of dragons coiled around the shafts, forever chasing the giant stone rosettes at the top.

Greny quietly dispersed the five ratchers among the pillars. Deetch, Queek and Zueel had joined Treek and Zetch after being hastily summoned from Scylax Tower. They were all visibly shaken by the death of Chemp and his companions at Spinbridge. He wished he could give them a little time to grieve the loss of their friends, but the current circumstances were too fraught for that.

The brass door was shaped like a yawning dragon's mouth. The heavy knocker was a golden rose. Greny lifted its stem and struck it against its rest several times, the clang echoing in the vaulted ceiling.

The door opened as silently as a creeping assassin.

"I'm here to see Okia on a matter of some urgency," Greny said as he swept by the butler.

A dozen servants stood to attention in neat rows on opposite sides of the foyer. They all carried knives and the black truncheons usually reserved for cordents. Their robes bulged with concealed armor. Elaborate white spiral tattoos covered their purple faces and bald pates. Their earlobes bore several triangular notches. They were obviously Nemonese Begriats, probably all from the same tribe, doubtless brought in great haste to Gyre to bolster Okia's safety.

Otherwise, the foyer, with its collection of statues and paintings bought and pilfered from across Noster, was just as Greny remembered it. While he waited for the butler to announce him, he pretended to admire a marble sculpture of a snake fighting a scorpion, all the while growing increasingly irritated by the scrutinizing stares of the guards.

The butler returned. "The meritocrat will see you in the garden," she said breathlessly.

As Greny followed her, two of the Begriats fell in silently behind him. He couldn't help glancing back at them. Tattoos covered their bare feet. *Odd. Are they tattooed all over?*

They emerged onto a large balcony adorned with rose bushes. The chill breeze of the Void completely swept away the intoxicating fragrance their profusion of golden blooms promised. Stairs led down to the lower levels of the garden that hung like a trellis down the side of the cliff. Almost hidden behind a circular marble table with its centerpiece of two naked men wrestling, Okia stood staring out over the balcony at the Void beyond.

She slapped both hands on the parapet and swung around.

"So, they sent you. I should have known. You come to my home in the middle of the night like an assassin, armed no doubt with lies and accusations."

"Who do you think *they* are, if you don't mind me asking?" Greny sat on a bench beside the table. He noticed a black chest at the feet of the stone wrestlers.

"Elca and Thespenilea, of course. They've made friends, it seems. Elca is particularly suited to her emblem of merit. The four-horned snake has shed her skin again. Without my help, she would be still Ratcatcher General, the lowest position in the Meritocracy. I always supposed you hated her so intensely because of that, being partial to rats."

Ratchers weren't rats, despite the superficial similarities in appearance, but now wasn't the moment to quibble.

Okia looked back over the balcony. The twinkling curve of countless distant shards crowned the sepia light of the inner sun. Dim stars splashed the dark vault above.

"I should have suspected Elca's sudden magnanimity toward Thespenilea," Okia reproached herself. "When she claimed she was building a bridge with the Short War Faction at this time of crisis, she gave no hint only she might cross it. She forsook Drinith and now she forsakes me."

"She says she still supports the Rhumgadian invasion," Greny retorted.

Okia smirked and slapped the parapet. "Of course she would! To say anything else risks alienating her followers in Parliament. But she proposes to send the Gadflies back to their homeland whether or not the Rhumgadian invasion went ahead. Do you know why Thespenilea hates the Gadflies with such passion? They are squatting on her property."

"I know she owns a substantial part of the Blue Quarter, yes."

"Thespenilea pretty much owns it all. She bought what buildings she didn't already possess on the shardlet by offering ridiculous sums to their owners. When the first of the exiles came to Gyre, she generously offered them the Blue Quarter as a home. They had money, or at least the veneer of wealth. When they became destitute, she changed her mind, but it was too late to evict them. She dare not enforce her leases lest she should spark a riot, and she couldn't find anyone foolish and generous enough to take her unwelcome guests off her hands."

Okia winced as if in pain. "And of course, Thespenilea is afraid. Her closest allies are dead, and many of the secrets and deals which held her faction together were lost with them. She's only too happy to accept Elca's overtures of friendship."

Greny made a calming gesture, but it was as lost on his host as a smile was to a dragon. "Did you receive an invitation to that ill-fated meeting in Osro's mansion?"

"I suppose Elca and Thespenilea have produced such invitations?" Okia asked tartly, folding her arms.

"They have."

"How terribly convenient for them," Okia said. She grabbed the chest, flung the lid open and, drawing out several slips of parchment, threw them onto the table.

Greny picked one up. It was embossed with the Onez winged siren.

Okia sat down on the bench and folded her hands together. She looked every bit her age and more. "I found these in a search of my home, along with two dead sunfinches and several dozen gilded feathers, no doubt planted at the behest of the true culprit. She hoped you'd find them if you searched the property. Hopefully, you will accept them instead as proof that I am innocent."

Greny couldn't help but smile. "Or very clever."

"I wish I was." Okia shook her head wistfully. "I was foolish to presume I understood the rules of this interminable game we all play, to imagine I was good at it. It's only now that I realize how pathetically naive I have always been. In truth, I lack the bitter ruthlessness of our peers. Where I might wound, they would gladly kill. Maybe they're right, and I really am a fool."

"So, it is your contention that Elca or Thespenilea masterminded this affair."

"I should have never trusted Elca," Okia said. "Look at how she punished the meritocrats who expelled her from the Vicenary Jury with such single-minded determination. She was cast out of the Iron Circle and yet managed to worm her way into the heart of Gyran power. If anyone had the patient ambition and callous disregard to engineer this plot, it would be her."

Of course, Okia had every reason to hate Elca after her act of betrayal. "In truth," Greny said judiciously, "any of you might be responsible for this string of murders."

"Sadly true," Okia admitted, walking over to the balustrade. "Or you, for that matter." At her nod, a Begriat gathered the sheets of parchment, placed them in the chest and handed it to her. She cradled it in her arms like a baby, then threw it into the Void.

Greny dashed to the parapet, but the box had already shrunk to an inconsequential dot. "You fool! That evidence might have been key in identifying the killer!"

Okia shrugged. "It was more likely to damn me."

"You speak as if you're powerless. You're the richest meritocrat in Gyre."

"The younger meritocrats and meritorians are besotted with Elca. The old guard is too few, too divided, and too distrusting of each other. Her alliance with Thespenilea leaves her unassailable. There is nothing I can do except retire to Noster."

"So, you just give up."

"Do you always play Angels and Demons to the last move? When facing inevitable defeat, it is more graceful to forfeit and congratulate the better player."

"This isn't a game," Greny groused.

"Elca hates you. She blames you for Ecethor's death."

"I'm leaving." Greny rose and headed for the stairs. The Begriats moved toward him, but halted at a flick of Okia's hand.

"There's a rumor that at the Vicenary Council tomorrow," Okia called after him, "there'll be a motion to expel you."

Greny stormed up the steps toward the mansion. *And I'll fight every moment between now and then to keep my seat. I won't give up like you, you old fool!*

44

—————

At Mileek's nod, Greny entered one of the many torture chambers in the Yellow Section of Inkeep. Sawdust covered the floor. Two ratcher guards, Riskeel and Kreevest, stood beside benches covered in knives, scalpels, metal clamps, needles of various sizes, and other torture implements. Strapped to a scored block of wood, the assassin twisted his head to study him with disdain.

Greny chuckled. "Glare while you can. Sight is the first sense we'll destroy. We'll leave your sense of smell until second, so you can fully appreciate the sweet putridity of your eyes being burned out. We take away taste and touch next. You'll greet that as a mercy by the time we're finished. You'll be a blind maggot crawling on the floor, waiting for some merciful boot to stamp out your miserable existence."

The assassin sneered. "Don't pretend you could even remain here while your rats people do the dirty work. You're too much of a coward to watch."

Greny laughed. "My would-be butcher talks of cowardliness. I won't be here, no. The smell of blood and burning flesh makes me queasy. But I will be close enough to enjoy your screams. Goodbye." He turned around and stalked toward the exit.

"Don't you want to hear what I have to say?" the assassin asked.

"No," Greny said without breaking his stride.

Riskeel ran a blade in slow strokes down a honing steel.

"Wait! Wait!" the assassin yelled.

Greny paused, turned slowly. "I'll give you one chance to tell the truth."

The scrape of metal stopped.

The assassin's lips moved silently, experimentally, but his moment of weakness passed too quickly. "I want no favors from you," he said through clenched teeth.

"I don't know why you're protecting the arch schemer who sent you to your death at Spinbridge," Greny said. "You might have killed me, but you couldn't have possibly escaped from the bridge alive. You were meant to die there, just like Drinith."

"I'm dead, anyway."

"Maybe not," Greny said. "I could be lenient, generous even, if you gave me the name of whoever betrayed you. I could arrange passage on a dragon—"

"To Beamstone," the assassin spat.

Greny smiled despite himself. "To anywhere you liked. Perhaps I could use a man of your talents. Working for me could be quite lucrative."

"Empty words. After your mother died, you promised my parents that you would retain them on your staff. Then one day, you locked them out of your tower, throwing what little they possessed into the street after them, and replaced them with your rats."

The blood turned to ice in Greny's veins. Cenmis's butler had once been a servant of House Scylax. Too much of a coincidence.

Suddenly breathless with fear, Greny nodded to the ratchers to ready their knives. "We'll get the truth out of you one way or the other." He dabbed the sweet-smelling ointment he carried under his nose in expectation of the scent of blood.

As the ratchers closed around the assassin, he grinned up at Greny in manic triumph. He laughed, he actually had the gall to laugh. "You're right. I was meant to die at Spinbridge."

Greny supposed his threat had finally brought the assassin to his senses. He signaled the ratchers to halt. "Who sent you there?"

"I should have never trusted your brother," the assassin declared gleefully. "You and he are both traitors to the core."

"No." Greny shook his head, though he could feel the truth of it in the pit of his stomach.

"That's right," the assassin said gleefully. "The man you seek is your own brother." His raucous laughter filled the chamber.

Greny snatched a springbow lying on the table and aimed at his tormentor, but the man only laughed all the harder.

Greny repeatedly pulled the trigger, but it kept sticking. *Damn contraption must be locked in some fashion.* When Riskeel stepped forward to assist, he roughly pushed him away. Greny ham-handedly fumbled with the knobs, trying to free the trigger, his frustration mounting.

He was just about to smash the springbow against the floor when suddenly the trigger snapped back; the springbow jolted in his hands, a bolt snapped against the wall beyond the prisoner.

The assassin continued to laugh, tears streaming from his eyes, as the springbow worked through its complex mechanism to reload. "You've let others do your dirty work for far, far too long. Just like Qilin sitting in his shop, playing with his birds, while he sends those who trust him to their deaths. Aah!" A second bolt had struck his leg, shattering bone. He bit back a cry, then laughed again, mirthless and defiant, and he kept laughing as Greny shot a third, a fourth, and fifth time. It was the sixth shot that struck him in the neck that finally silenced him, after a brief gurgle.

"Is he dead?" Greny asked plaintively. "Is he dead?"

The ratchers closed around the assassin and confirmed the fact with nods.

Greny stumbled backward into the table, placed the slippery weapon on it, and rubbed his sweaty hands together. Something caught in his throat, and he retched. Overwhelmed by the stench of blood and vomit, he fled the chamber.

~

GRENY CROUCHED against a wall outside the torture chamber and pressed his hands to the sides of his head. Dragons, his hands were wet with blood! He stared at his palms, but to his relief, only sweat made them slick. He had never gotten close enough to the assassin to get spattered.

Erphel, the fool, the deluded fool! Why had he gotten mired in politics again? Did he hate his brother so much that he sought to ruin him with another futile act of treason? This time it wasn't a naive, clumsy attempt to rile the commoners against their leaders and their betters. It was murder, callous and clinical. It was hard to believe that Erphel would forsake his precious code so completely and irrevocably, and yet the assassin's accusation made sense. The realization felt like a knife stabbed deep into Greny's heart. Sunfinch feathers would be exactly the sort of symbol Erphel might adopt; also, he was in an ideal position to recruit the servants Greny had banished from Scylax Tower. Osro, Cenmis, and Thaxen had been rivals for his love before Ricoen Zurin seduced and corrupted him. He would know them intimately, at least as young meritorians.

And yet he surely wasn't capable of contriving this plot. He was a follower, not a leader. His part in the Silverfish Revolt severed him from the Meritocracy a long time ago. Even with ex-servants of Scylax spying for him, he couldn't have the insight into the subtleties of meritocratic interactions of someone who moved freely in those circles. A meritocrat must be manipulating him—Elca, or maybe even Thespenilea. Greny needed to find his brother before Posaleum stumbled onto him. He needed the name of whatever meritocrat was behind this plot, and to save Erphel himself if it was possible.

If only Nayz were still alive. The man had a subtle mind and demonstrated absolute loyalty. Greny could have trusted him for something like this.

He glanced at the cell door across from him. Woad Glastum was locked in there. It had been a mistake to imprison him on Jarma's word alone. Greny walked over to the door and slid back the cover over the little grille.

"Woad?"

"What do you want?" Woad Glastum snapped somewhere in the cell's darkness.

"Drinith is dead."

Stunned silence followed a sharp gasp. He must be wondering why, if she no longer lived, he hadn't been sent to the Plank. His face emerged from the darkness within to fill the grille. "How?"

"She was murdered," Greny said, "by the same group I'm hunting. I have concluded that your services might yet be useful in bringing them to justice."

The ex-mercenary emitted a mirthless chuckle. "You what? Really promise to keep your word this time? You can't seriously expect me to trust you." He snorted.

"I'll release your wife as proof," Greny said. "She can walk free this very night."

"And Jarma?"

Greny repressed a grin at Woad's ignorance of her part in condemning him to Inkeep. "She's dead, too, unfortunately."

Woad Glastum's incredulous stare quickly hardened to grim resignation. "How?"

"She crossed me."

"The Oracle?"

"I'm not sure he's mine to release. Somebody else has a claim on him. Don't worry, he'll be safe."

"And what about Perian?"

"If you want," Greny said with a shrug. *An attempt at redemption, or at self-deception. Glastum wants to convince himself he's a good man and he had no choice but betray his friends.* "She's obviously aware of our mutual understanding. Of course, she isn't long in custody. A good dose of immemoreal would make her forget you."

"No," Glastum said firmly.

"You would burden her with the memories of being arrested and imprisoned? She's quite the blabbermouth, I understand. How long would it take for word of your role in her arrest to reach your dear wife?"

"Point taken," Glastum growled. "I want the Hax servants released, too. They did nothing wrong."

"Of course. Even the butler?"

"Not her. She can rot."

"She betrayed Drinith the wrong way, I suppose. Took pleasure in it instead of being tortured with guilt."

"For someone who wants me to work for him, you're pretty sharp-tongued."

For someone lucky enough to get a second chance from me, you seem peculiarly eager to throw it away. You'll accept, though. You're just trying to maximize the price of your fealty, and who could blame you? "I can send Fenvar to the Plank, if you so desire. You can avenge the wrong she did Drinith," Greny said.

No answer.

"I'll take that as a yes," Greny said. "If Drinith was still alive, she wouldn't approve."

"She's not," Glastum said. "Now, let me out of here."

Greny did so, but only after summoning Deetch, Mileek, and four other ratchers armed with springbows to make sure the Gadfly behaved. Woad Glastum emerged from his cell, grim and wary. "Let Tazran go. Immediately!"

A nod from Greny sent Kreevest and Riskeel scurrying down the curving corridor. "Cover her eyes." He grinned back at Glastum's murderous scowl. "Better she doesn't see you, don't you think? I'm sure you'd prefer to avoid awkward questions."

Glastum gave a hesitant nod.

The ratchers led his blindfolded wife down the corridor. Grim defiance pinched her mouth and tensed her jaw. She must assume she was heading for the Plank or something equally unpleasant—a round of torture, perhaps.

Glastum tensed as she neared. Conflicting emotions contorted his face—relief he had saved her, shame for his part in her arrest and Drinith's death, the nagging fear she might learn of it. He reached toward her, his hands trembling, but the ratchers swept her past him, and he didn't make a sound. He didn't breathe until she had disappeared around the bend. His shoulders slumped as if the weight of his guilt pressed down on them.

"And the others?"

"They'll be released, I promise," Greny said, "but we haven't time to watch them leave one by one. We have work to do." *We have to find my brother before he destroys me.*

45

Drinith woke with a start. A damp, warm sponge clung limpid-like to her injured face, bandages securing it wound around her head. She propped herself on her elbows to stare at Shelba, sitting on a chair, smiling sweetly. Had Drinith imagined her threat to summon cordents?

"How do you feel?" Shelba asked.

Drinith followed her glance to a silhouette sitting in a dark corner. He held a sword, its naked blade extending beyond the shadow to shine in the lampstone light. The figure leaned forward, revealing Rosel's face, taut with restrained anger.

Her pains had dulled significantly. "I feel much better, thank you."

"See, Rosel?" Shelba said. "I've not hurt her. I take my vocation seriously."

"That's why I found you outside calling for cordents when I came back," he harrumphed.

"Your meritocrat is wanted for murder," Shelba said. "I was just being a good Gyran."

"I know," Rosel said. "That's why I didn't run you through with my sword...yet."

Drinith winced at the pain in her side as she swung her legs out of the bed and sat up. A swirl of lightheadedness made her cling on to the edge. Rosel bounded from his chair to help her, but Shelba reached her first.

Cringing beneath his forbidding glare, she said, "She'll be fine. A little dizziness is normal."

Drinith rose unsteadily to her feet until the trembling of her legs, feeling like stilts of jelly, forced her to plop back down on the bed again.

"I'll give her a dose of Courtesar's Resolve." Shelba scurried over to the table and threw a dried sprig, two teaspoons of a black viscous syrup and three pinches of a black powder into a bowl. Then she selected a glass jar from her shelves and poured the red liquid it contained into the mixture. Straining the concoction through a sieve, she poured about half into a phial and offered the rest to Drinith. "This will help."

The medicine tasted sweet but left a bitter aftertaste.

"She's making a fool of you, Rosel," Shelba remarked. "Your family will never forgive you for aiding Meritocrat Orom's murderer." She nodded decorously at Drinith. "Begging your pardon, Meritocrat."

"Drinith had nothing to do with that," Rosel said, adding with a smirk: "I stake my life on it. The entire world makes a fool of the courtesar, but his honor makes a fool of the world."

"See where your honor gets you when every courtesar in Gyre wants to run you through."

Enough people sacrificed their lives for me. "Apart from the three of us," Drinith spoke up, "nobody knows that Rosel helped me."

"But they will eventually," Shelba said. "We can't sit here forever. You'll be caught and interrogated by truthscryers."

"You have nothing to fear from that, Shelba," Rosel said morosely. "Since all Drinith can attest about you is your betrayal."

"Try to rise now," Shelba said.

Drinith stood on firmer legs than before. She felt much stronger, her pains softened to dull aches. "Courtesar's Resolve is a potent medicine," she said. "I've not heard of it before."

"Courtesars use it to temporarily bolster their strength when injured," Shelba explained. "Some even take it to boost their prowess before a fight." Shelba glanced nervously at Rosel's deepening scowl. "Not that I would ever condone such cheating. It comes at a cost, though. When it wears off, you'll be twice as weak as you were, and your injuries will hurt as though you've been kicked by a casquar."

"How long will this potion last?" Drinith asked.

"Until morning, if you are lucky."

"What time is it?" Drinith asked.

"Past the second hour of midnight. The first nightebb bell shall sound soon."

Drinith rubbed the poultice bandaged to the side of her face. "Do I need this?"

"The cuts might scar without it."

That doesn't sound appealing. But no, it would draw too much attention. Drinith pulled the poultice off. "Rosel, I want you to guard Shelba until the first dawnbell. After that, I will renounce my love for you and any fealty you owe me will end."

A spasm of surprise flickered across Rosel's stern face. "If you insist..."

"I do. After the first dayrise bell, you will rejoin those hunting me. I'm unarmed. I need a knife."

Rosel's sword halted Shelba's lurch toward Drinith.

"She asked for a knife," Shelba pleaded. "I have one I can give to her."

"Point out where it is and let the meritocrat get it herself," Rosel said.

Following Shelba's trembling finger, Drinith found the weapon on the shelf.

"A courtesar gave it to me," the healer explained.

Drinith yanked the dagger from its ornate, rust-spotted sheath. A black patina stained the blade. "Gods, what a relic," she muttered.

"It was a gift in appreciation for my help," Shelba said, nervously rubbing her hands together. "I had no use for it, but I didn't feel right selling it."

With a parting nod to Rosel, Drinith headed out the door.

She hastened through the twilight-mottled city, avoiding areas brightened by the inner sun's glare as much as possible, clinging to the night. She carried the black blade in her hand, its handle quickly turning greasy in her sweaty palm. All the way to Qilin's shop, she struggled to come up with a plan to put everything right again. All she could think of was the vengeance she would take on that perfidious coward.

She approached the shop cautiously in case Erphel's outlook warned him, but no beggar lurked by the fountain. The shop was shut tight. She hid her dagger beneath her cloak and lifted her fist to bang on the door, but stepped back at the sound of footsteps inside rumbling toward it. At the sudden squeal and snap of the bolt, she slammed herself against the wall and dropped to the ground, where she curled into a ball, head down, so she might be mistaken for a sleeping beggar.

Through the narrow loop of vision her hood allowed, she glimpsed figures spilling out of the shop, four of whom had long, hairless tails. A fifth black-robed figure, judging from his stumpy build, must be Greny. Drinith hazarded a glimpse at the second human to emerge—Woad Glastum.

"So, he's gone, fled, leaving only an empty cage," Greny muttered. "Perhaps he's flown away. Or perhaps... Follow me. We may yet find our quarry."

Lead on, Drinith thought. *Take me to your traitorous brother.*

46

The restraining coffin swayed back and forth like a loping animal. The velvet lining was damp and stank of fear. In the smothering darkness, Jarma itched under her clothes, felt the dew of her stale breaths tickle her face.

Her exultation at wresting a damning confession from Greny dimmed as the vessel's journey dragged on. What awaited her when it reached its destination? Would it be the Plank and death, or might yet the Veiled Meritocrat intervene? She had promised to rescue Jarma once she left Scylax Tower, but Jarma was under no illusion about the value of assurances.

Versifer's book—she had forgotten it completely. The Veiled Meritocrat must have taken it. Gods only knew what secrets she gleaned from its enigmatic passages that might have rendered Jarma's testimony worthless. To her mysterious benefactor, she was merely another game piece for her board, to play with and dispose of when it was to her advantage. Anything might have happened beyond this wooden prison. Greny might be dead, or even the Veiled Meritocrat herself.

Jarma found equally appalling the prospect of plummeting into the inner sun and the prolonged terror of inescapable death. Some said those who fell into the Void cooked in the inner sun's heat before its flames ever touched them. Others claimed the fallers' hearts mercifully gave out from horror before that happened. The only certainty was that nobody survived.

To think I was once a maid, then a meritorian, and very soon I'll be just a scream descending into the Void. It will swallow every thought, every feeling, every memory, and nothing of me will remain. It will be as if I never lived.

She tried to draw comfort that she might yet meet her beloved Abecedar in the afterlife, but she couldn't see beyond the Void. He had been consigned to the inner sun after his death. A strangling terror built inside of her. The lining ripped as she balled it in her fists in desperation. She could feel herself slipping into the darkness's all-consuming maw.

The restraining coffin slapped the ground. Jarma couldn't speak. She couldn't even breathe. She listened to the screws on the lid squeaking as they twisted.

The lid lifted, and the cold, howling wind of the Crevast rushed into the vessel. Jarma's whole body became a scream.

A claw-like hand struck her face hard, stunning her into silence. The raw scratches the ratcher's nails had left on her cheek stung as he and a second ratcher hoisted her from the box. She recognized neither of them from the tower. Perhaps they were executioners. Behind her was Crimson Plaza and the monumental edifices that were the organs of the Gyran State—the Parliament of Merit, the Dragon Church, the Ducal Parliament, the Mortuary of Sin. What sin had she committed to be forced to walk the Plank? She burned with indignation at the unfairness of her execution. To think she was brought here in the middle of the night to die like some nameless pauper, unobserved except for a couple of disinterested cordents patrolling the plaza.

The ratchers turned her to face the Plank itself. It was red during the day, but the night turned its upper surface black, its edges limned by the inner sun's glow. Since Gyre's foundation, criminals had fallen to the death from it: murderers, traitors, would-be tyrants, and even a queen. Now it was Jarma's turn. As the ratchers shunted her forward, a paroxysm of competing urges gripped her. Did anyone care that she went to her death with dignity? Would screams elicit any sympathy from those few who heard them?

"Please, no," she said with mousy timidity. "Let me go. Please." But the ratchers kept pushing her forward. Their squeals and chitters sounded disconcertingly like laughter.

The cordents—redchecks—strolled over to watch. They doubtless considered her death a mild diversion on an otherwise boring night.

As they eyed her intently, a sudden resolve gripped her. *Damn them! I'll not be driven to my death like a sheep to the slaughterhouse. I shall choose the moment of my death. Let the Void take me!* A reckless ecstasy rose up within her as she ran along the narrowing Plank to fling herself into the Void's embrace. Versifer's third vision had predicted a woman falling to her death. Jarma would fulfill that part at least. The ratchers' panicked squeaks behind her made her grin all the harder. She would be the mistress of her own destiny from here to the end of the Plank.

"Stop!"

I will not!

"Stop! Stop!"

It was only when she had reached the very tip of the Plank that she paused, and she finally heeded the cordents' cries. She teetered there, feeling the pull of the Void, the breeze buffeting her as though she were a flimsy sail.

"There's no need to be afraid," a soothing male voice said. "Just don't move."

But all she wanted to do was fall. She was just uncertain in what direction. She seemed to be encircled by a precipitous drop. It was as if time had frozen at the moment of her leap into the Void.

The sudden touch of a hand made her lurch forward. More hands grabbed her. The sepia shroud of the inner sun filled her vision. But the hands gripping on to her anchored her to the Plank. Redchecks pulled her back from the brink.

"Silly cow nearly pulled us over with her," one of them grumbled.

"Watch your mouth," his companion snapped. "She's a meritorian, remember?"

"My apologies, Meritorian," the other cordent muttered.

As they moved back down the Plank to the Crimson Plaza, other cordents gathered around her, encircling her, protecting her. As she passed by the ratchers' corpses, she felt safe enough to burst into tears.

A meritocrat was waiting for her on the steps of the Dragon Church. She wasn't wearing a veil. Jarma grasped the significance of the red bar on the shoulder of her black dress before she recognized the slanted grin of Opriet Braesum.

With a gentle wave of her hand, the circle of cordents parted. With misting eyes, the cordent general descended the steps and enveloped Jarma in her arms.

"You are safe now," she whispered, her embrace as warm and tender as Jarma's own mother's.

47

Greny's party hurried to the nearest high canal, stopping only briefly to give their leader time to catch his breath. They commandeered the first two punts they encountered and set out for Mount Riddle. Greny, still panting after his exertions, sat in the bow of the lead boat and watched the quivering stars reflected in the gently rippling black water. Deetch sat behind him while Queek punted. Woad Glastum, Treek and Zetch were in the second boat. The tomb-pocked mountain expanded in the distance with irritating slowness. He had arrived at the shop not long after Erphel had left, according to the ratchers. His brother was no fool. Erphel must have guessed Greny would force the truth from his captured underling sooner or later. But eventually Erphel would go to their crypt. His dead twin was calling to him.

Unless Erphel had left Gyre altogether. If so, so much the better. We both would be safe. But the tightness in Greny's chest dismissed the possibility. Erphel would surely dismiss flight as abject cravenness. He'd rather die than live as a coward.

Could Greny kill him, his only brother, his own flesh and blood? He had promised himself in the aftermath of the Silverfish Revolt to protect Erphel. The prospect of breaking that solemn oath filled him with dismay. And yet he could never be truly safe while Erphel lived.

No, Greny only needed to imprison him in Inkeep. Or the Scylax Tower. Yes, Erphel could be his "guest" there for the rest of his life. It would be a kind of homecoming.

Mount Riddle loomed ahead, washed pink by the light of the twin moons. The tombstones and raised crypts spread across it made it look like a conical pile of misshapen skulls. No traffic disturbed the canal. Nobody but the dead had any business heading to the mountain at this time of the night.

Erphel might very well not be there, Greny thought. *I might be wasting my time.* And yet he clung on to this tenuous lead, as slight and fragile as a thread of spider's silk, hoping and praying it would lead him to his brother.

DRINITH KEPT BACK a good distance from the flotilla as it moved down the canal lest Greny's keen-eyed rodent servants should spot her. Following them was surely madness. What could she possibly accomplish against Greny, Woad and four ratchers, and maybe that traitor Qilin? And yet, what choice had she but to trail after them? No matter how dismal her circumstances, even when hunted in the tunnels of Ophigee or stalked by pentaculars, she had clung on to enough hope to survive. But this time, there was no hope to give up. If she wasn't dead by morning thanks to this quixotic pursuit, she'd be captured soon after and sent to the Plank. And yet she doggedly pursued the cordent general and his treacherous brother.

Something more than vengeance moved her. The insatiable desire to untangle this web of deceit, perhaps. She was like an arrow let loose from a bow. She simply had no choice but to fly toward her target.

By the time Greny's party reached the end of the canal, Neor, the white moon, had fallen from the sky and the bloody light of red-eyed Ruis alone bled over the mountain. Atop the entrance gate columns two stone dragons attacked each other, their necks knotted together to form an arch, their dorsal spikes stretching in multiple directions like monstrous teeth. On the fort on the back of the left one stood a hideous, leather-winged demon, while a sword-wielding angel graced the fort on the right dragon. Angels and demons locked in fierce combat sprawled across the metal gates. Its builders had likely intended it to scare off would-be trespassers, but Greny's mother had once told him that all mortal troubles ended at this gate. Greny couldn't help being jealous of the comfortable oblivion of the women and men interred beyond it.

They passed under the arch's fanged shadow and climbed the winding, branching path up the hill through a labyrinth of countless tombs. Here lay the ancestors of Greny's people, their corpses sown like seeds in the ground, flowering into magnificent stone, sinking roots deep into the earth. It was the Wealgiver herself who ended the practice of casting the dead into the Void and adopted landlubber burials. Here and there, anonymous mounds erupted like grassy boils through the stone, marking the graves of those early generations who left no heirs to move them to more salubrious tombs later on. On Mount Riddle, no space was wasted. Even the flagstones beneath Greny's feet bore names—beloved servants or friends too poor to buy a proper plot.

Here and there, more ornate crypt entrances bore familiar symbols—to the right, the Falier centicore, the Devaner knotted sepopard; to the left, the Reiner scale louse, the Ronad scytale; just ahead, the Visentar winged spider, the Rerato grinning crocotta. The party was close to the Scylax crypt—as close as Greny wanted his companions to get.

"Wait here," Greny said to Glastum. "The ratchers should be able to hear me should I call."

Rounding the corner, Greny found a cold blue glow in the open doorway of the crypt. Somebody was inside.

The Scylaxes' traditional emblem was carved above the entrance. This was the one place Greny, out of respect for his ancestors, had not dared to replace the Double-headed Axe with his wheel of rats, but seeing it guarding the door made him feel like a trespasser.

Two statues stood guard just inside, a man and a woman, ducalions four hundred years apart, back when holding that office honored one's family. Greny's mother had been named after the woman, his brother after the man. Greny shared his name with his mother's most fondly remembered lover, a lowly draker, not a courtesar.

Erphel stood in the middle of the crypt, head bowed, his old sword forged anew, transformed by the milk-blue lambency from the lampstone ledgerstones into another figure from those more heroic times. He looked up with a start as Greny entered, his sword leveled at the intruder. Sitting at his feet was a draped birdcage. Much smaller than the one Greny found in his shop, it reached up to his brother's knees.

"So, now you choose to come visit the family crypt," Erphel muttered, lowering his blade.

Drinith's wounds nagged her as she passed through the gates to the necropolis. What could she hope to achieve in coming here other than getting herself killed? In the past, the necessity to safeguard those who depended on her had given her strength, but now she couldn't even protect herself.

She had never felt so alone, so helpless, so pointless. All her life, she had been a gadfly of the rich and powerful. She had avoided their swats, but tonight she'd be finally crushed, stubbed out of existence.

Throbbing pain in her side made her lean against a headstone. Shelba's drug was wearing off much too quickly.

The black mouth of an open grave lay nearby, a waiting maw ready to swallow her.

Despite the overwhelming certainty of her impending death, she couldn't give up. She stumbled on up the mountain. *I am an arrow, and I must fly my course.* A last act of defiance beckoned.

"YET AGAIN, you put our family's honor in jeopardy," Greny said to Erphel. "I sacrificed so much to save you the last time, and this is how you repay me—murder and treason. Who are you working for? Who is this new love that spurred you to turn your sword against the Halcyon Republic again?"

But even as he asked, he sensed the answer. Erphel had never stopped loving Ricoen Zurin, pining for her. The Ducalion was up to her old tricks from inside the palace. They were communicating somehow. The birds! Of course: they were using the sunfinches to trade messages.

"Troubled by a guilty conscience, dear brother?" said Erphel.

"I'm simply trying to help you."

"Like you did during the Silverfish Revolt? By betraying me?"

"I saved your life," Greny said. "And Ricoen's too, for that matter. The Iron Circle would have burned Crimson Plaza and everyone on it, had I not intervened."

"But why help me now?" Erphel smirked. "After all, I orchestrated the murders of Cenmis, Thaxen, and Osro."

"And Ecethor."

"I had no part in Ecethor's death, but I did organize the attempt to kill you at Spinbridge." Erphel pointed the tip of his sword at Greny. "I could kill you here and now. Why would you now be suddenly willing to betray the institution you profess to love?"

"You're my brother. And you're a fine one to talk about betrayal. Have you forgotten the Courtesar Code?"

Erphel lowered the blade. "After it betrayed me in Crimson Plaza. I watched countless friends in the aftermath being exiled to Beamstone, or just disappear. I trusted the Code to protect them. I trusted your word."

"I, too, had my code." Tears pooled in Greny's eyes. "I was naive back then. I was lied to, too."

"But you chose to ignore it."

Greny nodded. "I protected you."

"The one good act that balanced out all the bad."

Greny reach into his tunic for a handkerchief but found none. Erphel, spurred by his chivalrous reflexes, offered his. Greny refused it with a sniff of disapproval and wiped his tears on his sleeve.

"You're both under arrest!" a triumphant female voice declared. Posaleum entered, flanked by two cordents armed with springbows. They must have been watching the crypt. *Dragons!* Greny lamented. *How did I miss them?*

"Arresting me over this is a bit weak, is it not?" he groused. "Considering my brother already tried to murder me."

"An obvious attempt to divert suspicion," Posaleum said. "You two have been working together to overthrow the Meritocracy."

Greny guffawed. "I've never heard anything so preposterous in my life! Do you really believe that?"

Posaleum lifted her chin imperiously. "I most certainly do."

"Yes, I suppose you would. It suits you to do so. And others will give credence to your absurd accusation because it suits them, too." He looked to his brother. "Tell her, Erphel. Tell her how—"

"You've got it all figured out, Posaleum. Yes, I admit it."

"He's lying!" Greny thundered.

"You can tell that to the Vicenary Jury at your trial," Posaleum said.

No need to be afraid. The truthscryers will clear you, Greny counseled himself. *You've led an exemplary life. You may have your embarrassing foibles, but nothing that would ruin you. They won't pry too much beyond the immediate matter. Everybody is afraid of the secrets you hold.*

A strangling horror wiped the self-satisfied smirk from his face. He had offered his worthless brother an opportunity to escape, and he had meant it. A moment of magnanimity had damned him! He had been an utter fool to squander mercy on that perfidious rogue.

"Raise your hands, both of you," Posaleum commanded.

Grudgingly, Greny obeyed. Erphel placed his sword on a slab on the floor—his sister's ledgerstone. He looked pained as Posaleum strolled over to the covered birdcage.

"Important evidence, this," she said. The birds under the cloth fluttered as she picked it up.

She led them outside, her two cordents keeping their weapons trained on their prisoners. Greny's mind raced with questions: *Where were Glastum and the ratchers? Why hadn't they warned me about Posaleum? Why didn't they come to my rescue?*

Greny's arms already felt heavy. "Do I really have to keep my hands in the air?"

"Be thankful I haven't bagged you or put you in a restraining coffin yet," Posaleum sneered.

Something cracked against stone. A bolt thumped into a cordent's chest, and he fell. For the briefest moment, everyone looked around in utter shock. A bolt struck Posaleum in the throat, sending her in a spiral to the ground. She ended up draped over a low gravestone, blood spurting from her crooked neck. The birds chirped and fluttered as the birdcage rolled away from her limp hand and shed its blood-spattered cover. Greny and the surviving cordent rushed for the protection of the crypt, but the cordent toppled before he reached it, a bolt jutting from his back. Greny reached out as the man crawled toward him, but three more bolts struck him in rapid succession. Greny sucked down the bile that surged into his throat and slunk further into the crypt.

Erphel, crouching, weaved through the tombs and snatched the birdcage. From behind a headstone he reached out, stole a dagger from the nearest cordent, and fled into the bloodstained night. Greny watched helplessly as bolts continued to strike the door jambs. He should have fled like his brother, but it was too late now. He was trapped. Who could these attackers be? Erphel's people? Associates of Woad Glastum? Greny should have never trusted him.

The clatter of bolts stopped. Shadows filtered through the lines of headstones toward him. They were coming to kill him. He was going to die in his family's crypt. He pressed his hands against his cheeks.

What to do? What to do? He picked up Erphel's sword, but he hadn't the strength to wield it. The tip kept dipping downward.

The crackle of springbow bolts resumed. One silhouette emitted a high-pitched yelp as it fell. The other two fled. One collapsed between two gravestones, the other melted into the distant night. Greny held onto the useless sword at the mouth of the crypt until he spotted familiar muzzled silhouettes approaching—the ratchers! Woad Glastum was with them, a springbow cradled in his arms.

Greny dropped the sword, its clang echoing through the tomb, and stepped outside to join them.

The dying attacker, wrapped in black cloth, wheezed painful breaths. Emboldened by his guards' presence, Greny knelt beside the figure and reached toward the mask with trembling fingers. The body spasmed. Greny let loose a childish cry and sprawled backward on his rump. He clambered to his feet with wounded dignity and barked: "Let me see his face!"

Kleest ripped away the mask. Greny gasped. It couldn't be, but it was—Opriet Braesum.

"Why?" Greny asked.

"My sons. She knew." She choked on the words, drowning in the blood spilling from her mouth.

"Everyone knew about your sons! Everyone knew!" Greny crouched down and, raising Opriet by the shoulders, shook her with a violence that shocked Glastum. "Dragons fry you! Who knew? Who sent you to kill me?" Greny slapped her face, once, twice. Opriet's eyes rolled back in their sockets; her swollen tongue lolled out. "Tell me, damn you!"

"That's enough, she's dead," said Glastum.

Greny, exhausted, let the corpse fall to the ground.

"My brother!" he raged. "Find him!"

Noise up ahead. Drinith dashed behind a headstone, the pain in her side making her wince. Three sunfinches fluttered like flickering sparks in the bloody moonlight above her. An empty birdcage rolled down the path, its door slapping open and shut as it banged down the steps. Qilin was staggering down the path, hunched to one side, panting and grimacing, a dagger wavering in his hand.

He halted some distance away. He must have spotted her.

Drinith stepped back onto the path.

Erphel gasped. "Is this a ghost come to haunt me for my sins? You fell to your death from Southspoke Bridge."

"Fate decreed otherwise, it seems," Drinith said.

"It was nothing personal," Erphel said. "I just...you knew too much. I..."

"It was Ricoen, wasn't it? She ordered my death."

A springbow bolt protruding from his shoulder gleamed red in the moonlight.

"You have little comprehension of the strength of the enemy we fight. The meritocrats we killed are like scales off a dragon's back. The wound we inflicted will scab quickly and the scales will regrow. We tried to change things peaceably. We really did. We acted with honor. And we failed. We had no choice..."

"I've heard nonsense like this before from someone who planned a massacre for my benefit. There has to be a better way than becoming worse than those you fight."

Movement further up the path—ratchers.

After a hasty glance over his shoulder, Erphel raised his knife. "I'm sorry. You know too much." He lurched forward.

Drinith tried to step clear of his sweeping blade, but, wracked by pain and exhaustion, she stumbled backward. A headstone thumped the back of her head. Through the blear of her pain, she raised her dagger, but Erphel slapped it aside. Something spattered her face— tears rained down on her as he raged through gritted teeth. For the briefest moment before his knife struck, she could see his face spasm with the struggle between his natural inclinations and his duty. The searing pain in her chest wrested her from her daze. Hollowing her whole body with a scream, she stabbed into the meat and bone above her until all she struck was air. Something metallic clattered against stone.

Erphel lay draped across the steps. The blood seeping from his chest in sinuous rivulets filled the blackened inscriptions, rewriting the names of the dead in red.

"Drinith!" Woad cried, his face drawn with shock, his eyes almost popping from his head. He smashed the butt of his springbow into the muzzle of the ratcher to his right. He swung the weapon like a club at the one to his left, but the creature dodged him and flicked its tail like a bullwhip, knocking him on his backside. As he reached for a headstone to arrest his fall, two ratchers pinned him to the ground.

"I thought you were dead," he said breathlessly as the ratchers bound him.

Greny strolled down the steps and shook his head. "A traitor to the last, Glastum. Too bad. I had high hopes for you. Now you'll have to walk the Plank with your dear wife and the others you thought you saved in our little bargain."

A wet whisper came from Erphel. "Greny, is Drinith dead?"

Greny stood over his brother, waved at Drinith to be silent. "She is." He beckoned to a ratcher, took its springbow. "Your secret is safe, whatever it is. Of course, I'll have to cover up your part in this little plot." He primed the springbow awkwardly and aimed. The snub of the springbow trembled in the breathless, bloodstained silence. He pulled the trigger, and the springbow snapped and snapped again. He moved Erphel's head with his foot, studied it for a while, then passed the springbow to its rattish owner.

"Take my brother's body to the family crypt and place it in one of the empty tombs," he said sadly. "At least he died with the grim satisfaction that his co-conspirator was safe in her palace. I guess we'll be getting a new Ducalion very soon."

"You knew?" Drinith asked.

"It isn't too hard to guess who could inspire my brother to become a murderer. I thought I had severed his lover's leash when I helped install her in the Ducal Palace. I guess I was wrong." He crouched in front of Drinith. "You don't look so great. I hope you'll last until your trial."

"But—"

"But but but. By my counting, six meritocrats are dead and you're already implicated in the deaths of most of them." *But who were the other two?* "I need someone to walk the Plank. The Iron Circle can quietly deal with the Ducalion, but there needs to be a public face for the Meritocracy to exert its anger upon."

Drinith's eyelids grew heavy. "If I am tried—"

Greny chuckled, his eyes gleaming with malicious glee. "Your trial will be held in private to prevent the Ducalion's involvement from becoming common knowledge. I'll spread rumors that you have amassed compromising material on several living meritocrats to make sure not even the Iron Circle will want to interview you. As you're marched off the Plank, you can say whatever you like to the crowd that gathers to watch you die. They'll be cheering too loud to hear."

Drinith struggled to keep her eyes open. She felt so terribly cold, as cold as the grave she lay upon.

Greny tilted his head to one side. "Unless you die before your trial, of course."

Her eyes shut, and the cold blackness engulfed her.

48

———————

The palanquin's gentle sway failed to soothe Greny as he headed, bleary-eyed and utterly drained, back to his tower. The cut on his arm twinged now and then, but the wound to his scalp ached constantly. He'd had too much to do in too short a time. First, his two prisoners had to be consigned to Inkeep, and he had to summon doctors to treat Drinith's wounds. Then, he sat down in Mileek's cramped little office and wrote his full version of events, outlining how he had hunted down his brother and captured Drinith, carefully piecing it together to absolve himself of any wrongdoing and put the blame squarely on her and the Ducalion. He wrote a couple of drafts before he was satisfied. This final version he would read to the Vicenary Jury. The Jury would doubtless edit it before percolating it in whispers throughout the Meritocracy. It would certainly omit the Ducalion. Drinith would be cast as the primary villain and the Blue Quarter would be cleared. Whether the Gadflies went to Rhumgad or Beamstone was immaterial to Greny.

Dragons! With Posaleum and Opriet now dead, more empty seats in the Chamber of Whispers would have to be filled. No matter. The Jury would quickly replenish its members. New meritocrats around the table brought new political currents, but he would worry about that later. For now, he was relieved to be headed home. He had sent Deetch ahead to ready the tower for his arrival, Zetch to deliver his report to Thespenilea, and Treek to summon a preservator to treat his wounds. He hadn't bothered with an escort, aside from Queek and a human yellowcheck driver. Greny was safe in this anonymous palanquin, and the threat of Erphel's machinations had died with him.

Strange, how little his death had impacted Greny. It was as if Erphel had died many years ago. Perhaps, in a sense, he had and the man Greny encountered in Mount Riddle was the ghost of his chivalrous brother. Greny had the body deposited in one of the vacant tombs in the crypt. He could only feel acute embarrassment at his lack of sorrow. He should grieve his dead brother, but Chemp's loss stung far worse, as did Nayz's, of course. Yes, Nayz had been a true friend. Greny would arrange payment of the death duty for his corpse and deposit him in the family crypt. If his grandmother could inter her favorite cat there, surely Greny could include the man who saved his life. *If only I'd realized he was my only human friend. That's the genuine tragedy.*

The palanquin halted outside Scylax Tower. He hopped out and, after dismissing the palanquin, hurried up the stairs. The doorbell went unanswered. He looked back for Queek, but the ratcher was gone. A creeping sense of vulnerability made him ring the doorbell with more determination. His first knock on the door made it creak open. A shiver shot up his spine at the reek of blood wafting from within. Something was terribly wrong.

"Deetch," he whispered. Silence. He hesitated, glanced around. Another squeak. He took a breath and opened the door fully. On the floor, Deetch, Zetch, Kleest, Zueel, Steevig, and Treek lay twisted into a crude circle. Greny rushed over to them, slipping and sliding on the congealing blood. Their tails have been knotted together in a mockery of Greny's sigil. They stared up at their master with lifeless eyes, their bloody mouths still agape with their death cries, their incisors missing or reduced to stumps. He tried to focus on each one as an individual but all he could see was Chemp's face in theirs.

The door slammed shut behind him. Heavily shod shadows trampled around him.

"Don't hurt me, please," he begged, covering his face with his hands. Metal gauntlets seized his arms and yanked them behind his back. He struggled as cord bound his wrists only to be rewarded with a knee to his kidneys.

"Who dares attack a meritocrat in his own—?" A gag tied roughly over his mouth turned his protestations into gibberish. A bag covered his head, plunging him into darkness.

His captors shoved him into a seat. He had to sit a little forward to avoid resting against his bound wrists. He recognized he was in a palanquin by its stuttering rock, but the noises of the city were disorienting. Greny couldn't make sense of them. He might be traveling through nearly any part of Gyre. The honking cries of casquars announced the palanquin's halt. Something large and multi-legged crawled under his hood—a giant spider. Greny screamed.

"If you don't shut up, I'll leave the gag on."

Greny froze. A gloved hand—*not* a spider—probed under the hood, touched his face. As it yanked the gag from his mouth, an urge to bite at it never strayed beyond fantasy. His captors had already proved they weren't the sort to be trifled with.

The bag lifted from over his head. A veiled figure sat across from him—a woman in a prim black dress.

"Who are you? Are you somebody I know?" he asked. He fruitlessly tested the bonds around his wrists again. It must be amusing to her to watch him wriggling about like a worm.

"I know *you*, Rat King," she said, her deep voice unfamiliar. "That's all you need to know." She lifted the curtain. Curiosity made him lean forward to peer out. The Yellow Section's forbidding entrance. "You're going to help me free Drinith Hax and her retinue."

"Her retinue as well?" Greny mocked. "My oh my, you are generous."

"She wouldn't leave without them."

Greny's blood ran cold. Maybe he was wrong about the Ducalion. "Are you Erphel's lover? Are you the same veiled lady who helped

Drinith escape Osro's clutches after she was arrested for attempting to kill the Ducalion?"

"Don't waste your time asking questions I won't answer. The only question you need to worry about tonight is, do you want to die like your rats or not?"

"What must I do?" he asked warily, already guessing the answer.

"You are going to order the ratchers inside to surrender to my men and to release Drinith and her associates into our custody."

The image of Chemp's gaping stare came to him unbidden. O faithful servant! Greny shut his eyes to dispel the memory, but it only grew more lurid. He knew it would forever haunt him.

"Have I your word the ratchers won't be hurt?" He blushed at the naivety of his question, but he owed it to them.

"Of course," she said, as if offended by any suggestion to the contrary, but he had no leverage to hold her to her promise. The courageous course was to refuse, to sacrifice himself to protect his servants rather than gamble their lives on her word. But Greny wasn't that brave.

"I'll..." He nodded, unable to speak.

The cab door opened and two hulking masked men reached inside. They pulled and shoved him out of the palanquin so forcefully he struggled not to fall. Hooded figures formed two lines up to the doors.

A hand clutched his shoulder and something sharp pressed against the back of his neck. "One wrong move and you're dead," the man behind him whispered.

"I...I'll behave. I promise." As he was steered toward the door like a blind casquar to the slaughterhouse, he entertained a sardonic thought: *Is this what it feels like to walk the Plank?*

"No tricks," the knife-wielder hissed in his ear as one of the other figures pounded on the door.

"I need to look up," Greny pleaded. "They need to see my face."

"Do it then."

He gently lifted his head, all the time fearing the blade might nick him. Beads of sweat rolled down his cheeks, tickling him like the knife as he stared into the mouth of the grotesque rat's head over the door. Through its jaws, a ratcher would be watching. Having already observed his captors and their treatment of him, the ratchers might not open the door. He had always assumed their absolute loyalty, but he had never been so dependent on it as now.

"Open up the doors!" he shouted. "Let me and my friends inside!" Fear rendered him unable to muster a reassuring smile for the guards.

The squeal of a sliding bolt sent a shiver through him. The veiled lady's servants bunched around him. The gate opened, revealing Mileek and Riskeel standing within. Greny's captor pushed him forward.

"Tell them to drop their weapons," the knife-wielder murmured. The ratchers must have heard that. They had excellent hearing.

"Cast aside your weapons. They're unnecessary," Greny said. The ratchers disarmed their springbows and placed them on the ground. Entering the central hall with its tiers of balconies was like stepping into a monstrous maw. Where were the other ratchers? A loud crack came from behind Greny. A warm, viscous drizzle sprayed the back of his head. The hand on his shoulder fell away.

As the invaders scattered and the balconies filled with movement, Greny stood where he was, aghast. A scream ripped him from his daze. He ran. The arm of a dead man tripped him and sent him sprawling across the floor. He tried to stand up, but a hand seized the back of his neck.

"Surrender or I kill him!" his captor thundered.

But the battle raged on.

49

———————

Drinith awoke to loud squeals, grunts, the clangor of metal against metal. As she leapt from her bed, something hard struck the door. The head of a crossbow bolt jutted through the wood. She had been betrayed too often to hope for the sympathy of the prison's invaders. She pushed the bed over to the door and propped the frame against it. Plaintive, inhuman screeches rose above the din of battle, only to be cut short in quick succession.

A terrible, deathly silence fell. Any moment now, the victors might break through the door and slaughter her. She pressed her ear against the door; nothing stirred. Was everyone out there dead?

She paced her cell, wringing her hands. Shouting out was as likely to attract unwelcome attention as aid. But she couldn't simply wait here, doing nothing, not when her friends might be in danger.

"Help!" she yelled at the top of her voice. No answer. She yelled again and pounded on the door. She stopped and listened. A distant hammering answered, perhaps another prisoner equally at a loss as to what had transpired outside their cells. Distant boots echoed in the corridor beyond. The river of footfalls flowed slowly toward her until it passed by. Something heavy rapped the door.

"Meritocrat Hax, are you in there? We're cordents with orders to liberate you."

If they intend to kill me, I can't stop them. "I've braced the door. Wait one moment while I remove the obstruction." She toppled the bed out of the way and the door opened. Beyond the nervous man in a redcheck's uniform standing in the doorway lay a mound of bloody fur.

He bowed. "I'm Captain Ketren at your service, Meritocrat. I've instructions from the Vicenary Jury to escort you to Meritocrat Trajar."

She followed him along the corridor, its floor mottled with bloody footprints. Ratcher corpses were piled in the middle of the corridor.

"What happened?" she asked.

"We don't know," he said, nodding to two passing redchecks. "We arrived here to find this…mess." They descended the stairs.

As Drinith reached the bottom, a figure dashed at her. Ketren leapt between them and pinned the man's face against the wall.

"Drinith, please, call them off," he croaked.

"Quiescat? Quiescat!" Recognition and relief surged through her simultaneously. "Let him go, please."

Ketren gave her a dubious glance but relented. Two more cordents raced up to them. "There he is!" one cried. "Apologies, Captain. He gave us the slip."

Quiescat rushed over and gathered her in a massive hug.

"Thank the gods!" he said. "I thought I had lost you."

Drinith stifled a chuckle as she gently freed herself. "I feared the same about you."

"Do you understand what's going on?"

For now, the less he knew the better. Ignorance might protect him from truthscryers. "It looks as if the Rat King has fallen out of favor," she remarked matter-of-factly, then turned to Ketren. "This man and all my other servants are to be released immediately."

Ketren sucked in a breath. "I was instructed to free you, Meritocrat, not your servants."

"Am I under arrest?" Drinith asked, repressing her anger.

His eyes widened with surprise. "You are free, Meritocrat."

"Then you have no reason to ignore my solemn command on this matter. My people must be released."

Ketren bowed. "Of course, Meritocrat."

"And Quiescat will accompany me to meet Elca or I won't be going at all." *I have no intention of facing that treacherous snake alone.*

"Yes, Meritocrat."

As Drinith emerged from the gaping mouth of her prison into the painful Gyran noon sun, the air had never tasted so sweet. She was lucky to be alive. Many of her servants sauntered behind her, haggard and grim, squinting like frightened moles in the unaccustomed brightness. How many would leave her service after suffering this indignity? Drinith couldn't blame them if they did.

"Were Woad and Tazran Glastum among the prisoners?" Drinith asked, scanning in vain the beleaguered, sullen faces that passed her.

Ketren nodded. "I released Woad Glastum myself. His wife was apparently released last night."

"I'll call on Elca as soon as I can," Drinith promised as she raced away, with Quiescat in tow. Tazran's discovery of Woad's betrayal would inexorably lead to one of them killing the other. Drinith had to find Tazran and tell her how Woad tried to rescue her, how he redeemed himself. She turned back to the captain and yelled, "Get me a palanquin at once! I need to go to the Blue Quarter!"

Drinith burst through the door of the Gad Moon Inn. "Tazran! Woad!" she called breathlessly.

Woad was sitting at a table, contemplating the contents of a metal thimble in his hand. His knife lay on the table. "She knows."

Standing across from him, Tazran cradled her springbow. She scowled over her shoulder at Drinith. "Thanks to your ex-maid's mother. As I left Inkeep, she approached me to plead for news of her daughter."

"You don't have to do this!" Drinith cried. "Woad tried to save me on Mount Riddle."

"*You* can forgive him if you like," Tazran said. "*You* can ignore his betrayal."

Drinith rushed to put herself between them, but Tarzan slammed the butt of her springbow into her cheek. Dazed, Drinith stumbled backward and fell. She managed to grab on to a table and landed in a sitting position on the floor.

"I thought Woad and Gelasin had trained you better," Tazran muttered. "Now stay down. This is between me and him."

"I'm sorry," Woad said.

"Do you know how hollow that sounds?" Tazran said. "I could forgive you for lying to me. I could even forgive your betrayal of Drinith, since she's plainly desperate to protect you. But your part in Gelasin's Crevastival attack..." She shook her head. "He intended to murder innocents, the more the better, and you just went along with it. Some sins just can't be forgiven. Some things can't be just wished away."

She aimed the springbow at Woad. "I really know how to pick losers."

Woad gulped down his drink. He stared into the empty cup. "We were desperate. Every potential ally had turned their back on us."

"And that makes it okay to murder children and pregnant women, does it?" Tazran howled, her whole body trembling.

Woad flung the cup across the room. "No."

"Get up," Tazran said.

Woad folded his arms. "You can shoot me just as easily while I'm sitting."

Tazran placed her springbow on a table and drew her knife. "I'm going to be fairer to you than you planned to be to those people on Crimson Plaza. Now pick up that dagger and stand."

"The chances of you beating me in a knife fight..." Woad shrugged. "Don't get me wrong, Taz, you're good and all..."

"Don't call me that! I'm the Widow to you. Maybe you'll win, or maybe I'll get lucky. Either way, this ends here and now."

Drinith looked on in horrified disbelief. *I must stop this madness. If I can grab the springbow, I might be able to delay the fight until Tazran's temper cools.* She scurried toward it on her hands and knees. A hard kick from Tazran to her stomach knocked her over and left her winded.

"I told you to stay down. If you kill me, Woad, I'm sure Drinith will forgive you. She might even help you dispose of my body. You can promise your undying devotion to her *again*. Funny, the first time we met her, it was in this very room. We had to dispose of a body that time, too."

Woad leapt to his feet, drew his knife, and flipped the table on its side. As Tazran circled it, he kept the table between them until she kicked it over on its top. He lunged over it, his knife thrusting before him. She parried his weapon with the pommel of hers. It flew from his grip. He grabbed hold of her armed hand. There ensued a battle of will and strength as both sought possession of the dagger.

Drinith dashed for the springbow, grabbed it. The mechanism jammed, but she pointed it at them anyway. "Drop your weapons!"

Locked in a shuddering embrace, the knife both clasped dangling above them, the pair took no heed of her empty threat. How she could pry them apart without killing one or other of them, or herself for that matter?

Tazran kept trying to kick Woad's legs from under him, but it was like trying to chop down a massive tree with her foot. The trembling blade moved in sporadic lurches inevitably toward her. "Do it!" she growled through gritted teeth.

The dagger suddenly reversed. Woad roared in pain as the slender blade slammed into his chest. As he stumbled backward, Tazran gasped in mingled anger and incredulity. "You backburning coward! You let me win!"

He collapsed on the floor, the knife still embedded in his chest, his dead eyes staring up at the ceiling, blood trickling from his wry grin. She kicked him and screamed. She fell to her knees, her shoulders shuddering with sobs. As Drinith approached her, she turned, her wet face ugly with rage. "Get out! GET OUT!"

Drinith tossed the springbow on the nearest table and stormed out the door. A small crowd had gathered outside, presumably drawn by the shouts inside.

"Get out of here!" Drinith shouted. "This is none of your business." And apparently, it was none of hers either.

Beyond the scattering crowd, the palanquin waited. Quiescat waved through the window of the cab. With a sigh, Drinith climbed inside.

Quiescat lifted one inquisitive brow. "Woad?"

"He's dead," Drinith said.

50

———————

As the palanquin slowly wound its way to Elca's mansion, curtains hung across its windows like widows' veils. They plunged the cab into a gloom that robbed Quiescat's eyes of their glassy sparkle, making him a mortal man again.

"We need to be careful dealing with her," he whispered.

Drinith bit her lip. He was right of course, but something about the way he said it irritated her. It was as if she couldn't see the danger for herself, as if she was still a child, even now, after all her travails. "Why did you conceal the cruelties of my ancestors?"

His eyebrows lifted. "What do you mean?"

"I read a history of Kaplar written for my great grandfather. It taught me what empire means. You never told me. You let me think my ancestors were heroes."

He rubbed the back of his neck. "When do you tell a child her father was a fool, her grandfather a monster, her great grandfather a murderous buffoon, and so on? When do you strip away that last vestige of innocence?" His inhuman eyes glistened as if touched by human emotion. "Yes, they were tyrants, but you're different from them."

"What makes you so sure?"

"I believe in you."

She smirked. "Put faith in gods, not mortals. Is that not the saying?"

"I've known you since you were a baby, and I've watched you grow into a capable young woman. You're better than your ancestors. They reveled in the atrocities you so deplore."

"What if you're wrong? What if I turn out no better than them?"

He shrugged. "Then Kaplar will be still better off under your rule than being throttled by the iron grip of Magian. The cruelties of your ancestors are paltry compared to his utter depravity. If we give up hope, we might as well jump into the Void."

"You should have told me, Quiescat."

"I'm sorry." He rested a hand on the window frame and stared at some distant point beyond the drawn curtain, as if he could see through it. He looked lost and sad. "Sometimes I wish I possessed the infallibility others' imaginations foist upon me."

The palanquin halted outside Elca's mansion. Ketren shifted uncomfortably as he waited for them to climb out of the cab. Before they reached the door, it was opened by a glum servant in dark navy livery. Ketren nodded to the servant and gave a curt bow to Drinith. "Excuse me, Meritocrat. I'll leave you in the capable hands of the house staff. I have matters I must take care of back at Inkeep."

"Of course," Drinith said despite an urge to ask him to stay. She exchanged a nervous glance with Quiescat. What might await them inside?

"Follow me, Meritocrat," the servant said, directing at Quiescat a critical eye verging on hatefulness.

"Quiescat will accompany me," Drinith declared with a firmness that forbade any further quibble.

Elca Trajar burst out of the parlor doors. "Drinith, it's marvelous to see you. And you brought Quiescat. How delightful. Come in, both of you."

The parlor smelled like a bouquet of brineflowers, sweet and salty at the same time. A thick black shag carpeted the floor. The furniture was mostly Nosteran, but there were also a few statues and vases of

Rhumgadian provenance. The seats were upholstered with white snakeskin. A queen's bust, presumably that of the Wealgiver, stared menacingly from the mantelpiece. A large, tattered map of Noster hung above it. On the other walls were more maps, select portraits of Elca's predecessors, and a tarnished sword with an ornate guard in the shape of a four-horned cerastes.

On a low table stood the smaller of Qilin's bird cages. It contained five chirping sunfinches.

Elca strolled over to it. "We recaptured some of Erphel's birds."

"Erphel?" Drinith asked.

"Quiescat's brother. You knew him as Qilin Pine."

"How did you know about them?" Drinith asked, pointing to the cage.

"Greny wrote a helpful report," Elca said with a wan grin. "We sifted the truth from his many lies." She signaled something to her servant, then invited her guests to sit. "This whole injustice Greny inflicted on you must have been very unsettling indeed. You can take some comfort that his crimes will not go unpunished. Obviously, his trial is too sensitive to be held in public, but I'm sure the other jurists will be as impressed as I am by the overwhelming evidence against him. Yes, he'll walk the Plank for high treason."

Drinith's throat tightened. *If truthscryers interrogate me...*

"No need to worry," Elca assured Drinith, as though divining her alarm. "You've suffered enough already, and your testimony isn't required to convict him. We have another witness."

The doors opened, and Jarma swept into the room. In her shock and delight, it took a moment for Drinith to reciprocate her hug.

"Poor Jarma has had quite a torrid time too," Elca said. "While Greny held her prisoner in his tower, he was indiscreet about his true feelings for the Meritocracy, something long suspected but unproven. Fortunately, we managed to snatch her from the Plank before his rodent minions could dispose of her."

"And what of Erphel's lover?" Drinith asked.

"Greny's cruelest trick. He wrote the letters to Erphel."

Nonsense! Drinith was about to blurt, but a circular motion—the symbol of the ineffable Iron Circle—of Elca's finger muted her. The Vicenary Jury had already decided that Greny's guilt was convenient. "Makes sense," she said.

"He never said that to me," Jarma said.

"We have other evidence relating to that," Elca said breezily. "Have no fear though. You didn't suffer in vain. Your testimony is critical." She lovingly stroked the cage. "I have other news."

"I hope it's good," Drinith said dourly.

Elca laughed as if she had cracked a joke. "I think you'll find it marvelous. I have come to an accommodation with Thespenilea. She has agreed to support the expedition to Rhumgad."

Drinith was stunned into silence for a moment. "What made her change her mind?"

"It comes with one simple stipulation. When you go to Rhumgad, you bring all your supporters with you. The Blue Quarter must be cleared."

It wasn't simple. There were exiles who had built lives in Gyre, who had businesses. "You don't expect them to blithely uproot," Drinith argued, "and start afresh? They will resist."

Elca shrugged. "It's either that or a transfer to the Beamstone colony, I'm afraid."

An icy shiver ran down Drinith's spine. The chirps of the sunfinches as they flitted about their cage hurt her head. She needed some quietness to think. *Pull yourself together.* "I'm sure we can manage that."

The lean smile beneath those two pale moon eyes stretched into a wolfish grin. "I have every faith in you. Tea?"

Five sunfinches in the cage. There were too many for them all to belong to Erphel. They seemed to Drinith to make enough racket for fifty birds.

"If you don't mind, I'd like to go home," Drinith said, rising.

"Of course. I'll bid you goodbye for now."

As Drinith and her companions fled, the bird's frenzied chirps followed her like demonic laughter.

51

———————

Greny sat up as soon as the lid lifted. He gasped the cool sweet air and mopped the tickling dew of perspiration from his face. Thank dragons, he didn't get sick in the restraining coffin! The stench of stale sweat emanating from its sodden black silk lining had nauseated him on the way here.

Only "here" wasn't where he had anticipated. He had hoped to emerge in the Parliament of Merit to stand trial before his peers and have his chance to tell the truth. It would destroy him, expose his indiscretions with his guests in his tower, but at least he might lance the pustule of treachery swelling within Gyre. This wasn't the parliament, however. It was the Mortuary of Sin, the tiny jail where the condemned were readied to walk the Plank.

"No, impossible!" Greny cried as the ratchers wrested him from the vessel. They almost wrenched his arms from his shoulders as they twisted his hands behind his back.

"There's no need for this," he pleaded as the cords cut into his wrists. "I won't make trouble."

He recognized one of his would-be executioners—Queek. The young ratcher had betrayed him!

Planted on his feet, Greny glimpsed Elca through the parting scrum. She leaned against a door, arms folded, legs crossed, a frightening glee on her starry face.

"This is outrageous!" Greny roared. "Am I to be denied a trial?"

"A trial took place. The testimony of your guest, Jarma, was more than enough to send you to the Plank."

Greny smirked. "If that's so, then everything else must have come out, including the Crevastival attack. Plenty to send your precious oracle to join me in the Void."

"I'm afraid that Jarma's interrogation was restricted to your crimes."

"That's impossible. The law—"

Elca's chuckle mocked him. "You forget we meritocrats are the law. I'm afraid you are a victim of your own reputation. Everyone feared you knew their secrets, so it wasn't difficult to convince the rest of the Jury to limit Jarma's interrogation to the treason you spouted in her presence."

"Thespenilea..."

"She and I agreed the evidence against you was overwhelming. Thanks for your report, by the way." Elca grinned with smug triumph. "It helped Thespenilea fit all the pieces together and convince me of your guilt."

"Traitor!"

"Your problem, Greny, is you've always been too aloof. Who will miss you when you're gone? Who'll weep as you fall to your death?"

"Nayz." *But Nayz is dead.* "I gave my life for this city. I sacrificed everything for it."

"And it'll remember you ever more as a traitor, your name as besmirched as your tower."

"And how will it remember you?" Greny snarled. "If it survives you."

"The lesson of the Old Noster Empire is that the glories of the nostalgic past are no match for the unsentimental realities of the present. To survive, a state must grow. My only ambition is that Gyre thrives, and Rhumgad is the key to that."

"All your talk of Gyre's welfare is gilded treason," Greny said. "No doubt you plan to seize the ducal throne."

"And become its prisoner? No, Ricoen will remain the Ducalion. Birds will continue to flit between her and her lover. As far as she knows, your brother is still alive but in hiding. She'll continue to preen herself in her gilded cage, scheming to seize Gyre and dreaming of their reunion. It's romantic and sad, in a sense." Her knowing smirk made Greny's skin crawl.

Greny charged at her head-down, like an enraged bull, but ratcher claws held him. "You planned this! You already knew about the birds! You've been intercepting them and swapping Ricoen's messages for your own. You corrupted Erphel. I should have guessed! Ricoen would never stoop to assassination."

"I helped establish the line of communication between the lovers. Not directly of course. An agent who had access to the Ducal Palace acted as an intermediary. I had been readying your brother for quite some time in case I needed a willing assassin. When the Short War Faction was in the ascendant thanks to Magian's proposal, I realized the time had come."

"And how did Ecethor's death fit into all this?"

"I was the senior partner in the brineflower venture that she enlightened you about. I only brought that silly fool into the business because my previous associate became indisposed."

"You murdered Ecethor."

"I was there the night you called. She intended to expose me, but your visit gave her little plan away. You left me no choice but to kill her."

"And you blackmailed Opriet."

"She had served me for quite some time. So had Posaleum. I never asked either of them for anything too taxing, you understand. You were the only cordent general I couldn't influence. Then Posaleum decided she'd cut her strings. She hated you so much she'd bring me down just to get you. I warned Opriet that Posaleum was going to expose her child swaps, and there was only one way to stop her."

"It was convenient for you that Osro discovered that dead sunfinch."

"I went to her with it. I was supposed to attend that night, but of course, I didn't need an invitation. Had it gone to plan, you and the other attendees would have died, and I would have blamed Magian for the murders. If that failed, the attack would have been traced back to Erphel, and maybe Ricoen. Unfortunately, you sent Drinith in your place and upset everything."

"Is that why you were so quick to forsake Drinith afterward?"

Elca produced a slim, battered leather volume. "This book belonged to Drinith and before her, the Rhumgadian poet Versifer. He was briefly Oracle of Godsdoor in place of Quiescat. The book contains five of his prophesies. Two had come to pass before the current crisis. The third prophesy, the one you wrested from Quiescat, foretold this crisis itself. The fourth predicts his return to Rhumgad. The fifth, I believe, foretells Magian's defeat. Neither of the remaining prophecies mention Drinith. Quiescat is the key, not her."

"You're deluded," Greny snapped. "Gyre couldn't even conquer its home shard in two hundred years of constant warfare. You expect now to subjugate a distant shard with the help of Gyre's bitterest rivals. Magian, whatever the else he may be, is no fool. Rhumgad is a trap." A thrill of realization passed through Greny. "Yes, it's a trap. The offer of the monopolies is merely the bait, the hint of weakness to draw Gyre in. You'll destroy us."

Elca's smile fell away. A scowl gathered over her enormous eyes as she slipped the book into a pocket in her skirt. "If that is so, you won't be around to see it." She turned and began to stroll away from him. "Goodbye, Greny."

"One last thing," Greny implored. "Just a moment, please!"

She stopped and regarded him coolly over her shoulder.

"How did you impel Queek to betray me?"

"He was my servant before he became yours. I managed to get two agents on your staff, but the second was killed at the Wealgiver Street. Fortunately, Queek did a great job insinuating himself into many of your private meetings, protecting Jarma from your drunken attentions, and leaving that secret entrance open for my people to storm your tower. Tomorrow, he returns to Nemon with a small fortune to retire on for a job well done."

"You forget every ratcher has overheard this conversation," Greny said triumphantly.

A broad grin spread beneath Elca's pale eyes. "They're well paid to be deaf. Besides, nobody listens to ratchers. That's why I needed Jarma."

"Betrayal is so easy for you," Greny spluttered as she walked away.

"Enjoy the trip to the inner sun. I hope you scream yourself to death before you burn."

Greny squirmed but couldn't shake off the ratchers' tenacious grip. "Elca Trajar's a traitor! Let me go! I must warn the Parliament!" he cried as they dragged him toward the exit.

Elca's voice filled the chamber. "Don't have them *throw* you off the Plank, Greny. Face your death with some dignity." With that, she departed, doubtless to take her place in the Gallery of Veils. *The best view in the house,* Greny mused sardonically.

The gates ahead opened, and the deafening clamor of cheers and howls and drums echoed down the corridor.

"Let me down," Greny whimpered. "I'll walk. I'll walk!"

Unmoved, the ratchers carried him onward. A peculiar terror gripped him, a horror of embarrassment. His own incongruous laughter shook him, echoing down the corridor, drowning out the jeers spilling through the open door ahead. But the laughter quickly shattered into sobs. He didn't want to die.

They dragged him down the hall and shoved him outside to the enthusiastic clapping and cheering of the crowd. The force of their exultation mesmerized him. His gaze scanned those raucous faces in vain for any hint of sympathy. A lone figure stood in silence amid the orgy of jubilation, staring at him with grim distaste. Her eyes narrowed with the realization that he was watching her. Jarma's contempt cut deeper than any of the taunts spat out by the boiling crowd. He grinned at the woman who had damned him. At least something good—she had escaped from the Plank and, dragons willing, would have a long, fruitful life—had come from this calamity. He had never wanted to kill her, not really.

A punch shunted him onward. Ahead, the long, clean ledge of the Plank sliced the emptiness beyond. Was he really going to walk meekly to his death? The only binds that held him were those cutting into his wrists. The rest, the intangible ones—the expectation of tradition, pride, fear—would die with him as soon as he stepped into the Void. And so would the truth. He turned and ran.

"Elca Trajar is a murderer!" He yelled as he dodged the guards' clutches and dashed toward the crowd, but he couldn't even hear himself over their baying for his death. A punch to the stomach knocked the air out of him. The ratchers' arms closed around him and lifted him up. In the Gallery of Veils, the Vicenary Jury stood watching, their faces hidden like mourners. Who had taken his place among them? Elca must be up there by now, smirking down at him.

He glimpsed the Ducalion and the other meritocrats high on the steps of the Dragon Church.

"Your lover's dead, Ducalion!" he roared. "Trajar will betray every one of you!" the crowd's laughter swallowed his every word.

The ratchers carried him to the edge of the Plank. They were about to fling him over, the ultimate humiliation. He tried to pretend it didn't matter. The shame would die with him.

Holding him by his limbs they faced him downward. The surface of the Plank slid beneath him as, to the mob's exultant cheers, they swung him toward the waiting Void. He swayed back and forth before the Void, a screaming pendulum, expecting each swing to be his last. The guards' grip suddenly vanished, and sky yawned before him. The crescendo of the crowd's celebration taunted his screams as he plummeted into the merciless jaws of the Crevast.

52

Drinith knocked on the door, braced herself for Perian's mother, Colyan, to answer.

The door squealed open. The old woman's features sharpened into a flinty stare the instant she beheld the meritocrat who had caused her daughter's imprisonment. Her lips worked soundlessly as though rage had stolen her voice, as if she couldn't find words vulgar enough to express her contempt.

Drinith jammed her foot in the door as the old woman shut it. She slammed the door thrice, but Drinith kept her foot in place. She had taken the precaution of wearing thick boots in case of this eventuality, but even so, it hurt.

"Leave us alone!" the old woman screamed.

"What's happening?" Perian demanded as she rushed to the door. She froze so suddenly when she saw Drinith, she dropped the clothes she carried on the floor.

Drinith stretched out a pouch of coins. "I've come with the wages I owe you, plus interest."

Perian's mother looked as though she'd rather spit in Drinith's face than accept her money, but Perian stepped forward and took it.

"I've also got a job offer if you're interested," Drinith said.

"She doesn't want your charity," the old woman muttered.

"I want you to be my new butler," Drinith said.

Perian arched her eyebrows. "I'm not trained… I wouldn't know…"

"You can learn. We'll figure it out together if we have to."

"You could hire a more experienced—"

"I don't want anyone else. I want someone I can trust. I want you."

Perian looked to her mother, but Colyan met her imploring gaze with a granitic stare. The younger woman appeared about to waver when Colyan suddenly sighed.

"Do whatever you want," she said. "But remember, being associated with *her* put you in prison. There are worse things that can happen." She glared spitefully at Drinith, as if willing her to walk the Plank. "You'll have a target on your back, daughter, if you take up again with *this one*."

Perian shrugged. "Not even meritocrats are safe in this city." She grinned. "I'll take the job, as long as I'm paid whatever Fenvar was."

"I'll pay you one and half times that salary," Drinith said. *Trust is priceless, and I can trust you.*

Jarma was waiting in the palanquin downstairs.

"Did Perian accept?" she asked through the window.

Nodding, Drinith climbed into the palanquin. She called to Nosdan to head back to Hax Mansion and drew the curtain.

"You were very quiet on the journey here," she said to Jarma.

"I had a lot on my mind." Jarma sighed. "I keep thinking about what happened, wondering if I could have done anything differently. I… This city corrupts everything. It makes me feel dirty. Greny is the first person I've ever killed." She quickly wiped away a tear. "I'm being silly."

"No, not at all. I feel like that all the time." *The boy in the darkness, the surprise of death.* "But you have nothing to be ashamed of. If you hadn't played along with the Veiled Meritocrat's scheme, we would likely all be dead now." *How many had died because of me? How many might yet die?* "Some things are beyond our control. We have to do the best we can and accept that, sometimes, our best won't be good enough."

"I just did what I needed to do to survive."

A deep sadness stirred in Drinith. And guilt. *Dare I tell you that the very deeds that cause you such terrible shame prove you're as capable as any of the meritocrats who sit in the Iron Circle. When the time is right, I shall....* She patted Jarma's hand.

They sat for the rest of the journey in gloomy silence.

Tazran was waiting for them on the steps of Hax Mansion.

"Wait here," Drinith said, leaping from the cab. Nosdan moved to follow her, but Drinith signaled him to stay at the palanquin. She couldn't help smiling when she spied Quiescat peering anxiously out a ground-floor window.

"A bit unusual being able to sit on a meritocrat's doorstep without being shooed away," Tazran observed with a sniff.

"I'm rather short-staffed at present."

Tazran stood up and, placing her hands on her hips, lifted her chin. "So I've heard."

"Come to apply?"

"Would you still take me?"

"You mightn't make the best maid, but I'm sure I could find something for you to do."

Drinith jumped at Tarzan's sudden seizing of her arm.

"When Woad pledged his loyalty, he made the promise of both of us. I intend to keep my word. I'm nothing like he is...was."

"I know," Drinith said.

Tazran nodded stiffly, her eyes reddening. "I think we're done here for now, yes?"

"Yes, of course. Call tomorrow at noon. We have much to discuss."

Tazran stalked away, across the plaza.

"I wasn't sure I should intervene," Nosdan said, strolling up to her. Jarma joined them.

"Nosdan, I need a favor," Drinith said.

"Of course."

"You've proved you're level-headed, and I can rely upon your loyalty. I need you to do more than manage my palanquin in the future. Nominally you'll be my senior driver, but you'll also act as my liaison with Tazran in the Blue Quarter."

"Of course," Nosdan said, grinning. "It would be an honor."

"It may be dangerous."

He chuckled. "I nearly walked the Plank only a few days ago. I think I can handle a little danger." Drinith's somber stare quickly sobered him.

"It *will* be dangerous," she said.

He nodded. "One thing, meritocrat, if I may be so bold..."

"Speak freely."

"You'll need a junior driver, yes? I'd like to suggest Jathar. He's quite a reformed character since the incident with the tattoo."

Drinith repressed the urge to dismiss the notion out of hand. "Do you vouch for him?"

He looked surprised, then nodded. "He's absolutely loyal."

"It's not his loyalty that worries me."

Nosdan stood ramrod straight. "You have my word, he won't let you down...or embarrass you again."

Despite her misgivings, Drinith trusted Nosdan. She patted his shoulder, squeezed it. "Then he has the job."

As Nosdan bowed in gratitude, Drinith and Jarma hurried into the mansion.

THE NEXT DAY AT NOON, Drinith and her circle of confidants sat around the table in the cellar room she had picked for their meetings. She locked the outer door at the far end of the hall and then the inner one. The chamber, used for storage, was cluttered and dusty, but it was secure from eavesdroppers.

"You four are the only people I can trust without reservation," Drinith said. Nosdan shifted uncomfortably. Quiescat had been against him joining this circle, but Drinith had overruled him. "I've something important to tell you."

As she explained the significance of Beamstone and the threat Elca made, shock and disbelief animated Perian's face. Nosdan looked sick and then violently angry. It was his people, his friends and neighbors, that Elca threatened. Already apprised by Drinith, Quiescat looked sad and weary, and Jarma maintained an inscrutable demeanor. The Widow appeared to take the news in her stride.

Nosdan stood and planted balled fists on the table. "So, our people are nothing more than playthings to be thrown away by the meritocrats when they grow bored."

"Calm yourself." Quiescat's murmur cut through Nosdan's rage; the latter sat down again, looking embarrassed.

"I'd expect nothing less," Tazran said. "We've always been interlopers here, nuisances...and Gyre didn't crush the Nosteran Empire by being nice."

"I'm sure I can moderate the threat to some degree so that a few of our people might remain here unmolested," Drinith said, "but the vast majority must leave. Our future lies in Rhumgad, not Gyre."

She wanted nothing more than to depart this city and walk on the same earth as her ancestors had, to inhale to sweet, salty air of the Wandering Sea and to face her true enemy—Magian. She'd had enough of fighting others' wars. The time had come to fight her own.

A WORD FROM THE AUTHOR

Want to find out what happens next? The best way to learn about future releases in this series and my other works my email list at https://photocosm.org/.

It would mean so much to me if you could leave a review wherever you purchased this story.

Feel free to email me at noelcoughlan@photocosm.org to ask any questions or share any comments you have about this book. I love to hear from readers.

Best wishes,

Noel

facebook.com/photocosm

goodreads.com/noel_coughlan

amazon.com/author/noelcoughlan

bookbub.com/authors/noel-coughlan

FATAL INVASION

Drinith finally returns to her native land only to discover that she's as much a foreigner there as the dragon armies invading it in her name.

Victory against Magian the Infinite finally appears to be within her reach. Yet, his imminent defeat threatens to replace one tyranny with another as the Republic of Gyre and its allies scheme to carve up the lands they claim to liberate.

Somehow, Drinith must stop them. But what can she do against the might of two hundred dragons?

Fatal Invasion is the next book in the **Champions of Fate** series.

THE GOLDEN RULE

Elf. Warrior. Saint. Heretic. Monster. Despised by two peoples, this pariah might yet prove to be the savior of both.

AscendantSun serves a dead god no longer. Adopting the religion of his human enemies, he haunts their mountains hoping to make amends for his violence toward them. Now, a figure from his past threatens to restart the ancient conflict he has struggled so long to put behind him.

War is coming again to the mountains, but this time he'll fight the legionaries he once commanded. Prophecy is against him. Numbers, too. But the greatest peril is the distrust of his human allies. Can he forge an effective alliance before the bright power rising in the east destroys them?

A Bright Power Rising and *The Unconquered Sun* compose **The Golden Rule**, a two-part epic fantasy for readers who enjoy unique and intriguing world-building.

SHORT STORIES

Fantasy:

No Escape

A desperate warrior carries a baby girl across a foreign desert. Although truth and honor are tattooed on his face, Tharo has abandoned both virtues in his quest to protect his charge. But it's only a matter of time before he fails her. Another man stalks them, a hunter no prey can escape, the dreaded Souldiviner.

(Prequel to *Fatal Shadow*)

The Parting Gift

Certamen's god is dead. His people, the Ors, are broken and enslaved. He finds consolation in the knowledge that they are safe... But not for much longer. Their masters, facing decimation by disease, are growing desperate. Desperate enough to kill.

(Prequel to *A Bright Power Rising*.)

The Fate Healer

Draston's master, Hamvok the Merciful, craves a royal ancestor or two to legitimize his tyranny. But every avenue of Draston's research has come to a dead end. To save himself from the tyrant's violent displeasure, he commits himself to a path of forgery and sacrilege, risking the wrath of not only the gods, but a far more terrible entity, the dreaded Fate Healer.

Science Fiction:

Alienity

Four short stories about aliens ranging from humorous to deadly somber.

Horror:

The Murder Seat

Dr. Herbert Marriott has a problem that only murder can solve. Luckily for him, the perfect weapon is locked away in his rundown museum, one too incredible for any court to accept. The cursed chair kills all who rest upon it. But will Herbert's victim be so easily drawn to her fate?

Hoard

Laura is Ger's last hope. His hoarding has ruined the lives of his neighbors and now threatens his own. As Laura and her team prepare to clean out his property under the glare of cameras, she is unaware that a sinister secret lies buried beneath the morass of junk, a dark truth waiting to kill her.

ACKNOWLEDGMENTS

I want to thank Kevin Cook and Pamela Cangioli from Proofed To Perfection for their editing work. I also must thank Alexa for proofreading the book.

I also want to thank Nick Lloyd for beta-reading the novel.

Finally, thanks to the good people at MIBLart for their fantastic cover.

ABOUT NOEL COUGHLAN

Noel lives with his wife and daughter in the West of Ireland. He writes epic fantasy, science fiction and horror.

From a young age, he was always writing a book. Generally, the first page over and over. Sometimes, he even reached the second page before he had shredded an entire copybook. And you couldn't even recycle all that wasted paper back then.

When he finally wrote and published a book, it took him fourteen years. *The Golden Rule* became two books so let us be generous and say he averaged seven years per novel. He has gotten a little faster since then. Honest.

His hobbies include writing, reading, and reading about writing. He has written about reading in the past, and he still writes about writing. He would happily stay at home all day writing, but the family dog, Ruby, insists on taking him for daily walks.

His pet hates include writing his biography and referring to himself in the third person.